Curse Not The

CURSE NOT THE KING

Evelyn Anthony

$\underline{\mathtext{C}}$

CENTURY

LONDON MELBOURNE AUCKLAND JOHANNESBURG

100658915

© Hutchinson Edition 1977

First published in Great Britain in 1954 by
Museum Press

This edition published in 1986 by
Century Hutchinson Ltd,
Brookmount House, 62–65 Chandos Place,
London WC2N 4NW

Century Hutchinson Publishing Group (Australia) Pty Ltd
16–22 Church Street, Hawthorn, Melbourne, Victoria 3122

Century Hutchinson Group (NZ) Ltd
32–34 View Road, PO Box 40–086, Glenfield, Auckland 10

Century Hutchinson Group (SA) Pty Ltd
PO Box 337, Bergvlei 2012, South Africa

ISBN 0 7126 9526 5

Printed in Great Britain by
WBC Print Ltd, Bristol

CONTENTS

FOREWORD

LIKE its predecessor, *Imperial Highness*, which dealt with the early life of Catherine the Great, this is a true story, the personal story of Catherine's son and heir, Paul of Russia.

In literature, as well as in life, the son has been overshadowed by his brilliant mother and the record of a relentless struggle for power and a bitter family feud has been eclipsed by the more familiar and notorious aspects of her long and fascinating reign.

The story of Paul is tragic and complex; the figure of the man has come down to us distorted by prejudice and fear, and by the need to justify one of the most dreadful crimes committed throughout Russia's history. The popular conception of Paul is best summed up in the words of his son's biographer, Paléologue, who excuses Alexander on the grounds that he was the son of that " suspicious degenerate, at once cruel and grotesque, that monster, that Death's Head, who was known as Paul the First ".

My study of Paul's life has convinced me that this verdict is untrue. Though written as a novel, it is a true story, with the exception of certain incidents which I have recorded in a note at the beginning of the book, and where accounts have differed, I have tried to select the version most in keeping with my own interpretation.

LONDON, 1954

AUTHOR'S NOTE

Most of Paul's biographers describe the Minister Panin as friendly to the Czarevitch, but in view of the fact that Panin betrayed his trust during Catherine's Revolution and could only expect punishment on Paul's accession, the other theory of his enmity towards the Czarevitch seems most likely.

In the first despatch delivered to the Empress in Chapter One I have mentioned Orenburg as the town attacked by Pugachev, when in fact it fell later on in the campaign.

The incident of Paul's intended arrest and Potemkin's intervention is fiction, inserted for dramatic effect and I hope excused by its probability under the circumstances.

Countess Bruce had lost Catherine's favour some time before the advent of Plato Zubov, but to avoid confusion by introducing a new lady-in-waiting I have ignored this.

I have found no record of Paul's attendance at Potemkin's last ball, though the descriptions are those of eye-witnesses, but I have assumed that on such an occasion the Czarevitch and his wife would have been present. They were travelling between Gatchina and the capital quite frequently at that time.

I have scarcely mentioned young Nicholas Panin, nephew of the old Minister and one of the conspirators in the plot to murder Paul, in order to avoid confusion with his uncle who had been dead for many years. Nicholas Panin's part in the plot was always subservient to von Pahlen's, and he did not take part in the actual murder.

EVELYN ANTHONY

BOOK ONE

The Heir

1

CATHERINE ALEXEIEVNA had been Empress and Autocrat of all the Russias for ten years. A decade had passed since a mysterious accident to her husband Peter the Third at his temporary prison in Ropscha had placed his crown firmly upon her head.

It had begun with many promises and plans, but in reality few changes had been wrought. Despite the upheaval of the throne, and the enlightened mind and Liberal leanings of the woman who had ascended it, the fundamentals of Russian life remained the same.

No less a person than the Empress herself acknowledged these facts; and she reviewed them one evening in 1773, seated before the dressing-table in her bedroom in the Winter Palace at Petersburg.

It was Elizabeth Petrovna's old room, and immediately Catherine pictured the dead Empress, the beautiful, vicious daughter of Peter the Great, and she smiled wryly at the memory.

The past seemed very close that night, and the Czarina could not account for it, for the habit of looking back was not one which she encouraged.

Perhaps it was the occasion itself which brought the ghosts of the last ten years crowding into her thoughts. She leant forward and regarded her own reflection in the mirror.

So many things had altered in her personal life, events had harried her almost without respite. Circumstances had delayed her splendid plans for the enlightenment of her country; expediency had decreed that she shelve her cherished project for freeing Russia's millions of serfs. . . .

Catherine frowned slightly. She had not forgotten her ideals, she merely waited until the time most suitable for their application.

It was an argument that she had found it necessary to employ too often in the beginning of her reign. Her conscience had been strong and strident then in its demands; she had been young and flushed with victory. The task of government seemed easy, her problems resolvable by honesty and reason. But the years had taught her the folly of that assumption, and the money she had intended to devote to the building of schools to educate her ignorant people had been poured into armaments for war; the reformer had plunged into a policy of ruthless conquest and expansion, urged on by the nationalistic leanings of her chief Minister, Panin, who had been one of the conspirators that had placed her on her husband's throne. But she remembered very well that her rise to power was never his original intention. In the beginning he had plotted for another . . . Her frown deepened at the thought.

The occasion was to blame for all these unsatisfactory musings. Years ago Panin and others had intrigued for her son Paul, and it was this night, when she prepared for the banquet to celebrate his wedding, that called the past so vividly to her mind.

Paul Petrovitch; he had been nine years old when she took the crown which should have been his on the death of Peter. Panin had forgotten that technicality as others had done, only too eager to participate in the fortunes of the new sovereign and to share in the spoils divided among her supporters. But the pale, ugly child had remembered, and that tremendous wrong had added to the intensity of his hatred. It was a mutual feeling, ungovernable on the side of the nervous, sullen boy, concealed and deadly in the heart of his mother.

They had never liked each other; they had begun their relationship as strangers and developed it as rivals; it had seemed impossible that there should ever be a truce between them.

She had closed her mind to the advice of those nearest her. He is rebellious and disloyal; he is his father's son in nature as he is in looks. Imprison him, put him to death. . . .

She had been forced in the end to murder one Czar. Ivan had been a babe in arms when he was crowned; he was scarcely two years old when the Empress Elizabeth's palace revolution had dethroned him and swept him into the darkness of imprisonment from which he had never emerged.

Elizabeth, whose cruelty was only matched by her superstitious piety, shrank from ending her hapless victim's agony and her own insecurity, so that Catherine discovered that, with the former's power, she had inherited her nightmare, a rightful Russian Czar, alive and in prison. Reports had dismissed him as mad, and Catherine, mindful of her own love of freedom and daylight, fully credited these tales.

Her instincts of mercy were instantly aroused; she visited the prisoner secretly, determined to free him, assured that the spectacle of his witlessness would render him harmless to her cause. But Ivan Ivanovitch was sane; backward perhaps, but in perfect health. The Empress had returned to her palace, the lie of his lunacy already prepared, but without the living proof. Within two short years the throne was rocking under her, revolt was threatening all over Russia, and the name upon the rebels' lips was Ivan. So Ivan had to die.

The burden of that dreadful deed had done more than anything else to safeguard the life and liberty of Catherine's son, Paul. Despite his faults, his disobedience and open enmity towards her, Catherine had spared him; she had no wish to take life unless she must, and for several years now she had been promised a solution. The doctors who attended upon the Czarevitch prescribed marriage as the cure for the ills of temperament, the nerves, discontent and violent rages to which the royal patient was subject.

Catherine had agreed; she had found him a wife, and that morning the marriage had taken place.

Was it possible that a solution had really been found to this rivalry between them? The Empress hoped so with all her heart. She had no love for her son; he inspired nothing in her but suspicion and dislike, yet she needed desperately the peace of mind his submission could give her. She longed for an omen of prosperity that did not have its origin in the wars her armies waged; she wished for a truce with her enemy, and above all for an heir from this marriage who could succeed him if the need to follow her advisers ever came to pass. . . .

The clock on the dressing-table struck the half-hour, reminding her that it was time to complete her toilette for the banquet, and Catherine rang for her ladies-in-waiting.

She sat quietly in her chair, watching their ministrations reflected in the mirror, examining the image of herself.

At forty-four she was still beautiful, though lines of concentration marred the smooth, high forehead, and the angle of her square jaw was more pronounced. It was a handsome face, fine featured, with vivid blue eyes and the clear complexion of a young girl; the sweep of hair which her ladies were arranging was still jet black; when her reflection smiled it radiated charm and grace. Yet the Empress knew her image to be nothing but a clever mask.

Beside the numberless cares and responsibilities of her position, Catherine had endured a personal torment which had only just been eased. For the first ten years of her reign she herself had been ruled, and the yoke imposed upon her had threatened to crush that indomitable spirit. Her ruler had become her lover when she was still Grand Duchess, a person as fabulous as herself in looks and reputation, the handsome, ruthless Gregory Orlov. Together they had planned the *coup d'état* which was to place her upon Peter's throne, and in his love for her Catherine had found the fullest satisfaction of her life. Cruel and barbarous he may have been, but his passion for her was undoubted. In adversity and danger nothing had come between them; it was in Catherine's triumph that his love for her had died.

He had expected consort's rank as the reward for his services, but equal power was the one favour Catherine would never give him. Money, lands, palaces and serfs were poured into his discontented hands, but nothing removed the stain of favouritism from his manhood. In the arms of countless mistresses, Catherine's lover sought revenge and consolation, and for ten long years she had suffered agonies of helpless jealousy, too much in love with him and too afraid of his power to discard him and end her servitude.

The previous year had seen the final outrage against her in the seduction of his thirteen-year-old niece, and Catherine, driven beyond caution, sent him on a mission and then banished him to his estates.

Her chief lady-in-waiting was securing a diamond coronet in her hair; the huge stones flashed brilliantly in the candle-light; a magnificent necklace was already gleaming around her throat. The Empress reflected suddenly that she would gladly exchange every jewel in her possession if she might safely return to Gregory Orlov's arms. But whatever the loneliness and nostalgia she felt, Catherine knew better than to weaken. Knowledge of her own temperament had dictated a measure which made Orlov's return impossible. She had taken another lover in his place.

"Your Majesty looks beautiful to-night. More beautiful than ever. Will you choose a fan?" Catherine looked into the mirror and smiled at the speaker's reflection. The Countess Bruce, her friend and confidante, the personification of discretion and loyalty; few people understood the needs of Catherine as she did, or pandered to them so efficiently. "Have you selected some for me to see, Bruce?"

"Yes, Madame. With that red gown, I thought perhaps one of these . . ." The Empress considered some half-dozen fans, a sample of the hundreds in her possession, most of which she would neither see nor use. After a moment she chose a painted chicken skin on gold sticks inset with diamonds.

"I wish to look well to-night. Remember, my daughter-in-law is very pretty!" Catherine laughed.

"No woman in all Russia can compare with you, Madame!"

"Now you know this little Natalie is quite charming! She's been much admired, and my son is infatuated with her. . . . It's strange, I never thought him capable of anything but hate. . . . Bruce?"

"Yes, Madame?"

"Could any woman care for him, do you think? Speak honestly. Everything may depend upon this marriage."

The Countess paused and met her mistress's eye in the mirror.

"Since you ask me, Madame, I don't think it's likely. No. I'm not squeamish, but even I wouldn't fancy him as a lover. . . . But she's young and pliable. They tell me she was carefully watched in Germany and nothing could be found against her. She may be content enough with him."

"I made sure of her virtue," the Empress remarked grimly. "I want no whores intriguing here, neither in politics nor in love."

At the stroke of twelve she rose.

Countess Bruce smiled admiringly at her.

"Shall I send for M. Vassiltchikov, Madame?"

Catherine Alexeievna nodded, unaware that this was the first of many names that the Countess would mention in the years to come.

"Yes," she said. "I am ready now. Call him to escort me to the banqueting hall."

In the ante-room the new favourite waited. He was a young

man in his early twenties, tall, well-built and handsome, and he bowed low over his royal mistress's hand.

On his arm, the Empress left her suite; she walked to the banqueting hall in a growing mood of optimism. It was the night of her son's wedding; all over Russia the people feasted and rejoiced; the streets of Petersburg were full of happy crowds, celebrating the event with the Imperial gift of tree wine and bread. From that moment she would put the past behind her; the shadowy end of Peter the Third, the death of Ivan; her lover's defections and final downfall—these would be forgotten. She smiled warmly at Vassiltchikov, and tried to summon a fleeting affection for the cause of her happy presentiment.

Paul Petrovitch and his new bride were waiting, waiting as she and Peter had done nearly thirty years ago on the night of their marriage, seated in the same chairs in the same banqueting hall.

But the resemblance would end there. The union would be successful, and fruitful, and she would try once more to make peace with her son.

Filled with these intentions, Catherine passed on to the banquet unaware that, three thousand miles away, the skies over the southern Urals flamed red with the fires of rebellion.

. . . . .

The heir to the throne of Russia was then nineteen years old, and that night, for almost the first time in his life, he found himself the centre of attraction in his mother's Court.

The Imperial table was at the head of the immense banqueting hall; above it, a crimson velvet canopy rose to the ceiling, surmounted by a golden double-headed eagle, supporting the crown between its dual beaks and clasping the royal insignia in each claw; directly underneath this Imperial emblem, the Empress sat on a magnificent throne, raised above the level of the other diners. Paul Petrovitch was seated further down the table, aware that hundreds of curious eyes were fixed upon him, and despite his pretence of arrogant composure, his sallow face flushed and one hand tugged nervously at his lace cravat. He was dressed with all the splendour of his state and with the elegance of an age of lavish male attire. His tight blue satin coat was fastened with large diamonds, and his broad chest blazed with an array of Imperial and foreign orders. The lace at his neck was priceless and secured by an enormous sapphire; all the wealth of Catherine's kingdom was symbolized in the person of her son, and with it the pitiable spectacle of a disinherited puppet, placed on show.

Since Catherine's accession Paul had been thrust into the background; insecurity had been the corner-stone of his early years and growing manhood, and parental love had been denied him. Ill health had weakened him and ravaged his features with convulsions that left a permanent nervous twitch behind them. Inevitably his stability had suffered; deprived of love and normal interests, Paul's thwarted mind had seized upon the dim memory of the man he thought to be his father, and his childish need had invested the cowardly, effeminate Peter the Third with an aura of martyrdom and fanatical worship.

Peter Feodorovitch had become his idol; in the end he had sunk to bribing his servants to tell him those things about his father that he wished to hear. The sordid, tragic history of Catherine and Peter had reached him through the medium of ignorant lackeys, and their stories raised the figure of a maternal demon to rank beside his paternal god. His mother was a usurper, they whispered, and the listening child would sit and clench his fists at the thought of her treachery.

When the tale of his father's murder was repeated to him, the Czarevitch was often seen to weep, though he knew every detail of the tragedy by heart; so, over a period of years, Paul's hatred of his mother grew in violence until it could no longer be concealed.

She had killed his father, taken the Crown which was his rightful inheritance, ignored and despised him, while she kept a low-born lover in the state which would have done honour to a king. It had become necessary to exclude the Czarevitch in order to avoid scenes which he never shrank from making, and Catherine added to his grievances by banishing him out of her sight as much as possible.

Despite his youth, Paul Petrovitch fully recognized the danger which threatened him as a result of his attitude and the Empress's dislike, and it was characteristic of his reckless courage that the knowledge urged him to try the patience of his mother and her ministers to the limit, daring them to take the course of imprisonment and death which he knew they contemplated.

But on this night he wanted neither recognition nor revenge. His only desire was to be alone with his new wife.

With his first sight of her, a weight of unhappiness seemed to have lifted from his life. Shyness, stammering, all the inherited curses of a shattered nervous system had impeded him in the early weeks of his courtship, and the timid little seventeen-year-old Princess from Darmstadt lacked the confidence to make the necessary advance.

Strangely, this inexperience drew the Czarevitch out of the shell of his own fierce prudery. His first reaction to the mention of a wife had been typically violent. No woman chosen by his mother would be acceptable to him, and only when he was presented to his betrothed did his hostility waver and finally collapse.

They had baptized her into the Orthodox Church, changing the harsh German names and titles to the flowing Russian of Natalie Alexeievna. Paul leant towards her and smiled, some formal query on his lips, love and admiration in his heart.

The new Grand Duchess was small and delicately made; her proportions were almost child-like in their fragility, and the oval face upturned to her young husband was exquisitely pretty.

Her dark hair was piled unpowdered on her head, Paul's wedding gift of pearls and diamonds blazed round her throat and cascaded down over her breast; white ostrich plumes and a white satin dress embroidered with silver and pearls emphasized the bridal motif. She sat at his side, as pale and fragile as a creature of the Russian snows and gazed at her young husband with eyes as blue as sapphires. Never had Paul seen anyone whose beauty so conformed to his ideal; pride swelled in his heart as he looked at her, increased by the knowledge that all men's eyes were turned on him in envy. She glanced up at him and smiled and his new-found solicitude sensed weariness, so that he touched her arm with a comforting possessive gesture.

"Are you very tired, Madame?" he asked anxiously.

Natalie Alexeievna managed to smile in denial.

"No, thank you, Highness. You show me too much kindness. . . ."

That at least was true, and as she looked at him, Natalie's

heart softened in gratitude and pity. For all his chivalry, his assumption of courtesy and grandeur, Paul Petrovitch of Russia was perhaps the ugliest man she had seen in her life. So ugly, indeed, that unlike his delighted reaction to their first meeting, his future bride had wept with disappointment. From his earliest years, the extraordinary likeness to his dead father Peter the Third had been a source of comment to the Court and of horror to his mother. Since birth, rumour had declared him a bastard, son of Catherine by a Russian lover, but seeing him there were few who doubted his paternity.

The Mask of Peter the Third, so a tactless observer had named him, and the remark was repeated to the Empress. It did nothing to lessen her hatred for the innocent boy. A reminder of treason and murder was growing up in her sight and in the view of all those who cared to remember the past.

But Natalie Alexeievna saw her husband with an unbiased eye; there was no memory of the dead Czar to influence her judgment. Paul Petrovitch strongly resembled his mother.

Every feature of the Empress was reproduced in her son; her broad forehead was there, only accentuated to the point of baldness, her fine Grecian nose had been inherited, but flattened and misshapen, giving the Czarevitch a cruel, juvenile look, and her splendid eyes were set in his head. They might have redeemed the travesty of his appearance, had their expression been less fierce and tragic.

To such a man Natalie Alexeievna had been delivered, and despite the heat of that vast banqueting hall and the weight of her elaborate clothes, the Grand Duchess shivered at the thought. His gentleness and generosity made the burden of her state a little easier to bear; in all the strangeness of that teeming Court, she had one friend. It was her misfortune that he must also be a lover.

From the comparative peace and security of Darmstadt, the seventeen-year-old Princess had been thrust into this background, and the only support offered to her had been the blind, clumsy devotion of the overshadowed Paul.

Instinctively she feared the Empress. Her youth and inexperience shrank before the immense personality of the older woman, and her narrow judgment recoiled in loathing from the crimes attributed to her.

Paul was frighteningly ugly, and physically the thought of him repulsed her, but she clung to him desperately, and in the few weeks before their marriage, a strange bond of fear and dependence had been forged between them. Left undisturbed, it might have grown into mutual love, but already events were moving to determine otherwise.

Among the young men who attended upon the Czarevitch was a certain André Rasumovsky. Son of a family ennobled by the late Empress Elizabeth, Paul's equerry was gifted with good looks only exceeded by his charm. Some four years older than his master, he was the perfect model of a young nobleman who had grown to maturity under the protection of Catherine Alexeievna. Cynical, gay and without moral scruples, he liked Paul Petrovitch as little as he understood him.

He was tall and gracefully built, carefully veneered by the manners and dress of western culture, but the narrow, hot, black eyes and sensual mouth betrayed him. A scratch upon the polished surface quickly revealed the lustful unscrupulous barbarian, true descendant of the savage Muscovite boyars whose adoption of European customs dated back less than a hundred years.

Fate opened the first phase of triple tragedy when it sent him among the escort which brought Paul's bride by ship to Russia. Rasumovsky had noticed her immediately, drawn by her personal beauty and by the novelty of her obvious virginity. Desire was easily kindled in him; but the treasure destined for his hated master was strictly guarded, so that the equerry was left at the mercy of his own sensual imaginings and a longing increased by the knowledge of the difficulties in his way.

In Petersburg, his duties kept him chained to Paul's side and he came near enough to Natalie Alexeievna to inflame his interest to the point of frenzy. Day by day he watched the Czarevitch with his beautiful betrothed, watched and listened to the clumsy, boyish gallantries that he longed to be allowed to make to her himself. Perhaps the greatest irritant was Paul's gruff admission that he was very much in love, accompanied by his usual nervous blush. Instinctively Rasumovsky had drawn himself up to his full height, conscious of the other's short stature, and congratulated him with an angry sneer that his master failed to notice.

Would to God that Paul Petrovitch was just another man and not the heir to the Russian throne. . . . He might then fear to match his manhood against André Rasumovsky. . . .

Thoughts like these, shot with hatred and treasonable design, possessed the mind of the young man as he endured the wedding banquet, staring at the Grand Duchess Natalie, his caution evaporating under the influence of quantities of wine. Beautiful, fragile, virginal, she aroused in him a degree of longing that was composed equally of attraction and the challenge of a man in love with what belongs to someone else. A faint element of pity crept into his emotions, and it crystallized sharply as he met her eye for a brief moment. Across the tables she stared at him, and the loneliness, weariness and uncertainty that he read there caught at his heart. The Grand Duchess looked away quickly, and Rasumovsky saw a hint of colour rise in her pale face. Then and there the wavering intention hardened into a fierce resolve: the wish to cuckold Paul, whom he hated and was forced to serve, became a vow to do so, and Rasumovsky was a man who had often risked his life in pursuit of his own will.

Little did he guess that the gentle, shy Grand Duchess, now firmly wedded to an infatuated bridegroom, was even at that moment staring at her plate in mingled confusion and despair at her own feelings.

Something stirred in Natalie at the sight of that young foreign nobleman, something quickened her blood and troubled her unawakened senses, so that she both longed and dreaded to come face to face with him. For all her inexperience, the Grand Duchess's instincts warned her that he was in pursuit and that her exalted rank and married state were no protection. Only Paul stood in the way, a safeguard against a danger that she suspected had an origin in her own heart.

She looked up at Paul, considering that grotesque profile, and for the first time an impression of something that was less than human came to her. It was a young face, but in it there was neither youth nor the composure of a mind which had matured. There was purpose in that grim, narrow mouth and arrogant chin, but it was of a quality that inspired uneasiness rather than admiration, and the expression in his pale blue eyes was empty and soullessly unhappy, as if his sight turned inward to some secretly contemplated grief. Only when he regarded her did his expression soften, becoming warm with tenderness and life. The knowledge of that transformation had done much to please her childish vanity.

She touched his sleeve and smiled at him; it was a subconscious gesture of defiance, aimed at his mother who despised him, and at men like the Minister Panin, but more than any of these, it served as a rebuff to that impertinent young Russian in Paul's service who dared raise his eyes to her in challenge and in pity at her fate.

.   .   .   .   .

Outside, the palace sentries stamped and shivered, closing their eyes against the sheets of driving snow. Beyond the walls, all Petersburg was celebrating, and the sound of singing drifted across the frozen surface of the Neva. By morning, many of those who feasted would be dead, frozen to death in their rags, slain by the cold and the free wine which lulled them into a sleep from which they never awoke. On this, the night of their future Emperor's happiness, the poor of his capital ate and drank their fill, and in the glow of these strange luxuries, they lay down in the snow and died. Death came mercifully to them at their first taste of plenitude: they were fortunate, these corpses that the next day's sun discovered, more fortunate than their Czarevitch, who might well have envied them their painless, peaceful end.

In the small hours of that morning a single horseman galloped through the outer gates and drew rein in the inner courtyard of the Winter Palace. He was covered from head to foot with snow and his mount stood trembling with fatigue.

A groom held the reins while the traveller dismounted and showed his warrant to a sentry, who examined it under the light of a spitting pitchpine torch.

"Royal Courier . . . You bring your congratulations late, messenger. The Czarevitch is most likely already tumbling in his marriage bed! Pass!"

"I bear no pleasant tidings. I carry despatches from the Urals and God pity me that I must deliver them. . . ."

He was a peasant, this courier, and when, in answer to his insistence, he was taken to the banqueting hall to deliver his message personally to his Empress, he hesitated on the threshold, blinking in the light of thousands of scented candles, his tired legs trembling under him.

He was the last of a series of couriers who had ridden for days across Russia, carrying with them the most evil tidings of an uneasy reign. His tired eyes saw the Empress, seated on the dais under the velvet canopy, and his heart bounded with fear. But she was merciful, he remembered. The people said of her that she had never caused an innocent messenger to be put to death or tortured, no matter how bad the news he brought. Pray God that this was so. . . .

A page led him to Catherine; with shaking hands he drew the despatch from its leather case, not daring to raise his eyes, and sank down on the steps of the dais.

The Empress turned to him, and seeing that he cringed with fear, smiled and spoke graciously.

"What message do you bring me?"

The courier looked up at her and stammered.

"Imperial Majesty. Little Mother . . . pardon me. I bring bad news. From Orenburg. . . ."

Orenburg? . . . The great fortress town on the Urals. Catherine held out her hand and took the scroll from him, aware that many eyes were watching her. With a murmur of apology to her immediate neighbours she broke the seal and began to read.

A lifetime of self-discipline enabled her to receive the news without a change of colour or expression. Calmly she folded the paper and passed it to Panin.

"I think you should see this at once, Nikita. I shall end the banquet now; wait for me in my room."

One of her aides went to the back of Paul's chair and informed him that the Empress was ready for him to retire with the young Grand Duchess. At the given signal Catherine rose, and the assembled hundreds stood while she left the room, followed by the Czarevitch and his bride.

The ceremony of preparing the new Grand Duchess for her husband was duly carried out. Catherine and her ladies undressed the exhausted Natalie, and according to custom the Empress gave her daughter-in-law her blessing and extended her hand to be kissed.

Sitting up in the enormous State bed, Natalie obediently touched Catherine's fingers with her lips, so tired that she was near to tears, and aware that the expression in the older woman's eyes was not unkind.

"Good night, my child. May God's blessing be upon your union."

A few moments later Paul Petrovitch entered the room. He

stood there shyly for a moment, the nerve in his left cheek twitching, as always in moments of stress. He had just parted from his mother, and their meeting had been marked by stiff formality. The Empress spoke no words of personal affection to Paul; there was no stirring of maternal sentiment in her heart. They bade each other good night with the phrases custom put into their mouths, antipathy and pride rising between them.

" God bless you, my son."

As Catherine had spoken the words the memory of the despatch which awaited her brought a harsh note into that level voice. A ghost stood at the Czarevitch's elbow, a stunted figure, wearing the outsize wig which accentuated his ugly physical proportions, and it seemed to the Empress as if the shadow of the murdered Peter the Third mocked her salutation, before melting into the living body of her son.

Thousands of miles from Petersburg another phantom had arisen; a man claiming to be the late Czar led an army of her discontented subjects in rebellion, and with this hideous reminder of the past which she had hoped to bury, Paul's fair colouring, his ugly features and nervous manner seemed a reincarnation of the man she had hated and finally done to death.

Her much vaunted rationalism always suffered a check in the presence of her son. The knowledge that the heir to Russia's throne was a bastard, the love child of her first liaison, fought a continual battle against the superstition which his appearance inspired in her. He was the son of a Russian courtier, Catherine reminded herself angrily, while her expression hardened with dislike and the empty words of affection and goodwill were exchanged between them. Though Paul aped Peter Feodorovitch, not a drop of Romanov blood flowed in his veins. The Empress had often reflected angrily that her son lavished loyalty and love upon the memory of a man who would have eventually put him to death for his bastardy.

Whatever Catherine's feelings, those of her son were rooted in implacable enmity, and as usual he made no secret of the fact. He was still tense and angry when he came into the bedroom and stood looking at his wife. Then he noticed the signs of recent tears, and instantly he softened. He sat down on the side of the bed and took his bride's small hand in his.

For a moment there was silence, then the Czarevitch raised his wife's fingers to his lips and kissed them gently.

"Are you unhappy, Natalie?" he asked her suddenly.

She managed to smile through her tears and shook her head.

"I am only tired, I think. Forgive me, my husband. . . ."

Paul gazed at her with such a mixture of pleading and adoration that she turned away, disconcerted and filled with an uprush of pity for the extremity of loneliness she sensed. If only he were not so ugly, she thought, and blushed as if he could read her thoughts.

"Natalie. Do you like me a little?"

He was like an animal, she reflected desperately, avoiding those sad, searching eyes; a creature starved of love, and pitiful despite the trappings of power and grandeur which disguised his state.

The heir to one of the mightiest European thrones sat at her side, begging for her approval like the humblest suitor, suing for what was already his by right. In all the short time that remained to them, she would never come nearer loving Paul than on that first night of their marriage.

"Indeed," she whispered, "indeed, I like you very much . . ." and it was only half a lie.

.   .   .   .   .

In her own suite, the Empress and her chief Minister, Panin, were discussing the despatch from the Urals.

The Count affected to minimize the danger. He assured Catherine that a few troops and cannon would scatter the rebels, and he treated the question of the self-styled Peter the Third with amused contempt.

"The reports say he is a Cossack named Emilian Pugachev," he remarked. "From my knowledge of your good subjects of the Don, he's apt to be above six feet in height and powerful as a bull. . . . I fancy he bears small resemblance to the illustrious Czar! Come, Madame, don't disturb yourself! It's unfortunate that such news should arrive on a joyful occasion, but I assure you these rabble will be put down and their leader captured within a few weeks. As for this Pugachev, we'll make an example of him that will discourage others from trying on dead shoes. . . ."

Catherine rose and began to walk up and down. She seemed restless and angry, impatient of Panin's soothing explanations.

"I cannot take your light-hearted view, Nikita. My people rebel against me; they follow a man they believe to be my husband! Don't you see what this means to me? What if you capture a thousand Pugachevs and put them all to death? . . . My trust in my people has been shaken by this. I believed them satisfied; God knows I have never played the tyrant! Ten years ago all Russia cried out against Peter: now they rebel in his name. . . .

"I have done my best, you know that, Nikita. Tell me, have I been harsh or cruel to my subjects? Haven't I made the name of Russia feared all over Europe, increased our power and possessions? Yet twice in ten years I have been faced with revolution. Not palace revolution, but disloyalty from the people themselves! "

Panin abandoned his pretence and followed the Empress's example in frankness.

"If I may speak openly, Madame, you've always been too mild. In Russia, obedience is only ensured by fear, and fear is something that you have never taught the common people. The Court, yes. They know you and they know me. They do not dare to plot; and since the death of Ivan there is no alternative to you but the Czarevitch."

"And no one would depose me to put him in my place, is that what you mean? "

Panin shrugged. "Only a traitor and a fool would think of deposing you, Madame."

"Don't flatter me, Panin. You tell me I've been weak with the people; would you have me become a tyrant? "

"It may be necessary, if you would keep your throne in peace."

Catherine stopped abruptly. She looked tired and drawn. Panin, whose fortunes depended upon her supremacy, begged her to sit down.

She seated herself wearily and accepted the glass of wine he offered her.

"I've tried to do my best, Nikita," she said slowly.

"I know, Madame, and if kindness has led you into error, it's no great fault. I beg you to place this rebellion in the hands of my brother, Peter Panin. He'll know how to deal

with this Cossack rabble. Only you must allow him to enforce what measures he thinks fit. . . ."

The Empress regarded him with hard, unhappy eyes.

"I won't tolerate ingratitude. As you say, Nikita, since my
subjects do not love me, then they shall learn to fear me. The
rebels are to be punished with the utmost severity, and their
leader must be taken alive. I wish your brother to forget that
there is such a word as mercy until the last follower of Pugachev has been hunted down!"

The Minister smiled and nodded.

"I shall draw up those orders, Madame. And I promise you
they will be most faithfully carried out."

Catherine set down her wine glass suddenly and turned to
him.

"Shall I never escape Peter Feodorovitch, my friend? Must
I be haunted by him for the rest of my life?"

"I assure you, Madame, this crazed Cossack . . ."

"I don't mean Pugachev," she interrupted. "He is one
form of Peter, but have you forgotten the other?"

"Your Majesty means the Czarevitch?"

"Who else? My enemy, Panin, and my rival. You say the
Court would never conspire against me in his favour; but what
of the people? If they'll follow an impostor like this Pugachev,
how much more dangerous is my son. . . ."

Panin moved his chair a little closer to her.

"Perhaps your Majesty sees the wisdom of the advice I have
given you these last few years. Imprison him, Madame.
Abandon your maternal scruples and send him to the Schüsselburg. Return this child from Darmstadt to her home and let
me arrest the Czarevitch. We can say he was implicated in
the Pugachev plot. . . ." he added.

Catherine smiled cynically. "You're very anxious for his
death, aren't you, Nikita? I'll swear there is a cell already
prepared for him. . . ."

"It has been waiting for the past three years, Madame.
Ivan's cell. . . . You have only to give the word!"

Catherine Alexeievna rose and walked to the window. She
stood with her face in shadow, and he waited for her to answer.

One word, one sign, and he would be free to remove the
greatest menace to her safety and his own. She was safe from
palace revolution, he had said, but the statement was a lie.

It was true that the Court feared her too much to plot against her yet, but in Petersburg as everywhere else, there were malcontents, men greedy for advancement and riches who had failed to receive them at her hands. And then there were the people. He had not expected her to reckon with them, for she lacked his knowledge of the seething unrest among the overtaxed, ill-fed masses, still labouring in serfdom. Paul Petrovitch was the answer to the seditious hopes of Court and country, should they decide to rise against the usurper Empress, and Nikita Panin and his friends would never know peace or security until they had persuaded his mother to put him to death.

"I'm going to disappoint your hopes, my friend. You are not to lay hands on the Czarevitch. Whatever his disloyalty, he is still my son, and I can't bring myself to shed his blood."

Panin bowed in submission, his fat face set with chagrin.

"As your Majesty commands. But I shall continue to have him watched, with your permission."

Sensing the anger in his voice, Catherine left the window and came to him. She smiled, and instinctively Panin's hopes rose.

"Because I refuse your request, don't think I disregard your warning. I have reason to respect your judgment, Nikita. . . . It's necessary that I should have an heir to stabilize the throne, you understand. When the Grand Duchess Natalie bears a child, we'll reconsider this question of my son's retirement from the world. . . ."

Apparently satisfied, the Minister kissed her hand and retired. On the way to his own apartments he passed the suite allotted to Paul for his wedding night and his pace became suddenly slower at the sight of a man leaning against the corridor wall, watching the entrance to the Czarevitch's rooms. A lackey stood guard by the ante-room door, and by the light of the candelabra which the servant held, Panin paused before the unknown.

"Are you keeping some vigil, friend, that you're not gone to your own quarters at this hour?"

The man he addressed raised his head and bowed unsteadily. To his surprise Panin recognized Paul's equerry, André Rasumovsky. He also noted that the young man was undoubtedly drunk.

"Well, André, what are you doing here? Watching over your master?" he asked smoothly, suddenly curious.

Rasumovsky bowed again.

"You must forgive my zeal, Count Panin. I came to offer my humble good wishes to their Highnesses . . . but I find them already retired. . . . Such haste is natural when the bride is so beautiful," he said, and his tone was as strange as his expression.

Panin regarded him attentively.

"I advise you to go to bed, André. The Czarevitch has no need of your attendance at this hour. He is surrounded by those who wish him well. Now go to your rooms."

Rasumovsky stepped away from the wall which had supported him and stood swaying in the middle of the corridor.

"I am obedient, my dear Count. I retire as you suggest. . . ." He turned towards the door of the bridal suite and swept the astonished lackey a deep, unsteady bow.

"God bless the Czarevitch," he muttered savagely.

"And grant him long life," responded Catherine's chief Minister smoothly.

Then he departed, walking with the soft-footed speed common to many fat men, and silence enveloped the dark palace corridors once more.

2

FOUR months after their marriage, the Grand Duke and Duchess followed the Empress to the Summer Palace of Tsarskoë Selo, and there, in a setting of perfect architectural and scenic beauty, Paul enjoyed greater happiness and freedom than he had ever known.

Etiquette was slack. Catherine herself relaxed from the business of affairs of State, gave intimate parties from which her son was naturally excluded, and generally left him to his own devices. He was at liberty to please himself, and the fount of all his pleasure, the mainspring of his life, was Natalie Alexeievna.

He was so hopelessly in love with her that his subjection

would have been ridiculous if it had not strengthened him in other ways. He insisted on her company for every minute of the day, dismissed his equerries and her ladies-in-waiting, and, clasping her hand in his, hurried her away into romantic solitude. He never tired of watching her, of admiring her beauty, of listening to the tone of her sweet voice, and he loved her with a passion that was almost frenzy.

His shyness had given place to manhood and growing confidence, his step was firm, his glance direct, and in his treatment of his wife, he was tenderness itself. And like all lovers, he was mercifully blind. The essential shallowness of her nature and weakness of character eluded him; he worshipped in happy ignorance of the fact that his bride was neither in love with him nor as trustworthy as he supposed.

He never suspected that their long rides through the snow were nightmares of exercise and endurance to the shivering Natalie; that she was as bored by his lectures on military tactics and Russian politics as she was unmoved by his lovemaking. And he also failed to notice that her eyes followed the figure of another man, and watched him with an expression that was absent when she looked upon her husband.

Before she left for Russia, her advisers had warned her to expect little personal happiness; a loveless marriage was the lot of royalty, and Natalie was prepared for indifference and neglect. She knew nothing of what love might mean, and Paul's devotion bewildered and frightened her.

His tastes were alien; he revelled in exercise which she hated, bored her with intellectual discussions which were beyond her understanding, loaded her with priceless gifts whose value she did not appreciate, and in the middle of showing her some treasure in his library, he often threw the books aside and took her in his arms.

She thought him violent in his enthusiasm and unbalanced in his hatred of his enemies. And inwardly she shrank from his devouring passion for herself.

For the first time in his life Paul had a confidante, and the full flood of his grievances and hopes were poured into his wife's ear. The weeks in Petersburg had been a nightmare to Natalie; her early dislike of the Empress was increased a hundredfold by the tale of treachery and hatred that Paul told her, and often he repeated the story of the late Czar's death until her flesh crept with horror; and sometimes, taking her arm, he pointed out one of Catherine's most favoured intimates, a gigantic Guards officer, with one side of his face furrowed by a jagged sabre scar. That man, Paul whispered savagely, was the one who had strangled his father.

The other brother, Gregory Orlov, had returned to court after their wedding, returned, so rumour said, to oust the Empress's new lover, Vassiltchikov, and regain his former place in her affections.

Natalie only spoke to him once, when he was formally presented to her; and despite her rank, she blushed under that impudent, lustful stare, and for a moment understood why Catherine herself, whose word was the law of life and death, had run from a palace ballroom and hidden in her Minister Panin's rooms, when she first heard that Gregory Orlov had defied her and come back to Court.

She had never seen such men as these—giants and barbarians, without fear of God or man; the immensity of their build and personality terrified her more than it fascinated; she was not Catherine, who could love an Orlov and yet remain free.

To illustrate the point of his mother's depravity and the kind of men she honoured, Paul repeated the old tale of the young Lieutenant Potemkin, another traitor who had helped the Empress to usurp the throne. He, too, had wished to become Catherine's lover, until the elder Orlov, Alexis the royal murderer, had dispensed with this rival to his brother's place by picking a quarrel with him during a game of billiards, and knocking his eye out with a well-aimed cue.

Armoured by inexperience, Natalie turned from the Empress and her Court in horror and disgust, unaware that her censure and dislike were rooted in jealousy and discontent. She hated Catherine, hated her for her brilliance and her power, for the freedom with which she ordered her life and arranged her love affairs, taking and discarding whom she would, while her daughter-in-law remained tied to an ugly, ardent husband and tried to pretend that her mind and body did not yearn for someone else.

At Tsarskoë Selo, Natalie finally ceased pretending to herself as well as to the world and to the unsuspecting Czarevitch.

The presence of this other man had destroyed her chance of happiness from the beginning. From that first exchange of glances on the night of her wedding banquet, the eyes of

André Rasumovsky had followed her everywhere, taunting her; his nearness and her almost daily contact with him had undermined her dignity and shattered her resistance. He spoke to her as often as he dared, he touched her as if by accident, so that she trembled and felt a burning, traitorous blush rising in her face, while the voice of her own rebellious heart told her that here was the man who could make the mockery of marriage into the reality of love.

This conflict within her only found peace in solitude, and since Paul sought her company throughout the day, Natalie was forced to invent a headache and escape to her rooms when she could; on those rare occasions when the Czarevitch went riding far out over the palace parklands, she slipped out of the Imperial suite and walked across the snow-covered lawns to the Grand Duchess's pavilion.

This was a small building, designed in the classical style; and despite the fact that it was unused until the summer months, the interior was luxuriously furnished. It stood on the edge of an ornamental lake, now frozen solid, where by tradition the Grand Duchess's swans circled gracefully on the pale water, and the ladies of the royal family spent the long hours of the warm summer days, feeding their birds from the steps of the pavilion.

The charming rooms had become Natalie's favourite retreat, a refuge from Paul, a haven from Rasumovsky and her own confused, often adulterous thoughts.

One afternoon in mid-January, she went there as usual, unaccompanied even by a maid, and since the palace servants knew of her habit, the pavilion was already prepared for her. With her eyes half closed against the dazzling glare of snow and ice, the Grand Duchess walked quickly up the steps and pushed open the heavy gilded door, brushing some of the feathery snow away with her gloved hand.

The room she entered was beautifully furnished, couches covered with exquisite thread embroidery lined the walls, tables of ebony inlaid with mother-of-pearl shone in the light of a gracious fire. There were mirrors in frames of solid silver hanging on the tapestried walls, and the inevitable ikons gave the chamber that air of incongruous piety peculiar to all Russian dwellings.

Natalie, who was beginning to hate the luxury and barbarity of the Imperial palaces, loved the pavilion, forgave it the riot

of colour in hangings and ornaments, dismissed the dim,
elongated Saints in their setting of jewels and gilt, and spent
happy hours of peace within its walls.

She now unfastened her sable-lined cloak, threw it carelessly
on a chair and advanced towards the wide fireplace, warming
her small, chilled hands before the blaze. Her black hair was
damp and shining, where stray flakes of snow had penetrated
under her hood, and the hem of her blue silk gown was wet.

Natalie leant against the mantelpiece and closed her eyes.
She felt exhausted and near to tears, two feelings which
attacked her immediately she was beyond Paul's unwanted
supervision. She wished for respite, for strength to bear the
odium of a loving husband and the torturing desire to take
refuge from him in the arms of an inferior. And above all, she
was ashamed, ashamed of her own weakness, and a surge of
vindictiveness grew out of her humiliation.

For the hundredth time she determined to have Rasumovsky
dismissed from her husband's service. One word to Paul would
be sufficient. She had only to express the wish, and without
questioning her motive, the infatuated Czarevitch would
release her from the strain of André's presence.

Natalie thought of him and trembled with simulated rage,
playing with visions of imprisonment and even death as the
fate which she could inflict on the destroyer of her peace.

In the midst of these hysterical reflections Natalie heard the
sound of a door opening and then swinging shut; a draught of
cold air blew through the room, and she swung round, suddenly
frightened, believing that it was Paul who had followed her,
Paul who had come into the pavilion to find her, to smother her
with his love and forbid even this refuge in the future.

But it was not the Czarevitch. The figure outlined against
the doorway was far too tall and as it came closer she recognized it.

Then for a moment there was absolute silence, as Paul's wife
and his equerry stood facing one another.

"I followed you, Madame," he said at last. "I've watched
you come here several times and to-day I followed you."

"How dare you, M. Rasumovsky! You know I'm un-
chaperoned. You must go immediately. I shall report this
to the Czarevitch. . . ."

They were brave words but her voice quavered uncertainly,
and Rasumovsky looked down at her and smiled.

"You won't denounce me to the Czarevitch," he said softly. "He would have me killed. You won't deliver me to that because I love you."

Natalie had begun to tremble. "You're mad," she whispered. "Mad. . . . For God's sake, André . . . go now. I'll say nothing to anyone, I promise you. . . ."

It was as much a plea for herself as for him, a plea to leave her in peace, not to do the thing she dreaded and yet longed for; even as she spoke she knew that it was useless, and in her heart she surrendered and was glad.

"I am mad . . . mad with love of you. And you're not indifferent to me. Don't pretend, Natalie, you have betrayed yourself a hundred times. . . ."

As he advanced upon her the Grand Duchess backed away from him and, turning, tried to reach the window. It was a futile attempt at flight from the inevitable. There was no one to hear her cry or see her signal had she had time to make one, for Rasumovsky sprang forward and caught her.

When he first touched her she resisted; her small fists struck at him and she strained backwards, trying to avoid his kisses. He held her tight against him as she struggled, murmuring his love and need of her.

"You are so beautiful . . ." he murmured, aware that her small hands were clinging to him and that her resistance was turning to response.

"André . . . Oh, André . . ."

He picked her up and carried her to a couch which was pushed back against one of the tapestried walls.

"I love you," he had said, over and over again, and for the first time in his life the empty formula had meaning. The fulfilment of desire had flooded him with a tenderness that he had never felt for any other woman, and in the face of this he became suddenly defenceless.

He looked up at her and smiled; they gazed at each other in silence for a moment, and in that moment expressed a love for which no words would have been adequate.

Rasumovsky raised himself upon one elbow, and touched her face with gentle fingers.

"You're more beautiful than ever, Natalie. They say a woman's beauty blossoms fully in the hour of love. . . . I am only afraid that anyone who sees you will suspect . . ."

"Beautiful? Like this . . . with my hair down like a

peasant girl's? " For answer he wound a thick strand of her dark hair round his hand and kissed it.

"I love you, Natalie Alexeievna. You are revenged. No woman has heard that from my lips before without hearing a lie. But to you, I tell the truth. I love you and before God, I'm afraid for myself. . . ."

"Why afraid, my love? " she asked him gently, and sat upright so that she leant against his shoulder.

"Because I've lost my freedom . . . because I feel that if you deny yourself to me I shall never know peace again. . . . Do you love me enough to forgive me for what I've done to you and to myself? "

"I love you enough not to care," she said calmly. "I must have always loved you, André. From the moment I saw you on the boat. Only I was a child then and didn't understand. With Paul I had no idea what love could mean. It was never love for me. But I know now, my dearest one."

He bent and kissed her and when the embrace was over she rested her cheek on his shoulder and smiled absently, tranquil and dazed with happiness.

"It is snowing again, my love," he said after a moment, looking out of the long window on the opposite wall.

"Thank God. It'll cover our footprints. Oh, André, why do we have to go back! I wish we could stay here for ever. Paul will be waiting for me, sitting in his rooms watching my door, like a lovesick dog. . . ."

"Don't speak of him! " Rasumovsky said savagely. "He has the right to you that should only belong to me. . . . I have to live with that. I have to wait upon him, see him looking at you, knowing that when you are alone with him he's making love to you. . . ."

"I'm not going to let him touch me, not now. I can't help it, André; I shall keep him away as much as I can. Then I can be with you. . . ."

"I have always hated him. . . . Now I could kill him, because you are his wife. Come here, my adored one, let me hold you again, forget the Czarevitch . . . forget everything but ourselves."

It was quite dark when they parted at last, parted unwillingly and with the promise of a meeting the next day to sustain them.

"To-morrow, Natalia."

"To-morrow, here and at the same time. I'll find some excuse for the Czarevitch. Farewell, my love. Until to-morrow. . . ."

Within a little while the fire in the grate flickered into a last false glow of life and then died out; the pavilion was dark and silent, its window panes coated with snow, the dim shapes of the furniture fading into a background of stillness and dusk, until it seemed a trysting place for ghosts, as if the lovers who had left it were already dead.

．　．　．　．　．

For a short period, Catherine returned to Petersburg, where Panin awaited her with grave news of the Pugachev rebellion. The troops and cannon sent to quell them had proved almost useless; the savage measures enforced against the rebels had done nothing to deter them; Catherine's lands ran red with blood and echoed to the hammerings of hastily erected gallows; the armies of both sides burned and slew without mercy.

But the revolt spread, thousands of starving, discontented serfs streamed to join the man they believed to be their rightful Czar, backed by the fiercely independent Cossack tribes.

Word reached the Empress that posters proclaiming her a traitorous usurper had been found in Petersburg itself, that daring voices had cried out for the Czar Peter the Third. And finally the dreaded sequel followed; the rebels in the Urals and the malcontents in the city had begun to mention Paul.

Panin and her councillors resumed their pleas for her son's imprisonment and death. It was the only way, they insisted; Pugachev was not the real danger; he would be routed, punished, publicly executed and the matter would end with him. But the true menace was the Czarevitch. It might even be that he was intriguing with his mother's enemies.

Catherine listened to them in silence, fighting the temptation to take their advice and humour her own wishes by serving her son as she had served her husband. Instead, she compromised. If Panin could show her that the Czarevitch was treating with her enemies, she would sign the order for his arrest and death within the same hour.

Satisfied, the Minister assured her that his spies were always active and departed, his heart lighter with the hope of catching out his enemy.

As an added precaution, he set a watch upon Natalie Alexeievna.

.   .   .   .   .

Early in spring the Empress returned to Tsarskoë Selo, and though she made frequent trips to Petersburg, and spent some time in Moscow, the Czarevitch and his little court remained at the Summer Palace. There were rumours of an impending change in Catherine's household, and the handsome favourite Vassiltchikov trod warily, confiding to some that the Empress treated him with growing indifference. Another rival had appeared, but no one knew for certain who it was.

While the Court gossiped and speculated, Paul pretended not to listen, and in fact those summer months at Tsarskoë Selo were among the happiest of his life. All those who saw him were aware of the change that marriage with Natalie had wrought in him.

The sullen, ugly boy, his awkwardness increased by an air of sour suspicion, had given place to a young Prince, a Prince who stood erect for all his short stature, and who had suddenly acquired dignity and self-assurance. Towards his mother and his enemies he did not relent, but his altered character now made his hatred a force to reckon with, and the court opportunists came flocking to right themselves as an insurance for the future. But flattery did not deceive him, for he knew its worth, and while accepting it he made a mental note of those to whom he owed past grudges.

One day there would be a reckoning; sinners who thought their crimes forgotten and unpunished would render him account in blood, and often his eyes rested menacingly upon the figure of the Guards officer, Alexis Orlov, and recalled that as a boy, trembling with hatred for his father's murderer, he had once vowed to match the jagged left-hand scar on Orlov's cheek with an identical incision, before the head was severed from the body.

But the matter of his revenge must wait, for love of his young wife took first place in his thoughts.

To him she was the embodiment of everything he worshipped; the missing comfort of his motherless childhood was waiting for him in her arms; she gave him the companionship denied the boy who never had a playmate or an animal to love, and she appeared the fair goddess of all adolescent dreams.

He was immensely proud of her, tender and unselfish, blundering only through ignorance, and completely blind to her tepidity and faults. Also he believed quite genuinely that she loved him with a passion as unbounded as his own.

Her health was the only blight upon his happiness, for his wife pleaded constant headaches and spent long hours ostensibly resting in her room. In his tenderness and anxiety, Paul humoured her lightest wish, and was comforted by the doctors when they assured him that though perhaps a little tired, the Grand Duchess was in good spirits and quite well. He became grateful for her companionship, and treasured their hours together; the smallest word or gesture of affection sufficed to please him, and since the physicians hinted that she was fatigued from love-making, he mastered his intense desire for her.

It was a courtier, Leo Naryshkin, for thirty years the devoted friend of Catherine, who noticed that the twitch in Paul's left cheek had disappeared. Others observed that the nervous habits had disappeared, the tricks of caricature were passing from his manner, and as a result the likeness to the dead Czar Peter was not nearly so pronounced.

Naryshkin, who knew very well the history of that old love affair, and the bastardy of the child ostensibly legitimate, spoke to the Empress one evening as the two were playing cards.

Leo, his hair now thickly streaked with grey under the powder, watched Catherine with admiring eyes. Thirty years of unrequited love had aged him, but the fire of his desire for her still burned.

The fall of Gregory Orlov had rekindled hope in him, and the knowledge that she was tiring rapidly of his successor brought Naryshkin to her side once more. But he was careful to say nothing of these things.

Instead, he talked of Paul.

Catherine put down her cards and listened.

" You find him much changed then? " she asked.

" Yes, Madame, almost beyond recognition. This child from Darmstadt has transformed him. God knows, I thought him a grotesque; now he has dignity, almost presence. One might remember who his mother is," he added, smiling.

Catherine's expression did not soften.

"He hasn't changed to me, Leo. He hates me still, calf love for Mistress Natalie hasn't altered him in that. She, too, looks on me with disapproving eyes, primed by my son. I'm not a happy mother, my friend. The children born of me, whether they are hidden bastards like Paul, or the son of Gregory, prove rebellious and ungrateful. You know Panin urges me to have the Czarevitch arrested?"

Naryshkin nodded.

"He's afraid for his own skin, in case your son succeeds you while he is still alive. If I remember, Nikita's safety was always his first consideration."

Despite herself Catherine laughed.

"You mean the morning of the Revolution when he hid in his bed with the covers over his head, pretending to hear nothing till one side or the other had won the people over? Ah, yes. Then he brought Paul to the Church of Our Lady of Kazan to swear allegiance to me. . . ."

"I'll vow that Paul remembers it as well as we," Naryshkin remarked drily. "Therefore Nikita seeks to bury the memory and the Czarevitch in the Schüsselburg. . . . Don't listen to him yet, Madame. Be patient with the boy. He's young and he may turn towards you."

Impulsively Catherine held out her hand to him, and Leo lifted it to his lips and kissed it. There was no shadow of formality between them.

"He'd never believe that you pleaded for him. He hates you, too, my dear friend; he told a lackey once that he was sure you'd been my lover, and that when he came to the throne he'd punish anyone who shared my bed. If I die and he succeeds me, what will befall you, then? What will he do to all those that I love who are left to his mercy?"

Naryshkin held her beautiful fingers in his, watching the jewels in her rings flashing in the candlelight.

"If what he thinks had ever been true, I would consider any punishment worth the payment. But it won't occur, Catherine. You'll live for many years to torment my heart. And you'll be ruling Russia long after I'm in my grave."

When he left her, Catherine sat alone at the card table, turning up the squares of pasteboard at random, thinking of his words and her own.

If Paul succeeded her, the lives of everyone she cared about would be in jeopardy. Leo, despite his extra years, the Orlovs, even poor stupid Vassiltchikov, whose dismissal was about to take place; he, too, would suffer for the two years he had been her lover. Scores of helpless men and women would become the objects of Paul's vengeance, and Catherine never underestimated the strength of his memory or the extent of his vindictiveness.

He was loyal, she knew that too, and ambitious, as she was herself. Many of her traits were in him, but until his marriage, his nervous disability had hampered their development. She had tried to make peace by giving him a wife, and the union was rapidly changing him into a dangerous rival.

She remembered that Panin thought him conspiring with Pugachev, and that the pamphleteers and street-corner voices who cried out, "Long live the Czarevitch, down with the Empress Catherine," did so with his consent. How true that was she did not know, but if anyone could discover it and trap him it would be Panin. And if it were proved, she could take action.

They would all be safe then, all those she loved and who depended on her, and if Paul were declared a traitor it would not plague her conscience; it would never haunt her like the death of Peter and of Ivan.

"Ah," said the Empress under her breath. "Let him make one false move, and I swear by God that Panin shall have his way."

.   .   .   .   .

Before autumn the Court was preparing to leave Tsarskoë Selo and return to Petersburg. Already an army of servants and lesser courtiers had departed to put all in order for the Empress's arrival.

The end of that long summer idyll was a source of dread to Natalie Alexeievna. Here, where etiquette was lax, her meetings with her lover had been easily arranged, the disappointed, trusting Czarevitch fobbed off with pleas of headaches and fatigue, and her ladies anxious to pursue their own paths and leave the Grand Duchess to herself.

From the moment of her surrender to André, Paul's wife dispensed with modesty or guilt. She loved the handsome equerry beyond all caution, and as her passion for the one increased, so her dislike of intimacy with the other deepened in proportion. Rasumovsky became less reckless as the weeks went by, sobered by the enjoyment of his prize.

It was necessary to keep up appearances, he told his mistress a little anxiously. It would be unwise to underestimate the Czarevitch; fool though he was, there was still a limit it was dangerous to overstep. She must coat the pill with sugar, and pretend to some wifely feeling for him. He was stupid enough to be content with very little, André argued. A few words, a little praise, a sentimental sop to set his mind at ease, and any amount of lies to keep him out of their way.

It was easy enough to dupe Paul, less easy to keep him out of her bed, but with a ruthlessness born of her love for the equerry, Natalie almost managed to do both while the Court stayed at Tsarskoë Selo. With alternate coquetry and excuses, she deceived and avoided him, until even Rasumovsky marvelled at the depths of duplicity and passion which dwelt in the gentlest of women.

He marvelled and became even more enslaved. Other mistresses had tired him, wearied him by their caresses and their words, but the Grand Duchess in her teens did neither. Their love was mutual, and it fed fiercely on itself until he who had counselled her to caution with regard to Paul, became a prey to savage jealousy once more.

Often they discussed the Court's return to Petersburg, talked of it with mingled anger and despair, aware that freedom would be much restricted for them both.

A thousand difficulties stood in the way of their meeting in the confines of the palace in the capital, where Paul and his household were subject to rigid discipline by the Empress. Never would the danger of discovery be so great as when they both became involved in the routine of life under the eyes of waiting-women with nothing to do but watch their mistress, and the duties of equerry to the detested Czarevitch would occupy most of Rasumovsky's time.

With that prospect before her, Natalie clung to him and cried, and the sight of her distress drove him to frenzy.

"We'll meet, my beloved," he promised her. "Nothing shall deprive us of our happiness together. I swear to you; we'll find a way as others have before us."

"We will, André, my love. We must. . . ."

So they resolved, desperate in their need of one another, and in happy ignorance that their intrigue had been discovered long before.

3

NIKITA PANIN sat at his desk, supporting one pendulous cheek with his left hand while he turned the pages of a thin dossier with the other. He knew the contents off by heart, and it made very curious reading. Six months of careful observation lay between the covers of that report, the work of the Minister's spies who had been lurking in the shadows whenever the Grand Duchess Natalie walked or spoke to members of her suite, whether she rode with her husband in the park at Tsarskoë Selo, or sat sewing with her ladies.

Sandwiched in between accounts of her most harmless activities, they reported the astounding fact that the virtuous bride of seventeen was committing adultery with a royal equerry within a few months of her marriage.

Nikita, whose hopes of discovering the Czarevitch engaged in treason were still frustrated, swallowed his astonishment and for the time being kept the information to himself. His opinion of feminine virtue could sink no lower for the revelation: he only marvelled at the stupidity of the girl who plunged into a love affair before a legitimate heir was born.

For six months he had waited, collecting the reports of stolen meetings; but at the end of that time, when the Grand Duchess was still childless, though possessed by a husband and an extremely virile lover, Panin decided at last that there was no more time to waste. If there had been a child, even if fathered by Rasumovsky, then a secured succession would have set many uneasy minds at rest, and opened the door of a cell to Paul.

But Natalie Alexeievna had not conceived, and for that reason Panin had decided to denounce her.

At five minutes to ten he heaved his increasing bulk out of

the chair, settled his wig firmly on his bald, bullet-shaped head, gathered up his papers in their proper sequence, and went on his way to the Imperial apartments.

The usual throng of courtiers was waiting in the ante-room of Catherine's suite; the air was stale with mingled perfumes, and the atmosphere was stifling. The Empress's subjects did not share her passion for open windows and the corresponding draughts.

As he passed through into the ante-room adjoining Catherine's own chamber, Panin's little eyes flashed shrewdly along the lines of those whom his Empress had favoured with the promise of an early audience. He noted two generals, her secretaries, Leo Naryshkin, whose friendship with Catherine was an institution, and then glanced sharply at a tall, uniformed figure which lounged ungracefully against the very pillars of the Imperial doorway.

He recognized the man who waited there immediately, even before the great head turned towards him, and he smiled blandly into that ugly, arrogant countenance.

In answer to Panin's nodded salute, the soldier barely moved. He was a man of massive build; his dress was careless to the point of disorder; his manner haughty and detached. His colouring betrayed a strong strain of Tartar blood, and though a patch covered one empty eye socket, the light of a fierce intelligence glowed in his remaining eye.

Panin was well aware of the rumour that Vassiltchikov was about to be dismissed, but he doubted if he had just looked on the Empress's new choice. He was far too ugly, with his sallow, Oriental features and clumsy giant's strength. However, it was as well to err on the side of safety.

"Good morning, M. Potemkin," he said amiably, and then passed through the doors to Catherine's private room, his mind already returned to the downfall of Natalie Alexeievna, unaware, as he went, that he had just given greeting to the man who was to prove his own.

. . . . .

"Before God, I'm astonished! After a few months she's creeping into someone else's bed!"

The Empress threw the Minister's report down on to her desk and regarded Panin, frowning and still almost incredulous.

The Count smiled at her, and his smile was a diplomatic mixture of sympathy for his mistress and censure for the culprit, whose real fault lay in having been discovered in her crime.

"It's most unfortunate," he agreed, ". and distressing for you and the Czarevitch. But I'm afraid there can be no doubt. The Grand Duchess is this young man's mistress; they're intriguing here in Petersburg. It pains me to have to shatter your Majesty's faith in the girl, but we can't afford to let this scandal continue. Now that we know she's unchaste, the Grand Duchess can never be trusted again. . . . Even if we punish Rasumovsky, as of course we must, there'll always be others."

"As you say, Nikita. There'll always be others. But what woman living will ever remain faithful to my son! As she was young and inexperienced I hoped she might settle down. But I never expected her to love him—I don't ask for miracles, my friend! "

"I know that, Madame. But I think the most vital point is being overlooked. There's no heir of this marriage. And you must have an heir! As long as your son remains at liberty, neither you nor those who serve you can be certain of their lives. . . . You said yourself that he was the greatest danger to you. There's a scandal and there's no child after a year of marriage. . . . Supposing the Grand Duchess is barren! We can't afford to wait; take her and the equerry and put them to death! That'll teach her successor a lesson in chastity and obedience. . . ! "

Panin sat back and wiped his forehead with a large lace handkerchief; he was sweating with his own vehemence and his little green eyes glittered with malice.

"Put them to death . . ."

The Empress regarded him intently and under that searching look he smiled uneasily and lowered his eyes. With her genius for reading human hearts Catherine divined the depths of spite that prompted his suggestion. Nothing had been proved against her son, and the hatred Panin bore him hoped to strike at him by shedding Natalie's blood and proclaiming the failure of his marriage to the world.

It was a mistake that he could ill afford to make with her, and he fell into such errors when he forgot that for all her failings she was never cruel.

"There'll be no open scandal, Nikita," she said firmly. "Rasumovsky shall be dealt with, but as for the Grand Duchess . . . if there'd been a child, I might have pardoned her, but in this, too, she has failed my son. Therefore he must divorce her. She will be shut up in the Novo Diévichy Convent for the rest of her life. . . ."

"And the succession, Madame?"

"As you hinted, my dear Nikita, we'll marry Paul to someone else before the year is out."

She touched the dossier, and then rose to end the interview.

"I shall keep this for the moment. Now be good enough to send the Czarevitch to me; I think I'd better break this news to him myself. And Nikita——"

"Yes, Madame?"

"Have guards posted round the Grand Duchess's rooms. It may be necessary to protect her against the fury of my son."

  .   .   .   .   .

It never occurred to Catherine that he might not believe her. She was prepared for a fearful storm of anger, for violent reproaches, even tears, for in moments of great stress she knew that he was still boy enough to weep.

Instead, he stood before her as if petrified and flung the damning report on to her desk. Her invitation to sit down had been curtly refused; his only concession to the tremendous shock of the accusation was to steady himself with one hand against the back of the empty chair.

He regarded his mother in silence for a moment, his eyes blazing with rage, the nerve in his left cheek twitching violently.

"I don't believe one word of this," he said harshly, and in spite of herself, Catherine started.

"Do you dare ignore the proof that I've given you? In God's name show yourself a man! Don't try to deny that Natalie's made a fool of you with one of your own suite, that she's abused your trust by adultery and deceit!"

Paul shook his head with bitter irony.

"No, Madame, my wife's not going to be ruined to gratify your whim or any other's. These lies haven't deceived me, nor the indignation you simulate so well. Must I remind you

of my father, of Prince Gregory Orlov, or a certain M. Vassiltchikov, to convince you that I'm not impressed?"

Catherine stood up slowly, her face as pale as his own, and
her mounting anger might have daunted many lesser men.
But Paul only saw that his insults had struck home, and he
smiled savagely, his heart pounding, a great wave of hatred
and nurtured grievance rising in him. Even as he spoke, the
old theme of his childhood wrongs repeated itself in his
throbbing brain.

She had murdered his father and taken the throne which
was his right; she and her adherents had neglected and slighted
him, with the thought of final imprisonment always in their
minds. Now she was trying to separate him from the only
human creature he had ever loved, and with the aid of forged
evidence she hoped to persuade him to sanction her plan.

If Catherine had judged him obstinate in the past, she little
guessed the power of the resolve forming in his heart at that
moment.

Instead she lost her temper, outraged by his allusions to
herself.

"How dare you speak to me like that! Don't presume too
far upon my gentleness with you. Even *you* are not beyond
the reach of my justice. Take care lest I send you to join
your bride in the Schüsselburg!"

Paul glared at her in fierce defiance, and a tinge of colour
stained his sallow cheeks. He trembled, but the cause was
reckless fury rather than fear.

"Ah, my mother. Would you murder me as you murdered
Ivan?" he said quietly, and Catherine shrank back at these
terrible words, catching at her gilded chair for support. It
was a deadly thrust and the accusation stung her to bitter
cruelty.

"You fool!" she spat at him. "Are you so blind to your
own ugliness that you think any woman could love you, or
feel anything for you but distaste? There's a mirror; look in
it and look at yourself. . . . Then think of André Rasumovsky! So tall and handsome! Think and compare! You
stand there prating of Natalie's virtue, when any numskull
would realize that she despises you and only submits to you
because she must! There's your proof, my son. There, read
it again and then admit that every word of it is true!"

Paul's answer was to seize the dossier and rip it across; he almost threw the fragments at his mother as he leaned towards her, white faced and quivering with rage and pain.

"How you hate me," he said hoarsely. "Is it because of all the wrongs you've done me? You taunt me with my hideousness, you say all women must see me with your eyes; that my wife must betray *me* as *you* betrayed my father, over and over again if rumour is to be believed . . . Well I say that you lie! You *lie*, Madame! What do you want me to do, divorce her, deliver her to you to punish? Ah, by God, if any man dares to lay a finger on her I'll murder him with my own hands!"

"Do you threaten me? I warn you, Paul, I warn you for your own sake . . ." Catherine interrupted, her voice trembling with fury.

He looked at her and laughed in fierce defiance.

"It's you who threaten, Madame! But this time you're powerless to make good your threats; I know how you hate me, I know what you'd like to do. You'd have me killed, as you killed my father, if only you were safe. But you're not safe! The people rebel, they rise against you in thousands! Harm Natalie, and you'll have to take me with her. . . . I dare you to arrest me! Follow your inclinations, my mother, shed my blood and separate me from my wife, for you'll have to do both I swear to you. Then take the consequences, for before God, you know that if you touch me now the people would tear down the palace walls about your ears!"

She sprang to her feet then, and all the tumult of terrible maternal loathing showed in her livid face and blazing eyes. Paul saw her fully for the first time in his life, saw the carefully cultivated mask of amiability fall to pieces, revealing the true nature of the woman, the greed and lust and fear which dwelt in her soul, warping and strangling the good qualities. He was too prejudiced to see that even in her rage she was majestic, and too much the child of her own courageous body to shrink from the consequences of that anger.

"Get out of my sight! Go, while you still have your life!" she shouted, and as she pointed to the door he turned his back on her and went without a word.

She almost fell into her chair, aware that tears of fury were running down her cheeks. She leant her elbows on the desk and covered her face with her shaking hands, ashamed because she wept, enraged by the loss of dignity and writhing at the memory of Paul's reference to the rebellion.

What he had said was true, and the knowledge ate into her mind like acid. Her people were restive, her kingdom riven by an impostor whose power was still unchecked. And her son, her ugly son whom she had cheated and despised, was as popular with the masses as she was hated.

"You'll live to regret this day. . . . By God, I promise you I'll make you pay for every word you've uttered. Only wait; wait until I've beaten Pugachev! Then I'll know how to deal with you."

.   .   .   .   .   .

Once outside his mother's room Paul began to run, careless of the astonished stares of those who saw him, his heart pounding with dread, afraid that even while he stood before the Empress, Natalie had been arrested.

The sight of two guards posted outside the entrance to their joint suite seemed to justify his worst fears, and he halted abruptly. Instinctively one hand flew to his little court sword and snatched the slender jewelled weapon out of the scabbard.

He stepped close to the tall soldier of Catherine's household guard and brought the tip of the blade on a level with his breast. At that moment he felt an awful, crazed strength flooding into every nerve and sinew, and with it the impulse to plunge the glittering steel up to the hilt into the heart of the soldier who barred the way to his wife.

"Where is the Grand Duchess?"

The Russian guardsman looked into the dilated eyes of his Czarevitch and blinked as the point of the sword pricked his tunic. Paul felt the first sensation of human fear that he had ever inspired, and subconsciously the impression went deep. Over and above it lay his terror for the helpless Natalie.

"Answer me, you dog! What have they done with her?"

The sentry grunted and stepped back as the tip of the weapon pierced his uniform and scratched his flesh.

"She is inside, Imperial Highness," he muttered.

"Out of my way, or I'll pin you to the doorpost. . . ."

For a second the soldier hesitated, faced with the prospect of a flogging for disobedience, or death at the hands of the Czarevitch. Relying on Catherine's leniency he chose his life and stood aside.

Paul flung the doors open and ran into the ante-rooms,

calling her name. He found her in her bedroom. She stood in the centre of the magnificent room, surrounded by the luxuries he had provided, rooted to the ground with terror, one trembling hand straying to her lips.

Her ladies had been sent away, her servants dismissed, and within a few minutes soldiers had replaced the lackeys who did duty outside her doors. No one had explained these measures; her tears and hysterical entreaties had been left unanswered, while the conviction that her intrigue with André was discovered brought her to the verge of fainting with fear.

As Paul stood there in the doorway, looking at her with wild eyes, his chest heaving, the little court sword in his hand, Natalie knew that they had told him, and in her terror believed that he had come to kill her.

"Oh, my God," she shrieked and fell on her knees, shielding her face with her hands.

Instantly Paul reached her. His sword clattered to the floor unheeded, and the shrinking Natalie found herself gathered into his arms. He held her closely, stroking her hair, soothing and comforting the distress he misinterpreted as the natural fear of innocence.

"Don't weep, my beloved. Don't cry like that. It breaks my heart to see you suffer. You're safe, Natalie. No one shall harm you. . . ."

Natalie Alexeievna clung to him, and made up in instinct for what she lacked in brain, by keeping silent, aware that by some miracle Paul was promising her his protection, and that her only hope of safety lay in his stumbling words of love and reassurance.

"What have I done? They sent soldiers, dismissed my servants. . . . I found myself a prisoner as soon as you went to the Empress. . . ."

The Czarevitch picked her up and laid her gently on the great canopied bed.

"It was a plot to separate us, my darling. My mother invented a foul accusation and tried to persuade me to repudiate you!"

Natalie's eyes widened with terror at his words. Repudiation . . . Divorce, she had heard what that could mean. . . .

"Oh, no! No . . . Paul, you're not going to listen to her . . . you can't believe her. . . ."

"My darling Natalie, how can you doubt me? I tore her false evidence in pieces before her face; I warned her I'd resist a separation from you with my life! Stop trembling, I beg you, there's nothing to fear. . . . I'll protect you, my dearest love. . . ."

He put fond arms around her and comforted her like a child, until she pushed him away in her anxiety.

"But what did she say when you defied her? What did she say I'd done? Please, Paul, tell me . . ."

"She was angry," he admitted, determined to soften the account and allay her fears. "But it will pass. . . ."

Natalie sat on the bed, one hand held tightly in his, and as he spoke her eyes glanced away from him, unable to bear that loving gaze, afraid that the admission of her guilt would creep into her expression.

Paul watched her for a moment, the explanation dying on his lips, and quite suddenly he doubted.

The memory of that sheaf of papers, of the revolting, detailed evidence, so utterly damning if it were true, the vision of the man they had named as her lover, handsome, carefree André Rasumovsky, all these returned to his mind, and the blind, passionate force of his belief in her wavered. Doubt pierced him with the impact of physical pain; for an instant his ugly face contorted. He watched her closely, and then under that unblinking scrutiny she paled and tried to turn away. At that moment the gentle, trusting dupe had vanished; instead he held her wrists in a tight grip and there was an expression in his prominent blue eyes that she had never seen before.

He hurt her and she wished to cry, to take refuge in the tears that always unmanned him, but this time she knew that something more was needed. For a second, Catherine faded from her mind; her greatest peril lay with Paul, the peril that looked at her out of that ugly face and made it alien.

"They showed me evidence," he said slowly, and he held her so that she was forced to look at him. "Rasumovsky was named as your lover. For the past six months. Tell me, Natalie Alexeievna, tell me this is not true. Swear to me that you have been faithful. . . . I wait," he added quietly, and Natalie froze with fear.

Desperation aided her then; instinctive mortal terror for herself and the man she loved gave her the strength and the talent to cloak her lies with the appearance of truth.

She slipped down and knelt at his feet. Humbly she lifted his hand and kissed it, and her answer came without a falter.

"Before God I deny it. I have loved only you, Paul Petrovitch, and no one else. Now deliver me to my enemies if you do not believe me. . . ." Then she leant her head against his knee and burst into a flood of tears.

Her word was sufficient, that and his own longing to have his doubts dispelled. He begged her to forgive him for having questioned her at all, and in a passion of relief Natalie did so, until the knowledge that victory over Paul was not enough forced more tears from her.

"What will the Empress do to me? Oh, my God, I know what will happen, I've heard of those dreadful convents where State prisoners are kept. . . . Paul, Paul, you must save me!" she cried, clinging to him, her delicate features distorted with terror, but though he soothed and promised impossibilities to allay her fears, he could not comfort her.

"Don't think of such things," he implored, almost weeping himself in the face of her anguish. "You've nothing to fear, I tell you, they can do nothing without my consent. . . ."

No qualm of suspicion troubled his mind when she rested her head on his shoulder and whispered that he must protect André Rasumovsky since he, too, was innocent.

"He shan't suffer, Natalia. I promise you he shan't be victimized; his safety shall be part of my terms. . . . Now dry your eyes, my darling, and have faith in me. As long as I live I'll take care of you. . . ."

With her arms round his neck the Grand Duchess bit her lips to restrain a hysterical impulse to shriek with laughter at his trust and the irony of that last guarantee.

How long would he, or any of them, live, with Catherine as their enemy. . . ?

.   .   .   .   .

The rumour of the Grand Duchess's arrest had run through the Court like wildfire, and those who hated Paul and despised his prim little German bride rejoiced. All that day they waited, the malicious, the curious, and the few who sympathized; waited to see the farce of a happy Imperial marriage end in betrayal and disgrace. And among the crowd, yet apart from it, Rasumovsky watched and listened in agony of mind, tortured with fear for his mistress and uncertainty for himself.

He knew that they had been discovered, and the punishment which must befall her would either be death or lifelong imprisonment.

But the hours went by and nothing happened. In the privacy of her suite Catherine told Panin of her son's reaction and pointed out that she was in no position to accept his challenge. The armies of Pugachev were advancing on Moscow itself: to do violence to the Czarevitch might cause a revolution among a people already restive, and decide the wavering loyalty of thousands in favour of the rebels. There was nothing they could do, she repeated angrily, and then added that if her forces triumphed she would remember her son's action and know how to punish it.

With that Panin had to be content, and in the weeks that followed Natalie remained at liberty and Rasumovsky also.

They never had another hour alone together. Paul kept his wife at his side day and night, overwhelmed her with attention in public and soothed her fears in private.

Life on the edge of a precipice was no new experience for him, and the basic human wish to see the mighty fall and suffer for their mightiness was only too familiar. For ten years Catherine's Court had been waiting for him to follow his father's way of imprisonment and death. Now they whispered and watched, hoping for the Grand Duchess as a victim. Paul placed himself between her and danger like a tiger at bay, and the knowledge of her desperate peril made her cling to him.

Most of their time was spent alone together; they dined quietly in their suite and in the effort to distract her Paul played endless games of cards or read to her aloud. Every member of their household was a potential spy and the Czarevitch drove equerries and maids of honour out of their sight with curses, and quite frequently with blows. Natalie had never seen the duality of his nature so clearly as in those terrible weeks of waiting. His fierce tyranny to others was only matched by his passionate tenderness to herself, and often the Grand Duchess, doubly imprisoned by peril and by love, felt tempted to scream or throw herself wildly into his arms.

"Come and play picquet, my dearest," he asked her one

evening when they had finished supper. Natalie rose and walked to the fireplace, staring blankly into the flames. Picquet. They had played every night for a week, and as always he had contrived to let her win.

"No, Paul," she answered, and her voice shook. "No, I . . . I don't want to play to-night."

Immediately he sensed the change in her, knew that her nerves were near to breaking, and he crossed to where she stood and took her trembling body in his arms.

"What is it? You are still worrying, still frightened . . ." Natalie leant against him, grateful for the strength of his arms and for the illusion of security it gave her. She said nothing for a moment, and in that moment closed her eyes, feeling the warmth of his body and the comfort of his hand caressing her hair.

Instinctively she slipped her arms round his neck and thought of Rasumovsky, thought of the preliminary embrace before their fevered love-making, an embrace as fierce and hungry as her young husband's was gentle and protective.

The comparison had been enough to send her hurrying out of Paul's reach in the days before this danger threatened her, but for some weeks her awakened senses had been starved of love, even from the Czarevitch, who unselfishly abstained from her for fear that it might tax her strength during the crisis. Quite suddenly the storm within her broke. She clung to him, her body burning, trembling and breathless; the whole mountainous burden of fear, uncertainty, frustration and guilt became concentrated in one surge of feeling.

"Kiss me," she begged him. "Paul, I need you, please please . . ."

He held her in a grip that almost cracked her narrow spine, the blood rushing into his face, his carefully disciplined passion shedding the bonds of self-control.

"Natalia, my darling, I have wanted you so desperately. . . . Oh, God, come to me then. Come now."

He never thought to question her experience, to wonder at the sensuous cunning of her caresses, of how her lips, supposedly untouched by any mouth but his, could inflame him with a kiss that he had never taught her. In the blindness of his love and the ecstasy of that night he accepted the transformation as a miracle; the passive, obedient bride had revealed herself as ardent and demanding of the love he only longed to give her; in the mutual fulfilment of their passion he fell asleep, unsuspecting and utterly content.

And Natalie slept also, slept deeply for the first time in weeks with Paul's head cradled on her breast, the barrier between them broken, but broken, as with so many human obstacles, too late.

.   .   .   .   .

Meanwhile, Catherine waited. She waited to trap Natalie and punish Paul's disobedience with the patience and clarity of purpose which had eventually cost Peter Feodorovitch his throne and his life. And towards the winter of that year it seemed as if the reckoning would not be delayed much longer.

The great Pugachev Rebellion had halted. The masses of wretched, ignorant people who had followed the Cossack leader had dwindled to a disorderly rabble of drunken looters; and the ending of the Turkish war provided the monstrous General Panin with a new influx of troops.

The danger had come very close to Catherine and she knew it. While her letters abroad dismissed the revolt with careless levity, and her cunning found a witty nickname for the shaggy, illiterate Pugachev, Catherine admitted angrily to herself that she would never trust her people again. With that admission, the first part of a new era for Russia began.

The second phase opened one evening in the Winter Palace.

As usual after dinner the Empress sat down at the card table with a select circle of friends, among them the intimate of many years, Leo Naryshkin, and the man lately returned from the Turkish wars, he whom Panin had saluted that morning many weeks before. No one could have called him handsome, yet none who saw him could help but look again. He was very swarthy, his nose aquiline and long in proportion to his face, and the black patch which covered the mutilated socket of his left eye heightened the general impression of a Turkish potentate turned pirate who had somehow wandered into the cultured environs of Catherine's Court. His physique was remarkable even in an age and nation of giants; his clothes were colourful and enhanced by many jewels, the whole effect upon the eye was extraordinarily vivid, vulgar and powerful.

He sat in the place of honour on the Empress's right hand, and Catherine turned to him, smiling and fascinated in spite of herself.

"M. Naryshkin thinks you must find Court life tedious after the excitements of campaigning," she remarked mischievously. Gregory Potemkin glanced across at the man he sensed to be a rival and nodded in acceptance of the challenge. The eternal suitor, he decided contemptuously, still waiting in Catherine's shadow, waiting and hoping for another's leavings. Potemkin noted his grey hairs and sneered with all the arrogance of youth.

"M. Naryshkin is mistaken," he said in his deep, resonant voice. "The source of all excitement, and pleasure, is to be found in Petersburg. A smile from you, Madame, and any soldier would declare the stimulus greater than cannon!"

Leo opened his mouth to retort, then the sight of Catherine's hand resting upon the other's arm restrained him. He examined his cards closely, struggling with his jealousy and the certainty of defeat. This ugly barbarian had already been selected. He knew it. At that moment he raised his eyes and found that she, the idol of his life, was looking at him; Catherine smiled and he read the message in that smile. It was a gentle, regretful, final 'no' and he acknowledged it with an answering smile, which promised that the war of words was at an end between him and the victor.

"I hope you'll forsake your battlefields and remain long in Petersburg, General."

Potemkin bowed.

"The length of my stay depends on the Empress," he said boldly and turned his single blazing eye upon her.

Catherine lowered her cards, sustaining that imperious, ardent gaze, aware that he had drawn very close to her, and that the fierce masculinity of the man transcended his appearance. The climax of twelve years of patient wooing was about to overtake her.

Now Gregory Orlov was gone and his old rival had returned, courting her by letter and in person, displaying gifts of charm that made the luckless Vassiltchikov seem even duller than he was.

"How much longer must I wait, Madame?" he whispered. Catherine stared down at her cards, hesitating, knowing that those who played with them were watching. The fate of Russia, the future happiness of the Empress, the ultimate destiny of Paul hung in the balance and were suddenly resolved.

"We've both waited long enough, my friend," she said

quietly. She threw down her cards and rose from the table.

"I'm tired to-night," she said. Then turning, she placed her hand upon Gregory Potemkin's arm. "General, will you escort me to my rooms?"

.   .   .   .   .

For weeks after that night the whole of Petersburg held its breath, watching the new favourite with the Empress, seeing the special marks of affection that had once been Orlov's privilege; and this fresh scandal thrust Paul and Natalie into the background.

When he heard of it, the Czarevitch told Natalie and raged against his mother. Every instinct of a son jealous of the love which was his due, no matter how he thought he hated, rose in rebellion at the sight of yet another common paramour: Catherine the ruler, symbol of power and authority, was bad enough, but the crude associations of sex filled him with repulsion and fury.

The men his mother loved were always big, tall and broad-shouldered like Russian Hercules—Orlov, Vassiltchikov, and now this Gregory Potemkin. For twelve years the favourites had towered above him, and a proud, primeval instinct hated to be overshadowed. As he had loathed Orlov and despised his unintelligent successor, so he became Potemkin's enemy.

And with this resolve Paul began a personal war that was to wage for over twenty years.

In December messengers hurried to Catherine with momentous news. Panin's opinion of human treachery and greed were fully justified at last: the huge reward of 100,000 roubles offered for the capture of Emilian Pugachev had proved too much of a temptation. As he lay drunk in the ruins of his camp, surrounded by those he thought to be his friends, his followers had seized him and delivered him to the forces of the Empress. He was already on his way to Moscow in chains.

The Court was in residence in the Wooden Palace in the heart of the old Muscovite capital, and Paul insisted upon watching the triumphal entry of the defeated Cossack. Unlike her ladies and the general populace, Natalie had no appetite for horrors and no wish to see the sufferings of the man who

had so nearly dragged the great Catherine off her throne. But
for once Paul would not yield. They could watch from a
window in the palace, he said stubbornly, and there was no
need for Natalie to sicken since his mother's talent for well-
timed mercy had changed the ferocious sentence of torture to
one of simple execution. Not even to her would he admit that
a doubt tormented him, born of rumours and uncertainty, the
phantom of his own childish longing for a miracle to raise the
dead. He wanted to see the man who claimed to be his
father.

They had put Pugachev into a great iron cage, and drew it
slowly along the streets of Moscow, ringed by troops to keep
the crowds at bay, and as he stood by the palace window Paul
Petrovitch watched the procession pass under a thin cloud of
gently falling snow.

For some moments he looked on the prisoner, chained and
exhibited like a wild beast: the man was a giant, black-bearded
and swarthy, his clothing in rags; with both hands he steadied
himself against the bars of the jolting, swaying cage, unable to shield himself from the showers of filth that rained in
upon him from the hands of the howling mob. The same
mob, as Paul thought grimly, who would have knelt to do him
homage in the streets had fate given him the victory instead
of Catherine.

There was a moment when the eyes of the two men met,
high above the heads of the crowd: the big Cossack, helpless
now, but savage with pain and humiliation, stared into the
face of an ugly young man, saw the fixed expression that none
might read, the prominent brow and flattened nose, caught
the brilliant flash of a great diamond in his cravat, and
insensible to anything but the ordeal of his approaching death,
looked on the Czarevitch whom his mad imposture had
claimed as his son, with uncomprehending animal eyes, dark
and wild with suffering.

As the cage passed, Paul turned and slammed the window,
to the great chagrin of his attendants, who wished to see the
execution. It was not until he took Natalie in his arms when
all had been dismissed, and kissed her with desperate tenderness, that the truth occurred to her.

Pugachev was beaten. At that very moment his head had
fallen, judging by the great shout which had gone up from the
crowd outside. The Turkish war was over, the rebellion

broken. Catherine was seated firmly on her throne and could afford to give the succession where she pleased.

Paul's threats availed him nothing any longer. Both he and Natalie were left at Catherine's mercy.

4

"IT's the waiting, Paul, the dreadful waiting, day after day, pretending that nothing is wrong, listening for footsteps, seeing their eyes on us! I tell you it's driving me mad! "

They were alone in their suite in the Wooden Palace, alone to all appearances, though God knew who spied and eavesdropped in the crevices of that grim building.

"I can't bear it much longer, I really can't. . . . I almost wish she'd have me arrested and get it over! "

He tried to comfort her, lying and making light of their danger, blinded by love to the selfishness of that refrain in which the dominant note was always of fear for herself.

"Please, Natalie, try not to worry. It's two months since Pugachev was executed and she's made no move. That's a good sign, my darling; it means she hesitates . . . I've told you she daren't touch you without harming me, that is our safeguard! "

"Safeguard! Oh, my God, Paul, you know that isn't true! She hates you, you said so yourself and now she can do what she likes . . . Oh, the suspense! And this palace! This awful gloomy place—caged in here for weeks on end—spied on . . . I know we're watched—my women watch me, I've caught them listening—and the Empress. I'm so terrified that when I see her I feel I'm going to faint. Oh, Paul . . . Paul . . ."

She came close to him and caught him by the breast of his brocade coat, gazing up into his face. He put his arm round her shoulders and kissed her tenderly on the forehead, his heart contracting with pity, for she was dreadfully pale and her eyes were dilated with fright.

"Paul, I have an idea," she said urgently, gripping him tightly in her agitation.

"What is it, my love?"

"Let's go to her and beg for mercy!"

"That would be quite useless."

"Oh, don't look like that . . . wouldn't it be better to try, wouldn't anything be better than waiting to be buried alive in some prison before they decide to murder us? If you went to her, Paul, if you humbled yourself . . . she might relent. . . ."

Gently he released himself and taking her hands in his, led her to a chair.

"Listen to me, Natalia. If I thought it would save you I'd go on my knees to my mother this moment; but all she'd do is pardon me on condition that I divorce you, and you know what that means. . . . Whatever we did or said, she'd separate us."

"But why? Why?" she sobbed. "She knows I'm innocent. . . . Why does she want to persecute me. . . ?"

One lover, Natalie thought desperately. And she has had so many, the hypocrite.

"Why does she hate me?"

Paul turned away from her and went to the window, unconsciously adopting Catherine's favourite attitude.

"I am the one she hates. I love you and you've made me happy, and that is something she can't bear. And there's no child of our marriage. I believe that is her main reason."

"No child . . . so that's why." She stared at his broad back and touched her dry lips with fingers that trembled.

"Then there's no hope for me. . . ." She might have betrayed Paul with a dozen men or stayed as chaste as he believed her, the result would have been the same. They wanted to get rid of her because they thought her barren.

"But I'm only nineteen," she whispered, so low that he did not hear. "Surely there is still time. . . ." There must be time, someone must beg the Empress to grant them a respite, and even as the thought of falling at Catherine's feet occurred to her, she saw the hopelessness of what she contemplated. Paul was right; Paul with his fierce pride and reckless courage, he knew that there was nothing to be gained by pleading or he would have sued for pardon long before in order to protect her.

"Natalie."

He stood before her holding out his hand and she rose with his assistance.

"Come in to supper, my little one, and I beg of you, eat something. You're growing so thin and pale. And try to calm yourself; God will protect your innocence."

The idea that Divine intervention depended on her virtue struck the Grand Duchess as a joke that André would have relished; André who worshipped nothing and believed in nothing. How he would laugh if she could tell him . . . if she could only get near him, see him for a minute, speak to him. . . .

Looking at her across the table, Paul noticed that her eyes had filled with tears, and that she had eaten nothing.

Would to God that she were pregnant, he thought, his heart breaking with love of her. Then they would have their heir, their substitute for him. And they could kill him if they wished, so long as she were safe.

.   .   .   .   .

Nikita Panin was becoming increasingly angry and uneasy at the Empress's failure to take advantage of her strength and strike down her son. Daily he sought Catherine out and begged her to seize the Grand Duchess and put an end to the situation. Imprison her, he urged, and then make the Czarevitch re-marry; he would have to obey, Panin argued; there were always means with which to bend a stubborn will . . . the threat of ill-treatment for Natalie Alexeievna, perhaps even of death for her, might persuade him into obedience. . . . If Her Majesty was listening to the advice of others, he implored her to heed his counsel rather than that of her intimates, who were perhaps more familiar with soldiering than politics. . . .

Catherine listened in silence, aware that the words whispered into her ear behind the bed curtains were carrying more weight than all the Minister's clever diatribes. And Panin was mistaken when he dismissed Potemkin as an ignorant soldier. He was proving to be extraordinarily cunning, far-sighted and shrewd.

He shared her patriotism, her ambition, her passion for debate, and for weeks he had been ridiculing Panin whom she knew he hated. She told him he was jealous of the Minister for the joy of seeing him caricature his enemy, waddling round her boudoir with a cushion stuffed under his tunic, admonishing her in Panin's irritating falsetto voice.

Jealous! Potemkin roared, half laughing and half angry, jealous of that squeaking bladder of venom! Let him choke on his malice against the Czarevitch and his wife! Wait, wait, he begged her seriously; give the criminals a few months' grace, let Russia settle down after the tumult of rebellion before a court scandal of such magnitude was loosed. And Catherine listened to him.

"As you advise, my beloved," she said to him. "I won't act against them yet, though Panin presses me to do so."

So she promised Potemkin, anxious to flatter, and deny him nothing. When he had left her she went to her writing-desk and made a note in her journal to separate Natalie from Paul in the course of the yearly migration to Tsarsköe Selo, and divert her to the nearest prison. The date was fixed for the middle of summer.

. . . . .

A few weeks before the time limit set by Catherine, Natalie Alexeievna fainted at a banquet. She was carried to her rooms, followed by the Czarevitch, who rushed from the table without waiting for permission. While the royal physician attended her, Paul paced up and down in the ante-room, the sweat running down his face.

The tremendous emotional strain of the past months had shattered his unsteady nervous system and in his anxiety he walked up and down, weeping, his grotesque features contorted with grief.

When the doors of her bedroom opened he started forward and confronted the doctor, unaware of the strange spectacle he presented or of the other's quick recoil.

"What is the matter with my wife?"

The doctor tried to withdraw his arms from Paul's fierce, shaking grip and smiled uncomfortably.

"There is nothing wrong with her, Highness. No cause for alarm. Instead there is reason to rejoice." He paused, until the strong fingers bit into his flesh.

Then, in one sentence, he reprieved his patient, and sentenced the listening Czarevitch to the fate his enemies had long intended.

"The Grand Duchess is with child."

.   .   .   .   .

The same night Paul went to tell the Empress.

"Madame, forgive me for disturbing you but the Czarevitch is in the ante-room. He asks to see you."

The Empress slipped her arms into the loose-sleeved Russian jacket that her robing mistress held out for her and then turned to the speaker.

"I will not see the Czarevitch," she said coldly. "I am expecting General Potemkin, Bruce, and I don't wish to be disturbed. Tell him to come to-morrow, and to seek audience like everybody else!"

The Countess shrugged.

"I have already said that, Madame, knowing that you were receiving the General. But he refuses to be turned away. He seems very agitated. He says it concerns the Grand Duchess," she added.

"Oh, I dare say! She fainted to-night during the meal and had to be carried to her rooms. Most edifying, in front of the English Ambassador, with my son running after her like a lunatic. . . ."

Catherine paused while her attendant fastened the red velvet jacket over her voluminous lace petticoats and smoothed back the écru lace from her breasts. Her ceremonial gown, stiff with jewels, had been put away, her diamonds removed, her hair brushed and loosened because it pleased her favourite to pull it down over her shoulders.

The Countess Bruce still hesitated, presuming upon her singular friendship with her mistress.

"I should see him, Madame; if only for a moment, to find out what he wants. . . . He might be willing to repudiate her now. . . ." she suggested.

"Repudiate her? No, Bruce, you don't know my son! Whatever he comes for, it is not to yield to me, be sure of that! Oh, very well then, admit him."

The Empress sat down in a gilded chair, her beautiful hands gripped the arms, her face set with hatred and suspicion. He had sought her out at last, after months of waiting, and demanded an audience with his usual arrogance. This would be their first private meeting since that hideous scene when she faced him with Natalie's adultery, and the memory of it made her heart pound with anger. I know, she thought grimly, I know, that little slut is ill with fear for herself and he comes to me to beg! By God, I'll prescribe a remedy for her that shall put her out of her pain, whatever Gregory advises. . . .

"Madame."

He was in the room, advancing towards her, his left cheek throbbing so violently that she frowned with distaste and looked away from him.

He paused in front of her, and then to her astonishment he knelt.

"It was very good of you to see me, Madame."

Catherine looked at him in surprise. She ignored his remark and said angrily:

"Why did you leave the banquet without my permission? Or have you come to apologize for your ill manners and breach of etiquette?"

"I have news . . . important news, about the Grand Duchess."

"Really? Then she's decided to admit her guilt, is that it?"

Paul looked down and bit his lip to stifle the furious retort that trembled on his tongue. How I hate you, he thought, how I would like to get up off my knees and spring at you, put my hands round your throat and squeeze the life out of your body as your friends did with my father. . . . He fought down the impulse, almost frightened by the suddenness and intensity of emotion which seized him as he listened to that mocking voice.

"My wife . . . my wife is pregnant. I came to tell you. . . ."

There was a moment of silence, broken by the musical chimes of Catherine's mantel clock. She counted twelve, her mind registering that the banquet had ended early, that by this time she should have been lying in Potemkin's arms . . . Pregnant, her son had said. Panin was wrong, they were all wrong; Natalie was with child.

She sat very still and said nothing.

Paul stared at her in desperation, trying to read that pale implacable face.

"I don't plead for myself," he said hoarsely. "I only beg of you . . . receive Natalie in friendship. She's ill, Madame, she scarcely sleeps or eats because of your displeasure. Now she bears my child . . . your heir. For her sake, not for mine, reinstate her and put her mind at rest."

Catherine looked on his bowed head and saw his hands clench to conceal their trembling.

"Go to the Grand Duchess," she said at last. "Go and offer my congratulations. Tell her that all is forgiven. I'll receive her privately to-morrow, if she is well enough. As for Rasumovsky, whom you persist in defending, I shall send him abroad. There is an end of the matter."

When he had gone she rose, hesitating with her hand on the bell-cord. Was it possible that he suspected what the birth of this child was going to mean for him, she wondered, and then dismissed the thought as fancy. No man was capable of love like that.

Within a year her problem would be solved and solved by means she didn't care to think about.

.   .   .   .   .

While the Empress lay in Potemkin's arms, Paul sat on the edge of Natalie's bed and told her that the danger of arrest was past. He held both her hands in his and reassured her eagerly, his voice unsteady with tenderness and pride.

"It will be a son, Natalia. I know that it will be a son. We will name him Peter . . . if that pleases you."

The Grand Duchess glanced down at the bedcover and assured him that it did.

In actual fact she scarcely listened. She was safe: the living nightmare of fear and suspense was at an end because of the coming of an heir for Russia, yet she who should have been delirious with relief could scarcely find the words to try and echo Paul's enthusiasm. She felt faint and ill, and the knowledge of what her slight body carried frightened her: soon it would grow heavy and stir with life, and quite suddenly Natalie flung her thin arms round her husband's neck.

He felt her tears against his cheek and held her close.

"What is it, my darling one, what's the matter. . . ?"

She lifted her head and looked at him and the sight of his ugly, worried face aroused the first spasm of genuine tenderness that she had ever known for him. She smiled forlornly, trying not to shiver.

"You're very kind to me, Paul Petrovitch," she said gently.

"I'm the most fortunate of wives. I only weep for happiness because of our son: and we will call him Peter as you wish. I think I'd like to sleep now, dear Paul."

With his own hands he covered her and snuffed out all but the two candles by the bed. When he had gone her eyes flew open and the tears welled up and overflowed on to the silk pillow; for some time she lay quite motionless and wept, staring up at the heavy embroidered canopy over her head, while a presentiment of tragedy enveloped her.

Paul was delighted, the Empress appeased. A new chance of life and liberty stretched before her, but in the candle-lit gloom of her great bedroom, the Grand Duchess Natalie Alexeievna stared into the future with wide, frightened eyes and wondered why she felt so cold.

Two days later, while she was still confined to her rooms, André Rasumovsky left Petersburg to carry out a diplomatic mission. He left in thankfulness and peace, aware that the woman he loved was safe and that his only punishment was this period of banishment. It would not last for ever and when he returned he hoped to resurrect the past.

As he passed out of the courtyard he raised his eyes to the windows of her suite, the panes aflame in the summer sunlight, hoping for one last glimpse of her, but there was none. So he spurred his horse and rode out of the city. He never saw Natalie Alexeievna again.

.   .   .   .

That summer the Court left Petersburg as usual and Natalie was forced to follow the Empress to Tsarskoë Selo with all its poignant memories of her absent lover. She travelled in a litter, drawn at the slowest pace so as to eliminate the jolting which might bring on a miscarriage, and Paul walked his horse at her side, leaning down to ask anxiously whether she were comfortable and well.

Natalie managed to smile and reassure him, before sinking back upon her cushions, sick and faint, trying to watch the interminable Russian landscape, and the hundreds of poor people who waited for days by the parched roadside to see their Empress pass. Hour by hour the vast procession journeyed on, led by the great gilded coach in which Catherine sat, smiling and bowing to the crowds, and those who saw the figure of a man seated beside the Czarina, nudged each other and whispered that that was General Potemkin, the new favourite.

Many times in the course of that short progress, the cheering for the Empress was half-hearted and spasmodic: oftener the people sighted Paul astride his horse; for all his lack of height and personal beauty, he rode with the arrogance of a king, and a sudden roar of welcome would burst from hundreds of enthusiastic throats.

"Long live the Czarevitch!"

For all their stupidity the masses were not long deceived. They knew the Empress to be sitting in another's place, their sense of fitness was affronted by the sight of her lover travelling in the Imperial carriage, and the tales of her troops' cruelties in the Urals were still vivid in the minds of men. As Empress Consort they had worshipped her, but now, after twelve years of rule, they were hostile and looking to her son.

Paul heard the people's plaudits and his sallow face flushed red with pride.

"Long live the Czarevitch," they cried, and in acknowledgment he raised one hand, aware that the demonstration of his popularity must gall his mother into bitter jealousy, and knowing that many Romanovs had suffered death because the masses showed them preference.

During that journey to Tsarskoë Selo he thought of his dead father for the first time in many months, mouldering forgotten in an unimportant grave, and told himself that all would have been so different had the late Czar lived.

But the dangerous worshipping reveries of his childhood did not last for long; the symbolic idol of his father had been almost entirely replaced by the living Natalie, and joined with her was the love growing in him for his unborn child. He, whose fury sent the culprits flying for their lives, nursed his wife with the tenderness of a woman, for as her time grew nearer the Grand Duchess became more miserable and ailing.

The fantasies that sometimes go with pregnancy took a strange form with her: she cried continually and couldn't bear the Czarevitch to go out of her sight.

To all his anxious questions she answered nothing, closing her swollen eyes and clinging obstinately to his hand, her slight body already heavy and grotesque.

Even André Rasumovsky seemed vague and far away, the

whole pattern of her marriage was a blur, the only reality was Paul who loved her and would protect her to the end. And in the closing months they drew very close together; for the first time she began to understand him, and since she knew her part in it must shortly end, Natalie viewed the future without personal fear.

Often Paul sat beside her on the couch where she spent all her days, his arm around her shoulders, one small hand clasped in his, and like that they talked for hours on end. He was full of plans, and his optimism saddened her unbearably.

With her head on his shoulder, Natalie stared out of the tall window on to the great vista of gardens that stretched around the Winter Palace at Petersburg. They had returned to the capital as usual and the first winter snows were falling.

"Promise me one thing, Paul," she said gently.

"I promise anything that will please you. You need only speak."

The Grand Duchess gripped his hand hard and turned a little more towards the window that he might not look down and see her face.

"I haven't been as good a wife as you deserve. . . . If you knew more. . . ."

With difficulty she restrained her tears and with them the hysterical impulse to admit that she was an adulteress, that she was utterly unworthy of the trust he lavished on her.

"But with all my heart I ask you this," she continued, silencing his protests. "Be careful of the Empress, Paul. Be careful. I have a feeling that she's planning to do you some injury."

For the first time she spoke of the thing that shadowed her, knowing that it would lend weight to her words in the future.

"If anything should happen to me, promise that you'll never plot against her . . . that no one shall persuade you to intrigue and give her the excuse to harm you. . . ."

Paul gathered her closely in his arms, turning her face towards him, and the strained, desperate expression terrified him.

"You're not to say that, Natalie. Never. Never speak of such a thing. I promise anything you please, if it will ease your mind. As long as my mother lives I'll stand aloof from all intrigue. You have my word. But I implore you, don't even think of danger to yourself. . . ."

He gazed at her wildly, holding her tightly against his heart.

"Why, if I lost you, my Natalia," he said hoarsely, "I think I should go mad. . . ."

.   .   .   .   .   .

One evening in April of the following year Natalie's principal lady-in-waiting hurried to the Empress, who was dining quietly with Potemkin.

The Grand Duchess's labour had begun, she explained, breathing heavily, for she had been running in her excitement. The Czarevitch was already in attendance upon his wife.

Catherine despatched her with the answer that she would come immediately, then she turned towards her lover and laid her hand upon his arm.

"My dearest love, I shall have to leave you and go to the lying-in. Finish your supper here and go to bed. I'll come back the moment it's over."

Gregory scowled in disappointment.

"I have no appetite without you and I certainly shan't sleep until you come. . . . Go then, beloved."

"I go," she murmured, resting her hands upon his shoulders to prevent his rising.

"Don't stand for me, Grisha . . ."

She bent down and pressed her lips against his mouth.

"And don't go to sleep, my bear! I shall want to celebrate with you. And pray, pray to all the gods and devils that it is a living, healthy child!"

As soon as the labour pains began, the ceremony for a royal birth was set in motion. The mattress was lifted from the great canopied bed and set down on the floor, the Grand Duchess was undressed and laid upon it, while scores of servants ran through the palace with the news. The Empress, the Grand Duke, the Ministers and officials of the Crown, the high Church dignitaries and all those members of the Court who could arrive in time, were permitted to crowd into the room and surround the mother on her mattress.

Paul was already at his wife's side, kneeling by the head of the mound of satin cushions and embroidered covers, trying to comfort her. Natalie paid no attention to him: she moved her head from side to side and moaned with pain.

The onset of the birth was going to be swift and her spasms were intense.

Vaguely she knew that the Empress herself was quite near, and that someone was bathing her forehead; she could hear a confused murmur from what seemed a vast crowd of people who were filling the room to overflowing, increasing the heat until it stifled her, and eating up the air she needed. There were periods free from pain when she opened her eyes and tried to focus on the wavering lines of faces, and instinctively she groped for Paul. His hot fingers found hers and closed over them in fierce tenderness.

With a great effort she looked up at him and whispered.

"The pain is so great. . . . Where's the physician. . . ? It comes again. . . . Get the physician. . . ."

Paul glared round him like an animal at bay. The sweat was running down his face and his great eyes were starting from his head with agony.

"She suffers," he said hoarsely. "The child will soon be born. . . . Where is the physician?"

The midwife, as anxious as he for help in the awful responsibility of her task, looked round helplessly and muttered that the doctor had been sent for.

The Empress turned to the nearest courtier and gave him a curt message. Human pain of any kind distressed her, and the spectacle of Natalie made her feel almost faint. In anger at the delay she phrased her summons carelessly, the hideous tortuosity of Russian minds forgotten.

"Go and find the physician!" she ordered. "Tell him if anything happens to the Grand Duchess I'll have his head!"

Then as the courtier pushed his way through the crowd, she turned to the mattress, and for a moment the eyes of mother and son met above the half-conscious form of the Grand Duchess. Paul was deathly white, his left cheek twitched convulsively, the hand holding Natalie's limp fingers trembled visibly, and when he tried to speak his lips moved but no sound came.

For a blinding instant it was the face of her dead husband that stared up at Catherine. Peter, the coward and degenerate, grown into a masculine travesty of himself . . . Peter, who hated her, gone mad with love and grief for someone else.

Quickly she stepped back, sick and furious, fighting a sudden onset of memories, memories of her own ordeal in that same room, lying upon the wide mattress, giving birth to the child Paul.

Everything to do with Paul had caused her pain, from that first dreadful day twenty-one years ago when bearing him had nearly killed her.

The terrible, primeval forces of hate and guilt rose in her like a burning tide as she stared down at her son: in her heart she hoped above all things that the coming child would live, no matter what befell the mother. Only let the child survive, and she would bury Paul in the darkest cell in the middle of the fortress where the guards had rid her of the burden of Ivan when she gave the word.

Slowly the hours went by, and the doctor who should have been attending Natalie repeated the Empress's ominous message to himself and hurried as far from the palace as he could.

If anything went wrong she'd have his head. . . . Examination of the Grand Duchess had convinced him very early that her chances of survival were almost non-existent. If she died, his ministrations could not be blamed as long as he wasn't there to give them.

And so, late in the night of the 15th April, aided by the terrified midwife and her assistants, the Grand Duchess gave birth to a son. One look was enough to tell Catherine that her plans against Paul had gone awry.

The child was stillborn.

Without a word she turned and left the bedroom pale with rage and disappointment: it mattered nothing to her what became of the mother; only the child was important, and the child was dead. Hurriedly the Court dignitaries followed in her wake, led by Nikita Panin whose annoyance was as great as Catherine's own. Within a few minutes the stuffy room was empty, except for the midwife, Natalie's chief lady-in-waiting, and the Czarevitch.

They had told Paul that his son was dead, but he gave no sign that he had heard. Instead he knelt by the mattress, his horrified eyes fixed on the face of his wife. Her skin was the colour of wax, and the surface shone glassily with sweat, the delicate, beautiful features were unrecognizable, her whole body lay broken and boneless under the coverlets. At last the midwife gave him her limp hand to hold, and he pressed it to his lips, his broad, short back heaving with sobs.

So great was his agony that he forgot that they were not alone, and his love and desperate pleading poured out in a flood of stumbling words, he chafed the small hand that lay between his own, and with shaking fingers tried to stroke her hair.

"Natalie . . . Natalie, my darling! It's all over, my sweet love; open your eyes and look at me, say one word that you will try to get better. . . . Here is my hand . . . here, hold it. . . . See, I am with you, caring for you. You will be well, my love, you *must* be well. . . ."

Some two hours after she had given birth the Grand Duchess turned her head; for a brief moment her eyes opened and she seemed to look at Paul. Then the tired lids closed over them, and a few minutes afterwards she died.

5

"THIS situation is ridiculous. I will *not* tolerate it any longer!"

Catherine was walking quickly up and down her boudoir, as she always did when angry or impatient. At the end of her sentence she stopped and swung round to the man who was listening, warming his back at the open fireplace.

That privilege had once been Panin's, but it was a sign of the times that it was no longer the Minister, but Gregory Potemkin, who held private counsel with the sovereign. While Catherine stormed, he said nothing, watching her out of his one eye, his ugly, expressive features set in thought.

He was so tall that his head topped the massive mantelpiece, his clothes were covered with gold and embroidery and blazing with jewelled orders, yet he was dishevelled and his wig lay carelessly upon a nearby chair.

"I have heard that he's grieving very much," he remarked after a moment.

"Grieving!" Catherine exclaimed. "His servants tell me that he's scarcely slept or eaten, that he spends his days shut up alone with her miniature and that sometimes they can hear him weeping through the door! It's ridiculous, I say; to mourn with dignity, yes, but this foolish spectacle has got to stop. . . . I sent for him this morning, Gregory, to tell him that I expect him to attend at Court in future." She paused, her full lips drawn into a line of unbecoming hardness.

"I also told him that he must prepare to marry again very soon."

Potemkin moved from the fireplace and poured some wine into two golden goblets.

"And of course he refused you, my love. Defied you, declared that he would love the late Natalie until the day of his death, and that he wouldn't hear the mention of another wife."

Catherine took the wine cup and nodded.

"Exactly. You've gauged his nature very cleverly, Grisha. Those were almost his very words. Oh, but he's such a fool! The girl deceived him with that young devil Rasumovsky within a few months of their marriage! I reminded him of it and he shouted that I was maligning the dead and rushed out of the room. . . . What am I to do with him? He must re-marry as soon as etiquette permits, but I don't think I can make him without using force."

"One thing I can vouch for, my adored," he said, "and that is that the Grand Duke will never yield to force. You may threaten, you may even act, but that's not the way to break his will. I am surprised, that for such a brilliant woman, you're always so stupid with your son."

The great Empress, before whom Princes trembled, accepted this rebuke and only looked at him appealingly.

"Then what do you suggest?"

"If you wish to bend Paul, it is Natalie Alexeievna who must be attacked. She is the obstacle. He clings to her, you see; it is the nature of loneliness, and without her he is very lonely. As you say, he was a fool, therefore we must enlighten him!"

"How do you mean, Grisha? I don't understand you."

"How many times a day do we write to each other, Catherine?" he asked, suddenly.

"Why, a dozen times at least," she answered in surprise.

"Exactly, though I see you so freely, I'm always thinking of little things to say and sending notes to you. And you send notes to me. Because we're lovers, my dear, and it is the way of lovers to put down their love on paper. You have kept my letters, haven't you, Catherine?"

"Of course, my dearest one. You know I have them all. They're there, locked in my bureau."

Potemkin put one great arm round her and smiled.

"Then doubtless that's where Natalie hid Rasumovsky's love letters. Have her apartments searched, and when you find your evidence, let it speak for you to the Czarevitch. . . ."

"My son has fought me successfully for years," she said, "but I believe he's met his match in you."

The following day Catherine's servants went into the dead Grand Duchess's rooms and made a thorough search. They unearthed a lot of fine jewellery which the Empress sent down to the Treasury, a mass of miscellaneous papers and household bills, and in a secret recess of her writing-desk they found a packet of letters tied up with ribbon.

That same evening Catherine and Potemkin retired early to her private suite, and one by one they read the letters, penned by the hand of André Rasumovsky to his dead mistress.

Potemkin folded the last of them and handed it to the Empress.

"No man's faith, however strong, can stand in the face of these," he said.

    .   .   .   .   .

Paul was in his study when a page brought him the package, with the message that these papers had been discovered among the late Grand Duchess Natalie's effects. The news that his wife's rooms were being searched had roused the Czarevitch to fury; that very morning he intended to go to his mother and protest, but instead he untied the piece of ribbon and, filled with fresh agonies of love by the memories invoked by anything belonging to his beloved wife, began to read.

At first he didn't recognize the writing. The opening words leapt at him with such force it seemed as if a voice had spoken them aloud.

"My adored one, my Natalia, I send this note to you because it might be a whole lifetime since we parted, though I know it is scarcely three hours since I left your arms. . . ."

He read on, almost mechanically, while the nervous tic in his left cheek awoke and began throbbing steadily.

"I love you more than ever, more than it is wise for any man to love a woman. In our meeting place I lived for the first time; here at Tsarskoë Selo, you have shown me that God's paradise exists on earth. . . ."

The phrases of flattery and passion ran on; he reflected quite impersonally that the writer had put into words all those emotions that he himself had never been able to express in speech or script. The signature at the end of the first letter stared up at him, black and bold and flourishing. "Your lover, André."

The piece of paper slipped from his fingers and floated to the ground; he sat quite still, the blood roaring in his head, the thunderous pulsing of his own heartbeat reverberating in his ears.

"Your lover, André . . . Scarcely three hours since I left your arms . . ."

In the letter it mentioned Tsarskoë Selo. He and Natalie had gone there for the first time a few months after their marriage. He remembered clearly that his young wife had not been well during their stay . . . No, he corrected himself, that was the second time, when she was pregnant; she was always ailing then and calling for him. The letter could not possibly refer to that period. It must have been the first visit, when they were newly married. And she *was* ill, he said to himself slowly; she had headaches and used to send him away for hours on end. . . .

Very deliberately, he picked up the second letter and saw that it, too, was written from the Empress's Summer Palace.

"Natalia . . ."

The name occurred every few lines, that pretty diminutive that he used to her himself, written by the hand of another, spoken by alien lips. The hand that drove the pen had touched her also, for the writer dwelt upon some intimacies that left no doubt about the fact. Intimacies received and given.

Phrases of passion that were repeated, incidents recalled, laughter and tenderness, he read them all, letter after letter, noting how the places changed from Tsarskoë Selo to the Winter Palace at Petersburg and to Moscow, and that quite often the notes were written in answer to ones which had been sent. He could not see these, he could only imagine their contents, and already his imagination was supplying him with pictures. Natalie Alexeievna, beautiful and frail, lying in another's arms, doing and saying the things which the writer described so vividly; he saw the pavilion at Tsarskoë Selo, saw his wife and his equerry, one dead, the other out of reach, saw them as lovers and remembered how often she must have come to him, warm from the adulterer's embrace, and submitted unwillingly to his own.

They had often talked of him, it seemed. The handsome equerry quoted her sayings on the subject, recording her complaints of mental boredom and physical distaste. And at the end, when discovery and danger threatened, he cautioned his mistress to bear with " the monster ", since both their lives depended on his blind stupidity.

Paul sat very still and stared in front of him, the letters scattered at his feet. He felt curiously numb and disembodied as if nothing of himself remained but that strange bursting in his head.

His gentle, chaste Natalie, his companion, the mainspring of his life. His lips parted in a ghastly smile of irony. His idol had just been proved a slut, a liar, the mistress of a coarse young libertine. She had betrayed him and brought him to the verge of imprisonment and even death to save herself and Rasumovsky. And together they had laughed at him behind his back.

With difficulty he stood up and walked towards a large mirror that hung from the opposite wall. For some moments he regarded his reflection, his brain quite cool, his thoughts collected. He saw the short body and broad shoulders; they reminded him suddenly of an ape, an ape in satin knee-breeches and coat, with a grotesque flattened face, from which the great blue eyes stared back at him, terrible in their pain and humanity.

" She never loved you," he said aloud. " Never. She hated you. Look at yourself, fool, and see how she must have hated you. . . ."

The lackeys on duty outside his door heard a sharp, tormented cry, followed by the shattering fall of glass.

When they entered, they saw their master kneeling by a chair, sobbing, with his arms over his head, and the blood running from a lacerated hand.

The wall mirror was smashed to splinters by a titanic blow from a madman's fist.

.   .   .   .   .

Three months later a crowd of several thousand lined the streets of Petersburg, watching the passing of a long procession of carriages and troops.

At the head of the line, preceded by an escort of Imperial Cavalry, the royal coach drove through the city, moving with the slow solemnity of a great gilded coffin, and he who sat in it remained as still and pallid as a corpse.

The people, cheering and shouting their loyalty, struggled to glimpse that silent figure in the foremost carriage, while lines of soldiers thrust them back with blows. The cries of the populace penetrated to the Empress herself, in the Summer Palace, so that she rose hurriedly from her desk and banged the window down. He was already out of sight; pray God, she thought angrily, he would soon be beyond earshot, and with that reflection turned once more to the affairs of State. The noise which distracted Catherine beat against the closed windows of the royal coach, but Paul Petrovitch sat upright, staring straight ahead of him, deaf to the tumult and blind to the sea of waving hands.

As always, the people acclaimed him; but for the first time he was unmoved. His expression was fixed and vacant, only the eyes glowed with life in his sallow face. He looked twice his twenty-one years.

He, whose wife was scarcely cold in her grave, was setting out publicly to bring home a second bride.

.   .   .   .   .

For some weeks after the revelation of Rasumovsky's letters, he had been ill with shock, physically ill, and tormented by sleeplessness and fits of weeping that gave place to periods of silent apathy.

Catherine's messengers had come to him during that time, demanding of the wretched victim whether he were prepared to obey his mother and take another wife.

"I will marry as soon as she pleases," he told them, and turning to the wall, he wept.

The Czarevitch was sick, they murmured to their mistress, but he was ready to do as he was told. Before them all, the Empress slipped her hand through Potemkin's arm and smiled her thanks upon him. Then she sent her physicians to her son with orders to rouse him and expedite his recovery. There was to be no malingering, she ordered sharply, and no soft treatment. The second Grand Duchess was already chosen, Princess Sophia of Würtemberg, and the Empress wished her son to be married again before the year was out.

True to instructions, the doctors did their best. Paul was bled and physicked unmercifully, then the refuge of his rooms was finally forbidden him so that he must exercise and appear in public. His bodily symptoms disappeared, he obeyed promptly and without demur, and the short-sighted among those who persecuted him assured the Empress that his stubborn will was broken.

There was a time in that period of his personal agony when all hope seemed dead within him, and with it the strength to resist his enemies.

Hour by hour, and day by day, Paul thought of Natalie and writhed with shame and fury. Phrases from those letters pursued him like hidden voices, whispering the hated words of love, conjuring up the visions which proved his short idyll of domestic joy to have been a loathsome farce. He had believed in her affection, trusted her word, defended her chastity with his own life in the delusion that in spite of his ugliness, she had found it possible to love him.

That faith had given him supreme happiness, confidence and health. His love for Natalie, and her imagined feelings in return, had been slowly dispelling the dark mental shadows of his appalling childhood and letting in the light of sanity and balance. Now, with one blow, Potemkin's action brought the precarious structure crashing into ruin.

The knowledge of deceit and inferiority stabbed at Paul's sensibilities like a sword, and his mind convulsed in the effort to withdraw from that probing point. But the wound was made, deep and quivering, and in the healing of that awful scar all that was sane and gentle was becoming warped.

The day came when no more tears of grief would flow, when the black indifference of despair gave place to a dull glow of inward fury, shot with streaks of murderous rage. Paul said to himself that he felt no sorrow, that even personal shame had vanished. An enormous anger possessed him, a sense of grievance so intense that only physical violence could bring relief.

Natalie Alexeievna. He said that dreaded name aloud, and clenched his fists, watching the scars on his knuckles whiten on the drawn flesh, and regretted bitterly that she had died the honourable death of motherhood when, had she lived, he might have strangled her.

And often when the image in his mind changed from his wife into his mother, and the avenging husband became the injured son, the ending to the fantasy was just the same.

Kindness was an error, mercy a mistake, and Paul resolved grimly that he would dispense with both these failings. If one wished to triumph in this world, even to survive, it was necessary to use the weapons of the enemy: harshness and fear.

The thought of marriage almost amused him and with a terrible, warped curiosity he asked about his future bride.

"Was she dark or fair," he questioned. They told him she was very fair and, satisfied, he smiled in his strained mirthless way. The first, the darling of his heart, had been so small and dark, with rivers of shining black hair that used to be his joy. Obediently he set out for Germany to bring her back.

He sat in the carriage, oblivious to the cheering crowds, clasping a miniature in his hands, a small faded picture in a frame from which the diamonds had been prised out years before, resurrected from the hidden drawer in which he kept his boyhood treasures. Peter the Third, Czar and Autocrat of all the Russias, betrayed by his wife and put to death at her behest. . . . It was the only portrait of his father that the Czarevitch possessed, and in the course of the first day's journey he looked at it earnestly.

"I will love what my father loved; I will live as he lived, and wait until the day comes when I can avenge us both."

Several times he said this to himself, until the interior of the coach grew dim and the miniature became a blur in the fading light. Then Paul hid it in his coat, where it pressed against his heart, deriving a strange comfort from the knowledge that this dear talisman travelled with him and that though the living had betrayed and persecuted him, he was not alone, never alone again, for he had the company of the dead which no one could take from him.

A month later Paul and his suite crossed the frontier into

Germany and proceeded to Berlin, where the King of Prussia, Frederick, who was already styled the Great, waited to receive them.

The meeting took place in Frederick's own apartments, and Catherine's greatest enemy rose from his chair and extended both hands in welcome to her son.

The King was taller than Paul; he was thin and upright, his features were sharp and his pale eyes cold and expressionless. Only his mouth belied the impression of freezing militarism given by his bearing and the tight Prussian uniform he wore. It was a sensitive mouth and it betrayed the nature of the man, for it was sad and twisted, a mouth that had more often been distorted by tears than lifted in laughter. Paul knew little about the Prussian monarch except that Catherine hated him, and since his view of all men was determined by their relations with his mother, he had come prepared to like him. He also knew that this strange, watchful man had been his dead father's idol, and that link with the past had determined him to enlist Frederick as his friend.

They sat down, one on each side of an immense fireplace eyeing each other over cups of wine, exchanging formalities of conversation. The King was a shrewd judge of human nature, and he very quickly sensed that for all his outward air of pride, the ugly Czarevitch was lonely, unhappy and pitifully insecure. Frederick watched him closely, noting that his fingers strayed continuously to the magnificent jewel in his cravat or smoothed imaginary wrinkles out of his brocade sleeve, and that his left cheek was twitching painfully.

The nervous habits were signs that the King recognized only too well, and while he asked Paul polite questions about his mother's health, he remembered the reports of bad feeling which existed between them, remembered also that the boy was said to revere his father's memory to the point of worship.

Frederick's judgment of Peter the Third as a foolish degenerate and a coward, who had lost his throne and his life through his own fault, was an opinion that he reserved from Paul, for he was very anxious to secure his confidence.

The tale of Natalie's adultery had reached his ears, and he was careful to avoid the subject. Instead, he wasted no time in probing Paul and finding out his interests. To his astonishment he discovered that they were very like his own.

The Czarevitch's face lit up at the mention of the Prussian

army; his stiff shyness vanished in a glow of enthusiasm and a flood of questions. For almost two hours they talked soldiering and discussed different systems of drill and general manœuvring, until Paul's angry criticism of the Russian methods gave the King the opening that he had been waiting for.

"Your father had already begun the reorganization of the Imperial Regiments when he died," he said calmly, and noted the deep flush that rose in his listener's sallow cheeks. "I always considered him a man of much ability. He would have been a great soldier. Had he lived . . ."

Paul leant forward, gripping the arms of his chair.

"I never really knew my father, Sire. I scarcely saw him and he died when I was nine years old. I, too, think he would have been the kind of sovereign that my country needs. . . ."

Frederick read the mingled grief and resentment in his face, and guessed that there was no need of subtlety.

"Though the Empress is German born, she seems to prefer the old Slavic system of sovereignty. She has destroyed all your father's reforms, and reduced the order he was trying to create into the former chaos. I have tried to advise her, but unfortunately she listens to nothing but her own will. And the counsel of this General Potemkin . . . Does she allow you any part in the government?"

Paul glanced up at him suspiciously, wondering whether the King mocked him with that question, and then answered truthfully and with great bitterness.

"I am neither consulted nor included in anything my mother does. Her personal hatred of me is so strong that it's doubtful whether I shall ever succeed her! You were my father's friend. You know that shameful history. But you have no idea of the persecution I have suffered at her hands. . . ."

Frederick stared across at the twitching countenance, and read a record of fearful misery out of those few words.

Something that was almost pity stirred in him, but stronger than his pity was his purpose and his cunning.

He got up and stood by Paul, resting one thin hand upon his shoulder in an almost fatherly gesture. And because it suited him, the advice he gave was good.

"Because you are Peter Feodorovitch's son, you are dear to me, my friend. As dear as the son I lack," he said, and he lied with such artistry that he surprised himself. "Will you listen to what I advise? I am old, and men say that I'm wily . . ." he smiled a little. He was wily, wily enough to help the Czarevitch against his mother, wily enough to fight her openly and in the dark, as he had done for nearly twenty years.

"First, do not underestimate the Empress: that was your father's error and he paid for it with his life. Above all, don't plot against her, you're not strong enough. Your only policy should be seclusion. Leave the Court with your new wife and live in the country where the intrigues of neither friends nor enemies can harm you and where you're not under your mother's eye as a reminder. . . . Opportunity will summon you, but until that moment comes, my advice to you is patience."

Paul sat in silence, considering, and he who was neither subtle nor deceitful, was astonished by the wisdom and simplicity of Frederick's plan. For the first and only time in his life, he acknowledged the merit of retreat, and in his heart he knew that his shattered nerves were crying out for rest, for a truce in the bitter struggle for survival in the face of personal tragedy, friendlessness and danger. He sighed, and when he looked up, the King saw that there were tears in his eyes and knew that Catherine's son was near to breaking point.

A faithless wife and a tyrannical mother . . . Frederick reflected that Nature had been very cruel to Paul, moulding him with spiteful fingers into a caricature of human ugliness, yet giving him the sensibilities to let him see and know and suffer. . . .

He pressed the boy's shoulder once more and then sat down in his own chair, facing him, and waited.

After a few moments the Czarevitch turned away from the fire and looked at him.

"I will do as you suggest, Sire. Immediately after my wedding, I'll ask my mother's leave to retire from Court."

"Good, my son. And never forget that I'm your friend."

"I know that, Sire. And believe me I have need of friendship."

Paul drank a little more wine, aware that the sudden uprush of emotion had subsided, that he felt warmed by the presence of his father's hero and calmed by a new sense of security. Here was one whom he could trust. One who had called him son and promised friendship. Frederick's manner and associations had disarmed him to the point of absolute confidence. And Frederick could talk of the subject dearest to his heart, his memories could bring the dead to life. With one hand Paul touched his breast, feeling the outline of the little battered miniature concealed under his coat.

"Sire . . ."

"Yes, my son?"

"Tell me about my father. . . ."

.   .   .   .   .

The following day, Sophia of Würtemberg was presented to her husband. She thought him hideous, prematurely old, hard-eyed and grim. Her first reaction was one of diffidence and fear, and these twin emotions were to characterize her married life. Paul judged her with absolute calculation. She was taller than he by several inches, which he disliked, plump, with very blonde hair and light blue eyes that made her general appearance so fair as to be almost colourless. No one could have called her pretty, and her conversation was confined to platitudes. The King of Prussia had recommended her as virtuous, obedient, and stupid. He was quite convinced of the last, determined to enforce the second, and cynical about the first. For her own sake as well as his, Paul thanked God that there was nothing in her to remind him of Natalie; neither beauty, delicacy, nor grace. It made the prospect of living with her easier to bear.

At the end of a very cordial stay, the Czarevitch set out for Russia, and he parted from Frederick with real regret.

Both men shared a passion for military reviews, and the displays organized for Paul's benefit aroused his fervent admiration. This, he declared to his host, was the model he would follow in the formation of his own country; the sense of order fascinated him.

Discipline for the army should be enlarged to include the whole state. Everything in this sparse, regimented country seemed the embodiment of masculine rule, while the corruption, sloth and laxity of Russia was synonymous with Catherine.

"You have shown me the road that I shall take, Sire," Paul said to Frederick when he left. "For that, as well as for your kindness and advice, I shall be for ever in your debt."

.   .   .   .   .

During the return journey to Russia, Paul saw little of his future wife and scarcely spoke to her; he had become the royal suitor of tradition, indifferent and strictly polite; the nature which had warmed with such a passion of love for the treacherous Natalie was frigid with reserve, and the sore, quivering heart of the Czarevitch was enclosed behind a façade of bitterness, boredom, inferiority and obsession.

He had long accepted the fact that love was not for such as he, that the ugly face and graceless body God had given him had placed him for ever beyond the reach of human tenderness.

Sophia of Würtemberg was certainly stupid, and it was fortunate that she was also insensitive. Though the prospect of marriage with this grim, silent young man depressed her to the point of tears, it never occurred to her to disobey or question the justice of her fate. But a streak of native sentimentality was outraged by his immovable indifference, his ugliness, and the rivalry of a dead first wife who was said to have been beautiful.

Her suite repeated their advice to concentrate on finding favour with the Empress; they hinted that Paul's life had always hung upon a thread, and that Sophia's first duty was to give the great Catherine an heir for her throne and ingratiate herself personally. Then whatever happened to the Czarevitch, she need not suffer with him. Please the Empress, ran the chorus, and all will be well.

With that object fixed obstinately in her mind, the future Grand Duchess Marie Feodorovna arrived in Petersburg.

On his return Paul found that many things had changed. During his stay in Prussia rumours had seeped through to him of some fresh scandal in his mother's private life, but, ashamed before Frederick, he pretended to ignore them.

From the first moment of Potemkin's conquest of Catherine, tongues had wagged hopefully of a rift between them, and Paul was too familiar with the explosive quality of their relationship to pay any attention. He had seen the Empress alternately smiling or in tears too often to believe that any scene could oust the favourite.

It never occurred to him, or to anyone else, that Potemkin might have tired of the association.

For months Catherine had showed signs of strain and frequent quarrels with the man she had overwhelmed with honours were not improving her temper, for he was becoming more demanding, jealous and moody as his power over her increased.

He accused her of infidelities until she wept hysterically, spurned her desperate advances and declared himself restless only because he knew he was unloved.

The logical, patient Empress retired utterly defeated by this neurotic onslaught, enslaved by her own need of him and made miserable by the suspicion that after two years of mutual passion, he was tired of her and wanted someone else.

Her premonition of his real reasons was well founded, and because her lover was Potemkin, inevitable. One woman, even a sexual Amazon like Catherine, would never be enough; she was beautiful, practised, passionate and devoted, but he was already bored by her body while still infatuated with her mind.

The strain of their relationship was slowly destroying a union that, without sensual ties, must raise them both to heights of glory; Potemkin knew this, for all his jealousy; knew that it was better to leave her he loved before the fires of passion sank into extinction, before his need drove him to infidelity and the fate of Gregory Orlov. His intuition and greed for power pointed the way to freedom, emotional freedom from Catherine whom he no longer really wanted, and freedom from the insane fear of his replacement by another.

With great tenderness and a sense of drama that almost convinced him of his own sincerity, Potemkin told Catherine that he had determined to renounce her. He preferred to lose her body and retain her heart, rather than try to possess them and end by forfeiting both. He loved her above all human creatures, he declared with tears and ravings, and the intensity of his passion would be their mutual ruin if it continued. He begged her to accept his sacrifice, to bind him to her side with ties of office and responsibility while setting him free from this intolerable bondage of the senses.

Held in his arms, Catherine wept and tried to protest, aware that the fundamental truth of what he said was shaking her resolve.

They could not continue as before. They could no longer love and bicker and then confer about affairs of State with coolness and impartiality. As a Minister he had become invaluable, Panin was obsolete, powerful in name only; everything she did and said in connection with ruling Russia needed Potemkin's guidance and approval before she felt satisfied and ready to proceed. Others might succeed him in the arts of love, but never as friend, counsellor and audience.

It was Potemkin, whose jealousy had caused them both such torments in the past, who suggested that she take another lover. He urged it as the sole possible solution and added that his only condition would be that she must let him choose the candidate.

While the Czarevitch was still in Germany, the General left for a visit to Novgorod. Meanwhile his mistress had tearfully agreed to take one of her secretaries, named Zavadovsky, as her lover while Potemkin was away.

The day of Zavadovsky's installation caused the General's enemies to rejoice openly about his downfall, only to discover that on his return, his influence with Catherine was as strong as ever.

It was a brilliant stratagem, the greatest test of his power that Potemkin's egomania could have devised, and to the Court's astonishment it worked. Another man occupied his official place, but Catherine's former lover still lived in his old apartments underneath the Empress's, and his grip on policies and influence over her mind became a stranglehold.

This was the situation facing Paul on his return. Count Panin's star was waning, but the substitution of Gregory Potemkin altered nothing; it only caused a sickening scandal, since he and Catherine and the rather diffident Zavadovsky were always on the best of terms. As soon as he knew the Empress to be satisfied with her new toy, Potemkin seduced his niece, the pretty, wilful Varvara Englehardt, the first of five sisters who were to enjoy their uncle's favours.

Paul's betrothal was celebrated with great splendour, and enhanced by a sudden flowering of domestic harmony rooted in fresh adultery and incest. The Czarevitch recoiled from it with incredulity and horror, refusing to speak to the young secretary who now sat at his mother's elbow and escorted her publicly to her bedroom every evening; and he insulted Potemkin as much as he dared.

Controlling her anger, Catherine decided to ignore him, and to pretend also that the spiritless boy who had left for Prussia many weeks ago had not returned a brooding stranger, as hostile and obstinate as he had ever been . . . and suddenly much older and more significant.

Paul's second marriage took place before the end of the year, and life at his mother's Court became a tremendous strain upon him; he had no stomach either for gaiety or for the spectacle of his wife's humiliation, for the failure of Marie Feodorovna seemed a reflection on himself, and he turned savagely upon those who did not show her honour.

She was shy and dull and perpetually shocked; shocked by Potemkin, who frankly termed her a sexless bore; clumsy and tactless before the Empress, whose good opinion she was trying so hard to secure, until the jibes and sarcasm of Catherine made Paul writhe with fury. They dismissed his wife as a fool, and the knowledge that she was every bit as shallow-minded and provincial as they thought her, hardened the Czarevitch into a show of amity.

The retirement he requested was denied him angrily; he merely received a warning that his marriage was expected to be fruitful, and there was nothing delicate about the bride this time.

So the weeks went by and the Grand Duke and Duchess remained in Catherine's shadow until the sombre, watchful presence of her detested son reduced the Empress to fury and exhaustion. She could no longer smother her feelings towards him, for her iron will weakened before the force of her own hate and irritation, so that she declared the very sight of him to be poisoning her pleasures.

Then in May, 1777, the Czarevitch came in person to his mother with the news that his wife was pregnant, and immediately Catherine's ill humour lifted. Their interview was brief and formal; if either remembered the last time Paul had brought such tidings, they gave no sign. There was no hint of pride or joy or pleading in the Czarevitch's words or his expression. Nor did he show fear, and for that the Empress labelled him a fool, for he should have been afraid indeed.

The death of Natalie's child had spoilt her plans, but this quick fertility resurrected them; and in the dark recesses of her mind, the door of a cell in the Schüsselburg swung wide and shut fast upon her son, never again to open while he lived.

6

O N the twentieth of November, Marie Feodorovna's labour
pains began. A messenger summoned the Czarevitch, who
found his mother already standing by the mattress and the
room rapidly filling with courtiers. Paul bowed stiffly to the
Empress and then saluted his wife.

"I wish you comfort in your pain, Madame," he said
formally. Then he turned towards Catherine, and for a
moment mother and son looked on each other with the cold
hostility that neither troubled to conceal.

"This time you shan't be disappointed; you shall have your
heir, Madame," he said quietly.

"I trust so," she answered him. "You owe me that, at least."
He walked away from her then, pushing his way through the
crowds who stood on tiptoe, watching the sweating Marie in
the indignity of childbirth, and stood by one of the long
windows, staring out with dilated, sightless eyes.

He knew what was to come, knew that this spectacle was
only the prelude to a drama that all Petersburg had waited
for for years. The birth of his child was to be the signal for
his arrest. Catherine had made up her mind; the resolution
looked out of her eyes when they rested on him, and sounded
in the tones of her voice. It would soon be over, this merciless
battle for supremacy between them, a battle rendered doubly
bitter by the natural antipathy they felt for one another.

He stood by the window, insensible to the sounds of activity
in the room behind him, certain that Marie would bring forth
a living child, and for a time he became strangely calm.

His father had died, at thirty-six, after ruling Russia for
less than half a year; the wretched Ivan Ivanovitch had
perished within two years of Catherine's accession to the
throne; now he, her only son and rightful heir, would follow
his predecessors' bloody path, being the youngest of them all
and never having donned the crown that they had worn so
briefly. . . .

He leant his forehead against the window pane and closed
his eyes, surrendering to a throbbing pain that pulsed in his

head, a pain that had seldom left him since Natalie Alexeievna's death.

Her image came into his mind before his will-power had had
time to banish it and a spasm of almost physical suffering
convulsed him.

He had been ready to endure this fate in order to protect
her; he might have died at peace believing that his wife whom
he adored and the child conceived in mutual love would live
on after him in safety, but even that false comfort was denied
him. Instead his ruin was being wrought by the stupid Marie
Feodorovna and by an infant for whom he felt no glimmer
of paternal feeling.

"I am accursed," he whispered, and two tears seeped under
his eyelids and ran down his ugly face.

Alone and unloved, his father's murder unrevenged, his own
destiny unfulfilled, his life was ebbing away with every passing
moment. It would be Catherine's final triumph that he should
die as he had lived, fruitlessly, achieving nothing. . . .

He felt a touch upon his shoulder and he stiffened, one hand
creeping to his sword.

"Your Imperial Highness . . ."

It was a page who stood at his elbow.

"You have a son. The Empress asks that you come and
bear witness." It must be legal, this important birth, he, the
father, must look on the baby and acknowledge it his before
the world. . . . Then when Catherine's men laid hands on him,
his child could be proclaimed Heir Apparent without the
danger of dissenting voices saying that Paul had been sup-
planted by a bastard or a changeling.

"I will come," he said, and with his hand still resting on
the pommel of his sword he walked through the staring, silent
crowd who made a lane for him to pass among them.

The infant Prince was already cradled in the Empress's
arms; Paul approached her and bent to look on the face of
his son.

For an instant he regarded the tiny, flushed countenance,
crowned by a fuzz of fair hair, and heard the baby's shrill
protesting cry against the misery of being born into the world.

Then he raised his head and met his mother's triumphant
gaze, squarely and defiantly.

"It is my son."

"Amen," murmured the voice of the Grand Duchess's confessor, and the next moment Paul had almost knocked him down as he thrust forward and began pushing his way out of the room.

They let him go without a word, knowing, by rumour, what he guessed by instinct, dismissing him as dead already, for he had begotten his own rival and successor.

The corridors were empty except for the sentries who stood guard at intervals; not even the members of his household dared to follow their master when he left the lying-in. Instead he walked to his own suite alone, listening to the eerie echo of his own footfalls on the marble floors.

His valet waited in his bedroom, and one look at the man's terrified face assured Paul that even his servants accounted him lost. They were all so sure, he thought grimly, so certain that he would be taken. . . . Certain, too, that he would submit without a struggle.

But in that last he would prove them wrong. A flood of desperate courage surged into his heart, born of the knowledge that he had nothing to lose which was not already declared forfeit by his mother.

Let them come then, he would be ready! His father had died secretly, outnumbered by four to one, and no man could swear to the manner of his death. Not so with him! He'd perish where he stood, and by God, a few of Catherine's soldiers should die with him. . . .

He turned to the silent, shrinking valet, and increased the man's terror by laughing aloud.

"Why do you tremble, Serge? It's not your head they want! Here, take off this coat of mine . . . it hampers me. I must move freely, no man can fight properly in a coat. . . . Ah, by God's Death, that's easier! Now withdraw my sword from the scabbard and give it to me! So. We will wait. But not for very long, I think. . . ."

But it was longer than he anticipated. His son was four hours old before he heard the sound of footsteps coming down the corridor, where they halted at the entrance to his rooms.

.   .   .   .   .

The first thing Catherine did was to send for Nikita Panin. Her grandson was in the care of his wet nurse. The mother, the least important factor now that her purpose was fulfilled, was sleeping peacefully, and Paul Petrovitch waited conveniently in his rooms. Panin, knowing his mistress's mind, hurried to his audience with a light heart, sure of the downfall of one enemy, hopeful of the decline of another.

She was going to follow his advice at last and make an end of Paul; he addressed a fervent prayer to his complacent Deity that the Empress's love for Potemkin was about to follow the same route as her maternal scruples, for his hatred of the Czarevitch was only equalled by his loathing and jealousy of the former favourite.

When Catherine received him, Panin's fat face was wreathed in smiles and he hurried to bow and kiss her hand, murmuring congratulations.

"God has heard your people's prayers, your Majesty," he said. "Not only a living child, but a son! My heart rejoices for you!"

"My heart rejoices too, Nikita," she told him truthfully. "Sit down, my friend. Here, beside me. Oh, Panin, I'm tired, but I'm so happy! At last we have the solution of our problem, you and I!"

"You mean the little Grand Duke, Madame?"

"My grandson, the heir I needed. And the physician says he's a fine, healthy baby. Nikita, you know what I've been thinking . . . The Czarevitch . . . He's been very strange these last months, have you noticed?"

"I've heard things; since the death of Natalie Alexeievna and his discovery of her adultery he's shown marked eccentricity. . . . It's said that he spends hours talking to a miniature of the late Czar. And Marie Feodorovna is terrified of him. . . . He seems to be developing his father's unfortunate tendencies. . . ."

"I know, Nikita, I've remarked it. He grows worse, more morose and intractable, more hostile to me. Now I think the time has come to take the counsel you've been giving me for many years. I think he should be imprisoned. For the good of Russia."

"I think so too, Madame. As usual, you're supremely wise."

Catherine looked down and smoothed a crease out of her skirt where none existed; for a moment it seemed to Panin that she was almost nervous.

"There is only one thing," she said quietly. "I am afraid that General Potemkin doesn't approve of what I contemplate . . . I mentioned the matter to him and he advised me to wait a little longer before taking drastic action. That's why I sent for you, my friend. To support me, to strengthen my resolution, for I believe that what I am going to do is the only right and safe remedy for us all."

Panin reflected briefly what he and others might expect if Catherine were to die suddenly and her dreaded son succeed her, and nodded vigorously.

"Oh, I agree with you, Madame, with all my heart! The General is a great soldier, but I fear his experience of statecraft is still limited. He's a sentimentalist; he doesn't understand the dangerous nature of the Czarevitch. Take my advice. Have your son arrested now, without delay! Once it's done, the General will have to see the wisdom of it."

Catherine listened to him and agreed, swayed by the dictates of her own insistent malice. Resolutely, she brushed Potemkin's objections from her mind. He told her to wait, he argued that her people and the whole civilized world would condemn such a tyrannical action as the imprisonment of her son without a shred of evidence that he deserved that awful fate. But he did deserve it, she countered angrily. He hated her and knew her for all the things she was, a usurper, an adulteress many times over, a party to her husband's murder.

Whatever Potemkin said, however great his anger, she made up her mind to defy him and have her own way.

Suddenly she rose, and tugged at the bell rope by the fireplace. It was the Countess Bruce who answered the summons, and blinked when she saw the superseded Panin sitting with her mistress.

"Send the Captain of the Guard to me," the Empress ordered, and understanding what this meant, the Minister folded his plump hands in his lap and smiled.

When the young Captain of the Ismailovs entered, Catherine wasted neither time nor words.

"Take an escort and arrest the Czarevitch. Convey him to a safe place in the Schüsselburg and then report to me! It must be done for the safety of Russia!"

The officer bowed low and saluted.

"Your Majesty, it shall be done."

"Thank God, Nikita," she exclaimed when the soldier had

retired. "Thank God! In a little while, we shall all be able
to breathe freely. . . ."

"I applaud you, Madame," he said solemnly, composing
his features with great difficulty, for he wanted to laugh with
relief. "Always remember that my advice is at your
service. . . ."

I have triumphed, he thought inwardly; she has acted against
Paul and defied Potemkin. And Potemkin will rave when he
hears of it. He'll abuse her, perhaps go too far. . . . She may
even dismiss him, but at least I've struck a blow at his
influence . . . a great blow, thanks be to God!

They were drinking wine together when Countess Bruce
opened the door without even waiting to knock. The confidante was pale and agitated.

"Madame . . . Madame," she stuttered. "The General . . .
the General is here!"

Before Catherine had time to speak Countess Bruce disappeared as if some powerful hand had dragged her back,
and the next moment the door crashed back and Gregory
Potemkin stood framed in the opening.

.   .   .   .   .

Catherine Alexeievna lay across her bed and wept. He had
swept into her room like a tornado; he had learned of the
Ismailov Captain's mission, for he had surprised the escort on
their way to execute it.

He had turned on Panin like a tiger, his great voice roaring
accusations.

"You damned eunuch! You'd destroy your Empress to
satisfy your woman's spite! Go, before I tear you limb from
limb for your treachery!" he bellowed, and Catherine, terrified for the safety of her Minister, urged him to leave them
alone.

When he had left the full weight of Potemkin's wrath fell
on her and it was an experience that utterly unnerved her.

He strode up and down her room, shouting and shaking his
enormous fists, his face suffused with anger.

Now, when the storm had subsided, the memory of it
haunted her; phrases flung at her in the heat of passion
repeated themselves in her aching brain.

He had called her a murderess, accused her to her face of

the late Czar's death, reminded her in the most brutal terms of the killing of the unhappy Ivan in his dungeon.

And then he told her savagely that she wished to shed Paul's blood to satisfy her personal malice. "Do this," he threatened, "and you'll go down in history as an infamous tyrant! Your name will be vilified for ever. Nothing that you've achieved will count for anything against such a crime. You have *no* excuse, Catherine! There is no rebellion, no plot, nothing to justify you. . . ."

The truth of what he said robbed her of argument. Instead she began to weep hysterically, unable to explain that apart from her own hatred of him, there was something about Paul Petrovitch that almost frightened her. . . .

Sensing that she weakened, Potemkin heaped reproaches on her, declaring that she had broken his heart by the discovery of her deceit, asking scornfully whether she wished to imprison him with her son and send them both to death. . . . She no longer needed him, he knew; her love for him was dead, his uses at an end. Then he would go, he announced, adding caustically that doubtless her soldiers were already waiting. . . . It was a shrewd, merciless attack; by linking himself with Paul he brought Catherine to her knees, and she ran to him, sobbing her denials, begging him to believe that he was still as dear to her as ever.

The General turned away, refusing to be convinced, knowing that if he hurt and frightened her sufficiently she would agree to anything rather than lose him.

"I am a broken man," he muttered. "I will go into a monastery and devote myself to God. . . ."

The fact that he had studied for the priesthood as a youth always lent weight to this most dreaded threat. For all her brilliance and her judgment, his sway was such that she was blind to subterfuge, and the menace to embrace religion and retire from her was still effective and he used it regularly when she crossed his will.

Catherine clung to him, imploring his forgiveness, beseeching him to stay, until Potemkin, who had never contemplated doing otherwise, allowed himself to be persuaded.

Her need of him always touched his heart; knowing that iron will and fearless temperament, he loved her for her weakness with him, though he traded on it shamelessly. What he had said and done to her was done for love; he had been brutal in order to save her from what he considered an act of desperate folly. In so doing, he had risked his influence, even his life, and he had won.

In victory he was generous; the full force of his great love for Catherine flooded him with tenderness and the need to make amends. He gathered his weeping mistress in his arms and treated her with an intimacy forbidden since they had renounced their old relationship.

And skilfully he put the blame upon Nikita Panin, assuring her that it was all due to his suggestions. His beautiful, wise, gentle Catherine was not to blame, he murmured, kissing her trembling mouth. She had been misled: but that would not occur again, and her whisper of agreement pronounced Panin's dismissal and disgrace.

But it was too late, she reminded him in sudden panic. By that time Paul had been arrested, but Potemkin smiled and shook his head. He had advised the Captain of the Guard to wait, he said, and asked her humbly whether she were angry with him.

Catherine acknowledged her extraordinary state of servitude to this dynamic man and shook her head. She was not angry; but she insisted upon one condition for Paul's continued freedom.

He must leave Petersburg, she told Potemkin. If her Grisha really loved her, he would arrange a speedy exile for her son.

With that promise Potemkin left her; and when he had gone, her overwrought nerves gave way and she wept. Paul was saved again, first by the death of Natalie's only child, now by the influence of the man he hated, a man who dismissed him as an ill-favoured fool whose unstable temperament rendered him an object of contempt rather than fear. But in her heart Catherine Alexeievna thought that judgment wrong, and in fact, of all the errors that Potemkin made in their joint government, the greatest was his opinion that Paul Petrovitch was not a person to be reckoned with.

. . . . .

When Paul heard the sound of footsteps halting by the entrance to his suite, he sprang out of his chair, sword in hand.

His pallor was grey and deep black rings of fatigue circled his eyes; the pain in his head was so intense that he could scarcely see.

"It is General Potemkin, your Highness," whispered his page, and Paul stared at him in momentary surprise.

Potemkin, come to supervise the order and report to Catherine. . . . Paul's lips twisted back in a strangely wolfish smile.

His mother's former lover, the royal pander before whom all men trembled; he gripped his long, slim weapon firmly, weighing it in his hand, his spirit lightened by a fierce resolve to thrust it through Potemkin's heart.

When the door opened he saw that the General was alone. Potemkin's one eye flickered in the direction of the other's sword, then he advanced into the room, ordering the page to close the door behind him.

For a moment he considered Paul and read the message written on that ravaged, twitching countenance.

"Put down your weapon, Highness. No one is going to harm you."

Paul answered him with a savage laugh.

"Where are your soldiers, General? Or do you come for me alone?"

Potemkin dropped into a nearby chair and thrust his hands into his coat.

"Enough of your heroics, in God's name," he exploded angrily. "Be thankful the Empress has seen fit to spare your life!"

The steel tip of Paul's levelled weapon lowered until it touched the carpet.

"Do you come to tell me this? Or do you try to trap me. . . ? Be warned, General, I can endure no more. Call in your guards, and then prepare for death! For I am going to kill you!"

Potemkin glanced up at him and then stared moodily down at the floor, the prey of a fierce reaction from his early fury; he was no coward and he respected bravery in others; for all his ugliness, Catherine's son had courage, and Potemkin conceded him that point at least. But he was tired, exhausted by his quarrel with the Empress and irritable with himself for having made her weep. He frowned, fighting the onset of one of his deadly fits of melancholy, his rage reborn in the knowledge that the cause of the unhappy scene stood before him, daring to threaten his life.

"I have a message for you," he said harshly. "You've angered your mother and she's decided to exile you."

The Czarevitch laughed shortly.

"To the Schüsselburg?" he sneered; and knowing how nearly right he was, Potemkin lost his temper.

"Hold your tongue!" he shouted, and sprang up, overturning his chair. "Another word and that's where you shall go! Now listen to me; after the christening you are to leave the Court, you understand? Make your arrangements, or by God, I'll make them for you! And watch yourself, Highness. . . . One more show of insolence towards the Empress and I'll rid the world of you myself!"

Then he was gone, and the door slammed after him with such violence that it broke the gilded catch.

Slowly the sword slipped from Paul's hand; he tried to shield his eyes with trembling fingers, suddenly blinded and almost insensible with the pain that stabbed upwards through his skull; the pressure increased in a matter of seconds until it seemed as if his eyeballs would shoot from their sockets. He moaned in agony and stumbled forward, blindly feeling for support until his feet caught in the legs of Potemkin's upturned chair and he fell face downwards to the floor. A few minutes later his valet found him, unconscious and livid, with a line of foam between his lips.

The mental strain that he had been subjected to had culminated in some kind of fit.

.   .   .   .   .

The baby Grand Duke was christened Alexander; the Empress poured out wealth to make the ceremony outstandingly magnificent in an age renowned for its extravagance, and everyone remarked on her attachment to the child. He was a beautiful infant, fair skinned and blond, with large, intelligent blue eyes, and Catherine, who had never loved the children born of her own body, held the baby in her arms and burned with tenderness and pride. He was her grandson, and she removed him from his mother and kept him in her rooms, forbidding the hapless Marie any maternal rights. The Empress nursed him, displayed him for the admiration of the foreign ambassadors and the Court, tended him and rocked his golden cradle with her own hands. She emerged from this domestic idyll to order that the country palace of Tsarskoë should be prepared for the reception of her son and his household. She ordered him to live there with his wife and stressed that his attendance at the capital was unnecessary except on State occasions. As for the Grand Duke Alexander, it was decided that he should remain at Court and be brought up with his grandmother.

A few weeks later Paul, accompanied by a weeping Marie Feodorovna, left Petersburg with a small retinue, departing into semi-banishment to the Palace of Tsarskoë which had been seldom used for nearly twenty years. Neither of them had been allowed to see their son.

The Years of Waiting

T H E days passed slowly, stretching forward into an interminable vista of weeks and months and years, years that followed one another at a creeping pace of boredom and frustration. Shortly after their retirement from the Court, the Empress gave them the Palace of Pavlovsk and they lived there with an extended household, but it was a household composed of all those whom Catherine considered dull or undesirable. The mediocre and the unimportant went to join the Czarevitch in his luxurious retreat. Occasionally they went to Petersburg or to Moscow, to find yet another youthful lover attending on the Empress, provided by the all-powerful Potemkin. And there Paul caught brief glimpses of his first-born son. The lovely infant had become a child of astonishing beauty, a serious, obedient, dignified little boy with a strangely opaque expression, who clung to his adored grandmother's hand and tried to turn away when his father approached. Catherine had added this factor to the long list of wrongs she had wrought against her son.

She had taught the Grand Duke Alexander to distrust and hate him.

And for Paul's part, they were mutual feelings. Somewhere in a corner of his mind there lurked a spark of jealousy, a subconscious resentment of his empty unaffectionate childhood, and the sight of his mother lavishing love upon his son roused him to fresh bitterness.

Another child was born to Marie, a second son, and he, too, was torn from them by Catherine, who named him Constantine as an earnest of her intention to subdue Turkey and ultimately make him ruler.

The crown of Russia, as none knew better than his father Paul, was destined to pass straight to Alexander on her death.

They were uneasy years for Paul, years of dangerous inactivity which encouraged brooding; there was nothing to do at Pavlovsk but ride, or regulate the household; no amusement but the pseudo-intellectualism of the Grand Duchess, who surrounded herself with mediocre poets, penniless writers bereft of major talent, and sycophants who flattered her with a fulsomeness that made Paul sick.

In 1781 the Empress sent for him. How would he like to make a tour of Europe, she suggested, and he hesitated, tempted beyond endurance by the promised change of scene, yet as always suspicious of her motives.

The years had not improved her; her beauty had faded rapidly, her supple limbs were fat, her expression hard and matronly. The same practised smile no longer suited her; it belonged to her vanished youth, to an era which permitted a young lover to stand behind her chair without the incongruity of twenty years difference in their ages. Go abroad, she urged her son, the accent of command emerging in her voice. Broaden your mind and take Marie Feodorovna to the Mecca of her intellectual dreams. Take her to Paris, and then to Vienna. Go, show yourself, my son, she ordered.

And when he had accepted she hurried to Potemkin with the news. Excellent, excellent, he applauded; let him descend upon the European capitals, equipped with all the eccentricities of manner that had grown so pronounced in the last few years.

Let them see him as he really was, a man so obsessed with the idea of assassination that a retinue of cooks and doctors and food tasters followed him everywhere; a master whose servants trembled in his presence and bore the marks of his fists upon their flesh.

He would be closely watched, the Empress added triumphantly; someone would hear him muttering aloud of his father's picture; he was certain to alienate and offend everyone with whom he came in contact. And later these things would be remembered as she intended they should . . . it would all help to smooth the path for her beloved Alexander. . . .

Paul and Marie travelled for twelve months under the pseudonym of the Comte and Comtesse du Nord and the journey turned into a triumphal progress. The plan of his relentless mother went completely awry, for no sooner did the Czarevitch pass beyond the Russian border than he became transformed. He treated his bewildered wife with gentle courtesy, smiled on his servants and overwhelmed his foreign hosts with graciousness.

In Vienna Catherine's ugly son displayed both gallantry and wit; even his enemies remarked that away from the hated influence of his mother, Paul's whole personality blossomed into amiability and humour. He breathed the free air of Austria and expanded in the luxury of being treated as an equal. He made friends among those most inimical to Catherine and so great was the impression of intelligence and dignity that he created, that his precautions against poison were treated with respect.

Once only, he betrayed himself. During a banquet in Florence Paul tasted something bitter in the wine and with a yell of terror he sprang up and made himself vomit, shouting that his mother's spies had tried to poison him.

For a moment the assembled guests glimpsed a less reassuring side of their royal visitor's mentality, saw his livid face and staring eyes, while the nerve of his cheek throbbed and throbbed, and his stolid wife sat speechless and trembling with fear at his side.

Receptions, banquets and balls were given in their honour and the delighted Grand Duchess found herself at last in France, in the centre of the brilliance and culture that she strove to imitate so desperately.

As for the Czarevitch, one memory of that Gallic visit never faded. For the rest of his life the mention of France evoked one picture, the picture of the lovely, laughing queen who had shown him especial graciousness, talking by the hour in her soft voice with the faint Austrian inflection, and on the day nearly thirteen years later when he heard that Marie Antoinette had died upon the guillotine, he turned away and wept.

When the time came for them to return to Russia, Marie Feodorovna sat in the carriage and cried; Paul only sat in silence staring moodily out of the window, the prey of resentment and despair. After a year of freedom, of friendship and honour, they were going back, back to boredom and uncertainty, to restrictions and idleness.

The Empress was in Moscow when they arrived; the reports of their success had infuriated her until emotion made her ill and she retired to bed to recover from her disappointment and rage.

As usual, Potemkin comforted her. Never mind the European tour, he argued; Paul was sick, sick in mind and, though the process was a slow one, he had thought of a way in which to hasten the symptoms. Pavlovsk was too small a residence; while it afforded no opportunities for plotting against Catherine, its lack of amenities prevented Paul from working mischief to himself.

Give him Gatchina, Potemkin whispered, and the Empress raised herself upon one elbow and repeated the name in surprise.

Gatchina? The home of Gregory Orlov?

Yes, Potemkin said eagerly. Orlov was dead and Orlov had died mad, fleeing from hallucinations of the dead Czar Peter the Third, crying out that the bloody ghost pursued him day and night. That vast gloomy palace would be excellent for Paul, with all its association of lunacy and horror. The Prince was a great believer in the power of atmosphere, and he had felt the dark oppressiveness of Gatchina for himself. Also, let the Czarevitch have men to play with, soldiers drawn from the lowest rabble, officered by petty tyrants renowned for cruelty and excess. Given these ingredients and a little authority over the inhabitants of the nearby town, the Czarevitch would fall into the infamous trap they set for him, and the stage would be set for Alexander after all.

So Paul moved into Gatchina, the great marble palace built for his mother's lover, the man who had helped to kill his father; and with him went a larger retinue of gentlemen and servants.

Among those was a nobleman of Tartar blood, the cynical, clever courtier Rastopchine, who had joined the Czarevitch's household against his own interests, because a quixotic streak of his nature sympathized with the fallen and despised the easy luxury of Catherine's Court. He was a curious, rather silent man who had managed to win Paul's confidence over the years, and the friendship strengthened in spite of Marie Feodorovna's jealous disapproval.

But the most evil influence in the household was also the most influential. A former Cadet Corps instructor named Alexei Araktchéief was transferred to Paul's service because of his brutal record, and he was joined by a low-born Turk called Koutaïssof.

The stiff, military despot, Araktchéief, his nature rigid with self-imposed discipline, whose ferocity to his underlings amounted to calculated sadism, was placed in command of the troops who were to keep order in Gatchina and the surrounding countryside. He entrenched himself in Paul's good graces by fanatical loyalty and blind obedience. He was a monster of cruelty, but his methods proved efficient; they transformed the savage collection of ruffians the Empress had allowed to enlist with her son into a highly trained force of men, men who obeyed the neglected Czarevitch as if he were already Czar of Russia, men who guarded him so that for the first time in his life he felt secure.

Koutaïssof became Paul's valet. He was cunning and ruthless, consumed with greed and the need to rise above his subservient station by any means available. He flattered his master, anticipated his slightest wishes, and loathed the Grand Duchess, who treated him with typical Nordic disdain. He was no soldier, no smooth-tongued courtier, but he was confident that his opportunity for usefulness would come. It came in the middle of 1788, just twelve years after Paul's second marriage, and it brought the precarious structure of his dull domestic life with Marie crashing into ruin.

BOOK TWO

Curse Not The King

7

MARIE FEODOROVNA sat in her music room at Gatchina making notes, while one of her ladies sorted out a pile of compositions and another read aloud in French. It was typical of Marie's methodical routine that no opportunity for cultural improvement should be lost, and while she muttered over her list she half attended to the reader's droning voice, nodding at intervals as if she appreciated and understood.

At last she raised her head and signalled the reader to stop.

"There, everything is arranged for to-night. You haven't forgotten the list of guests, have you, Anna?"

"No, Madame, I have it here, do you wish me to read it to you again?"

"No, that won't be necessary. They're all coming, aren't they? Including that horrible Araktchéief, I suppose; still, I had to invite him. Oh, someone must go to the Czarevitch and tell him I shall dine privately as I want to rest before the concert. . . . Who'll go to him? Well, in Heaven's name don't look so nervous; he objects to pages coming with personal messages from me and somebody has got to tell him. . . ."

"I will go, Madame."

Marie turned to look at the speaker and raised her light eyebrows contemptuously. It was the Nelidoff, of course, always willing to run errands, mild, stupid little creature; her gentle obedience and self-effacing airs always irritated Marie, who only wished to be surrounded by attractiveness and wit. Slight, dark-eyed Catherine Nelidoff possessed neither of these qualities, added to which she was an old maid of thirty without even a romantic scandal to her credit.

"Very well, go then, but hurry; I have things for you to do!"

The maid of honour slipped out of the room and began walking quickly along the dark, tapestried gallery which led to Paul's apartments.

Thank God for those messages of the wife to her husband,

messages which brought her into his presence and permitted her to see and speak to him alone. Though the occasions were rare and their duration brief, though he seldom looked at her or seemed aware that she existed, the insignificant lady-in-waiting lived for those encounters. She moved with remarkable grace, a grace that found expression in a talent for dancing that was preserved in an old painting commissioned by the Empress years ago after a performance by the childish Nelidoff had caught her notice.

But there was little dancing at Pavlovsk, where the Grand Duchess still spent several months, and none at all at Gatchina. She glanced round her at the dismal, Spartan furnishings and shivered; it was so gloomy, more like an enormous barracks than a home, its courtyard echoed to the tramp of soldiers, all day long the guards were being changed, companies were being drilled . . . and there were some days when she dared not look out of a window because some wretched criminal was being publicly flogged for an offence. Yet she preferred it to Pavlovsk, and though she shuddered in its atmosphere, she understood it, whereas the heavy, cloying air of Marie's Teutonic residence depressed her unbearably.

Pavlovsk was hideous, hideous in its attempt to appear tasteful: every piece of furniture, every ornament and painting was a clumsy sham, a replica of someone else's treasure. The gardens, which might have been beautiful left in their natural setting, were flattened and carved into the semblance of a French Tuileries.

Everyone in it was bored to death except Marie Feodorovna, and the Czarevitch was the most ill-at-ease of them all.

The Nelidoff paused before the entrance to his private suite, her way barred by two sentries of the Gatchina garrison, two snub-nosed Russian peasants, their bodies buttoned into elaborate Prussian uniforms, grotesque with powdered hair and monstrous conical hats. They recognized her and let her pass, springing back into position like clockwork toys.

A page directed her to his bedroom and she entered quietly, curtsying to the ground.

It was a large high-ceilinged room, dominated by two objects, the big canopied bed that stood in the centre and a huge portrait which hung on the wall opposite the bed, so that it was the first object on which the sleeper's eyes would rest when he awoke.

Catherine Nelidoff recognized the picture only too well; the irregular features, bulbous head and half-witted expression of Peter the Third were painfully familiar to the inhabitants of Paul's household. Quickly she glanced away, and seeing the Czarevitch seated before the fireplace, she advanced towards him.

He sat with his back to her, aware that she had entered, unable to turn round, because a servant was leaning over him, laying cold cloths on his head.

The servant looked up at her with inquisitive black eyes, and she recognized his valet, the Turk, Koutaïssof.

"Who is it?" Paul demanded.

"Mlle. Nelidoff, your Highness."

The valet answered for her, watching her intently.

"Tell her to come round where I can see her."

She approached him, careful to tread lightly, for his attitude was rigid with pain.

"I have a message from the Grand Duchess, your Highness," she whispered, and he opened his eyes with an effort and looked at her. For an instant she sustained his glance, noting the terrible pallor and strained expression, before the treacherous colour dyed her olive skin and forced her to look down.

"What is this message, then?"

"The Grand Duchess begs you to excuse her from dining with you this evening; she wants to rest before the concert."

He frowned and pushed back the compress from his forehead.

"What concert . . . what is she talking about. . . ?"

"A musical evening, Sir," the valet told him, never taking his eyes off Catherine Nelidoff's face. "'You were to attend, don't you remember. . . ?"

"Oh, God. . . . Yes, I remember. Well, since you're here, Mademoiselle, you may inform my wife that I have another headache and cannot be present. Also I excuse her from coming to dine with me."

"Yes, your Highness."

She curtsied again and backed out of the door, which a page closed silently behind her. Koutaïssof stared after her for a moment and then bent over his master.

"Sir . . . will you excuse me for an instant . . . only an instant?"

Paul motioned with his hand for him to go, and then closing

his eyes, relaxed in the chair, fighting the pains that tore through his brain.

The Turk caught up with her in a deserted corridor, still within the confines of the Czarevitch's suite, and seeing the slow walk and drooping shoulders, smiled momentarily before he spoke.

" Mademoiselle . . ."

She swung round, startled by the disembodied whisper, and seeing him, raised a hand to her eyes, which were quite red with recent tears.

" I must speak to you," he said urgently. " Please, Mademoiselle."

" What is it? " she asked him. Without answering he opened a door in the tapestried wall and motioned for her to enter a small ante-room.

" If you will come in here . . . I cannot speak where we might be overheard."

For all her timidity Catherine Nelidoff was curious; also he served the Czarevitch; it might be that Paul had sent him. . . .

" I speak on behalf of the Czarevitch," the valet said suddenly and saw that her pale face flamed at the mention of that name.

" Speak then, for the love of God! "

" He's sick, Mademoiselle. Very sick. These headaches are more frequent and he suffers greatly."

" I know," she murmured, and her eyes filled with tears, so that she turned away and would not look at him.

" I love him," Koutaïssof continued. " I would give my life to serve him. Therefore I lay it in your hands, and come to you."

She swung round on him then. " You come to me? But why . . . what can I do? . . . I am helpless, Koutaïssof. I have no friends at Court."

" I know that, Mademoiselle, and I come to you for aid of a different kind. l say that I love my master. I will say more. I believe that you, too, are devoted to him."

For a moment there was silence, while Catherine Nelidoff's heart pounded in mingled terror and determination. Then she faced the valet, her hesitation passed.

" I am," she said quietly. " Like you, I would give my life. . . ." Koutaïssof's narrow black eyes considered her, mentally appraising her attractions.

She was certainly not pretty, he reflected, but delicately made, with small hands and soft eyes. And her mouth was good; it was full and naturally red, and his considerable experience recognized that such a mouth bespoke sensuality. Perhaps even a virgin, he thought, and his confidence rose. It might be accomplished, if she was as love-sick as he thought her.

"The Czarevitch needs the affection you could give him. He needs a woman's comfort, Mademoiselle, and I know that you have already found favour in his eyes. Will you not come to him?" he asked her.

She had begun to pace the room while he was speaking, and seeing her wipe her eyes he knew that she wept. Again her reaction pleased him. Emotion was what his master needed after the stolid embraces of his hated wife. This gentle, sensitive creature could afford him boundless pleasure, and by reason of her nature, she, as well as Paul, would remain for ever in the valet's debt.

"What can I do, Koutaïssof?" she whispered through her tears. "I confess that I love him; that I have loved him for years, watching while he married two women, neither of whom were worthy to approach him!"

"Two women? You knew the first Grand Duchess . . . Natalie?"

"I was among her ladies. But no one noticed me; they just passed me into the service of her successor . . . I don't think he knew I was alive. . . . Now you say he needs me. Oh, Koutaïssof, help me!"

He came close to her then.

"I will help you, Mademoiselle. Do nothing until I give the word. And remember, you can trust me."

.   .   .   .   .

She was so late in returning to the Grand Duchess that Marie rebuked her severely, and dismissed her to cry in her room for the rest of the evening. But instead, Catherine Nelidoff lay in bed and dreamt wild dreams, dreams in which the central figure of Paul Petrovitch no longer viewed her from a distance, but approached close to her, his arms extended, asking to be sheltered, and finally slept with his head on her breast.

.   .   .   .   .

For three days the Czarevitch was ill; his head pained him and he remained in his rooms, sitting in silence before his father's portrait for hours on end, the victim of intense melancholy. Koutaïssof never left him; he served his master's food, barbered and dressed him, and persuaded him to go to bed at night.

And in the stillness and gloom of that strange sickroom, he whispered and hinted into Paul's ear, knowing that though he said nothing, the Czarevitch heard well enough and would remember.

On the evening of the third day, Paul Petrovitch left his chair and began to move around his room, one hand pressed to his forehead in the habit of pain.

"It's passing," he murmured to himself. "Thank God, it's going away. . . ."

He felt for the furniture as he walked, his inflamed eyelids half closed against the feeble light of a few candles and the brighter glow of the fire, and he stepped quietly with the instinctive care of a man who had known many hours of semi-blindness.

At last his groping hand found a small toilette mirror; it was too dim to see his own reflection and he moved towards a double candlestick, shielding his eyes with his fingers.

"I must look," he said aloud. "It will hurt for a moment, but I must see myself. . . ."

With an effort he opened his eyes and stared at his own reflection in the glass, the light of the wax candles illuminating his face.

The skin was bloodless and stretched tightly over the prominent brow and cheekbones; two deep lines of pain were cut across his forehead; his eyes, so fine and out of all proportion in their expressive beauty to the rest of that ravaged countenance, were red-rimmed and half closed against the light.

"Merciful God . . ." he said aloud. Mastering the impulse to hurl the mirror against the nearest wall, he put it down and turned away, his hand pressed to his throbbing head, the other outstretched, seeking for his chair.

A moment later his valet entered the room and bowed before the seated, motionless figure.

"Koutaïssof."

"Yes, Sir?"

"Send her away. I have just looked at myself." The valet's black eyes narrowed but his lips smiled down at Paul.

"The lady is already in your ante-room, Sir. She's too distressed to turn away. She begs to see you. . . . Just for a few moments."

Paul turned his head away into the shadows. Catherine Nelidoff. He tried to remember what she looked like but beyond the merest outline, his memory could supply no detailed picture. She was small, he thought, and not pretty. And after days of hinting, Koutaïssof had finally informed him that his wife's insignificant lady-in-waiting was in love with her Czarevitch.

Apparently she had cried on this account, and Paul smiled wryly at the thought. In his experience women's tears were weapons of deceit; they wept from fear, like Natalie, when she was lying and cajoling, or from greed like Marie, when she wanted something.

No one had ever shed a tear of love or sympathy for him. No one but this little creature Nelidoff who had sought out Koutaïssof as her advocate. Paul sighed suddenly; he felt ill and desolate in mind as well as body. Koutaïssof was insistent, he thought wearily, he praised the lady for her gentleness and good reputation; he also hinted that the Grand Duchess Marie bullied her, and knowing his wife's tendency towards petty domestic tyranny, Paul quite believed it.

"Please, Sir, see Mademoiselle Nelidoff. Just for five minutes. . . ."

A sudden temptation assailed him, urging him to listen to that smooth, prompting voice, to take advantage of the situation offered him. Perhaps she could comfort him; perhaps for once it would be pleasant to relax in the gentle company of a woman with the knowledge that he could dismiss her in an instant if she wearied him. . . .

"Very well. For a few moments then. When I ring for you, show her out."

Contented, the valet turned and vanished through the door.

When he returned, Catherine Nelidoff was with him. She stood in the centre of the room, uncertain what to do or say, paralysed by shyness, until the Turk pushed a small silver basin into her hands.

"Bathe his eyes and forehead, if he will let you. It soothes the pain. Go to him now."

Then the door closed softly behind him and she was alone with Paul. She was an emotional woman and her sense of awkwardness suddenly disappeared when she came close to him and saw how tired and ill he looked. She placed the bowl of scented water on a little table, and then knelt beside his chair.

Paul held out his hand to her and glanced down at her face. He saw the expression in it clearly for a moment, before the ache in his head and eyes forced him to give up.

It was a gentle face, as Koutaïssof said, and it was full of sympathy; he even fancied that he saw the gleam of tears.

"Thank you for coming to wait on me, Mademoiselle. It is kind of you."

She raised his fingers to her lips and kissed them.

"I hardly dared hope that you would receive me, your Highness. Only Koutaïssof encouraged me."

"He is faithful," Paul remarked slowly. "And he has spoken well of you."

She blushed, remembering that hysterical avowal of her love for him, made in that room off the corridor. Hope and fear of what that confession might bring her had become fused in quivering anticipation when she read the valet's scribbled message.

'He will see you. Come this evening and wait outside his rooms.'

She had come prepared to serve him in any way he wished.

There was silence for some minutes, and while it lasted, Paul found a certain tranquil pleasure in her presence in the room. It was comforting not to be alone; it affected him oddly to imagine the shape and features of the woman kneeling quietly by his chair. He tried to analyse the feeling, and in his attempt to do so, felt suspicion and discomfort rising in him.

She must want something, he said to himself; money, favours, vengeance on an enemy . . . he shifted uncomfortably, unwilling that these brief moments should be poisoned, however illusory they might prove to be.

"Koutaïssof gave me some scented water, your Highness. Would you like me to bathe your forehead if the pain is bad?"

Her voice was soft, and pitched low; a thin tremor of uncertainty ran through it which made her seem vulnerable, and the sound of it dispelled his evil thoughts.

"If you would be good enough, Mademoiselle."

There was a cloth in the basin; she dipped her fingers in the sweet-smelling water and wrung it out, then she stood behind his chair and wiped his forehead. For an instant her hand rested on his brow, and the tips of her fingers touched his eyelids. Her touch was light and extraordinarily comforting, her fingers cool and skilful at their task. Catherine, he thought resentfully: who had given her that hated name that suited her so badly? It conjured up visions of hands that bore no resemblance to those that soothed him at that moment. His mother's hands were beautiful, long-fingered and very white; when they moved the brilliance of diamonds dazzled the eye; but for all their beauty they were strong, ruthless hands, capable of directing men and armies, and they were pointed and sensual, made for amorous play. He hated her hands as he hated everything to do with her. . . .

"Put the cloth over my eyes," he said. "Then sit by me, if you please."

She obeyed him promptly and he heard the sound of her silk skirt rustling as she settled at the side of his chair once more.

"Have you any other name besides Catherine?" he asked suddenly.

"No, your Highness. But sometimes I am called Katya."

He smiled his rare smile, blindly, under the cover of the compress which masked his sight.

"Then that shall be my name for you. Katya. . . ."

"How is your head?" she asked him, trembling, because he used her foolish nickname and smiled at her, so that his ugliness seemed to have disappeared.

"Much better; you've soothed it, Katya. You have cool fingers; give them to me. . . ."

She caught hold of the hand he held out to her, and pressed it to her lips in a gesture in which there was no formality; then she held it against her cheek and leant on the carved wood of the chair arm, watching the firelight blaze and flicker in the marble grate. He moved a little and enclosed her hand firmly in his own.

"Stay with me, Katya."

"I will stay with you; rest now, my Prince. I'll stay with you until you send me away. . . ."

.   .   .   .   .

In his alcove off the Czarevitch's room, Koutaïssof waited, listening for his master's bell. When one of the palace clocks chimed, he counted the notes and smiled. She had been with him for an hour and the signal for her dismissal had not come.

.   .   .   .   .

In the weeks that followed, Catherine Nelidoff came to Paul's rooms almost every evening, slipping away as soon as she dared, often pleading illness to escape the Grand Duchess's service; though the servants watched and whispered, and the other ladies speculated, no rumour reached Marie of the reason for those absences and convenient spells of sickness. She scolded her lady-in-waiting when she remembered her existence, and remained in happy ignorance of the liaison which was being strengthened with every hour they spent together.

If others noticed that the plain little Nelidoff seemed happy, almost gay, Marie remarked nothing to excite suspicion. Instead she busied herself with preparations to return to her own palace at Pavlovsk, and broached the subject to the Czarevitch one evening when they dined together. Their meetings had grown rarer still since his last illness, and no one was more thankful for Paul's absence than his wife, but since permission to leave must be obtained, she sought him out.

It was a silent meal, occasionally punctuated by Marie's attempts at conversation which met with slight response. Privately she thought him excessively moody and abstracted, and longed fervently to turn her back on Gatchina and all it represented.

"I was thinking that Pavlovsk will be very pleasant at this time of year," she ventured, wondering why making a request of Paul always unnerved her, though she seldom met with a refusal.

The Czarevitch watched her with expressionless eyes, aware that she wished to leave him and as anxious for her departure as she was herself.

"I have no doubt of it. Do you wish to go there, Madame?" His directness always disconcerted her, and she blushed.

"Why, yes. If . . . if that would be agreeable to you."

"Perfectly agreeable. I shall remain here and join you in the middle of summer. You may leave whenever you wish."

The Grand Duchess masked her relief with a smile, and

even resigned herself to spending the night with her husband.

That night she lingered, expecting him to approach her, but Paul merely talked trivialities and made no move, and when she rose to leave he kissed her hand politely and wished her a good night.

As soon as she had gone he rang for Koutaïssof.

"Send for Mademoiselle Nelidoff. And hurry; it's already late." The valet bowed low to him and smiled.

"I have taken that liberty, Sir. She's waiting in my alcove in case you should desire her company."

"You're a good servant, Koutaïssof. I shall know how to reward you. Now send her to me."

The valet remarked his eagerness, and his black eyes gleamed with satisfaction. All was well; he was in love with the woman; he chafed in his wife's presence and refrained from inviting her into his bed even when she dallied in expectation of the summons, as Koutaïssof had noticed.

As he went to fetch the waiting Nelidoff, he decided that in spite of the evidence to the contrary, Paul must have made her his mistress as well as his confidante.

In this he was wrong, for that strange bond which existed between them had not been cemented by passion. Paul sat with her for hours, sometimes talking or listening while she read aloud in her clear soft voice, sometimes in silence, but always contented and at peace. He found her deeply sensitive to his needs, tender in a wordless, servile way, and the sensation of being mothered by her fulfilled an aching need. She was very gentle, yet capable of humour, with a ready laugh that pleased him on the rare occasions when he heard it. And she was virtuous; he sensed that precious quality in her and knew that he was not deceived by the lack of seduction in her manner and expression.

Also he missed her sorely when they were apart, and that night it seemed to him as if the tedious dinner with his wife would never end.

He was trembling with impatience as he waited for her, angry because so many hours of pleasure had been wasted through Marie Feodorovna, and suddenly uneasy for a cause he could not name.

When she came into the room he realized what disturbed him. Pavlovsk. That damned woman would be leaving very

quickly now that she had his permission, and Catherine Nelidoff would have to go with her.

Paul advanced to meet her and raised her up when she tried
to curtsy to him.

"I'm sorry you had to wait, Katya, but my wife stayed
longer than I expected. Come, sit down."

He examined her by candlelight, still holding both her hands
in his and sat beside her on the stiff-backed couch.

"You look pale," he said. "What have you been doing,
what's the matter. . . ? Tell me."

She looked at him and tried to smile.

"I'm only tired, Highness. It's been a busy day; the Grand
Duchess has already begun preparing to leave for Pavlovsk."

"I gave her permission to go there, this evening. . . . And
that's why you're pale . . . and low-spirited. Just tiredness,
Katya?"

She tried to withdraw her hands but his fingers tightened on
them and his eyes searched her face.

"I shall be leaving Gatchina soon. And I've grown so fond
of it."

"You disappoint me, Mademoiselle. I had begun to flatter
myself you might be sorry to say good-bye to me," he said
quietly, and felt her stiffen, and knew by the clenching of her
hands that she was trembling.

"Why do you make game of me, Sir, when you know this
separation from you will be like death?"

Somehow he had never expected to hear her say these words,
though he knew then that he had longed for that admission
and all that it implied. Koutaïssof had told him that she loved
him, but he had doubted, and tried to pretend that he did not
nurse a secret hope. No woman had ever loved him; neither
his mother nor his two wives. Araktchéief, his commanding
officer, his valet, some members of the garrison . . . they were
loyal, but they were men. He might be shorter than they and
uglier by far, it didn't matter, whereas with a woman all that
counted were the attributes he lacked. . . .

He gazed at Catherine Nelidoff intently, his expression
almost fierce, wondering desperately whether she too lied and
acted in order to achieve some object of her own.

Raising her eyes to his face she read the mingled longing
and suspicion there. "Try to forgive me," she said quietly.
"I cheated my way into your friendship, because I have loved

you secretly for years and something said to me by your valet
gave me hope. These last few weeks have been the happiest
of my whole life. Just to sit here and talk to you, to feel that
you needed me a little. . . . You can't imagine what that's
meant to me."

"To nurse a sick man, to spend hours in semi-gloom without
gaiety or entertainment . . . has that really made you happy,
Katya?"

She smiled ruefully, and withdrawing her hand from his,
moved a great silver candlestick that stood behind the sofa,
so that the light fell on her face.

"Look at me, Sir. Do you think there's been much gaiety
and entertainment for me? In order to succeed at Petersburg, it's necessary to be beautiful as well as nobly born, or
at least wealthy. I have no money, and as for beauty . . . you
can see that for yourself."

Paul looked and saw features which had begun to haunt his
dreams, an irregular nose, and the wide, brown eyes which
reminded him of a small, shy animal. Beautiful, no. But the
lack of physical grace was something that he understood as
gentle, sweet-faced Katya Nelidoff never would.

"I think you very pretty," he said solemnly, and she turned
away, playing with the embroidery on her skirt so that he
shouldn't see the tears which filled her eyes.

"I shall miss you, when you go to Pavlovsk," he continued
slowly. "I, too, have been very happy these last weeks."

She began to cry helplessly then, her narrow shoulders
shaking, all her poor defences shattered by that simple sentence containing the one lie she longed to hear above all others.

"I think you very pretty."

She saw them as they really were; two people with a common
bond of unattractiveness in a world that worshipped beauty
and flamboyance, both lonely, sensitive and proud. The great
Prince, the nominal heir to a throne, was as desolate in his
need as the plain maid of honour. And she fulfilled that need.
Here in Gatchina life held a purpose for her, a dangerous
purpose, perhaps, bringing the envy of the mighty in its train,
but even if they dealt with her as other favourites had been
dealt with throughout history, it would be worth the risk.

"I don't want to leave you . . . I can't, God pity me!"

For the first time Paul gathered her in his arms, murmuring
words of comfort, acutely moved by her distress.

He took his own handkerchief out of his sleeve and wiped her face; as he did so he discovered that the feel of her body was stirring and agreeable. She had left him in peace all these weeks, content to sit by him, talking or in silence according to his wishes, engendering in him the luxury of mental ease. Until that moment he had been content with that, afraid to test her feelings by a more intimate relationship in the dread that he would find them wanting.

Her wretchedness was the assurance that he needed, and his hot blood quickened as he held her.

Catherine Nelidoff gazed up at him, her fine brown eyes still wet with tears, sensing that his attitude had changed, knowing with the instinctive subtlety of women that she had reversed the process and reached his senses through his heart.

Inexperience aided her then; a practised movement or a flattering phrase would have destroyed the opportunity in a second. But instead she stayed still in his arms and said nothing.

Her mouth was beautiful, he thought passionately, full lipped and curved in lines of generosity and feeling. Suddenly he bent and kissed her, gently at first, holding himself in check while his desire increased as she stirred and murmured in his arms.

For all her shyness she was extremely sensual and under the stimulus of his embrace, her passion for him broke.

Her hands caressed his face and caught fiercely at the lapels of his coat as he began to kiss her with unrestrained desire, aware that she offered him an outlet denied him since the death of Natalie.

So Catherine Nelidoff surrendered to him, blinded by love and without the assurance that he could protect her from the final consequences.

.   .   .   .   .

The first indication that the domestic truce of her marriage was about to end reached Marie Feodorovna in the mid-morning of that day. She was writing letters in her study when one of Paul's pages handed her a note.

It was brief and written with his own hand. In it, he wished her a good journey to Pavlovsk, with the added injunction to leave as quickly as possible. He also informed her that

Mademoiselle Nelidoff would be remaining at Gatchina on his orders.

Marie Feodorovna sat rooted, the letter sliding to the floor.

She was to go, immediately . . . and her lady-in-waiting was to stay behind at Paul's command. . . .

"Oh, no!" she said aloud. "No. . . ."

When she recovered herself, and, blazing with fury, sent for the culprit, they found her room empty, and its occupant moved to another suite in the Czarevitch's wing, placed there out of reach by Paul.

There was nothing that the Grand Duchess could do, since he refused to see her, and only replied to her frantic notes by sending his own servants to expedite her packing and departure.

He stood by his window to watch her go, his face expressionless, until the last carriage disappeared from view, knowing that with the dismissal of Marie Feodorovna a turning point had been reached in his life.

.   .   .   .   .

By the end of the year rumours of a rift between Paul and his wife were so persistent that the Empress mentioned them to Potemkin, whom she had created Prince of Taurus the year before. The Court was in residence at the Wooden Palace in Moscow, and Catherine sat with her old friend in her study. It was a comfortable, almost domestic scene; the Prince's uniform coat hung over the back of a chair and his wig was pushed back from his forehead; he stretched himself in his favourite position on one of Catherine's cushioned sofas, helping himself and her to wine and sweetmeats which were placed at his elbow. He had aged and his fine muscular frame was soft and swathed in fat; bouts of gargantuan eating and sensual excesses had weakened his health, so that the Empress's beloved Grisha was often ill, and consequently very difficult and melancholy.

By contrast Catherine appeared in blooming health; her complexion was clear and ruddy, her shrewd eyes bright with an intelligence that no physical over-indulgence could dim. Rather she seemed to thrive on the mode of life that was sapping her old lover's strength. Catherine's lovers died or fell out of favour because their sixty-year-old mistress wore them out, but she remained alert, as avid for both pleasure and power as she had ever been.

"You know what's being said about my son," she remarked, and Potemkin nodded, stuffing a sweetmeat into his mouth.

"M—m—m. This woman . . . Nelidoff, is his mistress. And he's neglecting the elegiac Marie. I can't say I blame him. She grows more tedious every year. . . ."

"I don't like it, Grisha. The reports are not encouraging. Until the appearance of this girl everything was going according to plan at Gatchina. He made it into a prison . . . you know, a fortress in the Prussian style, rigid discipline for the troops, who not unnaturally relieved their feelings on the townspeople and tormented them in turn. As for Araktchéief . . ."

"The military schoolmaster with a bent for cruelty?"

"The same . . . Grisha, he has made himself so hated, and through him, Paul Petrovitch, that the civilians for a radius of several miles are deserting to other towns and taking refuge where they can. It was all excellent. Another year or two and there would have been a deputation from my subjects *begging* me to rescue them from my son. . . . Now this Nelidoff creature worms her way into his bed, upsets Marie, who God knows never interfered and did as she was bidden, and begins nursing Paul out of his mad humours!"

"Her influence is good, then?"

"Damnably good. She intercedes for Araktchéief's prisoners, stops the public floggings that do Paul so much harm and appears to be flooding Gatchina with gentle sweetness. . . . She's an adventuress, of course; probably very clever, for if I remember rightly she's sallow skinned and plain."

"What do you suppose she wants, besides the embraces of the Czarevitch?"

"Oh, most likely money, power, favours. In which case it might be possible to buy the little wretch away from him."

Potemkin swung his legs off the sofa and sat upright.

"You say she's ugly, Catherine? How ugly?"

"A more just description would be the one I gave you, sallow and insignificant. Why?"

He frowned and bit his nails as he always did when puzzled or concentrating upon some problem.

"From my knowledge of your sex, my dear, I should imagine

that if the lady is as unattractive as you say, she may prefer
the limelight as mistress of the second personage in Russia to
all the bribes that you can offer."

"Before God, Grisha, you're probably right! Then what are
we to do?"

"I suggest that we come down upon the side of morality
and lend our support to the injured wife. Order Paul to take
her back and surrender his little favourite into Marie's service
as before. If she can't be bought, she can be persecuted, or
if necessary frightened into retiring from Paul's household.

"Don't under-estimate the Grand Duchess, Catherine; she
may be a fool and a poseuse, but I'll swear she will find ways
to make Mademoiselle Nelidoff wish she had never been
born. . . ."

.   .   .   .   .

The Empress's wishes were communicated to her son at
Gatchina and his first reaction was to consign them to the
devil. He stormed into his rooms, livid with anger, his face
twitching convulsively, so that his gentle Katya shrank back
appalled, hardly recognizing the man she loved. He stood
before her, Catherine's letter crumpled in his fist, his eyes
blazing as if he stared at some intolerable inward vision, his
oaths and explanations turned into gibberish by the sudden
onset of a violent stammer.

"Don't," she begged him, terrified by his manner, "don't
upset yourself . . . whatever it is, it doesn't matter; only calm
yourself. . . ."

Even as she pleaded, the horrifying impression that he
neither saw nor heard her became a certainty, as he brushed
past her, and opening the door, shouted an order to the sentry
who stood guard outside it.

When he returned she caught his arm, clinging to it despite
his attempt to shake her off, rendered desperate by fear for him
and by the necessity to deny her own suspicions. . . .

"Paul . . . Paul! Listen to me!"

He looked down at her, and his expression altered from
anger to confusion, a confusion that melted into recognition
and confirmed her dread that until that moment he had been
unaware of her presence or identity.

"Katya. . . ."

He frowned, and encircled her with his arm, one hand pressed to his throbbing cheek, and she stared up at him in mingled tenderness and pain, knowing that he was trying to remember.

"I was so angry," he said slowly. "Did I shout at you, Katya?"

"No, Paul, no. A message came from your mother . . . a letter. You still have it."

He unclosed his fist, still holding her against him, and regarded the ball of tangled paper.

"Did I tell you what was in it?"

She shook her head.

"Let us sit down, my love. And before I begin, you're not to worry. I shall disregard every word of it."

She sat in her favourite position on a stool by his feet, resting her head against his knee and was glad that he couldn't see her face as she listened.

"I am to go on living with my wife and to visit her at Pavlovsk. It seems there are rumours of a crisis in my household and my mother is concerned. . . . As for you, Katya, you are to return to your duties with the Grand Duchess. . . ."

"That's not as harsh as I expected," she said at last and sat upright for fear that he should feel her trembling.

"Harsh! If you think that I am going to allow you to . . ."

"Please, Paul . . . don't get angry. Listen to me for a moment. I believe it's a fair solution; don't you see, the Empress might have banished me, imprisoned me! Instead, she offers us a way to be together without causing a scandal. . . ."

"Scandal . . . what is scandal to my mother? To the Messalina of the North! That's what they are calling her in Europe. Her name is infamous. . . . There is no vice that is not attributed to her. . . . Don't talk to me of scandal, Katya. This is another plot, another trick to deprive me of the slightest happiness. But she shan't have her way this time; no, by God, she'll not force me into Marie's arms and give you up to her to punish. . . . I sent for Araktchéief a few moments ago. We'll see how many men will be needed to fortify Gatchina. . . ."

She knew he meant it and her terror of what such an action would entail far outweighed her fear of the fate decreed for her by Catherine's order. One hint of rebellion, and all the force of that terrible maternal hatred would descend upon him and, justified before the world, deliver him to death.

"No. . . . For the love of God, Paul, what are you saying! They'd blow Gatchina and everyone in it to pieces in a few hours. . . . I beg of you, do as she says. Go back to Marie; we can still meet in secret. . . ."

"I am not listening to you, Katya," he retorted. "Araktchéief will be here in a moment; then we shall see what's to be done."

"If you do this thing," she said firmly, "if you do it, I shall leave you. I swear it, Paul Petrovitch. I will go into a convent and never look upon your face again! "

He stared at her, surprised by the vehemence in her voice; and, recognizing the immovable obstinacy peculiar to the weak and pliable when they are roused, he faltered in his purpose.

"You couldn't do that; you couldn't forsake me when you know that I can't do without you. You make wild threats, my gentle love, because I've frightened you with all this. . . ."

"It's no idle promise! " she told him, and he knew that if it meant her death she would not bend. "You can't fight the Empress with any hope of winning; no woman is worth the madness that you contemplate, least of all me. Think of your heritage. Think what you would forfeit; your crown, the crown that all Russia knows is yours by right already! You are my Czar, as well as my lover. . . . No, Paul, you will be reasonable, and patient. If I can bear it, so must you. . . ."

"I will not have you suffer, Katya."

"I won't; nothing can hurt me so long as I can come to you sometimes. Only promise that you won't desert me, and I can bear anything."

That thought alone sustained her while she argued, for no one knew better than she what treatment to expect from Marie Feodorovna. It can be endured, she thought desperately. I have had weeks of happiness. . . .

Often, lying in Paul's arms, she had thought that death would not be too dear a price to pay for what he gave her, and smiled at her own morbid fancy, uneasy because the shadow of ill omen kept recurring.

By the time a timorous page announced that Araktchéief was waiting to be admitted, Catherine Nelidoff had won. Paul's capitulation left her exhausted rather than relieved and filled with such an access of terror that for one dreadful moment she almost threw herself into his arms, entreating him to defend her as he wished, to do anything rather than deliver her to the Grand Duchess. But the moment passed and she sat passive, one lifeless hand in his, when the door opened and that dreaded, bloody name sounded in her ears.

"M. Araktchéief, your Imperial Highness."

He advanced into the room with measured steps, his shoulders back, his long arms stiffly at his sides, moving with the precision of a soldier on the parade ground. He was tall and deceptively thin, for that sparse frame was sinuous and powerful as a steel spring; for a moment his green eyes rested on her and the beetling black brows contracted with disapproval. He hates me, she thought and shuddered, unable to endure that freezing glance even for an instant. Abruptly he stepped before Paul and bowed low to him; then he inclined towards Catherine Nelidoff, and turned again to his master.

"Sir. You sent for me."

Paul nodded.

"Yes, but since I issued the summons, Mademoiselle Nelidoff has persuaded me to a different course to the one I contemplated. However, my dear Araktchéief, there are some matters which we may as well discuss."

He looked at the white-faced woman by his side, and his ugly face softened with tenderness.

"Go to your rooms, my love," he whispered. "I'll join you in a little while."

"You have promised, remember! You'll do nothing rash?"

"You have my word. Go now," he said quietly.

When the door closed behind her Paul rose abruptly, his expression hardening, and turned towards the soldier.

"She has a gentle influence," he muttered, and Araktchéief moved impatiently.

"It's not for me to discuss the lady with you, Sir."

"No, Araktchéief; by God, I know you're no friend to women. . . . You're loyal to me, are you not?" he demanded suddenly, swinging round upon the other.

The soldier looked at him and an expression of extraordinary passion flashed across his features. It was as if a sudden light illumined that arctic countenance, as if a creaking robot proved to have a living soul; for a second the man whose unspeakable brutality had made him the most hated of all the savage pedants who surrounded Paul showed himself capable of fanatical devotion, a love so abnormal and so strong that his enmity for Catherine Nelidoff had its roots in bitter jealousy.

"To the last drop of my blood," he answered.

"It is well, my friend. I need your loyalty. I need all men's loyalty, for my enemies begin to press their persecution of me. . . . I would fight them, Araktchéief, I would take up arms and die, rather than suffer any further at their hands. . . . But the Mademoiselle has entreated me to yield. And I have promised. So I shall not need your troops, my friend, not yet. Instead, give me your report."

"My men captured two civilians creeping into the town of Gatchina this morning. I believe them to be spies sent here from Petersburg."

Paul stared at him, and the colour drained out of his face; at the same time his left cheek became convulsed, the spasm tugging at the corner of his eye. Araktchéief, having learnt to recognize the symptoms, gave no sign.

"Spies, you say. Spies. Tongues have been wagging to my mother, Araktchéief . . . people have told tales. . . . I would discourage them."

Suddenly his voice became a roar of rage, his blue eyes blazed, and the blood rushed up into his face.

"Where are they?"

"In the cells under the guard-room, Sir," the officer replied, and his light eyes had begun to gleam, illumining his face until his expression seemed almost gay with some anticipation.

The Czarevitch was walking up and down, clenching his fists, tearing at his cravat as if he choked, watched by the silent figure of his garrison commander, whose punitive exploits had reached a climax on the day he tore off the ear of an offending soldier with his teeth.

"They shall be punished . . ." Paul said grimly. "They shall learn that it is dangerous to wrong their Czarevitch. . . . We'll make an example of them, Araktchéief, an example that may deter other traitors from spying for my mother. . . . Araktchéief!"

"Sir!"

"Assemble the garrison and as many of the townspeople as you can muster by to-morrow morning. Then bring out these swine and have them knouted till they die. . . ."

.   .   .   .   .

That night Paul went to Catherine Nelidoff, soothing her fears with promises of his protection.

When he slept at last, she lay wide eyed and restless, pinned down by the weight of his head on her breast, tormented by doubt and terror for the future, listening to the sounds of activity that went on inside the palace and within the great courtyard throughout the hours of darkness and which continued long after daybreak.

But fortunately Catherine Nelidoff did not look out on to the scene which Araktchéief had staged so expertly; instead she nursed her lover, who woke moaning with pains in his head, and cried out for darkness, since the light streaming through the window was torture to his eyes.

He lay in his mistress's arms, fighting the blackness of suffering and despair, while the two innocent citizens of Catherine's realm were flogged to death in front of the entrance of Gregory Orlov's old pleasure palace. The watching crowd was silent, mesmerized by fear, and some among them remembered standing in these precincts nearly twenty years before, when the handsome, wealthy Orlov had been in the heyday of his love affair with the new Empress and the ground at their feet had been splashed red with wine flowing from free fountains, instead of growing damp with streams of blood.

.   .   .   .   .

8

IN the apartments allotted to the Grand Duchess's ladies-in-waiting, Marie's confidante and childhood friend lay wide awake listening to a sound that penetrated through the wall of an adjoining room.

After a few moments Madame de Benckendorf, the Grand Duchess's " dear Tilly," raised herself on one elbow, and turned towards a figure outlined in an adjoining bed.

" Anna ! "

The second lady stirred sleepily.

" What is it? . . . I was almost asleep."

"Be quiet a moment and listen. Now, do you hear anything?"

Tilly Benckendorf's companion opened her eyes wide and sat upright.

"Someone is crying. In the next room."

Madame smiled triumphantly in the darkness.

"Yes," she said. "It is our presumptuous little Nelidoff. I fear she isn't happy with us any more!"

Anna Zanova slid down underneath the bedclothes and she too smiled.

"It is really very entertaining; I never thought the Grand Duchess could be so vindictive. And I never liked the creature. It amuses me to help torment her. Listen to her! And she can't creep to the Czarevitch to-night either, for Irena is in there watching her."

"It won't last," the Benckendorf declared. "In the end she'll ask to be relieved. And she's being punished as she deserves, the sly little vixen, trying to supplant my mistress with that ugly fiend. . . ."

Anna Zanova blinked nervously and suddenly the prospects of sleep receded.

"Sometimes, Tilly, I wonder if he knows. . . . If she tells him how we treat her. He's so savage. . . . Some of the things that happen in the prisons at Gatchina . . . even I can't look at them, and God knows I'm not squeamish! Do you know, Tilly, if he ever finds out what goes on with the Nelidoff, I believe he'd have us torn limb from limb!"

Tilly Benckendorf shrugged irritably. The thought of Paul's reprisal had occurred to her often enough and quite spoiled her pleasure in bullying and hounding the helpless Katya Nelidoff. In spite of her unwavering viciousness towards Marie Feodorovna's rival, fear of the Czarevitch chilled her enthusiasm and even imposed some restraint in her dealing with the victim.

"He doesn't know," she said sullenly. "She's too noble or too wise to tell him, since he can do nothing to spare her. And the Empress ordered a full reconciliation between him and the Grand Duchess. He's obeyed so well that she's pregnant, and I hope Mistress Nelidoff likes that!"

Anna Zanova pulled the bedclothes up to her ears and shivered.

"I wish I had your confidence, Tilly. I know he's submitted, but they say *she* persuaded him! And I don't believe he's really obedient. I think he's only waiting, waiting to spring on the Empress, on Marie Feodorovna, on all of us!"

"Hold your tongue, Anna! You know he is never going to succeed! The next Czar is Alexander, with the Grand Duchess as Regent. . . . Now go to sleep."

Obediently the lesser lady-in-waiting turned on her side and said no more, but she lay with her eyes wide open in the darkness, aware that while Catherine Nelidoff wept into her pillow in the next room, her chief tormentor, Tilly Benckendorf, tossed restlessly on her bed.

It was a long time before either of Marie's faithful ladies fell asleep.

.   .   .   .   .

Catherine Nelidoff's early life had been characterized by dullness. Then the brief interlude of passionate attachment at Gatchina taught her the meaning of fulfilment and for a time she was transformed; even after the dreaded order to return to Marie at Pavlovsk, she met her lover with smiles and tenderness, and surrendered herself to his outraged wife with an outward resignation she was far from feeling.

But for all her courage, her loyalty to Paul and her determination to endure his wife's anger patiently, Catherine Nelidoff's spirit almost broke during that first year.

Every humiliation which the Grand Duchess or her spiteful, partisan household could devise was inflicted upon the woman Paul loved. The meanest tasks were allotted to her, and her duties were increased till she could scarcely stand with tiredness. Where she was concerned, the stolid, autocratic Marie Feodorovna proved to be a vindictive tyrant, burning with injured pride and malice, who encouraged her women to add their persecutions to her own. She didn't care if he were angry, she declared to her friend and chief lady-in-waiting, the sympathetic Tilly Benckendorf, he should not humiliate her with the Nelidoff now that they were reconciled and she was once again with child.

And for months, Marie Feodorovna pursued this course, until her physical state induced a sudden aversion to Paul, an aversion so strong that she shrank from his casual visits and gave way to tears and fainting fits if he sent for her at night.

It was Tilly Benckendorf who summoned Catherine Nelidoff and told her that the Grand Duchess wished her to accommodate the Czarevitch while she was indisposed; and it was Koutaïssof who played the pander once again and brought the maid of honour to his master's rooms.

On the way he whispered words of encouragement, aware that the hated Marie Feodorovna had made his protégée suffer to the detriment of her looks and his advantage.

"The Czarevitch is so unhappy, Mademoiselle," he told her. "He has been like a man bereaved for all these weeks."

She looked at him quickly, her eyes enormous in her white face; the flesh had melted from her cheeks, her throat and shoulders had become painfully thin and she started nervously at every sound.

"Damn that spiteful German bitch and her pack of shrews!" the valet said to himself. "The girl has gone to a shadow. . . ."

"Then he doesn't blame me for neglecting him," she murmured. "Does he know I had no choice?"

"Oh, he knows, Mademoiselle," Koutaïssof promised grimly. "I've seen to that. . . ."

"Thank you, Koutaïssof. I know you are my friend. . . ."

When Paul received her there was no time for words between them. She ran to him and threw herself into his arms, sobbing uncontrollably, while he kissed her with blind fervour.

Paul held her close, feeling as if his heart would burst with tenderness.

"My darling Katya," he whispered, kissing her lovingly and without the impatient urgency of passion, once the mutual storm had risen to its climax and subsided.

"If you knew how I have missed you. . . . I was afraid you no longer wished to come to me."

"How could you say that. . . . This separation has been torture. But there was never a moment. . . . They watch me day and night."

"So Koutaïssof assured me. And when I sent for you, my love, the Benckendorf said you were ill and couldn't come. Katya?"

"What, beloved?"

"Has my wife been ill-treating you?"

It was a question she dreaded; even as she prepared to deny it, in order not to worry him she loved to the point of worship, the tears of weakness welled up into her eyes and her small body trembled in the circle of his arms.

She hid her face against his shoulder and lied.

"No, Paul. I promise you. I'm only unhappy because she keeps me from you. There is nothing else; I have my duties like the others, that's all."

But later, when she had left him and gone back to her room, the Turkish valet sat at his master's feet and told him what the Grand Duchess and her women were inflicting on his mistress. Paul listened in silence, his ugly face suffused with blood, rage rising in his heart.

"She would have told me herself, Koutaïssof. She knows they dare not treat her badly. . . ."

"You underestimate her nature, Sir. I believe Mademoiselle fears to bring more trouble on you by revealing how the Grand Duchess abuses her. But I tell you the truth, Sir; I know how highly you regard her. I know you would never permit anyone to make her wretched. . . ."

"You shall be rewarded, Koutaïssof. And I shall pay a visit to my wife to-morrow morning. . . ."

By the end of the year Marie Feodorovna gave birth to a daughter. But before the confinement Catherine Nelidoff was installed in a private room within easy reach of the Czarevitch's apartments.

.   .   .   .   .

When the Empress was informed that her son's liaison was still unbroken, she surprised her intimates by losing her temper. The terrible placidity of Catherine in the face of death, sorrow or danger had become a legend, and the fame of it had spread through Russia and across the world. Nothing disturbed this amazing woman, nothing ruffled that smooth forehead or wiped the smile from her painted lips.

Wars, revolution, the defection of her lovers, even the death of Gregory Orlov had failed to induce any but the most digni-fied reaction or a becoming grief. But Catherine had an Achilles heel. One man could be relied upon to shatter the façade of calm and that man was her son. In the days of her love affair with Potemkin, she used to cry, to rage and despair like other women, but that period was half forgotten. The beautiful, sensuous Empress, who then had still been in the full golden bloom of maturity, had now become a corpulent old woman nearing seventy, who dressed simply, ate and drank frugally in an age of gluttony, and loved to play the doting grandmother with Paul's two sons. Only at night this domestic pose was abandoned, and the ageing Empress retired to her bedroom with a lover nearly forty years her junior.

Outwardly serene, as secure in her power and as clear in her vision as a woman half her age, Catherine's inward disintegration only became apparent when Paul Petrovitch was mentioned.

The reminder of his existence was a searing irritant. He still lived, enjoying the sights and sounds of changing seasons, using the gift of the senses which she prized for herself above all others, while she had fought down the impulse to imprison and then to exterminate his hated person from the world for nearly forty years.

Potemkin had stopped her, thwarted her sovereign will, she reflected angrily, aware that at last she really did resent his interference, and that the extraordinary domination he had exercised over her seemed to be fading.

So the germ of wrath grew in her mind, nurtured by the stories of her spies in Paul's household, who reported that Catherine Nelidoff had stood the test; that though she wept and lost weight, she stayed under Marie's rule, until the Czarevitch had stepped in and rescued her. Now she occupied a nominal post with the Grand Duchess, and Paul's extra-marital idyll was resumed. Consequently his health had improved, they told his mother regretfully, but in spite of the Nelidoff, M. Áraktchéief's influence was still very strong. He was encouraging his master into greater severities and was even rumoured to be jealous of the gentle Katya's influence. But it was yet too soon to be certain about that.

Catherine listened and then began to storm with anger. It was the fault of Marie Feodorovna, who had mismanaged her opportunity, and of Gregory Potemkin for suggesting compromise as usual.

To intervene now, when the breach was outwardly healed, would make her look ridiculous, and to remove Mistress Nelidoff privately would only provoke her besotted son into rebellion. And she had promised Alexander that there should be no violence in order to achieve their aim. His father should disappear quietly when the time came for Alexander to step into his shoes. That was agreed and Catherine loved her handsome grandson too much to risk losing his affection by breaking her word in this respect.

Paul's future was secure; it had all been planned and discussed down to the last detail, and it was amazing how shrewd the fifteen-year-old Grand Duke proved himself in this matter of his father's disinheritance and death.

He begged her to avoid a scandal, and while expressing the most pious sentiments about his savage and unpopular parent, suggested that a group of gentlemen should be secretly nominated to arrest him in the future, adding that he should have the list of their names so that he himself could give the order in an emergency.

Potemkin was present at these interviews and listening to the soft-voiced suggestion, he glared at the beautiful, beardless boy with astonishment and contempt in his one eye.

For all his ruthlessness, his immorality, his cunning and his greed, there was a strong vein of natural sentiment in the great Tartar and the sight of Paul's first-born eagerly consigning his father to an early grave revolted him. There was something effeminate about the boy which he disliked, something opaque and unspeakably deceitful in that smooth, fine-featured face. And on occasions he suspected cruelty and cowardice existed in that secretive nature. But the impression was a fleeting one; in fact everything about the Grand Duke Alexander was shifting and indefinable, so that Potemkin, who loved reading men and putting them to his own uses, hated Catherine's grandson far more strongly than he hated Paul.

For almost the first time in nearly twenty years, Catherine did not consult her Minister about the domestic situation at Gatchina.

Instead she decided not to interfere, to leave Catherine Nelidoff in Paul's household, thereby punishing the Grand Duchess for her inability to dispose of her rival herself. And the Empress consoled herself with the fact that her son was surrounding himself with men of the worst possible character; she thought of Alexei Araktchéief and was comforted.

.   .   .   .   .

While Catherine Alexeievna contemplated Paul's destruction, while she discussed the manner of it with her grandson and kept a careful watch on that distant household, whose ill fame increased with every passing month, the pattern of life at Gatchina developed along ominous lines.

In his personal life Paul Petrovitch was happy, he found solace and pleasure with Catherine Nelidoff, and for a long period her influence over him was unchallenged.

But not even she could persuade him to abandon the Prussian discipline he believed in so fervently, and when she tried, he countered with stories of that distant visit to Frederick the Great, now dead but not forgotten while his disciple lived. As for the punishment system devised by Araktchéief, Paul sometimes modified it to please her, but his defence of it threatened to dissolve into an admission that he dared not make even to himself. Brutality appealed to him. It gave him a tremendous sense of power to see the sufferings of another human being and to know that he could increase or diminish them at will. Years of inferiority and the appalling strain of living under the shadow of imprisonment and death had culminated in this terrible reprisal against all men for what he himself had been forced to endure. Happiness, security, dignity and respect had all been stripped from him, first by the fate which fashioned him into a travesty of ugliness and by his mother who had deprived him of his father and his birthright. Her power and the malice of the men who surrounded her had never ceased to hound him, and Natalie Alexeievna, whose devotion would have saved his balance, had rewarded his love with selfishness and treachery.

Now Catherine Nelidoff gave him comfort, cradled his head in her arms when the attacks of blinding pain beset him, nursed him devotedly in his periods of sickness and, when he recovered, abandoned that gentle rôle and willingly assumed the guise of a passionate, adoring mistress.

And with all the strength of her love for him, she tried to save him from himself.

Often when she came to him in the evenings, she besought him for an act of mercy, risking his impatience, even his anger, to turn him from some savagery devised by Araktchéief.

"Paul, my beloved; is it true the sentry is to die?"

"You mean the man found sleeping at his post outside the stables? Yes, Katya, he has been sentenced."

"But they say he's to die by running the gauntlet. . . ." she whispered, looking into her lover's face, dreading the signs of implacable resolve she knew so well.

The unfortunate soldier was to run for his life between two lines of some three hundred men, all armed with clubs and flails, there to be beaten to death for the crime of dozing while on guard over the Czarevitch's horses.

"That is the penalty. . . ."

"But, Paul, it was only the stables, not even the household! If he must be put to death, couldn't you just have him shot?"

For the first time in their liaison, Paul answered her abruptly. The affection and indulgence always accorded her requests had vanished and an impatience that was nearly anger rose in him.

"Military discipline is not your concern, my dear. Oblige me by not interfering!"

She said no more, aware that the ties of their love were far more tenuous than she believed, and for a moment she shivered, remembering that she was not supposed to hector or advise. She was his mistress and her only hold on him lay in her own arts and his affection.

The lesson was a sharp one for Katya Nelidoff, and seeing her pale, downcast face, the Czarevitch relented, filled with his genuine love for her, admiring the qualities of womanly gentleness which prompted her to offer him advice he had no intention of following.

But he had hurt her, and like all lovers he was remorseful and full of the desire to make amends.

As usual, when anything upset him, his wrath fell on Marie Feodorovna, whose treatment at his hands was beginning to arouse even Catherine Nelidoff's pity.

Frantic with grief and humiliation, the Grand Duchess wrote to the Empress at Petersburg. Her position was intolerable, she wailed; the Czarevitch treated her with increasing harshness despite all her efforts to placate him and her toleration of his mistress. The letter declared hysterically that Mistress Nelidoff's influence was transforming the Czarevitch into a monster of violence and tyranny, as no doubt Her Majesty had heard. Therefore the Grand Duchess besought her to dismiss the woman and punish her accordingly. . . .

Catherine read the missive, and visualizing the misery and discord of that unhappy household, shook her head over Marie's pleas, and smiled. A monster of violence and tyranny. That was his own wife's opinion of him. "He *is* going mad," the Empress said to herself. "Nature agrees

with me that he's unfit to rule and he himself is proving it. . . .
A hundred Nelidoffs would fail to save him now. . . ."

And she told the Grand Duchess, when next they met, that
there was nothing she could do to help her; and she sent her
back to Pavlovsk, where Paul and Catherine Nelidoff were
living throughout the summer.

.   .   .   .   .

In the spring of 1791 the Czarevitch received two messages.
One was the official notice of his eldest son's forthcoming
betrothal to Princess Louisa of Baden and the second was a
private letter from his personal friend and partisan Rastopchine, who had left Gatchina to pay a dutiful visit to the
Court. In it, the courtier begged Paul to come to Petersburg
as quickly as he could. For it was rumoured that after twenty
years of supreme power and favour, the mighty Gregory
Gregorovitch Potemkin was about to fall.

9

WHEN Paul reached the Winter Palace, he sensed a subtle
change; it was an indefinable atmosphere, suggested by
the whispering, apprehensive members of Catherine's Court
and by an air of frantic gaiety. Petersburg's cherished reputation as a centre of brilliance and culture was no longer main-
tained by those who knew how to please their Empress. Instead,
the motif was amusement. Paul found the Court engaged in a
series of feasts and balls, each function out-rivalling the last
for magnificence and licence.

He reached the capital early in the morning, having travelled
from Gatchina without waiting for more than a change of
horses at posts along the way; for some time a sense of urgency
possessed him, often he felt as if some tremendous tide of
energy were bottled up within his chest, threatening to burst
the confines of the flesh with its need of an outlet, forcing him
to run rather than walk, to ride at breakneck speed with the

wind tearing at him like a living thing. To hurry, hurry, because time was short and his life already half spent in fruitlessness and inactivity. . . .

The Grand Duchess Marie followed at a more civilized pace, while the vanguard of his household rode ahead with their impatient master.

Paul's fierce sense of propriety forbade him to take his mistress to Court and flaunt her publicly; any hint of open condonation smacked of Catherine and her intimates, and the comparison decided Katya Nelidoff's fate. She was to stay behind, he told her regretfully, assuring her that his thoughts would dwell upon her constantly.

The first morning in Petersburg he hurried to his own suite, a suite seldom occupied, but now prepared for his reception, and there changed his travelling clothes for a dress cut in the Prussian fashion that so irritated the Empress. Rastopchine was not there to meet him, and Paul frowned, his sensitive pride touched to immediate anger.

Then they gave him a message from Rastopchine and he puzzled over it, his cheek twitching with nervous tension.

"I suggest that your Imperial Highness pays the new Adjutant General a visit. There he will find his most obedient and loyal servant, Rastopchine, who dared not omit this daily attendance to greet his master."

The Adjutant General. Paul Petrovitch tore the small piece of paper into shreds and threw them on to the fire. He understood that message well enough, and his sallow face flamed with shame and anger.

Even Rastopchine had been forced to bow, but not to Potemkin as of old; and there lay the clue to the rumoured ruin of the Prince of Taurus. Another had taken his place. The Adjutant General. For a long moment pride warred with expediency, until a third element, malice, came down on the side of common sense and decided him to take his friend's counsel and pay the visit he advised.

It was as well to see this new enemy and get his measure; and it would be a long-delayed revenge to witness his enemy's humiliation.

When he came to the ante-rooms of that infamous suite situated under Catherine's rooms, he could see a great crowd of people that filled the room and overflowed into the corridors. Paul might have been approaching the Empress's own suite

so great was the number of her subjects who pushed and
elbowed each other in order to squeeze into that ante-
room.

The loud hum of laughter and talk ceased abruptly as his
chamberlain announced him, and two of his household gentlemen pressed through the throng round the door, clearing a
path for him.

"Make way for His Imperial Highness the Czarevitch! The
Czarevitch! Make way there!"

They stepped back hurriedly, stumbling against one another,
and, having curtsied as he passed, the women stared after him
and the men grimaced. The notoriety of Gatchina and the
man who ruled it made him a figure of morbid curiosity, and
for a moment the carefree self-seeking nobles of Holy Russia
experienced an uncomfortable twinge of awe; a sudden gloom
had descended upon the packed chamber, stilling the shrill
voices and causing every knee to bend. Those who had laughed
at Catherine's ugly, unimportant son in the days of his youth,
now looked into that flat-featured face with the disfiguring
pulse beating steadily in the left cheek, and meeting the fierce,
cold stare of those prominent blue eyes, looked hurriedly away,
aware that in their hearts there was anything but laughter.

Thank God, they murmured to themselves, thank God, he
would never be Czar. . . .

Paul stopped before Rastopchine, and the soldier went down
on his knees and kissed his hand.

"God's blessing on the Czarevitch," he said, and Paul raised
him up, unable to conceal his affection for the man.

He was tall, this partisan of a cause all men judged lost, and
his features were too dark and saturnine for good looks. It was
an intelligent, ruthless face, the face of one riven by internal
contradictions. A wit and something of a scholar, a soldier
and a polished courtier, he was at once simple, cunning,
treacherous and brave; above all he was a patriot, and for this
reason he espoused the rights of the man he believed to have
been his country's lawful Czar for over thirty years. Instinctively Paul trusted him, where wiser men would have hesitated,
and in the annals of treachery and baseness which were written
in the years to come, that trust alone was justified.

Paul glanced round him contemptuously and then turned
to his friend.

"This might be twenty years ago, when first Potemkin

reigned. . . . Who is it? Just the 'Adjutant General' or something more?"

"In this case, that is enough," Rastopchine said quietly. "It happened quite suddenly. The Empress chose him, had him examined and tested by Countess Protassof, you know the ritual. . . ."

Paul, familiar with the degrading and cold-blooded routine by which his mother's lovers were selected, interrupted with a gesture of disgust.

"And then?"

"For a time all was well. The Empress was infatuated, but even that has happened before. . . . You remember: Mamanov, Lanskoy . . . they were all peerless, geniuses, the mainstay of her life. Until Potemkin told her to dismiss them and then the idol was pulled from his pedestal overnight. Well, the Prince took a dislike to this new favourite; it seems he was lacking in respect, so he suggested that Her Majesty replace him. And she refused."

"But she will capitulate," Paul told him in angry whisper. "She always has, and by God, you know that it matters little enough to her whether it is one scoundrel or another so long as he can satisfy her lusts! I'm afraid you're rejoicing too soon, my friend."

Rastopchine glanced quickly round him; those standing near had moved away, leaving the Czarevitch and his companion in a small circle of isolation. When the doors of the favourite's bedroom opened and he appeared among them, no one wished to be noticed standing too near the Czarevitch. . . .

"I'd stake my head his power is at an end. The Empress is besotted with her 'Adjutant'; the Court spends its mornings waiting here, instead of attending on the Czarina, who sends them to this creature with their requests! And Potemkin's apartments are almost deserted. . . ."

"What is his name?"

"Plato Zubov. But look, he comes!"

The gilded double doors guarding the favourite's bedroom were swinging slowly open, and at the same moment absolute silence descended on the crowded ante-room, and the hush spread out into the corridors. In an instant everything was quiet, except that the waiting assembly had divided itself in two, making a lane through which the privileged one could pass.

Paul stood very still, his eyes fixed on the doorway to that bedroom, a slow flush of anger rising in his face. He had lived too long away from Petersburg to view the scene with calmness, and all his fierce royal pride surged up in outrage at the honour paid to a vulgar Pompadour in masculine guise.

Yet when he saw the man his mother favoured, he stared despite himself.

He stood in the doorway, preceded by a bowing lackey, and a group of intimates hovered respectfully at his back; as he appeared, the watching courtiers sighed and a whisper of admiration disturbed their silent ranks. And even Paul, whose heart convulsed with instantaneous hate, admitted that Fate had gifted Plato Zubov with superb physical beauty.

He was above middle height, magnificently proportioned, and he moved with extraordinary, almost feline grace; his dress was splendid, and the breast of his gold brocade coat sagged with a weight of blazing jewels; an enormous order, encrusted with great diamonds, hung from a crimson ribbon round his neck, and within the circle of one arm he held a small monkey, collared in precious stones and tethered by a narrow golden chain. He stood outlined in the doorway, fondling the monkey and looking over the crowd with lazy arrogance. No one dared move while he was motionless. He wore a beautifully curled wig, but his colouring was very dark, and the hard, heavy-lidded eyes were black. By contrast to his muscular broad-shouldered body, his face was almost feminine in its handsomeness; the features were fine-drawn, the brows symmetrical, and the red-lipped mouth curved in an expression of extreme pride and superciliousness.

For all his splendour of looks and body, there was something indescribably vicious about Catherine's lover, so that it seemed to Paul that his great virility cloaked rottenness, and that he was in fact a travesty of what he represented.

In an instant his rage and loathing rose in a torrent, caution and self-control were swept away by an uprush of blinding fury, a fury streaked with a wild horror and disgust with his mother and what her association with such a creature indicated, that his hand was on his sword hilt and the blade half withdrawn before Rastopchine saw him. At the risk of his life, for he knew Paul, he seized his wrist.

"For God's sake! Don't. . . . If you touched him you'd be cut down. I beg of you. . . ."

Gradually Paul became aware of the pressure of Rastop-chine's fingers, and the sense of that frantic warning whisper sank into his boiling, muddled consciousness.

He'd be cut down. . . . Of course, his mother's favourites had always meant more to her than her son. . . . After a moment his hand released the jewelled sword hilt, and the blade slid back into its scabbard with a thin rasp that could be plainly heard throughout the silent room. At the same time Plato Zubov ceased playing with his pet monkey, and his haughty gaze rested upon the short dark figure of the Czare-vitch of Russia.

At the same instant he recognized him and a danger signal registered quickly in his mind. This was the madman of Gatchina, his fawning mistress's detested son. . . . Catherine had told him of her plans, for she told him everything, babbling State secrets like a garrulous schoolgirl in her anxiety to flatter him. Her son was not to succeed, she insisted, but in a second's lightning reflection, Zubov decided not to take a chance.

Catherine was old, weakened by flesh and overwork—exhausted by her own sexual mania. She might die. . . .

Turning, Zubov handed the monkey to an elderly nobleman who stood near, and this member of the ancient Boyar aris-tocracy creased his face into a smile and remained quietly waiting, while the animal screeched with rage and tried to pull off his wig.

Then facing the Czarevitch, Catherine's favourite swept him a graceful bow.

For a moment Paul stood rooted, so angry that he could scarcely focus, yet fighting for control.

Then he turned abruptly, presenting his back to Plato Zubov, and in a harsh, resonant voice, he spoke to the quivering Rastopchine.

"I suffocate. This place smells like a den of whores!" With these words he was gone.

.   .   .   .   .

In the weeks that followed, Paul Petrovitch saw Rastop-chine's prophecy fulfilled. Potemkin, who had abandoned his conduct of the second Turkish war to hurry back and dis-pose of his young rival, found his adored Empress completely

dominated by the pleasure Plato Zubov gave her. Outwardly
alert, as smoothly gracious as ever, Catherine's infatuation
with her lover was tragic in its senile submission.

Whatever her faults she had always been an honest sen-
sualist, treating her favourites with generosity and kindness,
even with motherly sentimentality in her later years, but in her
relationship with the twenty-five-year-old former Captain of
her Guard, there was no room for honesty.

Her senses were dulled by excess, but now for the first time
in years he gave Catherine the illusion of her lost youth and
fading vigour.

And in exchange Catherine seemed ready to sacrifice her
dignity, her independence, and the man who had loved and
served her so devotedly for twenty years.

Potemkin was her friend, her counsellor, the architect of
much that glorified her name in Russia; the greatest triumph
of her reign had been the Crimean Journey, undertaken less
than ten years earlier. Though the gaily costumed peasants
who stood waving to the Empress as she sailed down the
Dnieper were herded into carts and transported bodily to the
next stage of arrival as soon as the royal barge had passed,
there to repeat their welcome; though the towns which
delighted her eye were painted cardboard fronts, and the live-
stock grazing in such numbers were shipped out to grace
another spurious scene of prosperity a few hours later,
Catherine had no idea that what she saw was sham. Potemkin
had performed a miracle for her, transforming the newly
annexed Crimea into a paradise of riches and progress. The
fertile, thriving land she glimpsed from her barge and from
the window of her great sledge, was this extraordinary lover's
crowning gift; her glorification was his life's work and at the
time her pride and affection were unbounded. While the
impregnable fortresses she had admired crumbled and fell into
the sea at the first storm, since they were only built of sand,
and the skeletons of towns, hastily constructed out of wood and
plaster tumbled down and rotted, unfinished and uninhabited,
the Prince of Taurus reigned supreme at Petersburg, and his
position had never seemed more secure when he took command of his mistress's armies and went to win fresh laurels
for her against Turkey.

He returned to find her in the arms of Zubov.

·   ·   ·   ·   ·

During one of the frequent banquets given in the new favourite's honour, Marie Feodorovna sat at her husband's right hand, and for the first time since they left Gatchina her spirits rose and a natural colour dyed her cheeks. She was richly dressed, for Paul was never mean, and she was enjoying the gaiety and consumed with curiosity over the Empress and her favourite.

Another reason for Marie's transient happiness was the renewed contact with her two sons.

The younger, Constantine, was shy and silent; already his grandmother's adoring slave, he fidgeted in his parents' presence, and watched his grim father with suspicious eyes. His mother aroused some degree of affection in him, but the emotion was spoilt by feelings of guilt, as if he betrayed his grandmother, who had so often hinted gently that she did not care for either her son or her daughter-in-law.

But it was Alexander who filled the Grand Duchess with an access of maternal pride.

He was so handsome, she reflected, glancing covertly at him, where he sat close to the Empress; his looks were her inheritance, the stately height and blond colouring mirrored her Teutonic youth, and for that, as well as for his courteousness and grace, his mother loved him passionately.

She looked quickly at Paul, who sat slowly sipping wine out of a golden goblet, and following the direction of his gaze, saw that he watched his eldest son. He was unaware that she observed him, and Marie Feodorovna watched him with a feeling of horror in her heart, knowing that the man she had lived with and whose children she had borne was still a stranger to her, that only now, and that by accident, she had discovered that he hated his son Alexander.

For a moment terror enveloped her, and with it the confused wonder which defied analysis. Paul had no real power; he lived by courtesy of that omnipotent woman who sat at the head of the Imperial table, talking gaily to her handsome, sinister favourite; Marie knew this well, knew too that his chances of succeeding to supreme authority were non-existent, that that destiny was already reserved for the son she championed in her heart against her husband. Yet in spite of all, she was afraid of Paul.

The knowledge that he hated Alexander filled her with overwhelming terror on the boy's behalf. He was her son, she thought in panic, and her own ambitions to become Empress Consort vanished instantly in the face of her fear for the child of her body.

Then and there, Marie Feodorovna swore a private oath, her eyes fixed on the watchful, unreadable countenance of Paul.

If ever the issue arose which must decide in favour of the father or the son, she would declare for Alexander.

It was the only decision that she ever made which was to be of any consequence.

.   .   .   .   .

On April the 28th Gregory Potemkin was giving a ball at the Taurus Palace. Invitations to over three thousand guests were issued in his name, asking them to an entertainment devised in honour of their Empress, and it was rumoured that this was to be the most sumptuous spectacle ever witnessed in Petersburg.

In the privacy of his apartments, Paul was arguing with Rastopchine, and the invitation from his enemy lay on a marble table in front of him.

"There's no necessity for me to go. I know his talent for debauch, I've heard my mother praised and fêted in terms of blasphemy a hundred times before. I shall refuse!"

Rastopchine frowned, and his thin dark face assumed that worried wolfish look that was so characteristic of the man.

"Believe me, Highness, this is no ordinary occasion! All Petersburg is alive with rumours. They say that Plato Zubov will stand or fall at this ball; it is the Prince's final challenge to your mother, his supreme attempt to win her back and trample the favourite in the dust.

"God knows which way the Empress will decide . . . you *must* accept, Sir, for if Potemkin triumphs, he'll be more dangerous to you than ever, and if he falls . . . who had more right to witness his disgrace than you!"

"No man on earth," muttered the Czarevitch, and shrewdly, his friend waited for the suggestion to sink in and said no more.

"How will it end, do you think?" Paul asked him at last. The other shrugged.

"God knows. But if fortune smiles on us, the Tartar should fail. If anything happens to the Empress, we can deal with friend Zubov easily enough. But Potemkin would be another matter. I tell you, if Catherine abandons her Minister, the difficulties besetting your inheritance will be almost halved!"

"And my son, Rastopchine? What of my son?"

"May I speak freely, Sir?"

"I only fear lies, never the truth! Speak."

"The Grand Duke relies on his grandmother to take the burden of his treachery upon herself. I've watched him carefully, and I think him a waverer and a coward at heart. Equally, he has no scruples. With a man of action to direct him, he'd do battle with you for the throne. With Potemkin, he would probably win. But not without him. That is what I believe."

"And it is what I believe also."

Paul picked up Potemkin's invitation and stood, twisting the paper in his hands, until a sudden spasm of the powerful fingers shredded it to pieces.

"I have decided. I'll go to the ball. And if it is God's will, I'll see that one-eyed devil humbled and utterly destroyed!"

Bowing, Rastopchine left him, and went for a long solitary walk in the palace gardens, still frowning, and oppressed by a great weight of anxiety. "If Potemkin falls, the difficulties will be halved." So he had told Paul, but even with him, whom he loved, he chose not to be completely honest. Part of what he said was true, as it usually was. Zubov would be easy. They could murder Zubov, if necessary. And many of Catherine's Ministers might hesitate when it came to seizing the rightful Czar and putting that sly, pious stripling in his place. Thinking these thoughts Rastopchine beat his clenched fist against his brow, unconsciously imitating Paul's famous gesture.

If he could reason so, how obvious the risks must be to Catherine Alexeievna. And even the greatest fool must expect that she had made her plans accordingly.

But somehow, in spite of his forebodings, Rastopchine nurtured hope, and for all his astuteness he failed to realize that the source of his optimism lay, not with any well-laid scheme, nor even the pattern of the fates, which seemed as if about to turn to their advantage, but in the person of the grim, tormented Czarevitch himself.

.   .   .   .   .

In the monotony of Gatchina, enclosed by the gloom **and** discipline of Paul's fortress home, Catherine Nelidoff passed her days, sewing and reading her lover's letters.

The last letter mentioned the great ball to be given by his enemy Potemkin; it was a long letter, longer than any she had so far received and in it he expressed many of his hopes and fears, outlining the intrigues current in the capital, praising his good friend Rastopchine, and breaking the thread of his narrative to ask questions concerning his own household and its management.

Katya Nelidoff read it through several times, struggling to grasp the details which were so obviously important to the man she loved. At last she laid down the sheets of paper in her lap, and leaning back in her favourite position by the window, in her room, looked out on the courtyard below.

Squads of men were drilling in the hot sun, raising a low, yellow dust from the dry earth; she could hear the harsh voice of Araktchéief shouting orders, and unconsciously she shuddered.

For a long period she sat motionless, staring out at the visible forms of the things in Paul that had already driven a small wedge between them, while the tears ran down her face and soaked into that precise, detailed missive, in which he neither sent for her nor said when he expected to be back.

'   .   .   .   .   ,

That evening of April the 28th, Catherine Alexeievna was in her bedroom preparing for Potemkin's ball. A dazzling selection of dresses was spread over the huge bed and draped on chairs and couches; there were dozens of pairs of shoes on the floor, and a great jewel casket stood on a table, and one of the Empress's ladies waited, ready to hand each glittering tray of ornaments to her mistress so that she might choose from them.

In a corner of the room Catherine's hairdresser arranged his combs and drew a long switch of false ringletted hair through his fingers.

Meanwhile the Empress considered which gown to wear; Countess Bruce, hovering at her elbow, and the second and most notorious of her female confidantes, Countess Protassof, suggesting first one dress and then another for her mistress's approval.

Finally Bruce solved the problem.

"Why not wear scarlet, Madame? It's your most becoming colour."

"Scarlet. . . ." Catherine hesitated and smiled ruefully. "When I was young, Bruce, I wore nothing else. But scarlet for an old woman. . . ."

Behind her back the Countess clicked her tongue reproachfully.

"How can you say that, Madame! When Prince Potemkin beggars himself to please you and M. Zubov sulks with jealousy. . . ."

Five years ago Catherine Alexeievna would have answered the sly flattery with cynical scorn, but the mention of Plato's name reminded her of the necessity to paint the ageing contours of her face and confine the glandular fat which disfigured her body; she must appear young for him, she must smile and dance and feast to keep up with his youth and vigour; she must pander to his appetites for pleasure however old and tired she felt. . . . At odd moments lately she had found the effort increasingly difficult to make; there were times when her avid senses seemed at rest, when she acknowledged her weariness and the traitorous longing to send Zubov to the furthest corner of her kingdom and sink into the tender, platonic embrace of her faithful Gregory Gregorovitch Potemkin. . . .

"I'll wear the red and gold brocade," she said suddenly, and stood, resting both hands on Protassof's sturdy shoulders while they covered her ungainly form with the gorgeous material and laced her into it until she gasped for breath.

Then the coiffeur approached, and under his skilful fingers her thick white hair, still streaked with black, was piled high above her splendid forehead, and a long curled switch was secured at the back, so that the false ringlets drooped over her shoulder.

Catherine watched herself in the gilded dressing-table mirror with an inscrutable expression, her mind speeding back across the years, reviewing a succession of faces, dead faces, faces once dear and intimate in varying degrees.

Most persistent among the visions which swam across the surface of her mind was the proud, splendid countenance of the man who had died at Gatchina, died a raving lunatic, tortured by the shade of her dead husband. Brave, magnificent Gregory Orlov . . . of them all she had loved him the

best, loved him with the unforgettable passion of her vital
youth, plotted with him, marched with him at the head of an
army, and spent hot, breathless hours in his arms.

All that she had, he had helped to secure for her, and when
ambition and dissatisfaction finally separated them, another
had taken his place; a man as ugly as he was beautiful, yet a
giant in mind as well as body. He too had marched with her
on that momentous night; the tarnished sword knot of the
humble Lieutenant Potemkin still remained among her most
prized possessions. And he had loved her, made war for her,
fallen at her feet in worship, even as he bullied and raged at
her like a spoilt, jealous child, when he was thwarted. So much
lay between them; not the simple, blinding love which had
consumed her in the arms of Orlov, but a complex attachment, compounded of passion, of greed for power, of fierce
nationalism, indeed of all those things dear to the heart of the
ruler as well as the woman.

And no one knew better than Catherine what her Court was
saying, and how rumours declared this evening to be the great
Prince of Taurus's final challenge to the upstart favourite.

They watched her and whispered, wondering who would be
chosen, murmuring that Potemkin was laying siege to her
body as well as her heart, that he had abandoned all caution
and dignity to enter the amorous lists against the practised,
sinister arts of Plato Zubov.

Catherine turned to the jewel tray her lady held out for her
inspection and shook her head.

"Rubies," she said slowly. "I always wear rubies with red."

A great necklace of graduated gems encircled her neck, and
cascades of rubies dripped from her ears, while an enormous
peacock spray blazed from the top of her powdered head.
Each stone was ringed with large diamonds, and when she rose
her reflection flashed in the glass like a vision of fire.

"Your Majesty looks magnificent . . ." breathed Countess
Protassof and for a moment Catherine Alexeievna turned and
looked at her with the clear level eyes of the woman she had
known thirty years before.

"Don't flatter me, Protassof . . . send for my chamberlain.
I'm ready now."

When she had gone the two waiting women paused and
exchanged glances.

"Well," Countess Bruce whispered. "What do you think?"

Protassof shrugged.

"Who can say? All I know is, if Potemkin triumphs it will be the end of us . . . we recommended Zubov in the usual way, remember. . . . But only God knows what is in her heart. Or what she means to do."

10

POTEMKIN'S ball began at six o'clock, and a company of three thousand was assembled in the magnificent Taurus Palace by the time the Empress arrived.

Paul and Marie Feodorovna had already been received by their host, and for a few moments the attention of the guests had wandered from the drama about to be enacted between Catherine and her former lover, while Gregory Potemkin bent low over the hand of the Czarevitch, greeting him with the courtly grace he knew how to assume so well.

The Prince of Taurus was dressed from head to foot in crimson, the brilliant colour accentuated by a magnificent cape of black lace, his dark features were flushed, his one eye sparkled; pride and high spirits resounded in his voice and marked his whole bearing.

He, whose self-indulgence knew no bounds in anything, who sulked and stormed with petulant fury over trifles, concealed whatever anxiety and unhappiness tormented him behind a façade of sweeping confidence and gaiety. It was in this guise that he welcomed his greatest enemy that night.

"I am honoured, your Imperial Highness. Madame! More beautiful than ever!" he added, turning to the Grand Duchess, and for all her dislike of him, Marie Feodorovna blushed at the compliment.

Paul regarded him with a cold, hostile stare, aware that for the first time in their association, the ascendancy was his.

"You have prepared a magnificent feast," he remarked, and misunderstanding him, the Prince of Taurus bowed.

"No entertainment can be worthy of the Empress, Sir. However, I have tried."

For the first time that evening Paul Petrovitch smiled.

"It is always wise to honour the sovereign, Prince, rather than the favourite, as so many people have been doing lately. For M. Zubov is only the favourite, and favourites fall in time. . . ."

Then extending his arm to his wife, the Czarevitch passed on. Rastopchine, who had arrived with his master, and was standing a few paces behind, had heard his words, turned pale and edged out of Potemkin's view.

"Great God," he muttered, hurrying after Paul. "Potemkin will remember that jibe till the day of his death . . . if he triumphs to-night it will mean the end of the Czarevitch!"

Paul's courtier was not alone in his anxiety, for many hundreds trembled with him; men and women who had deserted the great Minister to fawn upon his rival, and who now thronged his palace and enjoyed his tremendous hospitality with the possibility of his re-emergence and subsequent revenge to spoil their evening's pleasure.

When the Empress appeared, the Prince fell on his knees before her and she raised him up with all her old graciousness, and, leaning on his arm, she entered the palace which his ingenuity had transformed for her delight.

But those who saw a portent in those marks of favour were soon confounded when Catherine stopped and beckoned Plato Zubov to her side.

The ball opened with a quadrille of forty-eight couples, among them the young Grand Dukes Alexander and Constantine; the sons of Russia's noblest houses partnered women chosen for their exceptional beauty, and the colourful eye of Potemkin had clothed them in alternate pink and blue and augmented their costumes with ten million roubles' worth of diamonds.

The ballroom was immense and brilliantly lit with the finest wax candles; the entire stock of candles in Petersburg had been bought up on Potemkin's orders.

A second room separated from the ballroom by a long colonnade had been transformed into a garden where trees and shrubs flowered as if by a miracle and fountains cooled the air. In the centre of the scene a great Paros marble statue of Catherine had been erected, and close to it an obelisk of agate, inlaid with her cypher in precious stones and ringed round with chains of solid gold.

Arm in arm with Potemkin, the Empress wandered into this artificial paradise, and though her steps were halting and it needed the combined strength of the Prince and Plato Zubov to support her on each side, she smiled and listened to her host with obvious pleasure.

And that night he was brilliant. All his gifts of laughter, wit, flattery and insight came to his aid, coupled with the indefinable childish, unruly charm that had held so many women captive, including the greatest woman of her age.

He made her laugh until the tears came into her eyes, and during the play and ballet which followed, whispered words of passionate longing into her ear.

He needed her, he murmured; his senses gave him no rest, his heart rebelled against their separation any longer. No woman satisfied him while Catherine's image burned into his tormented brain; he would discard them all, he declared vehemently, even his dear little faithful niece Branicka should be sent away, if his beloved Catherine would only close her eyes for one moment and remember the past.

From his place in the audience, Paul Petrovitch watched Potemkin's courtship of his mother, knowing how much his own destiny hung in the balance, and trying to read a verdict in the Empress's expression. Occasionally, he glanced at the pale, bored countenance of her young lover, who sat on his mistress's left, apparently indifferent to the blandishments of his deadly rival.

Observing him, Paul judged that elegant unheeding posture to be a clever pose; the defence adopted by a man who knows himself outmanœuvred in the field of wit and brilliant flattery, and who is content to wait until an opportunity favourable to a display of his own talents presents itself.

When the play ended Catherine retired to a room specially prepared for her, and rested there until the first serving of supper was announced.

The banquet was in keeping with the standards of magnificence Potemkin had already set throughout the evening. Six hundred of the noblest and most powerful of Catherine's subjects dined with her, and left the table to continue the ball while the next relay of guests went in to take their places.

Then, at two o'clock in the morning, the Empress signalled that she wished to leave. Immediately the great entrance to the Taurus Palace was crowded with guests, and on the arm of her smiling host Catherine Alexeievna walked slowly among them, pausing to exchange a word of greeting, stopping as always, to joke with her litelong friend Leo Naryshkin, whose ancient rivalry with Potemkin had mellowed into sympathy and admiration.

"My dear Leo," she said fondly, while he bent and kissed her hand, and when he looked at her she started, suddenly aware that the gay companion of over thirty years was in reality a tired old man. For a brief second while they smiled and murmured pleasantries as they had always done, the spectacle of age and death became personified in that one man who held so many memories of her early life. Her genuine affection for him saw that Potemkin's lavish feast had taxed his strength, that the humorous, loving gaze was dimmed by tiredness, and an extraordinary spasm of nostalgic weakness seized her, bringing the tears to her eyes. If she had ever loved him, ever rewarded that selfless, unswerving devotion with the gift of herself which had been so many men's acknowledged prize, perhaps her later years might have been dignified by serenity and love, instead of plagued by the desires of youth. It she had gone to Leo, perhaps Potemkin and his successors would never have come into her life . . . there might have been no need of such a man as Plato Zubov. . . .

"You are fatigued, my friend," she said gently. "My good Potemkin has overwhelmed us all this night. Go home, Leo. Go home and go to bed. . . ."

Then she turned to her old lover, to her companion-in-arms who had wielded the sword for her in many wars and laid his laurels humbly at her feet, to him whose genius had been the treasure of her reign, and whose love for her was to survive as one of the greatest passions of all time.

"I thank you," she said, "for the glory of this evening, as well as for so many other things. Good night, my dear Grisha. . . ." and at the sound of that familiar diminutive, the great Potemkin fell on his knees and holding her hands against his breast, he wept. No one among the hundreds who witnessed that scene knew whether he shed tears of sorrow or of triumph.

Long after Catherine Alexeievna's carriage had passed out of sight Potemkin stood alone on the steps of his great palace, the folds of his black cloak stirring in a sharp night breeze, staring out along the road she had taken.

.   .   .   .   .

When he returned to the Palace, Paul wished his wife good night with a finality that left her in no doubt as to his disinclination to discuss the evening, and shut himself up in his study. There he planned to write to Katya Nelidoff, but though the paper and quills were laid out on his desk, and the pleading sentences of her last letter echoed in his mind, he sat staring at the blank sheets of paper having done no more than write the heading.

"If you knew the impatience with which I wait for your letters you would correspond more often," she had reproached him, and remembering these words, he strove to formulate his thoughts, to drag them away from the great problems of that night, to dismiss the growing preoccupation with politics and his own destiny which so filled his mind that the figure of Catherine Nelidoff had almost receded into oblivion in the past weeks.

She missed him desperately, her letters said, and the note of loneliness and unease grew stronger in them as the intervals between his answers lengthened.

"My sweet Katya, I have been lost without you," he wrote, driving his pen slowly, aware that while true in one respect, the sentiment was yet a lie.

Physically lost, deprived of the solace of her unquestioning surrender to his wishes, he had even gone to Marie Feodorovna's bed since their stay in the capital began, but the gentle, womanly interests of his mistress had never wholly claimed his mind. She had come to him at Gatchina, assuaged his abysmal loneliness and diverted the destructive powers of his sick temperament; she was at once a soporific and a stimulant. But she was not quite part of the great world in which his exalted birth and heritage had placed him.

She belonged to his home, to quiet evenings of domestic peace, to interludes of passion which gave way to forgetfulness and sleep. In illness, solitude and neglect, she was the chosen solace of his life, he thought, while his quill laboured to finish the letter and his mind strained towards the puzzle of Potemkin and the consequences to himself. And she would remain so, he decided, signing and sanding the paper, for as long as he lived. But at that hour and time his destiny as Czarevitch came first.

His mother, always the principal enemy, joined now by his beautiful, treacherous son Alexander, had to be overcome, and every instinct warned him that the reckoning would not be long delayed. The wishes of the Empress, the guilty fears of her Court, and the persistent malice of all those who had despised and persecuted him throughout his life were all arraigned against him, barring his way to the throne of his father.

Before much longer he should know whether Gregory Potemkin could still be counted among that company.

.   .   .   .   .

The next morning a messenger delivered a personal letter from the Empress to her Minister. Potemkin's hands were trembling when he broke the seal; he had not gone to bed that night, pacing nervously up and down in his deserted palace in the midst of the ruins of his tremendous feast, waiting for the sign he knew would come. He read Catherine's note twice without speaking, and then sat down very slowly in the chair a frightened servant set for him.

"She thanks me," he murmured aloud. "She thanks me for the entertainment. For my farewell feast. . . . And she orders me to leave Petersburg. . . ."

Carefully Potemkin folded the small square of paper, and placed it in the breast pocket of his dressing-gown, as he had done with every scrap of writing she had ever sent him.

Then he leant back in his chair and laughed, laughed with all the roaring volume of his great barrel chest, while the tears streamed out of his one eye and seeped painfully from under the shrivelled sunken lid covering the empty socket where Alexis Orlov had blinded him for love of Catherine Alexeievna nearly thirty years before.

.   .   .   .   .

By the end of September the Czarevitch and his household returned to Gatchina, leaving the Empress's favourite victor at Petersburg.

Paul had remained in the capital long enough to witness the departure of his fallen enemy, ostensibly setting out to conduct the peace treaty with the Turks at Jassy, but in fact retiring from Catherine's presence at her order. Then turning to Rastopchine, the Czarevitch took his arm and walked slowly away from the window where they had stood to watch Potemkin's great coach taking him into exile.

"It is well, my friend," he said quietly; and glancing into his master's face, Rastopchine saw the savage triumph in his expression and decided that those who trembled at the thought of Paul's accession did so with good cause.

"Thank God, Highness," he said. "He will never return to power again."

"One less for me to fight, Rastopchine. And I've waited twenty years to see this day."

Quite suddenly he smiled, with that rare gleam of human gentleness.

"Thank God, indeed," Paul said slowly. "Now we can go home."

.   .   .   .   .

At Gatchina Catherine Nelidoff was waiting, and he held her in his arms once more, happiness filling his heart, forgetting that he had ever been able to exist without her. That first night she clung to him, crying with relief that in spite of her fears he had returned and proved himself as loving as before; for several days their old life together was resumed; their days passed walking or riding in the parkland, the evenings were spent in the privacy he loved so much, reading aloud or talking of the future, and if she noticed that this obsession with his destiny seemed stronger since his visit to the capital, Paul's mistress only listened and said nothing, stifling a persistent nagging fear that the coming battle for his father's throne might serve to separate them if it did not end in failure and death for her lover.

"Oh, God," she prayed when he had left her and gone to his own room before daybreak, "Merciful God, protect him! Let him stay with me, where he is safe. . . " It was a hopeless prayer, frantically repeated in the weeks that followed, when the spell of their reunion faded, and the Czarevitch spent hours in company with his commander, Araktchéief, drawing up military rules for his garrison, sitting in judgment upon

prisoners, many of them civilians convicted of some infringe-
ment of the lunatic regulations governing the palace and the
town it dominated.

And when she pleaded for Araktchéief's victim, Paul refused
her coldly, until the weight of his displeasure and the absences
which followed forced her to acquiesce, to be content with
loving Paul and following him blindly, unable to curb his
impulses or break the influence of those around him who
encouraged them. And her former friend Koutaïssof was foremost among these.

Then in October of that year a courier galloped into the
palace grounds and hurried to the Czarevitch, where he sat
dining quietly with his mistress.

The message, which he read to her, was brief, but the
contents were decisive.

Gregory Potemkin had suddenly abandoned the peace
negotiations at Jassy. Consumed by rage, heartbreak and
rebellion, he had set out in his travelling carriage, taking his
niece and faithful mistress, Branicka, with him, and thundered
towards the town of Octakov, the scene of his great military
siege and triumph in the late war.

Whatever the motives that impelled him to travel back
over the way of his old glory, his destination was never
reached.

He leant out of the window and ordered his coachman to
stop some thirty miles outside of Jassy. Immediately the
vehicles following with his servants and possessions halted
behind the huge carriage: there, on a bed of coats piled up
under a sheltering tree, with his great head resting on
Branicka's breast, Potemkin, Prince of Taurus, died by the
roadside.

.   .   .   .   .

" Protassof! "

" Yes, Madame? "

The Empress's confidante hurried into the study where her
mistress sat writing at her desk, and curtsied to the ground.

The Countess was a model of propriety in appearance and
behaviour, never by word or deed did she betray her deadly
knowledge of Catherine's weaknesses and her adroitness in
making the means of pandering to them available.

But for almost seven years this function of her office had

not been exercised; the death of Potemkin had left Plato Zubov in a position of unchallenged favour; his infatuated mistress hastened to take the honours of the dead and bestow them upon the living; the former Captain of the Guard was now a Minister and a Prince of the Holy Roman Empire.

In that year of 1796 all Russia grovelled at his feet.

"Protassof," the Empress said after a moment, and in that moment sanded a long document, shaking the golden sprinkler vigorously, her eyes still lowered to the paper; "Protassof, be good enough to admit the Grand Duke Alexander. And give orders that I am not to be disturbed."

While she waited, Catherine read over part of what she had just written, and then leant back in her chair and rubbed her aching wrist. When he entered, she looked up, her face illumined by a smile of tenderness and pride, and extended her arms to enfold him.

"Alexander," she murmured fondly, while he kissed her forehead and her hands, "dear boy, come and help me out of this chair. I've taken root at my desk."

Paul's son was now as broadly proportioned as he was tall, and he drew his grandmother to her feet: with one strong arm supporting her and the other encircling her waist, he led her to the sofa she indicated.

With a sigh, Catherine sat down, her tired heart pounding after the exertion of bearing her own great weight for even a few moments.

"Bring me that document on my desk, the top one, there. Thank you; now sit here by me."

Alexander, whose quick keen eyes had managed to read a few lines of the paper while pretending to search for it, handed it to her with an expression of smiling innocence, and a sense of wild excitement surging behind that courteous, false exterior.

He looked older than his nineteen years, for his handsome face was naturally grave and his blue eyes considered the world through an impenetrable filter of cunning, ambition, cowardice and deceit. His earliest instincts had been those of secrecy, characterized by an intense dislike of being understood or seeing his most unimportant motive revealed before the minds of others. He had set out to be an enigma, hiding from all men the true reason for his words and actions, pretending ceaselessly, with the desperate duplicity of a self-acknowledged rogue, subconsciously hoping that the day would dawn when he might perhaps delude himself.

The process was a slow one, but it was sure. Seated beside his grandmother, one arm linked affectionately through hers, Alexander thought of the contents of her will, which he had only glimpsed, and persuaded his conscience that his fierce, greedy joy was justified. Meanwhile his self-discipline enabled him to sit and talk of trivialities without betraying his impatience.

He told Catherine some details of his day, and she listened smiling, clutching that all-important paper in her plump, jewelled fingers.

"How is the Grand Duchess?" she asked him.

"In excellent health," he answered, on behalf of the Baden princess who had become his wife two years before.

"And you are really happy, Alexander?" His fine fair brows arched in surprise, but the ready smile and glib reply were there.

"But of course, Madame. Most happy." Sexually cold and utterly self-centred, his feelings for his wife were a comfortable mixture of indifference and content.

"I'm very pleased with you, Alexander. In all you do, you reach my expectations and conform to the standards of excellence I have set for you. Deliberately set, since the responsibilities I shall leave you will demand the utmost talent and devotion you can give. You know that, my dear boy?"

"Yes," he murmured.

"Good. Well, we've talked of this before, many times, since you were old enough to understand what I intended for you. Your father . . . your father is unfit to rule. You see that for yourself. And I have never contemplated delivering my country and my people into his hands. Since he was your age, my Alexis, I knew that he must never, never rule. For one reason or another I was weak with him, some call it mercy, but my own adjective is weakness. . . . There were reasons then, policy, unrest among the people, opinion abroad. But principally Potemkin, whose advice to me was most ill-founded. I listened to him, Alexis, until the opportunity had passed its peak and you were growing up. And you pleaded with me not to use force on your father. To please you, I must disinherit him legally, and that is what I have just done."

For a moment there was silence, while Paul's oldest son

stared down at the design on the tapestry carpet at his feet.

"How, my grandmother?"

"By will. Here. I have declared him mad and passed the succession to you at my death."

Alexander's tongue wet lips that were dry with apprehension and excitement.

"And what is to happen to him. . . ?"

"He is to be shut up in Löhde Castle. It is a very secure fortress and the precautions necessary to restrain a lunatic should ensure that he won't live long in prison. So there need be no burden for your conscience."

He looked up and smiled a beautiful, brilliant smile of relief. Then he lifted her hand to his lips and kissed it gratefully.

"How can I thank you . . . and you're so wise. You know I would never harm my father, you know my feelings for him are dutiful. . . . But my love for you comes first, that and my trust to safeguard your great work. It will be safe with me, grandmother. And I promise you that for all his faults, my father shall be gently treated. . . ."

"Not too gently," she interrupted, her hatred of Paul rising at the suggestion of clemency.

"Don't underestimate him. He's not too mad, and he is resolved and very dangerous. You mustn't be weak, Alexis. I know my son. . . . Promise me that you will be severe, that no false feelings of pity shall deter you!"

Alexander, who intended Paul's immediate murder in the Löhde Fortress, shook his head and promised, reluctance and resolution adroitly mingled in his words and manner.

Then, as always, he reassured his grandmother with the phrase that gave her most comfort in the face of her weakened health and advancing years.

"But all this lies far ahead, Madame. Far into the future. There's no need to think of it now. . . ."

Catherine smiled at him and nodded. "I hope so, Alexis, I hope to live for many years. But it's as well to be prepared. Put my will back on the desk; it must be filed with my papers where you can have access to it at any moment if the need arises. . . . Now come and listen to my plans for the French campaign."

Three years had passed since the heads of the King and Queen of France had fallen on a scaffold set up by the Revolution, and the Supreme Autocrat of Europe had been

content with protests and verbal condemnation, satisfied that
the system by which she herself existed should perish in
France, since in the process the influence of a major European
country was disintegrating, and the balance of power thereby
shifted further in her favour.

Catherine waited and watched, certain that the dangerous
Jacobin tenets of the Revolution would never take serious root,
that after the first outbreak of hysteria and blood lust, France
would be conquered by the avenging Austrians, whose prize
would consist of a country in the throes of economic chaos,
its people starving and leaderless.

This forecast had long since been proved wrong; the
Austrian invaders were repelled, France faced all Europe in
defiance, deriving her strength from the will of her ragged
armies to retain the freedom they had won. And when the
terror ended with the execution of its architect, Robespierre,
and the moderate party assumed power, a single figure
remained standing upright on the wasted shores of French
political life, like a great undiscovered rock revealed by a
receding flood tide.

France had produced a general, a Corsican of fierce drive
and extraordinary talent, whose name no civilized tongue
could pronounce properly or spell without error.

It was the emergence of this man which had decided
Russia's Empress to support her words with action. France
had committed monstrous crimes, she declared, and she shed
fresh tears over the fate of Marie Antoinette, then three years
dead.

She considered it Russia's sacred duty to avenge the wrongs
perpetrated by the Jacobins; and, accompanied by England
and Prussia, who discovered their consciences at the same
period, Catherine assembled her armies to make war.

At the head of them she placed the most celebrated military
genius of the age, the true victor of the Turkish campaign, the
eccentric General Suvarov.

All this she discussed with Alexander, and the young Grand
Duke listened attentively.

"This Bonaparte, Madame. . . . You really consider him
dangerous?"

"I do, Alexis. As you know, I distrust all forms of intuition,
but in this case I have seen my anxieties borne out by this
man's achievements. He may be very, very dangerous. That's

why I am going to war. I want you to take particular note of this."

"I will, Madame, I will," he promised seriously, and many years later in the terrible days of 1812, he was to remember Catherine Alexeievna's prophecy.

.   .   .   .   .

It was a happy day for Catherine, a day filled with industry and preparations for the great war against France, and her longing to disinherit Paul had taken concrete form. This time there was no one to interfere, to point out this or that reason for delaying, and when she thought of that intimate, affectionate interview with her adored grandson, Catherine's heart contracted with happiness.

He was so very handsome, so much a credit to her, unlike that dour, hideous son of hers, whose absence was her only solace for the fact that he still lived. In Alexander's eyes she was incapable of error, for though she sensed the elusive, impenetrable quality of his nature, Catherine felt herself secure in his admiration and his love. She was his model and the pleasure of fulfilling the rôle of heroine bound her to his side more closely. Admiration and affection; they were all she asked of those surrounding her, and all his short life Alexander had accorded her both. In return she had given him her kingdom and contrived the removal of his hated father down to the last detail. She felt unusually well that day, her vigorous mind was as keen as ever, her plans for the future unfolded like tentacles in her brain, and each one radiated glory and success. She would smash France to the ground, and then complete the dream shared by Potemkin and drive the Turks from Constantinople. Never had the thought of death been further from her than on that fifteenth of November, and that evening she gave a small supper party in her private wing of the Winter Palace to which all her old friends and her lover Zubov were invited.

It was a gay gathering, despite the fact that the most favoured guests were well past sixty, and that the smiling hostess, painted and jewelled for the occasion, could not move from her chair without assistance.

Plato Zubov sat beside her while they dined, and often she turned to him, laying one hand possessively upon his arm, her face upturned to his with the eager, sensuous coquetry of a young girl in love.

The two waiting women, Countess Protassof, Plato's huge, silent brother Nicholas, and Leo Naryshkin dined at the same table. After supper some of them sat down to cards as usual, and half-way through the game a page approached the Empress, who laid down her hand and asked him what he wanted. When she heard, she addressed Zubov, who sat opposite, fingering a rising column of gold pieces which he had won from her.

"Plato, he says there's a pedlar to see me . . . what is this? Some surprise you've planned for me?" Zubov shook his head.

"I know nothing about any pedlar. . . . Send him away, Catherine, and let's continue. Remember, I'm winning!"

But for once Catherine persisted.

"No, beloved. Let's have him in. My curiosity is aroused."

When he was first admitted Catherine did not recognize him; she saw only a bent figure wrapped in a shabby cloak, carrying a tray of trinkets in his arms.

"Your Majesty," he mumbled. "I have here a few baubles. . . ." For a moment she looked down at the cheap, gaudy ornaments he offered her, and then her keen eyes searched his lowered face and her ears recognized his voice.

"Leo! You wretch! Oh, my God, he quite deceived me. . . ." She sat back in her chair and began to laugh, while the grinning Naryshkin abandoned his pose and began extolling the virtues of his valueless wares to the richest woman in all Russia, in his own drawling, educated voice.

Catherine laughed and laughed.

"You fool, Leo . . . you dear fool, I should have known it was you playing a trick upon me. . . ."

The joke appealed to her so much that she abandoned all control and cried with mirth, until quite suddenly her face contorted in a grimace of pain.

Instantly Naryshkin was at her side, his tray of trinkets flung upon the floor.

"Madame, what is it . . . what's the matter . . . ?"

"It's nothing . . . nothing," she assured him, gasping for breath, one hand pressed to her side, the other clutching at her lover for support.

"I laughed too much," she whispered and stared up into Naryshkin's worried face with frightened eyes.

Countess Protassof was kneeling by her, holding a glass of water and the Empress drank from it, wincing with pain.

"I have a colic," she said, suddenly pitiful and strange in her distress. "It was the laughter . . . Plato, Plato, beloved, help me to bed. . . ."

She would allow no one but him to touch her; she collapsed into his strong arms, her face as white as death, her hands trembling and clinging to him. And when she had gone to her own bedroom, they stood in a disconcerted, anxious group, until the Prince himself assured them that the spasm had passed and the Empress was perfectly recovered. Then her ladies undressed her and helped her into the enormous gilt bed. Protassof lingered, conscious of her mistress's pleading gaze, frightened because the great Catherine had become almost childlike because of a stitch in her side.

"Protassof . . . send him back to me. I'm much better now. Much better. I want him, Protassof," she wailed. "I don't want to be alone. . . ."

"I'll send him to you, Madame. Rest until he comes."

A few moments later the Countess closed her mistress's door behind the broad back of Plato Zubov, and as she went to her own rooms, the waiting woman shook her head.

"She'd send for him if she were dying. . . ." she muttered, and then for some reason past her understanding, she began to shiver violently.

.   .   .   .   .

11

IT was very quiet at Gatchina on that afternoon of the 16th November. The Czarevitch had not been well; an unusually violent headache and a succession of appalling nightmares had tormented him for several days. He emerged from his sick room pale and wasted, consumed by nervous tension.

For once Marie Feodorovna sat with him in his apartments, drinking coffee and watching her husband anxiously. Five years of battling with him had drained the spirit out of the

Grand Duchess, five years of living under his displeasure had engendered a frantic desire for peace at any price, and the waning influence of the mistress had helped to assuage the pride of the discarded wife.

While she sipped her coffee, waiting for Paul to speak, Marie Feodorovna glanced idly out of the window, and it was she who saw a horseman galloping into the palace grounds, and, recognizing the rider, almost dropped her cup in astonishment.

"Paul! Paul, Zubov's brother is here!"

"What!"

Instantly the Czarevitch sprang out of his chair and rushed to the window. "Where?" he demanded and caught her roughly by the arm. "Are you sure . . . which brother?"

Marie looked up at his white face and, reading the alarm in it, began to tremble as she realized the possible meaning of such a visit.

"It was Nicholas, I think," she stammered, "Nicholas. . . . Oh, my God, Paul, what is it?"

"A deputation from my mother," he answered grimly, and then his grip on her relaxed for a moment and he regarded her with something strangely near to pity.

"We are lost, my dear," he said quietly. "This was how my father met his end . . . at the hands of the favourite's brother. I've felt it coming for days past. Go to your rooms, Marie, and stay there. They will be here at any moment."

"They . . . but he was alone," she whispered.

"Alone. . . ." Paul stared down at her frowning. "Are you certain?"

She nodded eagerly, realizing that no single man could hope to molest them in their own home, and at that moment she remembered Araktchéief's garrison and gave thanks for them with all her heart.

Almost immediately a page entered and announced that M. Nicholas Zubov sought an audience of the Czarevitch.

"Admit him," Paul ordered, and turning, he told Marie Feodorovna to sit down and appear undisturbed before their enemy.

The brother of Catherine's favourite was very tall and muscular in the tradition of the Guards, but he lacked Plato's grace and classical good looks. Nicholas, in company with the second brother Valerian, was fierce, brutal and of limited intelligence; his reputation for courage and unscrupulousness did nothing to reassure the fears of Marie or the suspicions of Paul Petrovitch when he first came into their presence.

For a second he hesitated, and as if in a dream the Grand Duchess heard the sound of horses stamping in the courtyard under their windows, and of voices shouting unintelligibly.

'He was not alone,' she thought mechanically, so terrified that her mind accepted the awful materialization of their lifelong dread with the detachment of one whom it did not concern.

'He brought men with him. . . . Paul was right.'

"Come in, M. Zubov. What brings *you* to Gatchina. . . ?" Paul's voice cracked ominously on the last words, and though his hand shook and the pain induced by any form of tension stabbed into his skull so that he winced, his fingers rested firmly on the pommel of his sword.

The brother of Plato Zubov did not answer. Instead he stopped close to the short, thick-set figure, rigid in the attitude of menace, and suddenly went down on his knees.

"God save the Czar!"

Marie Feodorovna's porcelain coffee cup fell from her hands and shattered to pieces; for a few seconds that seemed to endure for all eternity, that was the only sound in the room.

Then Paul spoke, spoke with difficulty, because his tongue was thick and stammering with excitement and unbelief.

"My mother . . . my mother is dead. . . ?"

"Not yet, Sire," Zubov told him. "But you must hurry to Petersburg if you would see her alive. She was found unconscious this morning, and they say she will not live for more than a few hours."

"Why do *you* come to tell me this? . . . Where are my Ministers? . . . Where is my son?"

"I come to offer my allegiance to you, Sire. The Grand Duke Alexander is in the capital, waiting for you. And already half Petersburg is on the way here to acclaim you Emperor."

Paul turned away abruptly and from the tall windows of his room looked out and saw a confusion of sledges being drawn up outside the palace; along the road into Gatchina a line of vehicles stretched back as far as the eye could see.

The sound of many voices came to him, the excited tones of his mother's courtiers who were at that moment besieging the entrance to his palace in order to throw themselves at the feet of the new Czar; those who had jeered at Catherine's ugly son and prophesied his disinheritance were now confounded.

The Empress who had begun to seem immortal had suddenly deserted them; she lay dying on the bed where Plato Zubov had made love to her the night before, the expected proclamation of her grandson Alexander had not taken place, and with the agility of rats abandoning a doomed vessel, the Court dissolved in a panic-stricken rush to make peace with the man who was already designated the Emperor Paul the First.

"It has come," he muttered, and standing by the window, looking down on the scene of fear and confusion taking place below, he struck his aching forehead with his fist, mastering a sudden unmanly desire to shed tears of gratitude to the God who had permitted him to see this day.

Outside his rooms a crowd had gathered, murmuring behind the door, barred from his presence by the Gatchina sentries; Paul heard them, and suddenly he smiled to think that in the course of a few hours the order of things could be reversed so quickly and completely. There was no Palace Revolution to dispose of him, Catherine lay speechless in the face of death, unable to say the few words which would wreak her final vengeance on her hated son, and Paul guessed that Alexander had not dared to give the order to seize his father without the Empress's authority; that, in a moment of crisis, fear had made him hesitate.

So he was to succeed.

"Sire. . . ."

Nicholas Zubov ventured to interrupt his thought, anxious that since he and his brothers had declared for Paul, no *coup d'état* in Petersburg should supplant him in his absence.

"Sire. You must set out for the capital immediately. There's not a moment to be lost! The Empress may recover consciousness. . . ."

She might indeed, Paul realized, and knew that a few words bequeathing the crown to Alexander might yet effect the ruin of all his hopes. But one question emerged from the turmoil of his thoughts, one query that might explain why the plans of the most resolute and methodical monarch in the world had come to nothing, with her son succeeding to the power she had intended for another. . . . Paul turned and stared into the dark face of Nicholas Zubov, who had no cause to love his Czarevitch and offer his sword to his service.

"Who sent you to me?"

Back came the answer without pause, delivered with the brevity of the soldier whose concept of obedience embraces all the vagaries of men and circumstances.

"Alexis Orlov, Sire."

.   .   .   .   .

The confusion in Petersburg was indescribable. Rumours that the Empress was dying, even dead, had seeped through to the people who left their homes and gathered outside the Winter Palace in shivering, speculative groups, watching the blind façade of stone and glass behind which Catherine the Great lay, spending her life with every halting breath.

No snow fell from the lead-coloured sky, so that it seemed as if the heavens had suspended their power and waited in unison with the people of Holy Russia for that one soul to pass into eternity; only a howling, bitter wind swept through the city, catching the dried snow off the streets and whirling it fiercely above the ground, creating a miniature blizzard. The Neva, frozen into a shining thoroughfare of solid ice, was dotted with sledges which cut across the great sweep of petrified water, passing the riverside entrance to the Imperial Palace where sentries stamped and marched to keep from freezing.

There were two currents of activity: the nobles deserting the Winter Palace and rushing towards Gatchina and an unknown future, and the humble gathered round the palace to pray for the woman who had ruled them for thirty-seven years.

There would be a new Emperor, the people whispered, but whether his name would be Paul or Alexander no one knew.

Paul—insisted the older of Catherine's subjects, the injustices of her long reign still fresh in their minds. Remember Pugachev, remember the horrors inflicted by her troops. Remember the ceaseless wars, the ruthless conscription of men for this new conflict against France. . . . Her extravagance, and her favourites—God save Paul!

But there were others who said nothing, others who had known the older Catherine Alexeievna and her handsome grandson, and to whom the name of the shadowy Czarevitch conjured up visions of savagery and madness, of vague crimes committed in the confines of notorious Gatchina. These gazed up at the great Winter Palace and in their hearts they prayed for Alexander.

The palace itself was silent, the vast, rambling buildings peopled only by servants, soldiers and a few who remained faithful to their Empress and kept vigil over her unconscious body.

Among these was her grandson, Alexander.

They had not allowed him to approach her bedside, and *they* consisted of men who had suddenly proved themselves friendly to his father and assumed control within the hour of hearing that the Empress had had a stroke and was about to die.

Rastopchine was among them, but Alexander had expected him to take the stand of loyalty; what he had never imagined was the emergence of Plato Zubov and his brothers into the ranks of the legitimist party, accompanied by his mother's Minister Bezborodko and others. Most fatal and astonishing of all was the action of that legendary friend of Catherine, the man whose hands were stained with the miserable Peter Feodorovitch's blood shed in that half-forgotten tragedy of nearly forty years before.

Alexis Orlov, who had more to fear from Paul than any man alive, swung the wavering balance in the Czarevitch's favour. Openly he urged Nicholas Zubov to ride at once to Gatchina and bring the rightful Czar to Petersburg.

"There's been enough bloodshed for this throne," he shouted in his still vigorous voice, so that the shrinking Alexander heard him. "I bear the stain of it, my brother Gregory died in torment because of what was done. Listen to me, who have nothing left to fear now but the judgment of God! Give your allegiance to the rightful Czar. . . !"

And they had listened to him.

With a murmur of excuses the Minister Bezborodko removed the Empress's private papers, ignoring the pleas of the young Grand Duke, who saw that precious will carried into an inner room out of his reach. Plato Zubov hurried to the bedside of his dying mistress and knelt beside it, while Nicholas Zubov, closely followed by Rastopchine, rushed from the State apartments, shouting for horses to carry them to the Czarevitch at Gatchina.

Then the panic set in, and in hundreds Catherine's courtiers fled the palace, commandeering any vehicles that were available, fighting to show their loyalty to the new and dreaded Czar, taking the long, crowded road to Gatchina and submission.

Watching that open doorway, beyond which his grandmother lay on her deathbed, Alexander knelt, and wept with fear and disappointment. It was all over, the brilliant dream that they had shared together and discussed so often, the dream of his accession. Catherine's crown had been torn from her head while she still lived, and placed on the brow of the man whose enmity was now become a deadly danger.

It had only needed one determined voice to cry out in his favour, one man quick enough to get him Catherine's papers and proclaim him Czar according to the terms of her will, and the thing would have been done. But the voice was raised, the loyalty evinced on behalf of Catherine's abhorred son, and thus Alexis purged himself of the murder of Paul Petrovitch's father.

Thinking these thoughts the Grand Duke continued to alternately weep and pray for his own safety, until the sound of a great commotion brought him quickly to his feet, wiping his swollen eyes.

The cry came faintly at first, as it preceded the tramp of many feet, until it sounded in the main ante-chamber.

"Make way. . . . Way for the Czar!"

For a single instant of hysteria and hate Alexander wanted to rush out and meet them crying that his grandmother still lived, that his father whom they had both hated was not Czar of Russia yet. . . .

But the spasm passed. A chill of icy caution froze the impulse and stretched the Grand Duke's pallid features in a welcoming smile.

It was too late, too late for anything now but submission with the rest. And like them he would submit . . . for the moment.

His fine, ringed hands straightened his cravat and brushed the knees of his breeches where contact with the marble floor had soiled them. Then he went out to meet his father.

.   .   .   .   .

At a quarter to ten Catherine's physician Rogerson informed the Court that the Empress was dead. Paul, who had been standing by the bedside, gazing down at the motionless figure of his mother, suddenly realized that the stertorous, painful breathing had stopped. As the lids were pressed down over the sightless eyes, a priest of the Orthodox religion lifted her hand for Paul to kiss, but with a gesture of impatience the new Emperor turned away, unable to pretend to sorrow or affection when his heart was bounding with relief and joy.

She was dead, and with her had died an era hateful to him in every detail.

A new reign had just begun and all the terrible resolutions formed for so many years in anticipation of this moment came rushing in upon him.

Away with vice, with sloth, with hypocrisy. . . .

Savagely he turned on the murmuring priest.

"Leave her!" he ordered. "She never believed in you in life!" Then he pointed to the Minister Bezborodko standing in a corner of the room.

"Get me my mother's papers," he commanded. "And bring them to me in here." Then he walked into an ante-chamber adjoining the room where the Empress's body lay, and there he received visitors who side-stepped the stiffening corpse with horrified glances. Most of those who were granted an audience noticed the boxes of papers which were broken open, their contents scattered as if a frantic search had taken place, a search that must have proved successful, for the fire in the marble grate was damped down by a heap of charred and blackened parchment.

It was all that remained of Catherine's will and Alexander's hopes.

At midnight the ceremony of swearing allegiance to the new Emperor took place, and afterwards Paul retired to the sovereign's suite in the Winter Palace, where a number of rooms had been hastily cleared of Catherine's effects and made habitable for him.

There he sent for those who were to set the pattern of his reign, the men whose past would indicate the future.

A crowd of weary courtiers waited in the ante-room of the Czar, afraid to go to bed despite the strain and exhaustion of the day until someone remembered to dismiss them.

Among them were men whose achievements in politics and war would be invaluable to the new Emperor.

But no call came for their attendance. Only two persons passed beyond the sentries from the Gatchina garrison who already mounted guard, and remained shut up with him for several hours.

Those whom Paul had chosen were Rastopchine, and the sadist, Araktchéief.

The reign of Paul the First of Russia had begun.

.   .   .   .   .

Three days after the accession of the Emperor, a tomb in the cloister of St. Alexander Nevsky Church was broken open.

Inside, the Czar's emissaries discovered a skeleton, identifiable by the remains of a mouldering boot on the left foot. With great care the brittle bones were lifted out of the rotting casket, a few shreds of decayed uniform cloth clinging to them, and laid in a magnificent coffin upholstered in velvet and inlaid with gold and precious stones.

Then the Emperor was informed that the body of the murdered Czar Peter the Third had been disinterred according to his orders.

Katya Nelidoff was with him when the report was made, and she listened, horrified, to the description of the exhumation of a man dead for almost forty years.

Paul sat in silence, staring at the floor while the witnesses spoke, interjecting a question as to the condition of the corpse. He was particularly anxious that the skull should be in a good state of preservation, and he was quickly reassured on this point.

Still gazing at the ground he dismissed the officials, and only then he raised his head and looked at his mistress. To her astonishment she saw that the tears were running down his face.

With a sudden surge of tenderness she caught his hand in hers, forgetting the changed status which had removed him to a still more distant plane from the old loving relationship of nearly nine years before.

"Oh, Paul . . . Paul, don't! Don't distress yourself. Let me pour you some wine. . . ."

He shook his head, but his fingers returned the affectionate pressure of her own, and for a moment the staring, arrogant mask of the past few days vanished, and she saw only the tired, sick countenance of the man who had become more dear to her than life itself.

"My father . . ." he said slowly. "After all these years in an unworthy grave, I can give him the burial that is his due. . . ."

Concern for him blinded her then; seeing that terrible pallor, the throbbing cheek and red-rimmed eyes, she thought only of his health, of the excruciating headaches, the fits of melancholy which sometimes tormented him for days on end, racking his body and casting a terrifying, illogical cloud over his mind, and in her anxiety to protect him from himself, forgot the lesson that many a miserable quarrel had taught her. There were some lengths beyond which no one might safely go with Paul, some subjects, however dangerous or exaggerated, which were sacred to him and which must never be questioned or belittled. Urged on by selflessness and love she plunged into folly, and the treasonable words were spoken before she had time to realize what she had said.

"Oh, God, what does it matter! Why disturb the dead, why bring all this grief upon yourself, remembering a man you never really knew! Beloved, bury your father's bones again and shut the past in with them. Begin your life and reign afresh; what's done is done, and since you've pardoned Alexis Orlov, what use is this morbid vengeance on your mother!"

For a moment he said nothing, but the hand holding hers unclosed and withdrew with a violence that almost threw her to the ground.

"What does it matter?"

The question was unspeakably menacing, spoken in that soft voice through which anger sounded like a distant warning note.

"My father . . . usurped and strangled, my inheritance delayed for thirty-seven years . . . a lifetime of persecution, of suffering, of living under the shadow of death. You can dismiss it so lightly, Mademoiselle. . . . You think it of no consequence. I have pardoned the wretched tool of my mother, the vassal who slew on her orders, pardoned his life because he helped to secure me my throne. . . . Therefore you suppose all is forgotten!"

He had risen and stood over her, his clenched fist raised as if about to strike her where she half knelt at his feet, staring up at him in terror.

"If you loved me, you'd never have spoken those words!" He had begun to shout, rage and amazement flooding his heart and mind with a torrent of furious suspicion. How often had she said she loved him, repeating the formula like a hypnotic chant that robbed him of his judgment; kissed and clung to him, her body performing the motions of a passion that was obviously as spurious as her avowals! And for nearly nine years he had believed her, fallen dupe to a deception which she had just revealed in its true light.

"You fool! Are you so blind to your own ugliness that you think any woman could love you. . . ?" Catherine's taunt, spat at him concerning Natalie Alexeievna, sounded in his brain as clearly as if she had returned to life and spoken it aloud.

And in that instant of unbalanced grief and temper, stung by the jibe delivered all those years ago and afterwards proved right when his adulterous wife was safely dead, Paul answered his own doubt concerning Catherine Nelidoff, answered it finally and accepted it like a death blow.

If she had really loved him, she would have loved and honoured what was most sacred in his life. If she had ever been sincere, she would have shared his grief and borne the burden of his hatred for those who had attempted his destruction. . . . Slowly his hands lowered to his sides, the blood drained out of his face, leaving it livid and contorted with pain.

"For the love of God, Mademoiselle. . . . Leave me, I beg of you."

She caught at his knees, weeping in an agony of distress, her excuses choking in her constricted throat.

He stepped back from her, and she fell forward on the carpet, sobbing.

"Paul . . . Paul, my love . . . please listen. . . ."

"As you persist . . ." he said, and walked into his bedroom, slamming the door shut.

A moment later she heard the bolt shoot into its socket; Catherine's chambers which had never been fitted with locks were now equipped with every device necessary to guard against assassination. With the sound of final exclusion in her ears, Catherine Nelidoff fainted.

.   .   .   .   .

The news of the favourite's disgrace spread like wildfire through the Court; within a few hours of the quarrel Marie Feodorovna heard that the liaison of many years had ended and that the unhappy Nelidoff was prostrate in her rooms, waiting for the Emperor's orders to go into exile.

The new Empress was far less pleased than her informants had expected; the violent storms of the past had subsided, her husband's mistress had long ceased to wield the main influence over him, her hold was sentimental as well as sensual, and lately the result of that placid relationship had been one of growing harmony between the trio.

Marie walked up and down her boudoir, frowning and biting her full lower lip, torn between wifely spite and the regret of her common sense which foresaw all sorts of complications should Paul replace the Nelidoff with a more ambitious woman.

It was too late for pride, she decided, and ordered her chattering ladies to leave her alone. Paul still slept with her at rare intervals, and her sexual jealousy of Catherine Neli-doff had died the death of acceptance and indifference to an unalterable situation. Gradually they had come to share him and, since he was Czar and prepared to endow her with the wealth and privileges of his Consort, Marie had not the slightest ethical or emotional objection to his making love to her unattractive maid of honour.

"Oh, dear Heaven," she murmured, "why must the little fool contradict him. . . . I'll swear that's what she did. . . . Just when we had all settled down in peace. . . . I can see I shall have to do something."

And she went in person to Paul to persuade him to take his mistress back.

He was signing papers when she entered, and the sight of Araktchéief standing behind his chair checked her words. Paul looked up and greeted her politely; he was very pale and his eyes were red-rimmed with sleeplessness. Marie noticed distastefully that the nerve in his left cheek was jumping visibly under the skin.

"Sit down, Madame, if you please. M. Araktchéief is just discussing a few matters with me. We will not be a moment."

The man who had just been created military commander of Petersburg bowed low to the Empress and regarded her with the hostility reserved for any woman connected with his beloved master.

Together they had completed the arrangements for absorbing Paul's loyal Gatchina garrison into the guards regiments, always the forcing house of plots and counter-revolutions, thereby rewarding the most notorious collection of military ruffians in the country with all the privileges and honours enjoyed by the Russian nobility. Also the proposed war against France had been abandoned, for Paul declared that he brought peace rather than bloodshed to his people. At the same time he ordered the imprisonment of one of Catherine's favourite footmen for having been a witness of her amours; and signed the warrant for his removal to the Peter and Paul fortress where he subsequently went mad in an underground dungeon. There were others, Araktchéief pointed out, while Marie sat on the edge of her gilt chair, her fear increasing with every moment as she listened to that cold voice, suggesting a long list of atrocities for the Czar's approval.

The late Empress's confessor was to be prosecuted, and had his Majesty forgotten that infamous woman whose part in the Revolution and death of his illustrious father would go down to history?

The Princess Dashkev, Paul echoed, remembering that his mother had abandoned her friend soon after the *coup d'état,* because her lover Gregory Orlov hated her. That old friendship had never really been resumed and the Princess now lived most of the time on her estates. " She is to be banished to Korotoya. I believe it is very cold. . . ."

Then two secretaries in the employ of Plato Zubov were consigned to prison, and having disposed of a host of lesser creatures, Araktchéief reminded the Czar of a much more powerful victim.

" What of Prince Plato Zubov, Sire? "

Paul looked up at him and smiled grimly.

" Patience," he said quietly, " patience. We will come to him later. And to Alexis Orlov. Go now, my friend. I will attend the parade in an hour's time."

Marie Feodorovna rose from her chair and went to him, her plump legs trembling under her, having witnessed the downfall of a score of persons being sanctioned in the course of a few minutes. Unimaginative and stupid as she was, Marie had seen the true nature of her position, of the position indeed of every living soul surrounding Paul. His displeasure had always been a source of dread, even in the old days of his powerless youth; now the loss of his favour could mean death or exile to Siberia, or, if his mood was cruel, incarceration in some dank, airless hole beneath the level of the ground until the blind and half-crazed prisoner prayed to die.

She who had quarrelled with him, complained against him

to Catherine, tormented the Nelidoff and incurred his wrath a hundred times in the past, now fell on her knees beside his chair, trembling in every limb, and tried to maintain their amiable truce and make amends for former folly, by pleading with tears for her old rival.

.   .   .   .   .

"Mademoiselle! Mademoiselle, the Empress is here and wishes to see you!"

Catherine Nelidoff raised herself on the bed where she had lain for twenty-four hours, the prey of utter despair, refusing food and comfort.

Listening to the agitated page, she jumped to the conclusion that Marie Feodorovna had come to gloat over her enemy, or even to deliver Paul's sentence of exile.

For all her weakness, her prostration in the face of her lover's anger, she possessed her own brand of courage.

"Beg Her Majesty to allow me a few moments' grace. I shall wait upon her as soon as I am dressed."

The page withdrew, and Katya Nelidoff fastened a long velvet robe over her nightdress, sponged her face with toilet water and combed her dark hair into some semblance of order. Then she went into the room where Paul's wife waited.

The sight of her fallen enemy shocked Marie Feodorovna, whose eyes were not deceived by the neat *déshabillé* and the formal curtsy with which the Nelidoff greeted her.

Instead she noted the desperate pallor, the nervously inter-locking hands, and reflected that the other woman's sallowness and irregularity of feature were now accentuated into ugli-ness by strain and grief.

"Sit down, Mademoiselle," she said and her tone was unexpectedly kind. "You look ill. I am quite concerned about you."

"I thank your Majesty," whispered the unhappy Nelidoff, the ready tears filling her eyes, aware that the words were free from sarcasm.

Marie coughed awkwardly, until the memory of Paul sitting signing death warrants overcame her diffidence.

"I have good news for you," she said. "I heard of your plight and interceded for you. The Emperor has decided to let you stay at Court."

Catherine Nelidoff threw herself at the Empress's feet and burst into a flood of tears.

"You interceded. . . ." she sobbed, overwhelmed with shame. "Oh, my God, how can I thank you. . . ? "

"Please control yourself, Mademoiselle. There's no need to cry now. I'll grant you a few moments to recover and then I would like to talk to you."

Paul's mistress wiped her face with a handkerchief and rising, rang for her page.

"Will your Majesty have a little wine? " she asked, and sensing the other's need of it, Marie nodded.

The Nelidoff seated herself once more, and drank a full glass of wine before the Empress judged her calm.

"I think the time has come for us to be quite frank with one another," Marie remarked at last. "Therefore I wish you to understand that however I may have resented your relationship with my husband in the past, I have no objection to it now. The Czar is . . . er . . . difficult sometimes and I am aware that your good offices are as necessary as my own to keep him placid. . . . In the circumstances I am prepared to take you under my protection and offer you my friendship. My first duty is to my husband and I consider you to be a benefit to him. . . ."

Catherine Nelidoff's face flushed to the roots of her dark hair as she gazed at the calm, colourless countenance of the woman who had been so long accounted a bore and a non-entity. For the first time she recognized a certain dignity and for an instant suspected that the Empress Marie was less of a fool than her enemies supposed her. That flash of insight was correct, for twenty years of living in the midst of fierce and tortuous intrigue had schooled the stolid German Princess in the art of guarding her own interests even at the expense of her pride.

The suspicion that she now befriended her rival in order to make use of her passed through the Nelidoff's mind and was swept away on a flood of gratitude and thanksgiving.

She went down on her knees and pressed Marie's plump fingers to her lips.

"You've been so kind, Madame; I'm in your debt for the rest of my life! "

"Not kind, my dear Mademoiselle," the Empress responded. "Just sensible. Now I advise you to go and repair your toilette

so that the Czar won't see a pale face and red eyes at the
reception this evening. . . ."

Once outside the Nelidoff's apartments, Marie sighed with
relief, confident that after that interview the lady's gratitude
would be unbounded.

"Thank God," she mused, "as long as she's with him I
shall be safe. And so will Alexander!"

Then she hurried to tell her eldest son that he, too, must
enlist the friendship of Paul's mistress.

.   .   .   .   .

It was a clever move, and for a time the strong and secret
faction who detested both Katya Nelidoff and the Empress
Marie were confounded by the outward reconciliation. As
always a crowd of parasites followed in the train of the Royal
favourite and the generous and unsuspecting Nelidoff had
secured posts for her relatives and friends in the Czarevitch's
Gatchina household and again on his accession to the throne,
thereby incurring the hatred of many of Paul's intimates who
coveted these places for themselves.

For a year or more the jealous eyes of Koutaïssof, now
waiting anxiously for the publication of his master's Coronation Honours; the interest of Rastopchine, who mistrusted the
truce existing between the mistress and the wife, believing
as he did that the Grand Duke Alexander might use his doting
mother for intrigue; and the deadly enmity of Araktchéief,
had been turned upon the problem of ousting the woman who
had held sway with Paul Petrovitch for nine long years. It
was not immediately apparent that Catherine Nelidoff's
position was only nominal.

Paul took her back in public, moved by the pleas of Marie
Feodorovna, who painted a pitiful picture of his mistress's fear
and misery as a result of his anger. He had loved her deeply
once, relied on her for tenderness and compassion, burying
his throbbing head in her breast and believing himself safe
in the compass of her disinterested affection. But that comfort
had been stripped from him; he no longer trusted her
desperate avowals of love, and, afraid to fall a victim to a
double practice of deceit, Paul gradually withdrew his confidence and affection from her in private, while saving her face
before the Court.

Paul danced the minuet with her, invited her to his table in public and showed her every mark of favour before the eyes of her enemies, for he could not bring himself to abandon her, and there were still moments when the beseeching gaze of those gentle brown eyes gave the lie to his suspicions. But thanks to the lesson of his first wife's betrayal, he was incapable of sustaining and conquering a doubt of that nature when it had once entered his mind, and when the Court receptions ended and the watch of prying eyes no longer followed him, the Czar more often wished Katya Nelidoff good night and passed into his heavily guarded bedroom alone.

At the most crucial moment of his life, he had retreated into solitude, bearing the burden of an immense kingdom in urgent need of reform, and endowed with a degree of despotic power which had turned the brain of many better balanced men. The throne was his, but among the fawning crowds who thronged his palace there were scores of potential traitors, friends of Catherine's and partisans of the Grand Duke Alexander; Paul had never trusted Alexander; the latter's submission on the day of Catherine's death had not deceived that fierce, suspicious mind; and lately, watching her fluttering devotion to her eldest son, the Czar no longer trusted Marie Feodorovna either. . . .

.   .   .   .   .

They talked of that terrible funeral of Catherine for months to come; the silent crowds of Petersburg, speechless with horror, the frightened courtiers, the ambassadors, who hurried to report to their respective governments that the Emperor of Russia was undoubtedly mad. And over the years the story persisted, unexaggerated even by the most colourful relater, for no imagination could have improved upon the dreadful symbolism devised by Paul.

The whole city was silent, the streets hung with black, the blinds drawn over every window as a sign of mourning, and in this setting, the procession of burial for the late Empress wound its way over a long route.

It was no ordinary cortège, for a great catafalque of gold headed the line, and in it lay a skeleton, the bones cleaned of dust and the grime of decomposing flesh, surrounded by guards who marched with their heads bowed in grief.

Immediately behind this ghastly bier, a tall old man walked alone, walked in the van of the poor remains of Peter Feodorovitch, and seeing him the people pointed, whispering.

"That is the murderer, Alexis Orlov. . . ."

That was the judgment pronounced upon him by the Czar, and with the coffin of Catherine Alexeievna moving after him, Alexis trod that road of public penance, his white head held proudly before the curious, accusing gaze of thousands, closing his ear to their murmurs.

"Alexis Orlov . . . the murderer. . . ."

Immediate burial was not Paul's plan, for an omission of his dead father's reign had to be rectified.

Peter the Third had never worn his crown; Catherine's rebellion had hurled him off the throne and into a premature grave before the ceremony of coronation.

Therefore Paul paid this gruesome honour to the dead, and while the cortège bearing Catherine's coffin waited, the skeleton of Peter Feodorovitch was wedged into the Imperial throne, and the magnificent, blazing Crown of Russia solemnly placed on the yellow skull in token of the legitimate rule which a usurper had interrupted.

Then, in the chapel at the fortress of St. Peter and Paul, traditional burial place of the sovereigns of Russia, the body of Catherine Alexeievna was lowered into a deep grave, and with her they interred the remains of her mortal enemy, and sealed this posthumous reconciliation by closing the tomb.

It was dark when the crowds dispersed, muttering in fear and wonder; and by the time that Plato Zubov sat with his brother Nicholas in the former's house outside the palace, it was nearly midnight.

At first they said little, the soldier drinking long draughts of wine, while Catherine's favourite ate sweetmeats and reflected.

"How safe is this place?" Nicholas Zubov asked suddenly.

"Entirely safe," his brother reassured him. "I am in mourning for the Empress. . . ." He gestured towards the walls of the room which were swathed in black drapery. "Wishing to be alone in my sorrow, and to talk freely while I am still at liberty, I have also dismissed my servants for a few days."

"What do you mean, still at liberty?" Nicholas questioned suddenly, and in answer Plato shrugged and smiled his handsome sinister smile.

"I don't altogether trust him . . . do you?"

Nicholas stared into the bottom of his wine glass and then set it down slowly, formulating his thought into words, reassured by the knowledge that there was no one in the building besides themselves.

"Plato," he said at last. "Plato, I think we made a mistake. . . ."

Catherine's former lover nodded, and his black eyes blazed for a second, before the lazy arrogance habitual to him filmed over them like shutters.

"I think so, too, brother," he said gently. "But mistakes can be rectified. . . . It may be possible with this one."

.   .   .   .   .   .

On the sixth of December the whole Court was electrified by the news that the Czar had ceased his enigmatic game of friendship with Prince Plato Zubov. For weeks they had watched in wonder, while the Emperor acted a sinister comedy with his mother's infamous favourite, setting out with the Empress to take tea with the Prince in his house, where the frightened observers reported that Paul treated his uncomfortable host with an amiability more menacing than threats.

It was a subtle revenge, more distorted and less bloody than his subjects had expected, and for those few weeks Paul sat and savoured the spectacle of the languid, insolent male courtesan doubling himself to the ground in the effort to placate his sovereign.

Then, suddenly he struck.

The Prince was dismissed his numerous posts, prosecuted and banished. And before the Court had recovered its breath, Alexis Orlov, who had also received the same marks of macabre favour for a short period, followed Catherine's lover on the road of exile.

Like a whirlwind, Paul's long-delayed revenge was loosed upon the more powerful of his enemies; the prisons were already filled with lesser creatures and within months of his accession the way to Siberia was crowded with soldiers, with statesmen and nobles, many of whom were being justly punished for rifling the coffers of the State during the previous reign. Even Potemkin's tomb was broken open and his remains thrown into the Neva. Every statue erected to his memory was destroyed, and any towns called after him renamed.

At the same time Catherine's son set out to redress Catherine's tyranny. The prisoners convicted by her courts were released, the exiles recalled, and the Polish captives employed under conditions of unspeakable brutality and hardship on the fortifications at Rogerwick were amnestied and sent home.

The nobility had always hated Paul, and Paul returned the sentiment with terrible intensity. They, the wealthy and high born, had laughed at him, snubbed him in his miserably unhappy youth; a dissolute aristocrat had seduced his first wife and turned the gentle virgin he had married into a deceitful whore. . . . They persecuted his people, ill-treated their serfs and squandered the country's funds when in office.

"No more!" he vowed to Araktchéief, his voice raised to a roar of anger. "They've had too much freedom for too long! But I'll break them, my friend . . . I'll break them!"

No sentiment could have been closer to the feelings of the Commandant, born the son of a poor country gentleman, and for every snub received by the great nobles in Catherine's day, he devised a humiliation which the Czar made law.

. . . . .

"Koutaïssof! Come here immediately. . . ."

The Turk had been dozing on a sofa in his master's anteroom, when the sound of that familiar voice, harsh and quivering with fury, brought him running to the Czar's study.

Paul sat at his desk, surrounded by despatch boxes which he had been opening; there were papers on the floor where his impatient hand had swept them, and with his knees knocking with fear, Koutaïssof bent to pick them up, only to be interrupted by a furious order to leave them where they were.

Paul's face was livid with anger, the bounding pulse dragged at the corner of his left eye as it always did when his temper rose to danger point.

He held a despatch crumpled in one hand, and he threw it at the Turk's head with the injunction to read it. Koutaïssof smoothed the sheets of paper and tried to decipher what was written on them, his brown fingers shaking with nervousness.

"Oh, God, how slow you are," the Emperor snarled suddenly. "Give it to me, if you can't read!"

"What is it, Sire? Only tell me. . . . Have I done wrong?" Koutaïssof quavered, preparing to prostrate himself and beg forgiveness before he even knew the nature of his fault.

"Not you . . . not you! What are you cringing for, fool? God's death, have I ever mistreated you that you cower like a whipped dog? Listen to this, Koutaïssof . . . 'Since the former King of Poland did not arrive on time at Riga, the banquet prepared for him was held in any case, as Prince Plato Zubov was passing through the town on that date. . . .' Zubov! Zubov whom I disgraced and banished, received at Riga and given royal honours! Ah, by God, no man shall dare insult me in that way. . . . Who is the Governor of Riga?"

"I don't know, Sire," the Turk replied, sweating with relief that this unknown was to be the culprit rather than himself.

"Then find out!" Paul ordered sharply. "Send for my secretary. I have a letter to dictate to this Governor who gives banquets to an exile. . . ."

And in due course, the letter was written, signed and despatched, and by that evening the incident had faded from Paul's mind. In fact while that letter, the most fateful in consequence that he would ever write throughout the short time that remained to him, sped on its journey to Riga by special courier, the Czar dined and attended a play in the royal theatre. Throughout the evening he was in the best of humours, his manner marked by his old gentleness so that a good many of those who hated him since his accession watched him and wondered, their hostility towards him weakening.

But the letter addressed to the Governor of Riga travelled across Russia, bearing a furious rebuke and an ignominious dismissal for the man responsible for the foolish act of courtesy to Catherine's favourite.

In a moment of rage, spurred by the jealousy, disgust and shame any reference to his mother's sexual weakness always aroused in him, however distantly connected with the subject, Paul Petrovitch had humiliated the most dangerous, vindictive and implacable man in Russia. The enmity of Count Von Pahlen, Governor of Riga, was to cost him his life.

12

THE coronation of Paul Petrovitch took place on a beautiful April day, a day on which the sun shone down from a perfect, cloudless sky, bathing the ancient capital of Russia in golden light.

The dense crowds assembled in the Kremlin Square looked up at that serene and lovely sky, and accounted it an omen for the new reign. Thank God for a Czar, they said among themselves; after fifty years of feminine rule, it would be good to have a man upon the throne. And a good man, by all accounts, a friend to the people, whose first thought had been the release of all his mother's prisoners, and who had delighted his subjects by filling the gaols and the hovels in Siberia with their former oppressors.

The people approved his morals also; remembering the scandals of Catherine's notorious amours, Paul's placid wife and unassuming mistress proved him a model of respectability.

On that day when he was crowned in the magnificent Cathedral of the Assumption, the citizens of Moscow cheered and waved with unaffected joy, delighted by the spectacle, the ranks of Guards in their gorgeous uniforms, the colour and dignity of the royal procession which passed down the Beautiful Staircase out of the Kremlin buildings on its way to the cathedral.

The Metropolitan of Novgorod and St. Petersburg performed the rite and placed the blazing diamond crown upon the head of Catherine's son. It was a moment of inexpressible solemnity; great clouds of sweet-scented incense rose to the distant roof, thousands of candles illumined the vast interior of the church and gleamed on the jewels and orders of the massed congregation.

The Metropolitan and his attendant priests stood on the steps of the High Altar, facing the still, lonely figure of the Emperor of all the Russias.

At the climax of the ceremony a deep flush rose in Paul's face, disguising the weariness and pallor; his head lifted proudly under the weight of the Imperial Crown and for all his lack of height his figure seemed to gain in stature and in dignity. The heavy velvet mantle, thickly embroidered with gold and lined with ermine, flowed down from his broad shoulders, and his breast was covered with glittering orders. A few yards behind him Marie Feodorovna waited, bearing the weight of her robes and the stifling, scented atmosphere with no sign of outward strain. The music, the ritual and significance of the occasion did not move her as it did Paul; unlike him she felt no surge of emotion, no mystical sensation of a great trust received and a sacred duty undertaken. She experienced a strong degree of satisfaction, of complacence in the assumption of her rôle as Consort, and moving from one tired foot to the other, regretted the Slavic passion for prolonged religious services. The knowledge that Paul was rigid in a kind of ecstasy would have amazed and horrified her. In all their years of married life, Marie had never understood him, never divined the loneliness and inferiority that his fierce exterior concealed.

As his love for Katya Nelidoff had been a mystery to her, too, so would she fail to grasp his reverence and fanaticism for the rôle which God had appointed him to play in the affairs of men.

When the ceremony was completed, the anointed Czar's special ukase was read out. In it Paul made the throne hereditary, ordering that from that day forward it should pass to the eldest son of the ruler on his father's death.

The Grand Duke Alexander listened with no trace of expression on his handsome face, realizing that Paul was trying to stabilize the succession and put an end to the system of revolution and bloodshed by which the Crown of Russia usually devolved from one Czar to the next.

He saw his mother's eyes upon him and knew that in her ignorance she was pleased, thinking this proclamation to be a sign of goodwill between the father and the son, whereas it only conjured up a vista of long years spent waiting for what he already coveted so fiercely.

His opaque blue gaze considered his father and grudgingly accorded him another twenty years of life as it acknowledged the strength of those limbs and remembered Paul's horseman-ship and physical power.

Headaches would not kill him, neither would melancholy and with all his heart Alexander cursed the God who had seen fit to inflict his hated parent with a disease that was not mortal.

His bitter reflections were disturbed by the reading of another ukase, and at the first sentences his acute wits sharpened and began to concentrate on every word.

As a token of his love for them, the Czar made a special pronouncement for the protection of his people. At the same time he restrained his nobility still further.

The ukase forbade landlords to work their serfs for more than three days in a week and ordered that they must be allowed to rest on Sunday.

Someone coughed in the congregation, and Paul's eyes scanned the packed rows of men and women with an angry stare that produced a paralysed silence. Then he gave the signal to end the service and the coronation procession re-formed. Walking back to the Kremlin, blinking in the brilliant sunshine, the Grand Duke followed the great gilded canopy which sheltered the sovereign, and repeated the amazing order to himself.

The serfs were not to be slave-driven any longer; and their masters, whose wealth was derived from the mass labour of these unfortunates, were destined to lose part of their income in order to please the insane humanity of the new Czar. . . .

"He's mad," the Grand Duke decided. "Only a lunatic would have made such a decree . . . the serfs . . . God in Heaven! No one in their senses would intervene on behalf of those animals and alienate every owner in the kingdom!"

As he visualized popular reaction to the ukase, Alexander's step grew light, and lighter still his heart, so that when he passed into the Kremlin in his father's wake, observers saw that he was smiling.

·   ·   ·   ·   ·

That evening the new Czar received the homage of his subjects. The audience took place in the historic Granovitia Palata in the Kremlin, and it was there in the setting of dark Byzantine splendour that Paul of Russia and the woman whose love affair with her Czar was to blaze like a meteor through his short reign, saw each other for the first time.

·   ·   ·   ·   ·

She stood in a line of hundreds of Court ladies ranged against one side of the hall, the wives and daughters of the nobility whose men were ranked on the opposite side of the great room, leaving a wide pathway to the raised crimson throne where the Czar would take his place.

When Paul entered she curtsied to the ground with the rest, her head lowered until he passed, so that her first sight was of his back, and the edge of his long robes trailing the floor. When he was seated she looked quickly up, and in the instant while she gazed upon his face her eyes suddenly flashed with excitement, retaining a picture of a stern, exalted countenance, of a level, searching gaze, and a fine strong hand—a single monster sapphire on the index finger—being extended for the kiss of homage.

"He is indeed a king," she thought, and only added as an afterthought that he was ugly.

When her turn came to be presented she sank down before the throne in an obeisance of perfect grace, her white satin skirts spreading on the ground like the petals of some shining flower, bending her supple body until her forehead almost touched the step of the dais, while the Court Chamberlain announced her name.

"Mlle. Lapoukhine!"

She raised her head and looked into his face, then her small fingers lifted the hand he offered her and she touched it reverently with her lips.

For a long moment Paul Petrovitch stared down at her as she knelt at his feet, stared with the expression of a man who sees the dead raised from the grave, returning not as a pallid corpse but warm-blooded and vivid with life.

His lips moved several times, but no sound came, until at last a hoarse whisper of astonishment escaped him, reaching the ears of the Empress who was seated on a lower level of the dais.

"Natalie. . . ."

Instantly Marie started, and looked more closely at the girl who should have long since passed to her and left the Czar.

Paul gazed at her as if bewitched, gazed into a perfect face of exquisite features and complexion, noticed a red, trembling mouth and the line of a delicate neck upon which her beautiful dark head was balanced like the bloom of a black rose.

Natalie . . . Natalie Alexeievna. . . . He repeated the name as he looked at her, aware that no rage rose in him at the resemblance, only a painful stabbing ache, as if some deep and dreadful wound had just reopened. Her movements, the proportions of her body, the bone formation of her oval face, with the straight nose and thin dark brows were almost identical with those of the woman he had loved and lost so many years ago.

"What is your name, Mademoiselle?" he asked her, and his voice shook.

"Anna Petrovna Lapoukhine, your Imperial Majesty."

Her answer broke the spell. The voice was not Natalie's; it was low-pitched, devoid of the distinctive German intonation. And then he realized that her eyes were not like Natalie's either.

They were as black as jet, huge and brilliant, vividly expressive.

"You may go, Mademoiselle," he said slowly, aware that his wife was staring at the girl and that a long line of courtiers waited for her place before the throne.

He could never remember who came after her, for that dark, lovely face was superimposed upon his vision long after his eyes had followed the small, graceful figure in the dress of bridal white and seen her vanish into the background of the crowded hall.

"Anna Petrovna. . . ." The words spoken in that deep-toned voice echoed in his brain, until he might have fancied that she whispered in his ear, and during the State banquet which ended the day of his coronation, Paul Petrovitch searched the long tables for another sight of her.

But he looked in vain; his head ached with the dull, threatening pain that turned to stabs of searing agony, and his tired eyes focused in a futile attempt to distinguish one face among so many hundreds, until they blurred and he succumbed to weariness, staring unseeing at the golden tableware spread out on the table before him, remembering another feast now long forgotten.

Then Natalie Alexeievna sat beside him, instead of his plump Empress Consort, and Catherine watched from the raised chair, under the golden eagle arms of Russia, which he now occupied. . . . Not in this vaulted chamber, with the frescoed walls, but in the gracious, glittering banqueting hall of the Winter Palace. . . . And Natalie, Natalie dressed in white like that other, who had appeared before him for the first time that night and yet personified an image that had never left his heart.

He knew that Marie Feodorovna watched him, and that her gaze was anxious, and he suddenly divined the motives which impelled her to defend her former enemy Katya Nelidoff, forcing upon him a relationship withering in disappointment and distrust, and that after that evening he would never, never want again. And, understanding, he was angry.

When the banquet had ended and he lay alone in the carved bed in the State apartment of the Kremlin, he felt more at peace; the throbbing in his head was a monotonous, dull pain, familiar enough to be borne patiently, and the low-ceilinged, ancient room enclosed him with an atmosphere at once alien and harmonious.

It was a sombre, magnificent room, with faded red walls trellised with golden mosaic and frescoed stories of the life of Christ, a room impregnated with memories of the past and into which the brittle, rational eighteenth century had never penetrated. A long line of Russian monarchs had slept within the wooden walls. Michael, the first of all the Romanovs, had lain where Paul lay, on the night following his coronation, and after him had come the tyrants and usurpers, the puppets and martyrs, who had since occupied the Russian throne.

The immense, airy palaces of Petersburg and Tsarskoë Selo reflected nothing of this brooding, ancient spirit; their pastel colouring, the profusion of bright gilt and coloured marbles, the gracious gardens, wore a façade of borrowed culture, a tribute to the feminine taste of nearly fifty years of female autocrats, who sought to escape the fact of their country's barbarism and their own, by living in the surroundings of the distant West.

Now one of the most tragic and ill-starred of all the Czars of Holy Russia turned in the old four-poster bed, remembering the young and lovely face of his new subject, and realized in triumphant hope that the limitless power accorded him in matters relating to the State extended to his private life as well.

.   .   .   .   .

At four in the morning of what was now the sixteenth of

April, the wife and daughter of the Senator Peter Lapoukhine were arguing fiercely.

The house in Tverskaia Street was a handsome building, for the family were wealthy as well as well-born, and the bedroom where Anna Lapoukhine and her step-mother were quarrelling was large and luxuriously furnished.

Madame Lapoukhine was a stubborn woman, hard-eyed and calculating, impervious to anything but greed and the embraces of her lover, an officer of the Moscow garrison.

Her domination of the household was unquestioned, the Senator obeyed her and took care to keep in her good graces. But Anna Petrovna was far from tractable.

"I've told you," Madame repeated angrily. "Your father has forbidden you to go to Court again!"

"You mean you've ordered him to forbid me!"

Anna glared at her step-mother, her beautiful face dark with temper.

The delicate grace which had so captivated Paul masked a fierce temperament, a bold tongue and a passion for taking risks. The firm mouth and obstinate chin revealed these traits, coupled with the liquid black eyes that could harden and blaze if once her will was crossed.

"You stopped me," she repeated. "You fool of a woman . . . didn't you see how the Czar looked at me?"

"Oh, I saw," Madame retorted. "And I also saw how the Empress looked at you while you knelt there, displaying yourself to her husband. . . . Do you suppose that by to-morrow he'll remember you exist?"

"Yes!" her step-daughter interrupted, stung by the jibe.

"You flatter yourself, Anna. Just because a few men here in Moscow lose their heads over you, you think the Emperor himself will do the same! Why, you foolish creature, the Empress Marie would dispose of you before he ever reached you! I was watching her and I've no mind to end my days in some fortress because the Czar might speak a few words to you and then forget about you. And I've heard that she's well content with this plain Nelidoff who gives her no trouble. What do you think would befall anyone who tried to upset that arrangement? The Czar would have to send for you personally before it would be safe."

"How do you know he wouldn't?" Anna asked her, and Madame Lapoukhine shrugged.

"If he did, that changes everything," she admitted and a sudden vision of the honours which must fall to the family of a royal favourite made her eyes shine.

"But the risk is too great. You're to stay at home, Anna. He leaves for Petersburg in a few days."

Anna Petrovna turned away from her, ashamed of the tears of disappointment that filled her eyes, feeling a sense of loss that was as sharp as a physical pain at the reminder that in a short time that strange, ugly, fascinating man would be hundreds of miles away.

"Very well," she said, and bit her lip to stem the tears until she might shed them in private.

"But I know one thing, Madame. He'll come back!"

But the Senator's wife was not listening, she was half-way through the door, satisfied, too relieved by the capitulation to heed the prophecy.

.   .   .   .   .

A fortnight after his coronation, Paul Petrovitch returned to Petersburg, and he made the long journey through cheering crowds and decorated towns in a mood of restless discontent. The Empress, who travelled with him, noted his humour and accurately guessed the cause.

No one was more thankful than the complacent, yet watchful wife when the Imperial Court left Moscow without the reappearance of that disturbing daughter of the Senator Lapoukhine. Marie had passed her days in dread of a meeting between Paul and the brazen, beautiful creature, whose resemblance to the Grand Duchess Natalie had been affirmed by her spies.

Having abandoned her pride and condoned the adultery with Katya Nelidoff, Marie was determined to keep the advantages which she had won by making Paul's mistress her protégée. And she thanked God that the momentary threat to her security seemed to have faded into the background.

Paul still remembered her and looked for her, the Empress noted that, and for a time she trembled lest he should send for the girl, but his diffidence with women and the endless State functions which filled every moment of their short stay averted that danger, until the day dawned when he left the Kremlin without having seen Anna Lapoukhine again.

While she smiled and conversed with him in her slow,

humourless way, Marie Feodorovna made a mental note to ensure that Mlle. Lapoukhine remained in Moscow and that any request from the family to come to Petersburg should be firmly refused.

But not only the Empress sensed his interest in the woman who had appeared before them all so briefly; another equally keen pair of eyes had observed it, and the man who had pandered to the need of the sick and lonely master of Gatchina by introducing Katya Nelidoff into his bed, now considered the problem of replacing her.

Koutaïssof's hopes of honour had been realized; in recognition of his many services, Paul had made him Master of the Wardrobe, a position carrying wealth and virtual control of the royal household.

While the Empress Consort journeyed back to Petersburg in the magnificent State coach, confident that the old order of domestic life at Petersburg would be resumed, Paul's former valet was certain that after that visit to Moscow the Nelidoff's reign could be ended with one decisive blow, and with her would crash the influence of the Empress and the uneasy truce concluded with her eldest son.

A new mistress was all the Gatchina faction needed in order to entrench itself in positions of unrivalled power, protected by a grateful Emperor. And should the influence of the woman selected to amuse Paul Petrovitch become too strong or deviate from the interests of her sponsors, why then she could be served as they meant to serve the Nelidoff. . . .

Koutaïssof was already wondering which fortress to recommend as suitable for her retirement, when the Guards escort rode into the streets of Petersburg.

.   .   .   .   .

Soon after her return to Petersburg, the Empress sent for the Grand Duke Alexander.

Whenever possible, Marie spent part of the afternoon with her son, and those few hours of his companionship were the happiest of her day. The great personality of Catherine no longer stood in the way of Alexander's friendship with his mother, and though in fact he felt neither affection nor respect for her, he was shrewd enough to see the wisdom of weaning her completely away from his father.

He knew that she loved him, and he exerted all his charm to flatter her vanity and increase her affection.

He went to her rooms regularly, stifling his yawns at her self-conscious attempts at erudition, discussed music and art with apparent enthusiasm, carefully concealing the superior knowledge of most subjects which the brilliant mind and advanced standards of education of his dead grandmother had ensured for him. With his fair head bent over some book and his cheek almost touching hers, Alexander humoured his mother and afterwards extracted much information from her.

That day they abandoned Marie's heavy-footed pursuit of culture to discuss Paul's ukase on the succession.

"But I thought you'd be pleased," the Empress questioned, and Alexander shrugged slightly.

"Oh, Madame, how happy I'd be if only I believed it genuine!" he said sadly.

"But of course it's genuine," she insisted and linked her plump hand through his arm. "Why else would he do it? Whatever his faults, your father's never been deceitful. . . . Besides, I'm always interceding for you, Alex. I never cease to tell him how obedient and loyal you are!"

He kissed her hand affectionately.

"I know that, Mother. But I'm afraid, and I can't help it. I don't believe he means me to succeed, I can't believe it! Every man in power around him is an enemy to me . . . Rastopchine, Araktchéief, the Chancellor Bezborodko. . . . But I don't like to worry you," he whispered, hesitating, and the Empress bent and kissed his half-averted cheek, her heart breaking with love of him and fear for his safety.

"Tell me, my son," she said in German, lapsing into that mother tongue which showed her to be still a stranger in the land her husband ruled. Understanding that spoken symbolism, Alexander answered her in her own and Catherine's native language.

"I've heard rumours that he means to have me arrested in due course and name Constantine in my place. It seems he hates me because the late Empress talked of passing the throne to me and excluding him. You know I would never have agreed to that!" he protested, and he lied with such vehemence that he surprised himself. "But since then he doesn't trust me . . . and you've seen what happens to those who fall under suspicion, Mother."

Marie sat in silence, holding fast to her son. She stared over his head and frowned, fighting the terrible suspicions that he had aroused, and even as she struggled to refute her doubts, remembered the expression in her husband's eyes when they rested on the son she loved so dearly, remembered that queer vengeance which tormented Plato Zubov with the promise of friendship and forgiveness before it stripped him of all honour and sent him in exile across the world.

"What can we do, Alexander?" she whispered.

"I need a friend at Court to help me," he said to her, his eyes averted, making the suggestion as casually as he dared.

"What friend . . . what for?"

"Someone who might counteract the influence of my enemies . . . a man my father might listen to, instead of them. . . ."

"Do you know such a person?" Marie questioned doubtfully.

"I've been trying to think," he lied. "And I remember a certain nobleman who used to come to Court while the old Empress was alive. I liked him, Mother. He was very witty and amusing. I think my father might favour him if once he came to Petersburg. And I know he'd be a friend to me. . . ."

"Then who is he? I could try and send for him. If he really did ingratiate himself it would be invaluable. . . . Tell me the name, my dearest boy, and your mother will see what she can do."

The Grand Duke rose and kissed her fondly before answering.

"He used to be Governor of Riga until he fell into disgrace for some slight fault which I've forgotten. His name is Count von Pahlen. . . ."

With Marie's assurance that she would secure a pardon and a summons to Petersburg for the Count, Alexander left her and hurried to his own apartments, for he felt the need to be alone.

It was a need that came upon him whenever he committed some wrong that even his pliable conscience would not excuse; and with the guilt of his action weighing on his soul, he knelt in his oratory and prayed for hours on end, until a condoning peace was granted him.

On that day he fell asleep before the golden ikon, worn out

with a long repentant vigil, unable to admit even to his God
that he had sent for the man he hoped would help him kill his
father.

13

THE State apartments in the Kremlin were being swept and
aired, the priceless furniture and pictures cleaned, while an
army of servants prepared the banqueting hall and the ballroom for a reception to which all Moscow had been invited.

They had talked of nothing else for weeks, consumed by
curiosity and delight at the prospect of a royal visit out of
season—until the inevitable rumour spread and gained ground.
The rumour became almost an accepted fact when it was
announced that the Empress Marie was remaining in Petersburg.

The Czar was coming to Moscow for reasons of his own, and
all those who had seen Anna Petrovna Lapoukhine's presenta-
tion recalled it and decided that they knew precisely what his
reasons were.

And for once, the gossips were correct in their assumption.

For months on end, whether engaged in governing his
country or walking in the gardens with the subdued, silent
Katya Nelidoff, the image of Anna Lapoukhine kept recurring
in Paul's mind. For a long period he fought against it, reminding himself that immorality had never appealed to him, and
then retreated in the face of his own argument as his restless
senses stung him and renewed their clamour. It was too late,
he insisted, disturbed by the discontent that possessed him;
had she appeared at Court a second time, or come to Petersburg, he might have acted, but the promptings of his heart
were only folly, dictated by imagination.

When he expressed these sentiments to Koutaïssof, the confidant smiled and shook his head.

It was never too late for the sovereign to have his will, he
murmured, unconsciously echoing his master's thoughts on the
night after his coronation. The Czar could command the lady
to attend at Court . . . perhaps if he saw her, his longing

might disappear. If it did not, why then it could be satisfied.

Paul listened, struggling against an overwhelming temptation to use his tremendous power and send the order out to Moscow, an order that no one would dare disobey. Then he frowned and shook his head. That was the tyrant's way, he answered, and it would not do to humiliate the Empress publicly.

But for these objections Koutaïssof had a ready answer. If the Czar went to Moscow, he suggested, he could see Mlle. Lapoukhine and make his choice. Provided that the Empress Marie stayed in Petersburg. With Mlle. Nelidoff, of course, he added quickly.

The next day couriers set out for Moscow, bringing the news of the Czar's visit, and carrying an invitation to the Senator Lapoukhine to attend with his family.

Anna Petrovna's angry prophecy had been fulfilled at last, but when they told her she was strangely silent. For once her spirited tongue refrained from comment, from expressions of hope or triumph. Instead she retired to her room, and shaken by some intuition of what her brief, momentous future held in store, she went upon her knees and prayed.

The Emperor's arrival was marked by a ball, and Paul, who loved uniform and despised elaborate costumes, dressed with unusual magnificence that night. Koutaïssof still attended him, performing the humble duties of valet, suggesting this choice of colour or that style of wig, watching his master with cunning eyes, divining the meaning of that dissatisfied, unhappy glance that always came to rest upon the mirrored reflection of an ugliness that no amount of jewels or lace could minimize.

What course would Paul's life have taken had he been born a handsome man, Koutaïssof wondered idly, a man that women could have loved and wanted for himself, instead of submitting to the lure of power and a great crown.

His mother had hated him for his resemblance to that other ugly man, the wretched Peter; his first wife had betrayed him, his second bore with him; and as for the Nelidoff . . . pah! Koutaïssof spat contemptuously. The shy, gentle creature, whose timid virginity had exerted a certain appeal, was now a sallow, downcast woman of forty years; the soft brown eyes were dim and red with frequent weeping and she clung to the good-natured toleration of the Empress to keep her near

her lover. Her former lover, he amended, for he knew that
for months past Paul had not gone to her bed.

But as he followed Paul into the ballroom he was well
content, satisfied that the Nelidoff was about to be ruined and
discarded, and that by providing his master with the object of
his desire, yet more power and favour would accrue to him.
Everything now depended on the cleverness of Anna
Lapoukhine.

.   .   .   .   .

They saw each other at almost the same moment.

Paul's searching eager eyes rested on her where she stood,
placed in a prominent position among the ladies of the Court,
and immediately the blood rushed into his face. Even as
he looked she turned and saw him, and her olive skin flushed
with an emotion the twin of his own. Then she sank down
in a curtsy, followed by the glittering ranks of women, and
he passed down the ballroom, acknowledging his subjects,
smiling and nodding to those particularly favoured, willing
himself to continue to the end of the great floor, without turning and sending for her where she waited, feeling her eyes
on his back as if their gaze were burning him.

Koutaïssof had talked of disappointment, and he himself
had dreaded it, afraid that the woman in his mind was less
beautiful and less dreadfully familiar than the creature of
flesh and blood that he had only once beheld. But now that
doubt was answered.

The likeness to Natalie Alexeievna was still there, but it
was a shadow, strong enough to wound but not repel, and
overlaid with a physical loveliness and a sensuous appeal so
strong that it was almost tangible.

Deliberately he hesitated, sipping wine and talking perfunc-
torily to a group of dignitaries, while his hundreds of guests
waited for his signal to begin the ball.

After some minutes he turned to a gentleman-in-waiting
who stood near.

"Ask Mlle. Lapoukhine to come here."

He saw her approaching without appearing to observe her
and managed to drain his wine goblet and set it down carelessly before he turned and found her facing him.

She curtsied, and the flower simile recurred to him as on
the first night that he saw her.

By this time the bloom was red. She wore a blood red Court gown scattered with some crimson stone, not rubies, he thought mechanically, and the wish to hang Catherine's gorgeous set of gems round that narrow, fragile throat flashed through his mind, as he acknowledged that his mother's favourite colour and therefore the one which most offended him, only enhanced the kneeling woman's beauty in his eyes.

" Mademoiselle, will you do me the honour of dancing with me? "

" The honour is mine, your Majesty."

He made a movement and the orchestra in the gallery began to play the first bars of a minuet. The great ballroom floor was empty, the guests were waiting for the Czar to lead and open the ball with the lady on whom he thus bestowed an honour usually reserved for Princesses of royal blood. He bowed to her, bowed deeply and with a grace surprising in one so muscular, and she placed the tips of her fingers on his sleeve and followed him on to the wide, polished floor, aware that hundreds of eyes were fixed on them in curiosity and envy.

For all her self-assurance she was nervous, the hand holding his in the set figures of the dance was trembling slightly; the phrases of flattery and wit so carefully composed and painfully rehearsed in weeks of waiting now deserted her, and while they danced he too was silent. Only his eyes betrayed him, for they never left her face.

" My compliments, Mademoiselle," he said gravely, " you dance excellently."

" Thank you, Sire."

Since she was fourteen years old, men had courted and complimented her and long before Paul's eyes beheld her Anna Lapoukhine had learnt the power and value of her own attractions.

No one had succeeded in subduing her spirits or possessing her body—for it suited her better to be no man's mistress and all men's desire—until a husband or protector of suitable means secured her favour.

But at that moment, confronted with the opportunity of every ambitious woman's dreams, Anna Petrovna's cleverness deserted her.

As a child she had heard of the Empress Catherine's son, listening to the adult gossip which described a distant palace named Gatchina where deeds of terrible ferocity were taking place; and as a young woman she had witnessed the wave of panic that followed his accession, spreading from Petersburg to Moscow, where the local nobility spent weeks in dread of what the Emperor Paul would do on his assumption of supreme power.

In company with everyone else, she had expected a cruel tyrant, and found that when she knelt before him she felt only awe and fascination.

Since that first meeting she had been fascinated by him, his ugly tragic face pursued her in dreams and the memory of his expression when he looked on her made her tremble with an emotion that she could not analyse.

Ambition, recklessness and egotism drew her to him in his absence and these sentiments she understood; but it was another element that urged her to defend him with all the asperity of a notoriously sharp tongue when those who fawned upon him to his face dubbed him a tyrant when his back was turned.

And now, when the object of her plans and fancies held her fingers in his own and danced the leisured figures of the minuet, she only followed him and trembled, her wit and charm dried up into a silence that she could not break.

Yet there was no fear in her heart, and she knew this, knew that this man, whose power could take from her by force what others pleaded for in vain, was shy in his pursuit and strangely humble.

He has been hurt, she thought quickly, and remembered an old half-forgotten legend of his first wife and a lover. . . .

When the minuet ended he turned to her and offered his arm.

"Will you take some wine with me, Mademoiselle?" he asked her and she nodded, thanking him with a sweet gravity that would have astonished those who knew her.

He ordered a chair to be set for her, and then sat down himself indicating that he wished to speak to Mlle. Lapoukhine without interruption.

Remembering the plain, uncertain Catherine Nelidoff, whose path to Imperial favour had begun on the platonic level of nurse and comforter, Koutaïssof observed Anna Lapoukhine and smiled.

She was extraordinarily beautiful, he admitted, his greedy

eyes considering the exquisite face upturned to Paul; and following the lines of her figure, he noted the pale perfect bosom and the narrow waist that a man's hands could measure.

His spies termed her hot tempered, wilful and shrewish, and for a moment his manhood regretted that so much spirit and potential pleasure should fall into the possession of a man who would never know how to tame the one and make the best use of the other. . . .

For all his innate fear of Paul, Koutaïssof permitted himself the luxury of a secret contempt; his cunning had divined Paul's weakness years before, and he, whose use for women began and ended with the satisfaction of his lust, viewed the Czar's need of affection with cynical scorn.

As successor to that incarnation of sentimental virtue Katya Nelidoff, his master had chosen a black-haired hussy, attracted by some fancy that recalled the passion of his unhappy marriage to an unfaithful slut, and with his gutter estimates of all human values, Koutaïssof judged her reign would last till she was found in bed with someone else.

But for once his calculation erred.

Anna Lapoukhine sat quietly, talking to the man already known as the Death's Head Czar, and found him gentle, unassuming and, despite his dignity, pathetic in a way that made her long to give him tangible comfort.

The impulse to touch his hand, to press her lips to that disfigured left cheek, was so strong that her eyes filled with tears, and the struggling, half-acknowledged feeling which had stirred in her that night so many months ago flooded her heart in a torrent before which ambition, hauteur and self-interest were torn up and swept away.

He had given her nothing and promised nothing, but she, who had reserved herself for wealth and power, sat at his side and fell in love with him, eager to offer rather than receive, aware that had he been the poorest and most unimportant man in Russia, the lack of ceremony would have made her surrender all the sweeter.

"Why have you never come to Petersburg?" he asked her.

"My father's duties keep him here, Sire."

For a moment Paul's hand strayed to his cravat in the old nervous gesture.

"I could give him a post in the capital, if you would like

to visit Petersburg," he said, and seeing that she hesitated, his confidence began to waver.

"Understand me, Mademoiselle Anna, I do not command," he told her simply. "Only come if you wish. . . ."

"I do wish, Sire . . . with all my heart! "

"Then I am very happy," he said, and he turned the great sapphire in and out upon his finger; it was a trick he often used in order to conceal that his hands shook. . . .

"It would please me very much to present you with what you need for the long journey," he added.

Anna Petrovna looked at him and smiled for the first time, and the gentleness of her expression softened her lovely mouth and bold black eyes, endowing her with something more than beauty.

"I need nothing, Sire, except to be near you. But I fear my family will prove very greedy. . . ."

"They shall have whatever they ask. And I repeat, you have only to express a wish and I will see it gratified . . . it would please me very much if I could grant you something."

"You can," she whispered. "Let me be near you here in Moscow."

.   .   .   .   .

The time spent in Moscow was the happiest Paul Petrovitch had known for almost twenty years, and to those who knew him he seemed a man transformed. Anna Lapoukhine, already his acknowledged mistress, was as gay as she was beautiful; no sign of melancholy was allowed to develop into moods or depression once her sharp eyes detected it, and Paul was teased, and caressed into laughter, until he took her in his arms in token of capitulation. From the moment of their first illicit meeting after the Kremlin ball, a meeting contrived by Koutaïssof on the Czar's instructions, a fierce mutual passion had flared up between them, and the difference in age and temperament dissolved before the intensity of their desire for one another.

Whatever Paul's dignity in public, or the hauteur and wilfulness of Anna Petrovna, who was making scores of powerful enemies, the moment the doors of the Imperial suite closed behind them, they forgot everything but the need to rush into each other's arms, and there acknowledge that the longing had tormented them all day.

He was bewitched sensually, fascinated by her boldness with others and her unfailing tenderness with him, gratified by her refusal to take money and mystified by the contradiction when she greeted the gift of some of Catherine Alexeievna's marvellous jewels by dancing round the room with pleasure.

And sometimes, when she was quiet, and thought herself unobserved, the memory of the woman she resembled so much in face and yet differed from so sharply in character, returned to him as he watched her features in repose, so that the pain of that old heartbreak stabbed at him and made him wonder why he didn't hate her.

But for some strange reason it only served to increase his love and sometimes an odd fancy entered his head that Natalie had come back to pay her debt and erase the wrong she had done him, content to be a mistress whose pedestal was no higher than her Emperor's bed. . . .

And what a mistress she had proved to be!

"I am the happiest of men," he told Koutaïssof. "Come, help me think of something else to give her. . . ."

"Jewels, Sire," the Turk murmured, and his master shook his head.

"I've given her my mother's rubies; she shall have the rest later, when we get to Petersburg. No, something different. Think, man, think. . . ."

Koutaïssof wetted his lips; it was the only sign of nervousness he ever gave, but every instinct warned him that now was the moment to complete the plan worked out by Rastopchine and himself, with Araktchéief's sanction.

"If I may suggest, Sire, your best gift to the lady would be Mlle. Nelidoff's suite in the Winter Palace. . . ."

Paul turned and stared at him, his blue eyes narrowing, all his good humour gone.

"What do you mean by that?"

But the Turk's courage held and he continued.

"It may be a little difficult for Mlle. Anna with the Empress, and I venture to suggest—most humbly, Sire—that you remove the Nelidoff to some convenient place before Mademoiselle arrives in the capital. That should resign Her Majesty and convince the lady that you do not intend to abandon her. . . . I am sure, Sire, that she would prefer not to find Mlle. Nelidoff still in Petersburg."

It was a daring move, but at the same time insinuating and

shrewd. Paul's heart was soft where a weeping woman was
concerned, even an outworn mistress might prove troublesome
if her pleas were fortified by tears and the entreaties of that
pompous, pandering wife. . . . He had been tired of Catherine
Nelidoff for countless months, yet out of sentiment he kept
her in her old estate. Therefore it was imperative to place
her out of sight and reach, to prevail upon the Czar that it
was necessary to be cruel and forceful in order to be
kind. . . .

"Why don't you send her to a convent?" the Turk
whispered.

But Paul scarcely listened; instead he pictured Katya Nelidoff waiting in the Winter Palace, prepared by advance
rumours for the coming of a young and lovely rival, and
envisaged the bitter struggle for his favours which Marie
Feodorovna would force on the unhappy woman. Whatever
his past feeling for her, it was irrevocably dead, blighted by
doubt of her motives, by an utter satiation of her body that
he only fully realized since the advent of Anna Petrovna into
his life.

She must go, he decided, and go before his adored Anna
could be angered by the sight of her; and he appeased his
conscience with the promise that she should have all the
money, luxury and favours she desired to soften her dismissal.

And his wife, that pious procuress of dubious loyalty . . .
she should accept Anna Lapoukhine and do as she was told, or
else prepare to be got rid of in her turn. . . .

.   .   .   .   .

The day that Catherine Nelidoff left Petersburg, the Empress
and her eldest son were sitting together in her rooms as usual.

Marie had been weeping; even her stolid, calculating nature
had been stirred by the sight of her old enemy and recent
ally going into exile. She had been very brave, the Empress
admitted to her curious son. She had not railed or wept, but
her acceptance of Paul's gently worded order reminded Marie
of a woman hearing the sentence of her death pronounced.
And in that same, listless obedience, his mistress and companion of ten years packed her possessions and departed, her
narrow shoulders bowed, and a message of loving submission
to the Emperor on her lips.

She travelled to the Löhde Fortress, where magnificent apartments in the palace buildings were prepared for her, equipped with every luxury and treasure that the orders of the Emperor could devise; she resided there in freedom, wealthy and assured of his protection, and until her voluntary retirement to the convent of her distant youth, Catherine Nelidoff slept in a soft gilded bed, a few hundred yards from the fetid cell which Catherine Alexeievna's will had designated as the tomb of her son Paul.

.　　.　　.　　.　　.

The Emperor did not return to Petersburg immediately. He went on manœuvres, an innovation detested by the Russian army and abhorred by the guards regiments whose former indolence and inefficiency were being remedied by exile and the knout. Then he visited Kazan.

In the meantime the Lapoukhines prepared to move to the capital, and while Anna controlled her impatient heart and senses as calmly as she could in the interval, Paul's wife and eldest son sat in Petersburg and trembled.

"What a misfortune!" Marie Feodorovna raved, twisting her plump hands in despair, while the impenetrable Alexander listened. "This woman Lapoukhine is most undesirable! I've heard all kinds of disquieting things about her. They say she's arrogant and vain, that her family are swallowing money and honours as fast as your father bestows them . . . and I'm told he's completely under her sway. Oh, my God, Alexis, why couldn't he have remained with the Nelidoff!"

Alexander put his arm round her unwillingly, somehow revolted by the lack of pride in his mother that bewailed her late rival so openly.

The fact that most of the wretched Marie's anxiety was actuated by her fear for him counted for nothing with her son.

"I should never have written that letter forbidding the creature to come here, after Katya left," the Empress mourned, "it made your father so angry!"

"It *was* foolish," Alexander agreed coldly, knowing that the tactless impulse had made an enemy of this powerful new mistress and infuriated her royal protector.

"But I did it for you, Alex! Nelidoff was your friend as well as mine. . . . I didn't want a different influence being exerted over the Czar. Supposing this woman dislikes you, my dearest boy? Supposing your enemies, Rastopchine and that vile Araktchéief, bribe her to work against you ... Oh, merciful God! Even I mightn't be able to protect you then! "

The Empress had begun to weep, and her son, always the victim of surface emotion, wiped his own eyes.

" Whatever my father does, my conscience is clear," he said. " But I'm not really frightened for myself. Dear Mother, have you never thought that if this Anna Lapoukhine is as beautiful, and my father is as infatuated, as they say, he might end up by divorcing you and marrying her? "

Marie Feodorovna's face turned deadly white for a moment, then a reserve of stolid German courage aided her and she released herself from her son's treacherous embrace and began to walk up and down.

" No, I had never thought of that," she admitted. " Not even in the worst days, when he was so ill at Gatchina and so strange, and so violent over that miserable Nelidoff, I never thought he'd put me away if he came to the throne."

" But you didn't expect him to succeed, did you, Mother? " the Grand Duke interrupted softly, drawing the contrast between the wish of a powerless and unpopular Czarevitch, and an omnipotent and decidedly self-willed Czar.

" No, but he has, and *everything's* been upset since he quarrelled with Katya. But there's one thing I want you to know, my son," she said, and stood facing him, her solid jaw set in determination. " Whatever happens, nothing shall harm *you*. Without me, you'd be powerless here, but if I have to kneel to this slut he's bringing back from Moscow, I'll try and secure her good offices and keep my place as Empress. You can be assured of that! "

" I don't want you to humiliate yourself, Mother," he whispered, content to despise her methods and take advantage of the results obtained by them at the same time.

" I know that," she told him, returning to his side and linking her arm through his.

" But you can leave all that to me, Alexis. Promise me you won't worry, my dear boy. Paul won't get rid of me; I'll always be here to speak for you and safeguard your interests. I'll give this Lapoukhine presents and flatter her; she'll be complimented, you'll see! And even if ... if anything should go wrong with your father and myself, *you* must give me your word that you'll be sensible and not endanger yourself in my defence!

"I can bear anything, providing I know that you, my own darling son, are safe and in friendship with the Emperor!"

It was a vow he knew she meant to keep, but his only true reactions were a confusion of contempt for the stupidity which imagined it could patronize a woman of this Anna Lapoukhine's mettle, genuine fear lest his threat to his mother might come to pass and his most devoted advocate and spy be enclosed in some convent where she could no longer help him, anxiety for himself as usual, and the knowledge that he had succeeded in frightening the Empress even more deeply than he had hoped.

She was very much afraid and he knew it, despite her phlegmatic show of courage and her nauseating, self-sacrificing mother love. The idea that Paul might decide to get rid of her and marry someone else had terrified her on her son's account and her own to such an extent that Alexander counted on it to undermine whatever scruples she still possessed where the life of her husband was concerned.

That was the real purpose of his words to her that day; it had been his purpose all the time. He was deliberately frightening her, tearing her with anxiety and suspicion and gradually sowing the seeds of acquiescence to the plan which had been formed by Catherine Alexeievna and which her grandson was already plotting to put into practice.

His schedule differed from the old Empress's in only one respect. There would be no outward show of abdications, no lull while Paul's blood was shed in prison, after the palace revolution had removed him from the throne.

He must be struck down by sudden death, killed with the savagery inspired by fear before a hand could be raised to save him. Only then could his son hope to take his crown in safety.

And in that year of 1798, just eighteen months after Paul's accession to the throne, the last phase of his destiny opened with the arrival in Petersburg of Count von Pahlen.

Marie's request, made before the Czar left for Moscow to seek out Anna Lapoukhine, had been carelessly granted. If the former Governor of Riga was really sorry for his fault, then he might come to the capital and be restored to favour. So Paul decided, his mind distracted by thoughts of his

journey, and by longing for the woman he had dreamed of
and desired for months; he was ready to please Marie Feodorovna, since he intended further infidelity; and thereby opened
the door to the man Alexander hoped to cast in the assassin's
rôle.

Soon after his return from Kazan, the Emperor held an
evening reception at the Winter Palace and it was there that
Paul Petrovitch and Count von Pahlen met for the first time.

The Count was a tall man, his bearing was erect, as befitted
a soldier, and his high colour and genial expression radiated
good humour and benevolence. These factors disguised the
thin nose, and the narrow-lipped mouth, flanked by two curv-
ing lines as if he laughed continuously. A fan of wrinkles, the
badge of a merry disposition, showed at the outer corner of
each flat blue eye, so that, looking into his eyes, an observer
failed to notice their opaqueness and the fact that, whatever
the Count's mood, no light or alteration was ever reflected in
their depths.

He bowed almost to the ground when brought before the
Emperor. Paul stared at him with the suspicion habitual to
him when viewing strangers, remembering his promise to his
wife, recalling also that this big, red-faced man had dared to
thwart him by showing honour to that Plato Zubov, whose
practices had engulfed the old Empress Catherine in ever-
lasting infamy.

For a moment a great rage stirred in Paul's breast, and an
instinctive, violent impulse to shout for the guard and watch
them drag the Count von Pahlen from his presence by the
heels. . . .

It was an unreasoning urge, born of some buried sense of
self-protection and it drained the colour from his face and
caused the pulsing under his left eye to leap under the skin.

But such impulses were only too familiar; for years now
they had assailed him, their intensity increasing. He had
learnt to know the signs of anger, the murmur in his head that
rose to a raving bellow of suspicion, of fear, of blind resentment that transformed the object, whether innocent or guilty,
into an enemy of half-remembered form that must be struck
down, exiled, beaten . . . for some crime he knew it had
committed but which his boiling brain could not distinguish
at that moment.

He knew the signs, and with all his strength he fought them, often successfully, or when disaster overtook him and an order of barbarity escaped his lips, seemingly spoken by another will than his, he hurried to the victim's rescue, horror and contrition in his heart.

The terrible events of the next two years hung in the balance while Paul struggled with his hysterical, sick predilections, and at last conquered them, pardoning the man who stood before him, in apparent humility, with hatred, vengeance and murder seething behind his flat little eyes.

"Welcome to Court, sir," he said at last, and the Count bowed again. Then he faced the Czar and smiled, making a good-humoured mask of honesty, portraying the bluff soldier, eager to be pardoned for a fault most bitterly regretted.

"I thank you, your Imperial Majesty. Due to my own folly I never hoped to hear those words. Now I can offer my old carcass in your service. . . ."

"The past is forgotten, Count."

Suddenly Paul's features relaxed, the last phrase, ringing with loyalty and gratitude, had touched him.

"I shall be glad of your service. And the carcass you mention appears young enough to render me many good years yet!"

"As you please, Sire. . . . But I'm close to sixty! However, I trust you'll find use for me, however humble. I am your servant, Sire, till death. . . ."

Paul stepped forward, motioning the Count to walk with him, and the royal entourage melted away to let them pass.

"I admire humility in a man of courage, Count von Pahlen, and I need faithful friends on whose loyalty I can rely. You've admitted your error, and I assure you you're completely forgiven. We will have some wine, Count, and you shall tell me about conditions in Riga."

They talked for nearly half an hour, and several times an astonished, watching Court heard the sound of Paul's infrequent laughter, followed by the Count's hearty uninhibited guffaw.

Meeting the Grand Duke Alexander's eye, Marie Feodorovna raised her brows and smiled encouragingly.

See, my son, what a good impression your Count Pahlen has already made upon the Czar! See, and take heart!

That was the message he read in her anxious, maternal gaze, and seeing his father's hated figure, topped by the

Count's superior height, he gained in confidence and hope, answering his foolish mother with the gentle smile that served to mask his true emotions.

Clever Pahlen! So bluff and honest featured; the very picture of a soldier, guileless, brave, obedient and jolly. His jollity was Alexander's marvel and abhorrence, for he knew it covered a nature of extraordinary ferocity and vindictiveness, capable of sustaining the most reckless and implacable resolve.

And as he watched him with the Czar, conversing with just the right mixture of ease, interest and respect, Alexander forgot his fears of Anna Lapoukhine and the reversal of Court influence that must follow in her train, for he felt that here, at Paul's side, stood a man capable of withstanding and conquering a dozen women, however beautiful, and in whom stiff, fanatical Araktchéief, and even the supremely wily Rastopchine, would meet their match at last.

That night, when the reception was ended, von Pahlen shut himself into the privacy of his bedroom in a friend's house on the Nevsky Prospect, and sat down heavily upon his bed.

No valet attended him, for he wished to be alone, to collect his thoughts and review his progress; the inconvenience of undressing himself was a small price to pay for valuable solitude at such a moment.

Once alone, his whole appearance had altered, changed as if a tight-fitting mask had been peeled off his face. The sharp features were hard and pinched with fatigue and his flat eyes considered the floor in unseeing, inward concentration.

The dominant trait in Pahlen's soul was pride, an egotism so intense and so insanely sensitive that, once wounded, he knew neither peace nor mercy until the insult was revenged.

The Emperor Paul had humiliated him; the abusive phrases of that fatal letter of dismissal still rang in his head, and the memory of his public disgrace and the amusement of his enemies in Riga reduced him to a state of apoplectic fury.

But with the cunning of the monomaniac, he hid his feelings, enjoying the popularity his genial manners won him, content to masquerade before an audience of dupes, until the moment to reveal his talent came. He played at honesty, practised his loud, ready laugh with the attention of an actor mastering the smallest details of a character, and meanwhile watched himself, fascinated and lost in self-admiration for the skill of the performance.

He thought of the Czar of all the Russias who had received him with such graciousness that night, and sneered with angry malice. He, who was tall, and in his youth judged rather handsome, pictured the short, ugly son of Catherine Alexei-evna, and raged in fresh resentment that the man who had humiliated him resembled nothing so much as a tragic monkey who had succeeded in frightening a lot of pampered courtiers with his bursts of temper. . . .

But the Empress Marie was afraid of him, Pahlen had seen that immediately, and his handsome son watched him with uneasy eyes. Even Plato, who for all his viciousness was no coward, spoke of the Czar as a man to be reckoned with.

Yet the stories of ruthless purging of corruption, coupled with disciplinary measures for the army and civilians which raised even Pahlen's far-from-squeamish brows, were contradicted by the tales of Paul's gentleness to his first wife and to the younger children Marie bore him.

What manner of man was he, the Count wondered, who struck so fiercely at the privileged aristocracy and passed extraordinary laws for the protection of the serfs. . . .

It was Pahlen's experience that in order to destroy an enemy it was necessary first to understand him, and then to become his friend. He had never failed to accomplish either object, and he had never hated any man as much or owed him such a debt of vengeance as he did Paul Petrovitch.

But it was also his experience that all rulers shared a common weakness; it was a lonely destiny, devoid of the comforts of disinterested affection for which all human beings longed. He was already sure that Paul was no exception, that the man who could win his friendship was the man who could eventually stab him in the back. And even if it took him years, Pahlen determined to fill both positions. Upon that resolution he fell asleep.

14

T H E Court was at Tsarskoë Selo when Anna Lapoukhine was reunited with her lover, and there, in one of the most beautiful of all the Imperial palaces, they enjoyed a brief, personal idyll.

The Empress had retired to Pavlovsk so as not to intrude upon her husband and his favourite, determined at all costs to herself to maintain friendly relations with Paul and to placate the new mistress.

No sooner had Anna arrived than she was hurried to her lover's rooms, accorded almost royal honours by the Court, who took care that their murmurs of admiration were audible to her ears. But Anna neither heard nor cared. Naturally cynical, suspicious of flattery, and ruthless in her treatment of self-seekers, she almost ran down the long corridors, longing to see Paul, to rush into his arms and repeat their own magic formula of passion and laughter, safely enclosed in the compass of the love which had flared up between them and in which opportunism, power, or notoriety had no place.

He embraced her immediately, forgetting his worries, the insistence of his English and Austrian allies that he should resume his mother's plan and go to war with France, the sudden hostility of his old friend Rastopchine to the likeable, trustworthy Pahlen, and a hundred other problems of varying importance.

The moment he held her against his heart, his burdens lifted, and as he kissed her eagerly, he noticed that even his persistent headache seemed to have lost its throbbing impetus. . . .

"Why were you so long? I've counted every second, waiting for you . . . Anna, Anna, my darling. . . ."

"They wouldn't hurry. My parents, I mean. I told them I'd leave without them in the end! Oh, Paul, I'm so pleased to be with you, so happy now, my lover! And I want to tell you everything and hear everything. . . . Oh, let me go, Pavlouchka," she whispered, "let me **take** off my travelling dress. . . ." And with the perversity that was so great a measure of her fascination, she locked her hands behind his head and clung to him, even as she asked to be released.

Later they dined together with the informality so rare and now so dear to Paul, and while she laughed, alternately tender and impudent, her conversation spiced with gossip and bouts of wicked mimicry of friend and enemy alike, he sat and watched her with indulgent, loving eyes, aware that whatever she said or did he only loved her more, that even her faults, her pride, her outspoken, often outrageous tongue, her impetuosity and her harsh judgments never affronted him as they would have done coming from any other woman.

"I've so many things to tell you, Anna," he said, when the meal was finished. "Come, sit by the fire with me."

When she did, it was the gauge of the difference of temperament and relationship between the two women, that she sat on her Emperor's knee, instead of adopting Katya Nelidoff's humble stance and resting on the floor at his feet.

"I'm not going to trouble you with politics," he began, and she knew that he longed to discuss them, and demanded details.

"I'm afraid I may have to go to war, Anna. War with France. I hoped for peace; Russia needs it badly, my mother and her advisers nearly bled the country white with conflict after conflict. . . . She was going to attack France when she died. Now England and Austria are pressing me to send troops against this French General Bonaparte."

"Is he so dangerous, then?" she questioned, and Paul laughed.

"Dangerous to them, my love. That's why they want war, quickly, to crush him before he gets too powerful. I intended to remain neutral, to act as mediator if necessary, but now I shall have to take action. He's not only beating the Italians out of the field, but his troops occupied that island in the Mediterranean . . . Malta, and the Knights have appealed to me for help!"

"And must you grant it?"

"I must. I gave my word."

"It's odd that you should be so honourable; honour doesn't worry me," she remarked, and he chided her with a smile.

"But don't be too honourable, my Paul. Believe me, it can be traded on, just like a weakness. At least if you must keep such standards, allow me a little vulgar wickedness on your behalf!"

"Would you commit a crime for me, Anna?" he asked, half mocking and half serious, playing with one of the great diamond earrings he had given her.

"I'd do anything for you.   And not just because I love you, but because to me you're the Czar, and therefore God's anointed.   Whatever we do and say to one another, though I lie in your arms and we make love, you're still sacred to me. You are still the Emperor.   Does that seem strange to you?"

"Do you believe in the Divine Destiny of Kings, then?" he asked her, astonished by that firm avowal which suddenly elevated him above the rôle of lover which he had occupied so happily.

"I do.   If you'd never even spoken to me, if I'd never seen you, I would consider myself bound to you in loyalty until death," she answered.

"Only the people have those feelings," he said grimly.   "Not the nobility.   Undue reverence for the sovereign never troubles them!   How many rulers have been assassinated, imprisoned and murdered in the last two hundred years?   What of my father?   He was God's anointed, as you say, but they shut him up and strangled him. . . . And they'd do the same with me," he added, and the pain began thudding in his head while he spoke.

"But I'm well guarded, my Anna.   I know them.   I've fought my enemies since I was old enough to understand, and I know how to protect myself.   I've got my own troops, loyal troops, not these indolent swine of the Guards who were never trained to do anything but make love to an old woman, in case my mother sent for one of them!   And Araktchéief . . . I'll present him to you to-morrow, he is loyal to me.   He protects me. They hate him, Anna, and by God they fear him!   Even as they hate and fear me.   No, my darling, don't contradict me, I know what my Court feels, I read their minds and see the treason written there, while they fawn and smile before my face!   They long to be rid of me; then they'd put Alexander on the throne and be able to idle, oppress and exploit the country as they've always done.   Anna, when I was Czarevitch I knew my mother wished to kill me.   I had food-tasters, guards, strong bolts fitted to my doors, every precaution to defeat assassination, and now, when I'm Czar, the danger still exists.   But I know how to circumvent it, I know how to ensure my safety until I've discovered the last of my enemies and broken them, until the whole core of this corrupt and evil Court is cleansed and pacified! "

" What will you do? " she asked him, her face grave and drawn with anxiety, as his dread infected her.

" These palaces aren't safe," he said. " There are too many staircases, passages, secret entries . . . the guard system is inadequate. I've given orders to demolish the old Summer Palace in Petersburg and for a new building to be erected on the site. A safe building, Anna, made of stone, encircled by a moat, fortified like a castle! There'll be no holes for murderers to hide in, no secret passages for traitors. It'll be impregnable! I've named it the Michael Palace."

Anna Lapoukhine leant her cheek against his hot forehead and said nothing, thinking of the fortress which was to stand in the beautiful city of Petersburg, and where the man she loved would live, surrounded by guards as if he were a prisoner rather than a king.

" My head aches, Anna," he said at last. " God knows, it's always aching," he added, half to himself, and he covered his eyes with his hand, shielding them from the soft candlelight.

She slipped off his knee, and blew out the offending tapers, watching him with anxious eyes, the rumours of his continuous illnesses returning to her mind.

For a moment she shivered, then her courage returned. If the conditions mentioned by Paul really existed, then she supported whatever methods could best combat them. And no one would prove as fierce and cruel as she, if the life of Paul Petrovitch was the price of mercy. . . .

" I'll send for your servants, you must go to bed . . ." she said quietly, and when Koutaïssof and the new valet answered her bell, she waited while they undressed the Czar and helped him into bed.

Finally, when Koutaïssof lingered, she dismissed him curtly. " Go! Leave His Majesty with me! "

Then she came to her lover's side, and drew the covers over him.

" Sleep now, my beloved lord," she whispered, and through his pain he heard her, and his fingers groped for her hand.

She bent and kissed them, holding the strong palm against her cheek, ready to weep at the sight of his helplessness, equipped though he was with such bodily strength. But her tears were vitriolic with rage; the pitying gentleness of the

Nelidoff was an emotion of which Anna was incapable. Instead she regarded her lover, and recognizing pain and weakness, grew venomous with anger at the thought of danger to him.

And while she stood beside his bed, Paul's mistress made a private vow. No one and nothing should be allowed to harm him. Neither the courtiers he distrusted, nor the eldest son who might be selected to replace him. The ties of friendship or of blood should count for less than nothing, and any living creature whose existence menaced Paul, whether innocent or guilty, should be disposed of without mercy. She, Anna Lapoukhine, would see to that. . . .

"Anna," he muttered, and swiftly she knelt so that she could hear him.

"Anna. . . . Thank God you came . . . I missed you so. It's good that you're here . . . and Anna, there's a soldier, an excellent fellow . . . trustworthy . . . von Pahlen. Remember that name, Anna. Von Pahlen. We can trust him. Go now, my darling."

"I go," she told him. "Sleep well. Von Pahlen; I will remember."

.   .   .   .   .

"The Commandant is here, Sire."

Rastopchine's lackey bowed, and having received a sign of assent from his master, admitted the military commander of Paul's capital. Rastopchine rose to meet him.

"My dear Araktchéief! Come and sit down. I'm so glad you found time to make this visit."

"It is a pleasure, Count."

The most dreaded man in Petersburg sat stiffly in one of his host's elegant chairs, as always extremely ill-at-ease in comfortable surroundings, wishing dourly that necessity had not forced him into friendship with this well-bred, contradictory man whose cunning had so far been the impetus of their intrigues.

They drank wine, and watched each other in silence for some moments. Rastopchine, observing his visitor over the rim of his glass, decided that the rigid soldier might have been dismissed as an unimaginative boor, if the experience of meeting those cold pale eyes, set like twin agates under the thick brows, had not revealed a mad and almost demoniac spirit. . . .

'If you are what is said of you,' Rastopchine thought, at

the same time, smiling and refilling his guest's glass, 'you may have to be got rid of, before your tendencies carry you too far. . . .'

But aloud he conversed on different lines.

"I asked you to come and see me, my friend, because I thought it time we reviewed the situation. Without the encumbrance of the admirable Koutaïssof, who is becoming quite unbearable!" he added.

The jealous susceptibilities of Araktchéief immediately raised the matter which displeased him most, though its achievement had been part of a plan to which he had agreed.

"This Anna Lapoukhine . . . I think she is gaining too much influence with the Czar!" he stated, and knowing the hatred any mistress of Paul's must inevitably incur from Araktchéief, Rastopchine smiled and shrugged.

"All the better," he said. "She's friendly to me already, and she approves of you, because you protect the Czar. In fact I'd be prepared to trust her to a certain extent for I believe she loves him. In any case, remember that she is of our faction, whereas the Nelidoff was not! There will be no friendship with the Empress, no interceding for the good Alexander in this case. That was the danger before. The more I watch these two the less I trust them . . . that woman idolizes her son; so much so that it is beyond her power to hide it even in public. And you know what I think of him!"

"If the Emperor listened to me, he would have nothing to fear from that quarter," Araktchéief said coldly.

"Our views agree, my dear Commandant. . . . And in time they may prevail. It only requires a little patience, and a mistress of the stamp of Mlle. Anna to add her persuasions to our own. . . . But what I really wished to discuss was the favour our Emperor is showing Count von Pahlen."

The Commandant stood up and began to walk towards the window; the preference shown by Paul for this newcomer had upset him, and the knowledge that others recognized it, and were probably laughing at his discomfiture, had ensured his undying enmity towards the Count.

"I have noticed that he's often with the Czar," he said.

"Too often," Rastopchine added. "I don't like him; I don't trust any man of that kind who has been humiliated and then comes fawning to kiss the hand that struck him. He's too bluff, too jovial. It doesn't agree with his reputation as a soldier, and his devotion to Paul Petrovitch is less likely to be genuine when you remember that he loved the old Empress enough to risk his head by honouring Plato Zubov!"

"What do you suspect, then?"

"I don't know, yet. A self-seeker perhaps, ambitious and hoping for favours from the Emperor. . . . Even then he's a menace to us, for we have one thing in common, my friend, despite our other differences—and it's a thing shared by Anna Lapoukhine, unless I'm much mistaken.

"We love Paul Petrovitch, and popular or hated, sick or well, we mean to keep him on the throne! That is the difference between us and the rest. . . ."

Rastopchine too had risen, and for a moment the underlying hostility and misunderstanding that existed between two men of such opposite character dwindled to insignificance in the face of that admission. He did love Paul, not with the feeling of Araktchéief whose warped mind had transformed his Czar into a mental image not far removed from God, for whom he would willingly die, and willingly kill; that was not Rastopchine's bondage, but a personal affection, borne of years of intimacy; the tie sometimes forged between men of opposite temperaments, and which not even the influence of a woman can completely undermine. However violently Rastopchine disapproved of Paul's militarism, of his severity, even of his odd reforms, which gave the miserable common soldier the right to a court martial and to complain of ill-treatment to his superiors, he accepted the contradictions, the innovations, and the occasional instances of brutality of which the Czar was guilty, and knew that by comparison with his devotion, they were of no importance.

It was something more than mere jealousy or self-interest that warned him when he watched Count von Pahlen with his Emperor and friend. It was an instinct that recoiled in baffled fear and mingled with it was a feeling that he would find the Empress Marie and the Grand Duke Alexander implicated if only he knew how to set about making the discovery.

So he and Araktchéief talked, promising to watch the interloper and to put in a word against him whenever they had the chance, until the discussion veered to politics and the possibility of war with France.

.   .   .   .   .

When the Court returned to Petersburg, Paul's wife and mistress met in public at an evening reception.

The encounter had been eagerly discussed for weeks by Marie's enemies and by the scattering who vaguely sympathized: how would the Empress receive Anna Lapoukhine, and what would be the attitude adopted by her eldest son? . . .

Anna knew that the whole Court would be watching that night, many of them in the hope that the arrogant, spoilt favourite would suffer some humiliation, and she prepared accordingly.

Aggression was Anna's remedy for any situation; she flung herself at her enemies without expecting quarter even as she gave none, and she already hated Paul's wife with a loathing that was both temperamental and instinctive. She had failed to make her husband happy, she was boring and respectable, and somehow more clever than she seemed, since so many violent domestic storms had raged in her vicinity and yet left her unscathed. And she had borne this son Alexander who was a menace to his father.

Women of that kind were always inimical to her; incapable of placidity or moderation where emotions were concerned, Anna Lapoukhine had already made up her mind to hate Marie Feodorovna, unaware that her enmity had its roots in jealousy, that she, beautiful, witty, unscrupulous and indulged in everything by Paul, was bitterly envious of the plain German princess for the simple reason that she was her lover's wife. . . .

Any hopes of conciliation that Marie nursed concerning her rival were finally dispelled that evening in the Winter Palace.

The famous Mlle. Lapoukhine was dressed with exotic magnificence, her dress cut outrageously low, while the Czar, whose prudery was a byword in the uncomfortable Court, watched her admiringly; and as a supreme impertinence she wore a set of the old Empress Catherine's priceless jewels, jewels which should have been given to the Emperor's Consort.

When Anna was presented, she curtsied briefly, and her dark eyes stared up at Marie Feodorovna with an expression of open hostility.

Still the Empress delivered her set speech of welcome and preserved her bovine calm, while she fought down and mastered her anger and her fear, knowing that this fierce and lovely Russian could never be won over, that this was no Nelidoff, who would respond to a favour with endless loyalty and gratitude.

Alexander, standing close to his mother, considered his father's mistress and frowned uneasily. She would be difficult, he decided; a haughty, ambitious, ruthless woman, equipped with every weapon that the Empress Consort lacked. And Paul Petrovitch worshipped her. Perhaps her fearlessness was the secret, the Grand Duke thought; everyone trembled before the Czar; even the gayest became stiff and uneasy in his presence. The gloomy, stern man who ruled in Catherine's place punished crudity or moral vagaries as promptly and harshly as he dealt with the dishonesty, sloth and inefficiency which had been a privilege of the well-born for countless generations.

Also he was religious, and, most ridiculous of all, tolerant to those whose faith differed from his own. Even the Catholics, so savagely oppressed in former reigns, were permitted to worship as they pleased under his protection.

The effect of such a personality, backed by the power of such men as Araktchéief, had paralysed the Court with fear, beneath which the bolder members matched their dread with boiling resentment of the change in their mode of life enforced by his rule.

Yet it was typical of his father, that paradoxical, damnable man, with his Puritan dislike of promiscuity, to fall in love with an impudent wanton, to make her his mistress openly, to overwhelm her with treasures, and to laugh indulgently when she snubbed his nobles, affronted his wife, and took personal liberties that no one else in Petersburg would have dared to contemplate.

"She's a danger," the Grand Duke decided; "a great danger. I hope Pahlen realizes that a woman of that character could ruin everything. . . ."

But he need not have worried. Von Pahlen had been watching Anna Lapoukhine for weeks, and his estimation of her quickness and ambition were on a par with Alexander's. Also she disliked him, not openly, for he guessed that Paul had spoken in his favour, and she was still trying to fathom him, hoping to find the quality that had captured the friendship of the Czar.

That achievement was his greatest triumph; often, lying awake in his room, Pahlen thought of how much Paul Petrovitch seemed to like him, and smiled unpleasantly in the dark. The incident at Riga never left his mind; his humiliation festered in his imagination like a sore, and nothing the Emperor did to make amends could heal or alleviate that constant stinging need for vengeance.

Also Pahlen hated him as a man; despised him for his ugliness, watched the signs of nervous strain that often eluded his self-control; and, conscious of his own iron stability, sneered inwardly. He dismissed Paul's reforms as the whims of an irresponsible madman, an opinion justified by this absurd decree to lighten the load of the serfs; detested his military innovations, not for their severity, but because they demanded discipline for the officers as well as the men; and considered him a tyrant consumed by bourgeois morality which he did not apply to himself.

Pahlen had made a shrewd study of Anna Lapoukhine, but his prejudice refused to admit the possibility that anyone could find the Emperor tolerable, far less love him. . . . She slept with him for wealth, for power, for advantages for her family, and for the sheer love of notoriety. At the moment her influence was unbounded, but with every day and hour his own was growing, and that was a fact Mlle. Anna had yet to learn. . . .

"How beautiful she is, Sire," he said quietly, and Paul nodded, still watching her where she stood in the centre of a group of fawning courtiers.

"Yes," he said. "Yes, Pahlen. Everybody spoils her, but who can blame them? . . . Imagine it, the child wants to waltz!"

The Count raised his eyebrows in surprise, well aware that Paul had forbidden the new dance as immodest.

"But surely that's prohibited, Sire?"

"Not if she wants it, my friend. If it will really please her, all Petersburg shall dance nothing else! Come; let us go over and talk to her."

Von Pahlen followed Paul across the room, and after a few moments managed to speak to the Empress Marie, who was sitting by her eldest son, pretending that she was impervious to the success of the Lapoukhine.

"Your Majesty," he said, kissing her hand, and bowing deeply to the Grand Duke Alexander.

"I believe that I owe you a debt of gratitude that I can

never hope to repay.   Your intercession with the Czar secured my pardon."

"It was my son's suggestion, Count Pahlen," she said quickly. "And since you seem to have His Majesty's ear, I hope you will recommend the Grand Duke to him.   That will balance the little favour we did you."

"Be assured of that, Madame."

Then seeing Anna Lapoukhine's eyes on them, the Count withdrew. The evening ended in triumph for Paul's mistress, and tears for his wife, which she shed profusely in the privacy of her rooms, while the poisonous suggestion first voiced by Alexander returned to her mind and deprived her of sleep for the rest of the night.

Supposing Paul decided to divorce her. . . .

"Oh, my God," Marie wailed into her pillow. "What would happen to me and to Alexander then? . . ."

That notion, so dreaded by the Empress, was just beginning to occur to Anna Lapoukhine.

But his love and the wish to protect her from scandal drove Paul into making a fatal error. Before he had time to realize that he wanted her as his wife, he arranged a marriage of convenience which raised Anna to the rank of a princess and invested her position at Court with an outward respectability.

At first she resisted his wishes; she wept and stormed, terrified that this passion for convention was only the initial stages of dismissal, and when he finally convinced her that the marriage must be in name only, she still refused, afraid to admit to him that a husband was an extra bar to the plan on which she had set her heart.

"I won't marry, I won't!" she raged. "I don't want a title, and I don't want to be tied to someone else. . . ."

He, who for two years no man had dared to contradict, took her in his arms and reasoned with her gently.

"Please, my darling, do what I ask. You can't live at Court in this position, at the mercy of every scandalmonger in Petersburg; you have no rank, no proper status. If you marry Gagarine you'll have both, and you need never see him afterwards. . . . You must do it, Anna. It's the first favour I have asked of you. . . ."

At last she gave in, still reluctant and angry, while Paul's love for her increased by reason of the opposition he had tried so hard to break down; he thanked God for her jealousy, which found vent in accusations that he was tired of her, that this marriage was only the beginning of the end. . . . She behaved with the recklessness and rage of a woman in love, deluging him with tears and fits of savage sulking, often refusing his embraces, unaware that her hold on him was enormously strengthened by this conduct.

In return for her obedience, she extracted one promise, a promise which left the door to her ambition still unlocked.

" Give me your word that you'll have this miserable marriage annulled if I'm unhappy," she demanded, and he agreed instantly, wondering why the loophole pleased him, still ignorant of the desire to fulfil his love for her by placing her on the throne at his side.

And while he arranged his domestic affairs, and decided that war with France must be declared, while the reorganization of the army proceeded under the efficient eye of Araktchéief, and the Ambassadors who had written home that Russia's Czar was mad, after witnessing that ghastly funeral, now worded their reports more cautiously, Paul's son Alexander and Paul's good friend von Pahlen began to plot against him.

The conspiracy was slow in starting; the Grand Duke, always unwilling to commit himself, talked to Pahlen for hours on end, probing and calculating, waiting for the older man to make the first move.

For his part, Pahlen played Alexander's game for several months, determined to force that evasive personality into a position from which it could not retreat, wondering whether he dared presume upon the hatred that he sensed in Paul's son, and reveal that his sentiments towards the Emperor were the same.

In the early part of 1799 he was made Military Governor of Petersburg, a position that raised him to real power, and ranked him among the men who helped Paul rule his kingdom. Pahlen accepted the honour with every appearance of gratitude, and went out of his way to be gracious to the new Princess Gagarine, whose dislike of him was becoming very obvious.

Then, backed by the authority his victim had vested in him, he revealed himself to Alexander.

They both attended parades, an exercise which the Grand Duke enjoyed in spite of himself, and which Pahlen loathed as synonymous with Paul, and it was after they left the parade ground one morning that the new Governor suggested a walk in the palace gardens.

"I love Petersburg," he remarked as they turned down a broad path flanked by trees and lawns that swept down to the carved river parapet beyond which the great Neva flowed.

"It has many happy memories for me, Highness. Memories of your illustrious grandmother, and of the days of Russia's glory. . . ."

Alexander's fair skin flushed red and then faded into a pallor that indicated his mingled excitement and fright.

"No one here speaks of Catherine the Second," he said.

"I speak of her," Pahlen retorted. "And I think of her often. I look on this city, I listen to the endless drilling, marching, I see the lines of *khibitas*[1] leaving for Siberia with your father's prisoners closed inside them, and I remember Russia as it used to be when Catherine Alexeievna reigned!"

"Why do you say this to me, Count?" Alexander questioned, still hedging, tormented by a sudden impulse to withdraw from the situation he had schemed so long to bring about. He had sent for Pahlen, knowing his nature, and had prayed that a means might be found to pull Paul off his throne and kill him, so that he might ascend it himself; and it was typical of him that when his desires were on the point of being forced into the light, he could not bear to acknowledge them.

"Because you remind me of the Empress," Pahlen answered. "Because when I heard of her death I expected to come here to do homage to you as Czar of all the Russias. I never thought to find your father in your place. . . ."

"It's not my place, Count Pahlen," the Grand Duke whispered. "That is treason. . . ."

Von Pahlen stopped and faced him, gazing directly into Alexander's averted face. His flat, cold eyes were glittering with excitement; for the first time he portrayed himself and gloried in the moment of revelation. He stood before the Grand Duke as the man he was in fact, hard, proud, merciless, a man for whom risk or humanity were of no consequence at all.

"It was treason to the Empress to let her son ascend the throne. It was treason to you, Sire, and treason to Russia. . . .

[1] A closed carriage for prisoners.

Now I have said what all Petersburg thinks. You can go and denounce me to your father if you wish! "

Slowly Alexander looked up at him, his handsome features haggard, his blue eyes pained. Pahlen, the consummate actor, was not deceived by this hypocrisy, and seeing the signs of sorrowful reluctance put on for his benefit, knew that he was safe and Alexander's complicity assured.

"I would never betray you, Pahlen. You know how my father's severity sickens me; I can't bear to think what he would do to you."

"What he has done to others," Pahlen said grimly. "Death by flogging. A thousand lashes with the knout, watched by friend Araktchéief. That's how I should die, Highness, for *I'm* not a prince of the royal blood. But when his hatred of you ends with your being taken to the Schüsselburg, you'll be as helpless as I am at this moment, having talked treason to you, and put my life in your hands! "

"You have nothing to fear, Pahlen, I swear it! I am your friend."

Pahlen bowed and lifting the Grand Duke's hand, he kissed it as if he did homage to a ruler rather than a prince.

"I only fear for you, Highness, and for your brothers and sisters, and for the Empress Marie. I know the Emperor's mind, God help me, and I tremble for all of you! "

"We all live in fear, Count," Alexander answered. "The Imperial family, the whole Court, the army, everyone! He's a sick man, very sick . . . my grandmother used to tell me that even as a child he was violent and unreasonable, that he suspected plots against his life. . . . We must have pity for him, Pahlen; we must remember that these fancies of the mind make him severe."

"He isn't fit to rule," the Count said, and his little eyes watched Alexander closely. "A sovereign sick in mind is worse than one crippled in body; and no one can cure him now, Highness. Princess Gagarine knows now, if she did not before; she's nursed him when his head has troubled him, she's seen him blind with pain, wandering in his thoughts like a man with some fever. . . . The others know his condition, Araktchéief, Rastopchine, but they only think of themselves! They don't care what happens to Russia or to you while a madman holds the power of life and death! "

"If he would only abdicate," murmured Alexander, and

Pahlen smiled. "It might save him, as well as many others. . . .
He could live somewhere in peace, be properly tended. . . ."

"And you could ascend the throne and complete your
grandmother's plans, Highness."

"But he'd never agree, Pahlen! To hint even at such a
thing would mean death!"

"There are some circumstances where he might be persuaded to listen to reason. I could arrange it. Given time."

"What of Anna Gagarine, Rastopchine and the rest? They'd
never advise him to give up the crown."

Pahlen folded his hands behind his back, and they resumed
their walk, while he considered.

"I've thought of that, Highness. And that's the first thing
we must do. We must separate these adherents from your
father. I think that is something you can leave to me. . . ."

It was not an idle promise, and the Count proved it by
getting rid of Alexei Araktchéief in September of that year.

15

PAUL'S great fortress was rising on the site of the old
wooden Summer Palace; the labour of thousands of workmen had built the foundations and raised part of the walls of
a huge stone edifice.

Crowds gathered to watch the work in progress and to murmur that this was the Czar's new home, specially constructed
in the style of a medieval castle, surrounded by a deep moat.
Here he would be safe from the dangers that threatened him,
dangers so real in his mind that police infested his cities, spying and arresting. And in the atmosphere of terror and suspicion that was spreading throughout Russia, thanks to the
savage zeal of Araktchéief, the Emperor's reforms were over-
looked.

The serfs in whose favour he had legislated were treated
with appalling harshness by their owners, who vented their
anger with the Czar upon them, so that their plight was almost
more wretched than before. In their misery and ignorance,
the people blamed the Czar, their fear and misunderstanding

fanned by persistent propaganda issued by Pahlen, who, as Military Governor of Petersburg, ordered the most frightful and absurd barbarities, at the same time proclaiming them to be Paul's instructions.

The legend of the "Death's Head" Czar was spreading fast and gaining a firm hold on the minds of the people, until the severities which had always been a part of peasant existence and the lot of the Russian soldiery were traced back to his order, and he was reviled accordingly.

Also, the war which had broken out with France destroyed the country's hope of peace after the expensive wars of Catherine's reign.

For a time the shadows cleared when news of the great victories won by Suvarov heartened the populace and pleased the Court. But even in this the balance tipped in Paul's disfavour.

Suvarov, unorthodox, brilliant, devoted to the memory of the dead Empress Catherine, before whom he made the Sign of the Cross when received in audience—Suvarov had won for Russia. And Suvarov hated the Czar, jeered at the new Prussian discipline, laughed at drill as the amusement of parade ground soldiers, and, following the magic Russian formula of eccentricity, piety and a God-given instinct on the battlefield, routed the armies of Republican France and offered the Corsican General Bonaparte his first serious challenge in the war. Suvarov had brought victory to the Russian arms, but it was no credit to the Emperor Paul. . . .

Once or twice a week, the Czar drove to the site of the new Michael Palace to watch the progress, and accompanied by Anna, Princess Gagarine, he walked among the skeleton foundations, describing the towers, the thick doors and impregnable walls of his stronghold.

Anna, who loathed the gloomy building, humoured his enthusiasm, wondering why his persistent childish trust in the safety of the Michael Palace always filled her with unhappiness and dread.

"It will be like a prison," she told him one afternoon, as they stood by their carriage, watching hundreds of workmen shoring up the sides of the freshly-dug moat.

"Nonsense, my darling. It will be the safest place in Russia. No memories of revolution, no ghosts of my predecessors to haunt it. Nothing! We'll begin a new life there; I can't wait to take up residence; and when I show you the plans drawn up for your apartments you'll like it too! ”

A much more enthusiastic response was provided by von Pahlen, who often suggested to his Emperor that they should visit the building. Paul was delighted and flattered that the project should interest his friend as much as it did himself. In fact there was something miraculous in the similarity of taste and sentiment that existed between them, the man he had once disgraced had gradually enlisted his affection and secured his trust to an astonishing degree, for Paul was naturally suspicious, and deeply sensitive to atmosphere. He lived in his disloyal, discontented Court and sensed that they hated him because he had disarranged their extravagant, careless lives, and that with all their hearts they wished him dead. He knew instinctively that the passive indifference of Marie Feodorovna had been replaced by watchful partisanship for her eldest son, that though she humbled herself to Anna Gagarine until the spectacle of her indignity disgusted him, the motive was only love of Alexander. And above all, he suspected the Grand Duke.

There had been a surface truce between them, played out far too convincingly by the new Czarevitch, and it had lasted uneasily for the first year of Paul's reign. Now the pretence was fading; everything about the smooth, effeminate grandson of Catherine Alexeievna seemed spurious. Open rebellion would have secured the Czar's respect; hostility, even insults, he would have understood and seen in them some shadow of himself in his fierce, fearless youth, when all the power of Catherine had not been strong enough to make him bend. But the sly, evasive tactics of his son repelled him, filling him with angry hatred, while the reports of Alexander's wishes to retire to Switzerland and live in private with his wife aroused his father's rage and disbelief.

He confided his loathing of his son to Anna Gagarine who echoed it, and to Pahlen, who listened at first and was noncommittal. Then he began to agree, apparently regretful, adding an occasional poisonous word that fanned Paul's suspicions and directed his thoughts to more sinister channels.

Lately the Czar walked with his arm linked through Pahlen's and stood by the site of his stone palace, leaning on his worst enemy, sometimes pressing his other hand to his eternally aching head.

"It will be a glorious building, Sire," the Count declared. "Where will the Grand Duke Alexander's apartments be?"

Paul looked at him, and his mouth set ominously.

"I haven't made up my mind, Pahlen," he said slowly. "They may yet be in the Schüsselburg."

The Count's face was expressionless, but he made a mental note to repeat the remark to the Grand Duke.

"Come home, now, Sire, you seem tired," he said solicitously, and Paul smiled and nodded.

"We'll go then; you're a good fellow, Pahlen. I believe I grow more fond of you every day . . . you and Anna. God's death, how bleak my life would be without you both! I wish you'd try and make friends with her; it would please me if you liked each other better, you're both so dear to me."

"I will try, Sire. I have always tried, for I admire the Princess and I'd give anything to win her favour. But she's a woman, and jealous, I think. You mustn't heed her, Sire; it's quite natural that since she loves you, she hates me . . . she can't bear to share you, even with an old man!"

That explanation of his mistress's dislike banished a doubt which had been tormenting him for some time. She was jealous, Pahlen said. Of course, that was it; jealousy! Therefore in this case her instincts, usually so sure, need not be trusted. . . .

"They say it will take another year to finish," he remarked, looking back at the shell of the palace named after St. Michael the Archangel, the guardian of God.

"Perhaps less, Sire. I'll see what can be done to speed the work. . . . Take care, Sire, take care! You nearly stumbled on that beam. . . . Permit me, take my arm once more. . . ."

As Paul entered his carriage the Count turned quickly and looked once more at the great stone building, surrounded by the muddy, yawning moat, and smiled behind his master's back.

As Paul said so often, no one could possibly get in, but by the same rule, if the assassins should chance to be inside, no one could possibly get out either. . . .

.   .   .   .   .

The fall of Araktchéief had left a void in Paul's household and for many weeks it seemed to the uneasy Court that that dreaded personality, so long synonymous with the reign of the new Czar, must suddenly appear in his old place, restored to favour and vested with all his former power. But the months went by and no word reached the exile, while Alexander's confidence in Pahlen steadily increased.

A tiny slip had caused Araktchéief's downfall; he, the inhuman instrument of Paul's will, had allowed himself a little family feeling. He concealed the theft of some military stores to protect his brother who was in command of the post, and that gave Pahlen the chance to ruin him.

The Count murmured the story to the Czar, explaining that an innocent man had been blamed for the crime, with Araktchéief's knowledge. He felt it his duty to prevent an injustice, he declared uncomfortably, even though it pained him that he must expose his master's lifelong friend. Paul's reaction had been doubly violent in proportion to his trust; Araktchéief, on whose complete loyalty and integrity he had relied for countless years, had proved himself a liar and a cheat, ready to sacrifice a subordinate to the punishment merited by his own kin. . . .

Blinded by anger and disappointment, Paul banished and disgraced the one man who might have protected him, and most ironically, transferred his trust to Pahlen. And when the Count befriended a certain Hanoverian German named Bennigsen, the Czar received him and gave him a place at Court. Bennigsen was a tall, harsh-featured man, with a violent and bloodthirsty nature, ready for any kind of crime, provided profit to himself were guaranteed.

He hated Paul, who had punished him for inefficiency before Pahlen had rescued him, and he was quite prepared to help his benefactor murder him, so that the Emperor lived from that day onwards with his two assassins at his heels.

Together they laid their plan, while each of them sounded his friends in the army and the Court, enlisting support for what they meant to do, hinting that the Grand Duke Alexander was the power for whom they spoke. And those who had lost privileges under Paul, who saw in him a menace to their comfort, or disapproved of his policy, gave their consent to the project for his assassination.

Pahlen insisted upon one condition; they must wait until the Czar had moved into the Michael Palace, for he had determined that Paul's stronghold should prove to be his tomb; and to this malevolent proviso the rest of the conspirators agreed.

But there was one man whose favour with the Emperor stood as high as Pahlen's, one man who could never be frightened or bought over from his master. Rastopchine held the position of Postmaster General, which enabled him to keep a watch on all correspondence, thanks to the rigid censorship; and he also controlled the Foreign Ministry. His removal was an absolute necessity, and only Pahlen, whose determination matched his hate, believed that it could be brought about.

It was Bennigsen who queried the fate of Anna, Princess Gagarine, while her royal lover was being done to death.

Pahlen shrugged. "She's only a woman after all, perhaps a little dangerous, but easy to deal with when the time comes. *I* have our precious Emperor's complete confidence, and nothing she can do can shake it!"

But of all Paul's friends, friends gradually disappearing into banishment or given conveniently isolated posts, thanks to the tireless counsels of Pahlen, it was Anna Gagarine who struck a decisive blow to save the Czar.

.   .   .   .   .

Paul had not tired of her, as their enemies had hoped. Instead his love for her increased with time, and his enjoyment of her deepened through intimacy. To her he first confided the secret plan of making peace with France, and admitted that his mother's nationalism was already stirring in him. England, Prussia and Austria had strained his patience and roused his suspicions: he was tired of shedding Russian blood, when no real danger menaced Russia. Often, a strange dream recurred to him, a dream of conquest as wild and enormous as anything ever conceived by Catherine, the greatest of all eighteenth-century Imperialists, and this vision he shared with his mistress.

"Peace with France, my Anna! Why should I fight Napoleon for England and Austria, when I can ally myself with him and share the spoils of the world? France and Russia together . . . there's nothing we couldn't do! He can have Europe, my darling, and I—I shall turn to the East!"

"The East?" she questioned.

"India! That is my plan."

"You would take India from the English?" she whispered in amazement, and he nodded.

"While they fight France I can invade and conquer India. In the meantime the great European powers would be waging a war that must leave them all weakened, no matter who wins. Then Russia would be master of the world, my love! "

His ugly face was flushed, his eyes bright, and the nerve in his cheek throbbed with excitement; he held her in his arms and kissed her, and for a moment they were silent, each envisaging the same dream.

"If I succeed, I'll lay the treasures of the earth at your feet, Annushka," he said, pressing his lips against her hair.

She drew away from him then, gently, so that he knew her troubled rather than angry.

"There's only one treasure that I want, Paul Petrovitch, and you've already given it to someone else."

"It shall be taken from them. Name it! "

"Put away Marie Feodorovna and make me your wife. Let that be your gift to me when you take India! "

He came close to her, encircling her with his arm, and looked intently into her face. "Marry you, Anna . . . make you Empress. . . . Is that what you ask? "

"It is what I beg," she corrected him, and her rare humility touched him. Still he was silent, until she asked him, "Are you angry, Paul? "

"Not angry, my darling, only thinking. It's been done before, many times. I didn't wish to marry her, I have never loved her, nor she me. . . . And for a long time I've mistrusted her."

"She's not loyal to you," Anna said fiercely. "She is a hypocrite, who would betray you to-morrow if it favoured her son! That's the one she loves, Paul: Alexander—and I've always hated them both, you know that; I dared to tell you so from the beginning, and if you really want to safeguard yourself, you'll cease thinking of danger from without and look to your enemies in the palace. That's where you'll find the assassin you've always dreaded, not among the people! "

"Then you suspect my wife and my son, is that what you tell me? "

"I do," she answered, "and not only them. Above all, my heart distrusts von Pahlen! For the love of God, don't trust him as you do! "

"No, Anna, you're wrong," Paul told her firmly. "The Empress and the Grand Duke, yes, but not Pahlen. I'd stake my life that he is loyal. . . ."

"That's exactly what you *are* staking! Your life! Oh, Paul beloved, even if you don't want to make me your wife, get rid of them. Get rid of them all, before they do you some harm. . . ."

"Imprison Marie and Alexander? By God, Anna, you give terrible advice! My wife and my heir. . . ."

"Traitors, both!" she interrupted. "Listen to me, my King. I love you, and in the last twelve months I've not been idle. Nor has Rastopchine, who *is* your friend. We've set spies, and from their reports I believe there is a conspiracy, headed by Pahlen, whose arm you lean on and whose counsel you follow; Pahlen is in this plot against you and many others with him. And they have the approval of your wife and your son!"

He had turned pale, and his mouth, so recently smiling and gentle, was drawn into a tight line of savagery and fear. He moved aside from her and began walking up and down, frowning, his blue eyes becoming almost black in colour as the pupils dilated; he struck his fist against his forehead on which the veins were swelling visibly, so that Anna knew that an attack of pain was just beginning.

Lately these attacks had grown worse; at times he became quite violent, raging and incoherent, until he fell into his servants' arms, almost unconscious, and while the spasms lasted, he sometimes looked at her with a stranger's eyes and called her by an alien name. Natalie. . . . Koutaïssof had told her what that meant, and received a furious box on the ear in return for the unwelcome information. Now she watched Paul, as frightened in her way as Katya Nelidoff had been, but the strength of her purpose did not waver.

"What mercy would they have shown you, if the old Empress hadn't died suddenly?" she persisted. "None at all. And that's what you should show them!"

"What proof have you of all this? What is it but hearsay, Anna?"

"Do you need evidence against that miserable, snivelling son of yours, when you know he had agreed to your deposition in his favour? And Marie Feodorovna . . . how many hours does she spend with him, what does she ever do but lie to you to ingratiate him. . . . She's tried with me, Paul, many times. Presents, jewels, little notes full of promised friendship, if only I will speak in favour of the Grand Duke! You don't need proof against them, you have it! As for that devil,

Pahlen, give me a little time and I'll get proof enough to hang him times over!"

"Stop it, Anna, stop it!" he roared. "Pahlen is my friend; I won't listen to you trying to poison me against him. God's blood and death, would you take even that away from me . . . making me a man accursed, without one human soul that he can trust. . . ."

He held his burning head between his hands, and immediately she went to him, steeling herself to pursue the subject to the end, however much she hurt him or even endangered her own place in his affections. She put her arms around him and rested one cold palm against his throbbing forehead.

"There are many who love you, Paul Petrovitch. Millions of your people, all over Russia. The Father of so many children can never be alone . . . remember that. Remember also that there is one who loves you more than life. And warns you for your own sake."

"I know that," he said slowly. "And I listen to you, Anna. I've been thinking a great deal about my eldest son. And my wife. But for the last time, don't accuse Pahlen unless you can prove him false. And if that day comes, I promise him a death that will satisfy even you, Anna Petrovna!"

"I am satisfied," she said. "You shall have evidence. Now, come, sit down. I'll ring for some wine."

He sat within the circle of her arm, sipping a little wine, with his eyes closed against the glow of the fire that blazed in the carved marble grate, his head resting against her breast.

"How is the pain?" she whispered.

"Not too bad," he muttered. "I shall go to bed, I think. Only my thoughts race round and round, like mice on a toy treadmill. . . . There's not room in my head for them all. Anna?"

"Yes, my beloved?"

"I think I'll send my wife to the Novo Diévichy Convent. . . . Then you can have your marriage with Gagarine annulled. . . . Do you know that it's nearly seventy years since Russia had an Empress Anne? . . .

She did not answer him; her triumph and joy were so intense that she could find no words, but in her emotional way she wept with happiness. And within a few weeks the rumour crept through Petersburg that a cell in the Novo Diévichy was being prepared for a new and illustrious occupant.

16

ALEXANDER and his mother were alone in the Empress's apartments. He had come in answer to an urgent message and found Marie Feodorovna sitting straight-backed in one of her gilt chairs, embroidering, apparently quite placid. A closer inspection showed him that she was haggard and pale, and that her hands, usually so skilful, wielded the embroidery needle with trembling clumsiness.

When he bent to kiss her she threw the piece of framed cloth to the floor and clung to him.

"What is it, Mother, what's the matter? . . ."

Marie Feodorovna stared up at him in open terror.

"I had to send for you, my son. . . . Alexander, have you heard this rumour?"

"What rumour?" he asked her.

"The rumour that a cell is being got ready in the Novo Diévichy Convent. . . . They say it's being prepared for me!"

He knelt beside her and took her hands in both his own.

"Oh, my God," he said slowly. "Then the rumour that he is going to marry Princess Gagarine must be true. . . . That's what I was afraid you had heard. . . ."

Marie Feodorovna held on to him and it was the first time that he had ever seen her show real fear.

"You warned me long ago that this might happen, my Alex, and I didn't believe it," she quavered. "But now I think it's come at last. And when he's got rid of me and made this whore his consort, what will become of you, my darling? If she bears him a child, what will happen to all my children?"

"I dare not think," he answered, and this at least was true. If Anna Gagarine became Empress of Russia his life would not be worth a kopeck; she was ruthless, she hated him, and adored his detested father; lacking Pahlen's insane prejudice, he saw and recognized the strength of her love for Paul, and he knew that she would get rid of him at the first opportunity. Already Marie Feodorovna's days were numbered.

He put his arm round his mother's shaking shoulders, and comforted her, assuming the rôle of protector which she had filled so long and faithfully for him.

"I'll never let him do that to you, Mother. . . . Never!
Even if he is my father, I would kill him first!"

"Jesu forgive me, my son, but it may be necessary to do
so. . . . For your sake as well as mine," she answered and he
nodded. Then he began to talk to her quietly.

Late that night, the Grand Duke approached his father's
Minister during the interval of a play performed in the royal
theatre, and murmured that the Empress Marie was ready to
give full support to their plan.

Pahlen smiled, but said nothing. Then he hurried to the
side of the Emperor who waited for him and took his arm
affectionately. But afterwards he added Marie Feodorovna's
name to a long list he had compiled of persons wishing to
dethrone the Czar.

That list was a piece of indiscretion that he could not bear
to destroy; it gave him the keenest pleasure to look down the
column of names, and to add another to their number, indulg-
ing in a vindictive fancy that he was passing the death
sentence on his enemy. His spite and his passion for order
kept the document from the flames to which he should have
consigned it months before, and provided Anna Petrovna
Gagarine with the proof she had promised her lover.

.   .   .   .   .

By the end of 1800 the war with France was over, and even
skilful diplomatic sabotage could not any longer prevent the
threatened friendship between the Corsican First Consul and
the Czar of Russia. Paul and Rastopchine prepared to abandon
their old ally England, to whose advantage they found they
had been fighting, and the Emperor confided to his friend
von Pahlen that plans for the invasion of India were already
forming in his mind. Pahlen listened and echoed his master's
enthusiasm, while his uneasiness increased.

It would be difficult enough to kill the peace-maker, but
impossible to murder a Czar who had seized one of the richest
prizes in the world for Holy Russia. The popular picture of
a ferocious madman which his propaganda had induced in
men's minds would be replaced by an image not far removed
from the early Catherine Alexeievna, an image which had
earned her the sobriquet 'Great'. No, Pahlen decided, while
he agreed with Paul's suggestions, they would have to act

quickly before this tremendous project fired the imagination of even those who had previously sworn to take their sovereign's life. . . . There were dozens of conspirators, he thought angrily, who were capable of abandoning the plan and even betraying the ringleaders if popular feeling switched in favour of Paul Petrovitch. He needed men like the Zubovs as well as the adventurer Bennigsen.

It was then that the solution came to him. It emerged in his mind with perfect clarity, and with the daring and single-mindedness that had defeated all his enemies so far. Pahlen turned to the Czar in the middle of their conference and risked his whole future on a suggestion.

"Sire, I have an idea! Why not increase your glory by an act of mercy on the eve of this great operation? Peace with France, an alliance with Bonaparte, the capture of India. . . . Why not grant a general amnesty to prisoners and exiles and have all your subjects at your side when you go out to conquer?"

Paul looked at him and hesitated. "An amnesty . . . No, my friend, you're too kind-hearted. Pardon would never change my enemies."

"But think what a gesture it would be, Sire," he urged. "You can afford mercy; as the greatest monarch in the world, what have you to fear?"

"Assassination," came the answer, and for a moment Pahlen's colour deepened; then he smiled.

"If you allowed me to supervise the list of pardons, I would take care who reached Petersburg and who remained behind. You can trust me, Sire, to guard your life as if it were my own."

Paul leant back in his chair and rubbed his forehead; Pahlen watched him and wondered coldly how severe his headache was that day.

"I should like to be merciful," he said. "Above all I should like to rule as if my mother had never polluted this Court, turning everyone about her into traitors, lechers and thieves! Most of her intimates have gone, thank God, Pahlen. They're either dead or banished. As you say, some could be over-looked. . . . An amnesty. It might indeed bring down God's blessing on this enterprise!"

"As His anointed, Sire, I think it would be fitting," the Count said simply.

"I think so too. Once again, my dear friend, I'm indebted

to you for an excellent suggestion. There shall be an amnesty. All those punished since my accession may return! I leave the arrangements in your hands."

When he left him, Pahlen's mind was much relieved, and not even to the Grand Duke Alexander did he reveal that he had sent a secret summons to the Zubovs, Nicholas and Plato, to come to Petersburg as quickly as they could.

On the first of November, Paul issued the decree of general pardon. The purging, the vengeance and punishments were over, people whispered, and this impression was confirmed by the news that Alexei Araktchéief, whose cruelty had made the Czar responsible for so much bloodshed and brutality, was not among the penitents called back to Court.

By the end of a week the roads into the capital were choked with exiles, some travelling in battered carriages, while others, whose punishment had ruined them, came on foot. A small proportion of them reached the Czar, and then the general air of relaxation ceased abruptly with the news that Pahlen's troops were arresting the remaining unfortunates at the gates of the city. By order of the Emperor.

In ignorance of the travesty being enacted in his name, Paul held his Court and reinstated many who had lost his favour, unaware that Pahlen's casual reference to a few incidents of disorder among the crowds covered so much human misery for which his Minister was seeing that he got the blame. No one disputed it; Rastopchine, too busy with his plans for France, dismissed it, and Anna Petrovna, preparing for the annulment of her marriage, scarcely heard of it at all.

At the same time, messengers arrived to tell the Czar that the last stone of the Michael Palace had been laid in place.

.   .   .   .   .

"Gentlemen, Prince Plato Zubov!"

The conspirators were gathered together in a house which was situated some versts outside Petersburg, and it was here that Plato Zubov and his brothers were living since their return from exile.

"I have explained the situation to the Prince," Pahlen was saying, "and he and Count Nicholas Zubov are prepared to join us. Let us sit down, gentlemen. I have some good news for you."

Pahlen poured out some wine and handed it to his guests; he was smiling and confident, radiating cheerfulness.

"What news, Count?" Plato Zubov demanded impatiently.

"I have found the means of ruining our friend Rastopchine! Does that interest you?"

There was an excited chorus: "By God, Pahlen, how?"

Pahlen smiled and deliberately sipped his wine.

"He dislikes a member of the Foreign Office, young Nicholas Panin—he's one of us, gentlemen—Rastopchine believes he was trying to thwart his plans with this French upstart Bonaparte. So, not being a very scrupulous fellow, he has forged evidence of treason against him which he is going to present to the Czar!

"Not *real* evidence, thank God! Only of intriguing politically. Just enough to get him sent to Siberia and perhaps knouted. . . . But dishonesty doesn't pay—does it, gentlemen? Because when our Emperor, who is the soul of honour, hears about this despicable trick, it will be Rastopchine who goes to Siberia, not Panin, eh?"

Plato Zubov did not join in the uneasy laugh which followed.

"When are you going to tell him?"

"Immediately I return to the capital. He has already moved into the Michael Palace and the time has come when we must strike. At any moment Marie Feodorovna will be repudiated and forced into the Novo Diévichy, and Anna Gagarine will take her place. The arrest of the Grand Duke Alexander would follow in a matter of days; perhaps even mine with him, for the lady hates me, and she's not inclined to scruples any more than her friend Rastopchine. But once he's gone, she won't be able to protect the Czar!"

"Are you quite certain that we can trust the Grand Duke?" Plato interrupted. "I've no mind to do him a service and be sent to a fortress as a reward!"

"We can trust him," Pahlen assured him. "His own life is in danger; we'll hold the power of Russia in our hands when this maniac is dead. Alexander is a weakling, believe me; he'd never dare to turn against us!"

It was then that Bennigsen, usually so stupid, made a wise remark.

"There's no such thing as a weak Czar. . . . The blood of Catherine Alexeievna and Paul Petrovitch runs in his veins, remember."

"I am quite confident, Bennigsen. And if he should prove difficult, he has brothers and sisters. . . . What happened to the father could overtake the son. . . ."

"And our immediate plans, Count?" Zubov questioned.

"The disgrace of Rastopchine. Then we must all gather in Petersburg where we will decide the date on which our tyrant shall be removed."

Plato Zubov looked up quickly.

"As the confidant of our late Empress, I must claim one point. The honour of killing her son is the privilege of my family. . . ."

Pahlen bowed.

"When the time comes, Russia's liberator shall be a Zubov! That is agreed, Prince Plato."

The date of that meeting was the middle of February. And on the twentieth of that month Rastopchine received a furious order from Paul to retire in disgrace to his estates. All his posts were given to von Pahlen. He was not allowed to see the Czar, who was inflamed with anger at the disclosure made to him, and, with his going, only Anna Gagarine and the former valet, Koutaïssof, remained to stand between Paul and his murderers. But Koutaïssof was now ennobled, well rewarded by his master for his services, and himself involved with a demanding mistress, who persuaded him to keep aloof from all intrigues. Something was bound to happen to the Emperor, the lady argued, and Koutaïssof followed her advice by pretending not to see or hear. So that it came about exactly as von Pahlen had predicted.

Only Anna Gagarine was with her lover at the end.

.   .   .   .   .

The walls of the Michael Palace were still damp when they moved in. The Emperor's obsession to live in his new home discounted the pleas of his architects who begged him to delay, and panelling was laid over the damp stones, pictures hung and furnishings arranged until a mist of steaming vapour filled the rooms. Nothing deterred Paul, and he transferred his Court to the Michael Palace, taking the Empress Marie and the Grand Duke Alexander with him, and installing Anna Gagarine in a suite of rooms communicating with his own.

And it was there, in the unhealthy, fetid atmosphere of her magnificent apartments, that the servant who had been spying on von Pahlen came to Princess Gagarine and told her that the Count kept a list of names which he always carried with him and sometimes added to in private. The spy had been too terrified to steal the paper, but if the Princess could secure it, she would find evidence of treason.

She went to Paul immediately.

"Araktchéief betrays me; then Rastopchine, and now you say you can prove Pahlen a traitor. . . ." he said at last. "Very well, Anna. Where is this evidence?"

"In his pocket. When he comes to you to-morrow, demand to see what papers he carries. If he refuses, force him, and see what you'll find! That's all I have to say."

She put her arms round him and looked into his face, and her love for him softened her triumph. She kissed him tenderly, and he stroked her hair.

She said that Pahlen was a traitor. Since Rastopchine's fall he was almost ready to believe it; she had put the doubt into his mind and as he held her in his arms he promised her the test she asked.

"When he comes to-morrow morning, I will ask him, Anna . . . Anna, my darling. . . ."

When he had left her, as an added precaution he sent a letter recalling Alexei Araktchéief to Petersburg.

.   .   .   .

On March the ninth Pahlen went to the Czar's apartments to make his report as usual and receive orders for that day. He walked through the long corridors whistling softly, glancing at the patches of damp that discoloured the painted walls, and smiling to himself at his own thoughts, as he expressed a private wish that his victim might not die of pneumonia contracted in his unhealthy stronghold before Pahlen had time to see him killed.

So the Zubovs wished to commit the murder, he reflected. Well, let them! Far better that the actual blood should be on their hands rather than his, when the time came to proclaim Alexander. . . .

Not even his interception of the Czar's letter to Araktchéief had disturbed him, for his new position as Postmaster General enabled him to suppress it. And before any enquiries could be made, Paul Petrovitch would be dead. . . .

When the Emperor received him, Pahlen knew at once that there was something wrong. But his own favour was so secure that the possibility of danger to himself never occurred to him.

Paul was sitting at his desk, and he regarded him with hard, unblinking eyes, the nerve in his cheek throbbing angrily; he did not acknowledge his Minister's bow but only stared at him, turning the great sapphire ring round and round on his finger.

Pahlen stood before him and waited, while his composure faded as the minutes ticked by audibly on the clock that stood on the Czar's desk, and still no word was spoken. He knew then that something indeed had gone very wrong, and that the ordeal by silence, which inspired so much terror in Paul's victims, was at last being applied to himself.

He shifted slightly, and cleared his throat, holding the Emperor's unwavering stare and reading the accusation in it, while the sweat seeped out over the palms of his hands.

"Pahlen."

The Count's whole body stiffened at that tone.

"Yes, Sire."

"You were here in 1762? When my father lost his throne?"

"Yes, Sire." Pahlen's mouth dried up and he swallowed with difficulty.

Paul rested both hands flat on the top of his desk and said levelly:

"Empty your pockets, Pahlen, and put the contents here for me to see."

The Count's heart leapt in his breast and for a moment a deep, incriminating tide flooded his thick neck and spread over his face to the roots of his powdered hair. The fingers of his left hand strayed in the direction of his sword, while the temptation to fling himself upon Paul and murder him passed through his brain and was immediately discarded. For a single blind second, panic overwhelmed him, with the knowledge that his list of conspirators reposed in the breast pocket of his coat. Then the coolness and courage which had distinguished him in battle aided him in that moment of mortal danger. He had been betrayed; no excuses would avail him with his victim who had so suddenly become his judge. He dared not refuse, and he could not hope to hide that terrible document; instead he risked everything on absolute boldness.

"What is the matter, Sire? Of what am I suspected?"

"Of a conspiracy against my life," the Czar said coldly, and for the first time Pahlen trembled. But his nerve held, and with incredible composure he bowed low. Then his flat, blue eyes looked squarely at his accuser and he answered.

"There *is* a conspiracy against you, Sire. I am a member of it. The list of those implicated is in my pocket." And he put his hand into his coat and withdrew the paper on which his name, and that of everyone pledged to the assassination was inscribed.

Paul took the document from him and held it, unread, while he stared at the man who had just admitted so calmly the most dreaded of all crimes in an autocracy.

"Do you admit this, then?" he said hoarsely, and Pahlen nodded.

"I have known a plot to murder you existed for some months, Sire. The only way I could uncover it and save you was to join in it myself!"

"Merciful God in Heaven! Pahlen, Pahlen, why didn't you tell me?"

Paul had risen and he came round the desk, twisting the paper in his fingers, his disfigured face convulsed with emotion. He struck his fist against his forehead and repeated his words in a voice that shook with incredulity and horror.

"Why did you hide this? Don't you know what I might have done to you if you hadn't explained? ... By God's death, Pahlen, I cannot look at you, I am so filled with shame!"

There was a ghastly moment when the Count suddenly wanted to laugh, to stand and rock back on his heels with laughter, as he listened to the Czar of Russia begging his forgiveness, turning from him with tears in his eyes because he had suspected him unjustly. . . .

But the fact that Paul still held the list sobered his unbalanced sense of humour, and he decided once again what course he was to take. He went down on his knee to Paul and kissed his hand, bending his head as if some most unpleasant duty weighed upon him.

"I've had that list for weeks, Sire, and for weeks I've been adding to it. It is complete, but I couldn't bring myself to show it to you, and thereby break your heart!"

" My heart is broken, Pahlen. . . . I am beyond all pain from human treachery. What are you trying to tell me? "

" Sire. Open it and read."

He watched the Emperor as he unfolded the paper and saw that his eyes focused upon the top of the written column and remained there, reading and re-reading several times.

" My wife and my eldest son. . . . They head the conspiracy against me. . . . My wife and my son. . . ."

He turned and sat down slowly, and this time he read every name; Princes, Generals, members of the Diplomatic Corps, men he had trusted as well as those he had at times punished and forgotten. There were sixty persons listed on that crumpled piece of paper. At last he put it down and motioned Pahlen to sit beside him. His colour was livid, and his eyes were almost glazed in their expression.

" What were they going to do, Pahlen? "

" Murder you, Sire, and put the Grand Duke Alexander on the throne. They intend to act before you divorce Marie Feodorovna. The time was set for after Easter. I was supposed to guide them to your apartments where they would kill you."

" Very well, Pahlen, my friend. We will anticipate them. They shall die *before* Easter, and you shall choose what you want out of the wealth and estates of them all. . . . That should make you a very rich man, my dear Pahlen, as well as a very loyal one. . . . My personal reward to you will come later. Now be so good as to sit down at my desk if you please, and write out an order for the arrest and execution of Marie Feodorovna, and another order for the arrest and execution of my son Alexander."

For some moments there was silence, except for the steady scratching of Pahlen's quill as he formed the words of the warrant.

" That the former Empress Marie Feodorovna, being proven and judged a traitor, shall, by the order of His Imperial Majesty Paul the First, Czar and Autocrat of all the Russias, be conveyed to the Schüsselburg Fortress and there be put to death for her crimes against the person of His Imperial Majesty. . . ."

" Anna was right," Paul muttered, " she warned me, she begged me to do this long ago. . . . She was right about them all, all except you, Pahlen! But how could she know. . . ? "

The Count listened as he wrote, pausing to dip his pen deep into the golden inkwell so that the name of Alexander Pavlovitch, Grand Duke and Czarevitch of Russia, stood out black against the paper as he traced an order similar to that relating to the Empress.

"I have finished, Sire. May I make a suggestion? "

Raising his head Paul looked at him and nodded; it surprised Pahlen to see that he was smiling and that the expression was more terrifying than any conventional sign of rage.

"Say nothing of this to anyone, Sire. Not even to Princess Gagarine; unless you tell her that you are satisfied with my loyalty and that in a few days all Russia will have tangible proof. But don't tell her of these warrants, or of the other warrants for the rest of the traitors which I shall prepare immediately. No one must escape, Sire, and if word of your intention towards the former Empress and her son gets out, the conspirators will scatter and some may escape punishment. . . . Will you trust me with this, Sire, as you have already trusted me with so much, and let me make sure of arresting them all at the right moment? "

"How long will you need, Pahlen? "

"Three days, Sire. In three days there will not be a man or woman on this list at liberty. Beginning with the two names at the top."

"Three days, then. That will be *long* before Easter, my friend! "

As Pahlen left the room he heard the Emperor laughing, and the sound of that fierce, crazy laughter followed him as he literally ran down the corridor, with the two death warrants and the list of traitors stuffed safely into his breast pocket.

That afternoon he arranged a hurried meeting with the Grand Duke Alexander, and when they met in a private part of the new palace, Pahlen wasted no words but opened the signed warrant for the arrest and death of Paul's heir and handed it to him.

He watched the Grand Duke's fair skin flush and then drain to an extreme pallor; then he held out the document condemning Marie Feodorovna to the Schüsselburg and execution.

"Take that to the Empress, your Highness. You have three days before the sentences are carried out."

"Why this . . . so suddenly? Why, Count? " Alexander's voice was shaking.

" The plot is discovered. He has everyone's name, including my own. I've managed to clear myself for the moment but it's only a matter of time till he thinks again and I follow you to the scaffold. No sane man would have believed me, but thank God, he's more than a little mad. . . . Delay or panic now will cost us all our lives! Within forty-eight hours we must act! Have I your permission to give the word, Highness? " he demanded.

Alexander looked down at the warrant in his hands and folded it carefully. It occurred to Pahlen that after the first shock of the revelation he seemed very calm. In a man of tougher mettle, such composure might almost have been termed cold-blooded. . . .

" You have my authority, Count. I will answer for the Empress, my mother. God go with you! "

Pahlen bowed very low. " Highness, by the twelfth of March, you will be on the throne of Russia! "

.   .   .   .   .

In the few hours that remained of that day and throughout the one following, messengers informed the scattered conspirators that they must be prepared to put their plan into action. The date fixed by Pahlen was the eleventh of March and the hour, just before midnight. They were to assemble in the house of General Talysine, in an annexe of the old Winter Palace, there form into three groups, and set out for the Michael Palace.

.   .   .   .   .

The eleventh was a beautiful day, the temperature milder with the first softening of the Russian spring, and a pale golden sun shone down on the city of Petersburg.

Even the Czar's new palace seemed less grim and out of place, for the outside walls were painted and gilded in the Baroque style that distinguished Tsarskoë Selo and many public buildings, where the Czarist passion for colour and ornamentation assumed real splendour because of the immense proportions. Paul's fortress was set in a parkland, surrounded by trees where hundreds of birds nested, the main building ringed by a wide moat and spanned at intervals by drawbridges, the whole place honeycombed with guardrooms through which an intruder would have to fight his way. And never, as on that eleventh day of March, did the Czar of all the Russias feel so happy and secure.

In the morning he worked as usual, smiling sometimes as a tender thought of Anna Gagarine distracted him; his whole personality soothed and softened after the night they had spent together. Several times he laid down his pen and allowed his mind to dwell on her, and he thanked God for his happiness. The treachery of Marie, whom he had already determined to repudiate, no longer hurt him, and the betrayal by his eldest son was only what he had a right to expect of Catherine Alexeievna's grandson and disciple.

They did not love him, and they had no claim on his pity or his duty any longer, now that their names had appeared on that list.

Within a few days his treacherous wife and son and a host of others would be dead, and before setting out to conquer India, Paul would make Anna Petrovna his wife.

Thinking of her he shook his head, amazed at the power of her fascination for him, the perfect fusion of inflammable desire and practical tenderness that characterized their whole relationship, until he wondered how he could have ever thought of anything but marrying her and placing her on the throne at his side where she belonged.

That afternoon he dined with the Princess, and took her into his room to show her where workmen had bricked up the door which communicated with the Empress Marie's apartments, a link that had only been a formality. But, on Pahlen's advice, Paul was taking no risks with his wife, and the doorway was blocked.

"What's the matter?" Anna Gagarine implored him, "you never told me what Pahlen said to you, and yet you talk of a secret that I shall soon know. . . . Tell me, my beloved, please tell me. . . ."

For a moment he hesitated and then shook his head.

"No, Annushka, my curious one. You'll know soon enough. Come riding with me before it grows dark."

And together they spent what was left of the day, laughing and lighthearted in their enjoyment of each other.

Meanwhile word reached the Grand Duke Alexander that the reign of Paul the First would end that night.

"Go to your rooms and sleep," Pahlen instructed. "And when it is done, I will come for you."

That evening the Imperial family dined together as usual, and Paul, who had been so happy that day, became moody and preoccupied at the sight of his wife and son. He sat in silence, glancing from one to the other, his face twitching with anger, and he noticed that Marie Fecdorovna's hands were shaking. His rage with them was dull and deep; it boiled in him, but he controlled it, believing truly they were in his power. Thank God for Pahlen, he said to himself, while his considered stare turned from Marie to his son; they had not counted on the loyalty of his friend. . . .

Alexander avoided his father's glance; his pale blue eyes were concentrating on his plate for fear that even at the last moment Paul might intercept the hatred and excitement that seethed in his heart. Never had he loathed his father more or wished so fervently for his death; with the climax so near his self-deception failed him, and he acknowledged freely that he longed for the moment when Pahlen and the Zubovs would make certain that that ugly, crazed, detested man would give up his life as well as his throne.

After dinner the Emperor walked down the Gallery of Apollo which led to his own apartments, and Princess Gagarine followed him. The palace was very quiet; even the guards stationed in front of the enormous main staircase were less active than usual, and the warmer temperature of the day had increased the humidity of the damp walls, producing a haze that seeped through panelling and tapestry. In the library preceding his bedroom, Paul stopped before the guardpost. The troops were Horse Guards, commanded by Colonel Sabloukof, and they sprang to attention at the Sovereign's approach.

The Czar looked at them in silence for a few minutes, then he felt in his pocket for a note sent him before dinner.

"The guards on duty in the library are not to be trusted with your safety. I beseech your Majesty to dismiss them this evening. You have nothing to fear, everything is in my hands. Pahlen."

He turned to their colonel.

"The post is relieved! I wish the regiment to leave Petersburg to-morrow. Have two footmen take their place for to-night."

Then he passed through the library door into the closet leading to his own apartments.

In Paul's bedroom a bright fire was burning, and the high-ceilinged chamber was comparatively cheerful; it was panelled in white wood, and some magnificent paintings, which were the Emperor's joy, glowed on the walls. At the entrance to his apartment there was a little staircase leading to Anna Petrovna's private suite.

She went in with him, and the Emperor's valet closed the door behind them, and prepared to doze; from his knowledge of the Emperor and his mistress the Princess would not emerge from his bedroom for several hours, if indeed she left before dawn.

When they were alone Paul held out his arms and enfolded her closely; she reached up and drew down his head, kissing him on the mouth, her fingers caressing his face.

"You looked so gloomy to-night," she said at last. "I longed to do that all through that dismal meal. . . . Pavlouchka, when can I know this secret of yours, why won't you tell me now?"

"You shall know it to-morrow, my Anna. Come to the window with me; shh! Do you hear the birds out there? What a noise they're making . . . I wonder what's disturbing them. . . ."

"Probably they're changing the guard," she said carelessly, but with his arm round her waist she walked to the window and pulled back the brocade hangings. Outside it was very dark and raining.

"You ought to have those trees cut down," she remarked. "That'd get rid of the birds. . . . Listen to them! My God, no wonder you don't sleep!"

"It's not usual," he muttered. "Something's frightened them. . . ."

He was often suspicious, she reflected, often disturbed by sounds and fancies, especially when his head troubled him. Even there, surrounded by guards, cut off from the city by a system of medieval fortifications, he still kept a sword in his bedroom, insisting that he might one day need to defend himself.

She turned in his arms and embraced him, and this time her slim arms tightened round him as if she held a child to her for comfort.

"I had better stay with you here," she whispered. "To-night we can sleep, my darling; our ride has tired you out. . . ."

"My head's aching again," he admitted, resting his cheek

against her hair. "But I'm restless to-night, Anna. I don't know what's the matter with me. . . ."

"You'll feel better to-morrow. Come, let me ring for your valet and get you to bed. It's after eleven, your clock is just striking."

He held her without answering, while the delicate chimes of the last hour to midnight sounded and were still.

Then he looked at her, and touched her face very gently with his finger, so that the great sapphire he wore flashed in the candlelight.

"I love you, Anna Petrovna. You've given me all the happiness I've ever known . . ." he said quietly.

"Why do you say that . . . why do you look at me in that way? We might be parting, to hear you. . . ." She was trembling suddenly and her hands caught at his coat and clung to him tightly.

"I want you to go up to your own room, Anna. Go up and in a little while I'll come to you. But leave me alone now, my darling. I want to be alone now."

Slowly she released him, and then, with a flash of her usual spirit, she smiled, and kissed the hand that rested on her shoulder.

"I'll go, and I'll wait for you. But come to me quickly."

At the door she turned to look at him, smiling, with some endearment on her lips, and found him standing by the window watching her. She mounted the stairs to her bedroom and slowly undressed; then she sat down to wait.

.   .   .   .   .

The conspirators had been gathered in General Talysine's house for several hours before Pahlen arrived. Most of the officers who were going to the Michael Palace to depose their sovereign had been drinking steadily, but Plato Zubov and Bennigsen were coldly sober.

"I wish to God these fools would stop drinking!" Bennigsen said. "One sound at the wrong moment and we might ruin everything."

"They haven't the stomach for revolutions that their fathers had," Plato sneered. "The thought of a little bloodletting and they fly to the wine bottles for courage. . . ."

"Well, he *is* the Emperor," the Hanoverian shrugged.

"Bah! Sovereigns are only human beings, my dear fellow. Very human, believe me. I slept with one for nearly seven years and I assure you they're just like anybody else. Look, there's Pahlen! You're late, my friend; these stalwarts'll soon be too drunk to stand up, if you don't stop them."

Pahlen looked round him and frowned. The crowd was noisy and drunken, when stealth and precision were so vital to the success of his plan. He stood on a chair and shouted for silence.

"Gentlemen! Gentlemen! Listen to me, please! Listen carefully. This is the outline of our plan for to-night."

They were all quiet then, and Pahlen continued.

"There are three parties; General Talysine will lead one, Prince Zubov the second, and I'll take the third. Now, this is what we have to do. Talysine, you march to the Michael Palace and spread your troops through the outer gardens—deal with any sentries you meet, but for God's sake do it quietly—and be ready to repel any rescue attempt from the town. At the same time, Prince Zubov and his men will approach the Saskaïya drawbridge. You, M. Argamakof, will demand admission. You say there'll be no difficulty?"

Paul's equerry stepped forward out of the crowd.

"None, Sir. It's my duty to report to the Czar if anything goes wrong in the city. I often go to him at night. I'll be admitted without question."

"Excellent," Pahlen said. "Prince Zubov and the rest of your party go with you, overpower the guards on the drawbridge, raise it, and enter the palace by a side door which I have arranged shall be unlocked. Thanks to the Emperor's fancies, that part of the building's still so damp that not even a servant can sleep there, and the inside staircase leads to the White Salon. Adjoining is the library. Usually, there's a strong guard posted in there," Pahlen paused dramatically and then smiled. "But I sent our Emperor a note advising him they weren't to be trusted, and told him to dismiss them. . . . So you'll meet no opposition there. The library leads into the Czar's bedroom. After that, I leave it to you, Prince Zubov. In the meantime, I'll take a small body of men and march to the main drawbridge. They'll certainly let *me* in, and when they do some of my men will seize control of the drawbridge, and I'll lead the rest upstairs. We'll join up with the Prince in the Emperor's suite.

"I must impress upon all of you," he continued, "that the slightest noise would be enough to give the alarm. The whole point of this plan is that it's both quick and silent. Your route into the Palace is deserted, and you ought to be able to dispose of the few men at the Saskaïya drawbridge without letting them cry out. If you should meet anyone on your way to the Czar's room, kill them! But do it quietly. That's all. With Talysine outside in the gardens, our men in control of both drawbridges, no one can get in or out. It should be all over just after midnight. Are you satisfied, gentlemen? Has anyone a question?"

Then one of the younger officers spoke up; the deposition of a reigning sovereign was not part of his experience, for Catherine Alexeievna had been on the throne for fourteen years when he was born; the Revolution and death of Peter the Third were part of history to the boy, who found himself preparing to enforce the same fate on that miserable monarch's son. And though he had been drinking with the rest to still his conscience, he asked the one question uppermost in all their minds.

"What will happen if the Czar resists?"

Pahlen stepped lightly down off the chair, eased his sword in its scabbard and picked up his gloves before replying.

"You can't make an omelette without breaking eggs," he said. "God save the Emperor Alexander! Come, gentlemen. Let us go!"

.   .   .   .   .

Everything went as Pahlen planned. The Saskaïya drawbridge was lowered to admit the treacherous equerry, its guards silenced in a few seconds, and Plato Zubov and his men crept through the unlocked door and began advancing into the heart of Paul's palace.

They were mounting the stairs when hundreds of rooks in the gardens began to scream with the abruptness of a thunderclap. For a moment Plato stopped and stood motionless, while the birds' cawing became a crescendo of protest and alarm.

"God's death," he snapped in a whisper. "We forgot those damned rooks in the garden. . . . That's Talysine's men arriving. The fools have disturbed them. . . . Come on, curse you, hurry! We've got to get upstairs before someone goes out to investigate!"

Inside the palace it was very quiet, their route was deserted and badly lit by torches placed at some distance apart. The vapour seeping out of the walls was so thick that in places they could hardly see each other's faces.

"The crazy devil," Bennigsen muttered. "He's built himself a death-trap. . . ."

"Be quiet, damn it!" Plato swung round on him. "That's the White Salon, there at the top of these stairs." He opened the door and looked through the narrow crack. "It's empty. Come on."

When they crossed the room, Zubov paused by the double doorway leading to the Emperor's library.

"Supposing there is a guard post there," one of the officers whispered. "Suppose Pahlen's wrong and he didn't dismiss them. . . ."

Plato put his head against the panels of the door. Then he straightened and his handsome features relaxed in a small, cruel smile.

"Don't worry, friend. He did as Pahlen told him. There are no troops in there. I'm going to open the door. Now!"

The lackeys on duty in the dim, spacious rooms were overcome before they had time to raise a cry. One of them fell under Nicholas Zubov's sabre as he turned to reach his master's bedroom.

In the little valet's closet, they found Paul's personal servant cowering. With one look at the drawn swords of the intruders he fell on his knees.

"Spare me, for God's sake, gentlemen. . . ."

"Where's the Czar?" Zubov demanded, his hands twisting the man's coat collar until he almost choked.

"In his room, Sir. . . ."

"Alone? Where's the Princess Gagarine?"

The valet's face was livid with terror; he twisted his head helplessly to escape the throttling pressure.

"She's upstairs . . . in her room. Excellency, Excellency, you're choking me. . . ."

Zubov flung him aside, and he fell heavily against the wall.

"Someone go upstairs and barricade the Gagarine into her room. Come on, my friends. There's the bedroom door. We're going in!"

After Anna Gagarine had left him, Paul's mood of restlessness increased. He walked up and down for several minutes, listening to the angry screaming of the birds outside his window, repeating the question to himself. 'What's disturbed them? . . .' and then answering in Anna's words: 'It's nothing, probably changing the guard, it's only my cursed fancy. I'm always hearing noises. There's nothing, Anna's right. There's no use rousing the guard because of a flock of birds. But I'll have those trees cut down to-morrow. To-morrow morning!'

Then he remembered that there was a letter to be written to Prince Weimar in Paris, before he could mount those stairs and lay his aching head on Anna's breast and try to sleep; he sat down at his bureau and took up his pen.

And while he wrote his thoughts began to riot, until he found that he was fighting an extraordinary impulse to think about his mother and his early life. When the image of Natalie Alexeievna appeared, he pressed his hand over his throbbing eyes in a vain attempt to shut her out, to close his mind to the associations of unhappiness and failure that crowded into his brain, holding up mirrors, showing him himself as he had been that day when a real image had mocked him from a looking-glass, and he'd driven his fist through the reflection.

Then Catherine came to him, smiling and lovely as a young woman, with her handsome lover Gregory Orlov at her side, two splendid phantoms before debauchery destroyed the one and lunacy the other. But though four years had passed since he had buried her, enclosing her body with the remains of the man she had murdered, he knew that death had not diminished his hatred nor understanding softened his resentment and disgust. For all her glory, she was nothing now, her name preserved in infamy; as for Potemkin, thanks to the action of her son, no man would ever find his bones to honour them. . . .

He was revenged upon them all, but the years of his youth had been wasted in idleness and gloomy introspection, both marriages had failed, even his son had proved a traitor, and when he thought of Alexander his mood hardened. The sudden weakness, the sense of loneliness that even Anna's presence in the upstairs room could not dispel, were superseded by bitter rage. Marie and Alexander. Three days, Pahlen had promised, wait for three days and then they shall be punished. He had waited, and by the next morning that time limit would be reached.

Betrayal and suffering were part of his past, but by God, he swore, sweeping the pens and paper to the floor in his excitement, there'd be no place for them in his future. He had come into his birthright and he was going out to conquer and enrich his country at the expense of the most powerful nation in the world. He was going to marry Anna Gagarine and if she bore a child, that child should inherit the throne of Russia; it was the future that mattered, he insisted, and at forty-four he was still young, a man with many years to live. . . .

It was then that he heard the sound of voices outside his bedroom door. The tones were loud, which was unusual, considering the late hour, though no word of what was said could be distinguished. For a moment he thought it must be Pahlen. . . . But no, he knew it was not Pahlen, for there must be several of them on the outside of that door. He moved into the middle of the room, listening, waiting for the valet's knock upon the panels before he announced who sought an audience. But no knock came. Instead he heard a scuffling sound as if a man had fallen in the tiny corridor.

Automatically he began to walk forward to turn the key in his door, until the realization came to him that he had never had a key. It was not necessary, Pahlen advised him at the time, when a guard post kept watch in the library and a servant slept by the entrance to his room. Then he remembered that there *was* no guard post. He had dismissed them himself only two hours before. There were no troops protecting him, and something had happened to his valet on duty in the closet. . . . Someone had got in.

The sweat broke out all over his face and the nerve under his eye gave a tremendous leap, and then suddenly, for the first time in twenty years, it stopped, and the twitch was still. He turned slowly and stared at the archway in his bedroom wall, where the door communicating with the Empress Marie's suite had so recently been bricked up. Beyond that door there was a little ante-room, always filled with troops during the night. But he could not get to them nor they to him. If he shouted, they might not even hear him.

It flashed through his swirling brain that Pahlen had insisted that he block that entry; an entry which was also an exit as he recognized too late.

"I am trapped," he whispered, glaring round the huge, white panelled room, a room with windows high above the ground, a room with enormously thick walls through which no cry could penetrate. . . . A room with only one door. And then he knew beyond a doubt what lay beyond that door, as he had known all his life. The horror he had been fleeing in his mind had turned into reality, and finally caught up with him.

And with that acceptance, all fear left him. He wiped the sweat out of his eyes; he picked up the sword that always rested on a chair by his bedside and unsheathed it, then he stood facing the entrance.

At almost the same moment the handle of the door began to turn. His last thought before it opened was thankfulness that Anna Gagarine was safe in her own room.

.   .   .   .   .

She too had heard voices, and she sprang up in her night-dress and threw herself at the door. Her fingers caught at the handle which seemed held in a vice, and in an access of terror, she knew that someone was outside, jamming it.

"Paul! Paul!" she screamed, beating her fists on the panels, pulling and struggling to wrench the door open against the strength of her unseen captor. "Paul, look out! It's a trap. . . . Oh, God, you swine, you devils, let me out. . . . What are you doing to him!"

The man on the other side of the door held the handle easily with one hand while the imprisoned woman dragged on it.

By then she was hysterical, her hands were bleeding where the carved door panels had cut them, and her shrieks drowned the noise of falling furniture, and the single, hoarse yell of rage and defiance which was suddenly cut short. At last Anna stopped; she clung to the wall tapestries, listening to a terrible silence.

"Paul . . . Paul," she whimpered. "Oh, Merciful Jesus. . . ."

.   .   .   .   .

When Pahlen arrived he was met by Bennigsen at the entrance to the Imperial bedroom. The Hanoverian was very pale, and to his astonishment the Count saw that the intrepid and pitiless old man was trembling.

"Why weren't you here?" Bennigsen snapped.

"Is it over?" Pahlen ignored the question. He could not see into the room properly, but he knew that Plato Zubov was standing over something.

Bennigsen moved back. "Look for yourself, Count!"

Pahlen walked in and stepped over the legs of an upturned chair. He saw a sword lying in a corner and recognized it as the Czar's. Then he stared down at the body which lay on its back on the carpet, staring sightlessly at the ceiling, with an officer's sash knotted round its neck. There was blood on the clothes and on the floor. . . .

Pahlen looked round him.

"Why did you have to sabre him as well as strangle him?" he asked coolly. "It'll take hours to make the body look respectable. I see he tried to defend himself."

Plato Zubov said nothing, he only sheathed his sabre and walked to the window; he seemed as if all interest and energy had gone out of him. It was his brother Nicholas who answered.

"There was a struggle," he said slowly. "When we came in he was waiting for us, sword in hand. Plato told him he was to abdicate in favour of his son. . . . He just laughed like a madman. He shouted, 'You'll have to kill me first, damn you,' or something like that and he lunged at Plato. . . . Then he fell down. . . . There was great confusion, Count, it's difficult to tell what happened. . . ."

Pahlen regarded him and smiled unpleasantly. "I can well imagine, my dear Nicholas. However, it's very well done. I suppose no one can remember who put the scarf round his neck?"

Nobody answered. Pahlen nodded, still smiling. "Of course not . . . and just as well, it might be awkward if Emperor Alexander were to ask. . . ."

At the door, he looked back over his shoulder, his eyes focused on the ground, and the ends of the bloodstained yellow sash. "He always tried to imitate his father," he remarked. "It's curious that he got his wish in death. . . ."

Then he went to inform the new Emperor.

On the morning of the twelfth of March, 1801, the Emperor Alexander the First appeared in public at the Winter Palace. He was very pale, and witnesses whispered of terrible scenes of grief when the news of his father's death was first brought

to him.   He fainted, they said, and refused to take the
crown. . . . He was not really responsible at all, the rumours
insisted.   It was the Courlander Pahlen and the German
Bennigsen who had planned and carried out the murder.   And
a brutal murder it was, for though the physician Rogerson
spent six hours preparing the body, it was possible to see that
the Czar Paul had not only been choked to death but beaten
and stabbed as well. . . . No wonder the young Emperor looked
so grieved and ill. . . .

Pahlen knew what was being said, but he walked at
Alexander's side and pretended not to hear.   He was still
confident, assured of his protégé's gratitude, and he proved his
talent for organization in the hours that followed the death of
Paul.   Orders were issued to arrest Koutaïssof; and the Princess
Gagarine, who had heard so much but seen nothing, was given
into her husband's charge.   The country, Gagarine was informed, would be the best place for his wife. . . .

Unlike her eldest son, the Empress Marie remained calm,
while her unimaginative mind refuted the details of her
husband's death.   He was gone, his mistress banished, and
her beloved Alexander safely in possession of the crown.   Her
gratitude for their deliverance took on a pious form, and in
consequence she found the presence of Paul's murderers an
increasing inconvenience.

Within a week she went to the young Emperor, and embrac-
ing him in her familiar way, proceeded to advise him on his
future conduct.

Alexander listened quietly; he looked ill and his fine eyes
were red-rimmed.   In fact his capacity for shedding tears had
served him well; he wept publicly and presented a picture of
grief and distraction that deceived many who should have
known better.   He took the crown of Russia with humility and
an air of duty unwillingly done, while he rejoiced in his heart,
and could scarcely wait to destroy all traces of his hated
father's work.

His only genuine emotion was the regret foreseen by Plato
Zubov; someone had been found to do the thing he dared
not do himself, and now that it was accomplished, and their
uses at an end, he discovered that hostility rather than gratitude was all he felt for them.

Marie crystallized his feelings with her question.

"What are your plans for Count Pahlen, my son?"

Alexander stared over her head; she suddenly noticed an expression of obstinate hauteur that she had never seen before.

"I am considering, Mother."

"Won't you discuss it with me, Alexis, after all . . ."

" No, Mother. I don't intend to discuss it with anyone. The Emperor's decisions are his own. If you will excuse me, now. . . ."

He rose and offered his hand which she took and kissed like any subject. For a moment it did not seem possible that this cold stranger was her son. He bowed to her and walked over to the window and drew back the curtain to look out. The attitude reminded her instantly of someone else who used to adopt that stance when thinking. As she left the room, she remembered who it was.

It was the Empress Catherine Alexeievna.

Alexander heard her go, but he did not turn round. His mother was hurt, and he only hoped that her sense of rebuff was seasoned with fear; the necessity to bear with her had passed, it ended that night on the eleventh of March, when Pahlen and Nicholas Zubov burst into his room to tell him that the Emperor Paul was dead. . . .

Pahlen, the Zubovs, Bennigsen. . . . They were the principals, he thought, and frowned. Even his mother, whose intelligence he despised, had seen that the presence of these men around him was unseemly. So would the world see it, and public opinion would declare that the monarch who spared the murderers had contrived the crime, and that was a judgment Alexander was very anxious to avoid. He looked out of the window and his frown became a scowl. Pahlen was the most dangerous, and what Pahlen had dared once, he might even dare again. . . .

For a long time the Emperor Alexander remained by the window, looking at nothing. But when he finally turned away, his face had cleared, and a resemblance to Catherine Alexeievna was suddenly evident in the line of his jaw and the expression in his eyes.

He went to his desk and made a little note in his diary, dated a few months ahead.

He had made up his mind.